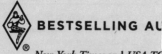

BESTSELLING AU

New York Times and *USA TO...*

D0377546

DIANA
PALMER

THE
BEST
IS YET TO *Come*

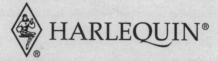

HARLEQUIN®

TORONTO • NEW YORK • LONDON
AMSTERDAM • PARIS • SYDNEY • HAMBURG
STOCKHOLM • ATHENS • TOKYO • MILAN • MADRID
PRAGUE • WARSAW • BUDAPEST • AUCKLAND

Recycling programs
for this product may
not exist in your area.

ISBN-13: 978-0-373-38988-9

THE BEST IS YET TO COME

Copyright © 2010 by Harlequin Books S.A.

The publisher acknowledges the copyright holders
of the individual works as follows:

THE BEST IS YET TO COME
Copyright © 1991 by Diana Palmer

MATERNITY BRIDE
Copyright © 1998 by Maureen Child

BESTSELLING AUTHOR COLLECTION

In our Bestselling Author Collection,
Harlequin Books is proud to offer
classic novels from today's superstars
of women's fiction. These authors have
captured the hearts of millions of readers
around the world and earned their place on
the *New York Times, USA TODAY* and other
bestseller lists with every release.

As a bonus, each volume also includes a
full-length novel from a rising star of series
romance. Bestselling authors in their own
right, these talented writers have captured the
qualities Harlequin is famous for—heart-racing
passion, edge-of-the-seat entertainment
and a satisfying happily-ever-after.

Don't miss any of the books in the collection!

CONTENTS

To Tara, with love

THE BEST IS YET TO COME

New York Times and *USA TODAY* Bestselling Author

Diana Palmer

DIANA PALMER

got her start as a newspaper reporter and is now the prolific author of more than one hundred books. A multi–*New York Times* bestselling author and one of the top ten romance writers in America, she has a gift for telling the most sensual tales with charm and humor. Diana lives with her family in Cornelia, Georgia.

Chapter 1

The bleak winter landscape was as depressing to Ivy as the past few months had been, but she felt a sense of excitement as she watched the long country road. Ryder was on his way. Guilt wrenched her heart as she gave in to the need to see him, to listen to him, to love him. She'd always loved Ryder, even as she feared him. It was her secret passion for Ryder that had sent her running scared into a tragic marriage that had ended six months ago in the death of her husband. This would be the first time she'd seen Ryder since the funeral, and she was torn between delight and shame.

She'd lost weight, but that only made her more attractive. She was tall and willowy, with long black hair that waved around her shoulders, and a complexion like fresh cream. Her eyes were as black as coal—a legacy from her French grandmother—framed by lashes that were thick and long and seductive. Ryder always said that she looked like a painting he had in his living room—an interpretation of the poem "The Highwayman," depicting Bess with her long black hair. But Ryder was fanciful at times.

Ryder had been at the funeral, down in Clay County, Georgia, near the banks of the wide Chattahoochee River, a good half hour's drive from Ivy's home in southwest Georgia. They'd buried Ben in the cemetery of the little Baptist church he'd attended as a child, under a canopy of huge live oak trees dripping with gray Spanish moss. Ivy had stayed close beside her mother, trying to ignore the tall, commanding presence across from her. Ryder had been at the house as well, and she'd had to pretend not to notice him, to pretend grief for a man who had made her life a living hell.

Ryder couldn't know that his very presence had been like a knife in her heart, reminding her brutally that her secret love for him might actually have led to Ben's death. It had hurt Ben that Ivy couldn't respond to him in bed, and because of that, he drank. The accident that killed him had resulted from one drink too many, and Ivy felt responsible for it.

She thought back to her teenage years, when Ryder had been the whole world and she'd worshiped him. He'd never guessed how she felt. That had been a blessing. She smiled, remembering the tenderness he seemed to reserve especially for her. He wasn't the world's most lovable man; he had a quick, biting temper, but Ivy had never seen it.

"That's the first time I've seen you smile in weeks," Jean McKenzie observed dryly, staring at her daughter from the hall. "It does improve your looks, darling."

"I know I'm a misery," Ivy confessed. She went over and hugged her mother, ruffling the thick salt-and-pepper hair that framed eyes as dark as her own. "But you're a doll, so don't we make the perfect pair?"

"Ha!" Jean scoffed. "Pair, my eye. The very last thing you need is to stay here for the rest of your life." Her voice softened a little, and she frowned at the faint panic in her daughter's eyes. "Listen, baby, it's been almost six months. You have to start looking ahead. You need a change. A job. A new direction. Ben wouldn't want this," she added meaningfully.

Ivy sighed and moved away from the older woman. "Yes, I know. It's getting easier, as time goes by."

"I know that, too. I lost your father when you were only a toddler," Jean reminded her. "In a way, I'm sorry you and Ben couldn't have had a child. It would have made things easier for you, I think. It did for me."

"Yes. It was a shame," Ivy murmured, but without really agreeing. A child would have been a disaster. At first, Ben had been a good friend, but he'd never been a good lover. He'd been always in a hurry, impatient and finally harsh because Ivy couldn't feel the passion for him that he felt for her. She'd cheated him by marrying him, and it was guilt more than any other emotion that had haunted her since his death. She'd never felt passion. She wondered sometimes during the last miserable weeks of her marriage if she was even capable of it. She'd promised Ben that she'd go to a therapist, although she couldn't imagine what one would find. Her childhood had been uneventful, but happy. There were no emotional scars. She simply didn't want Ben physically, because she belonged, heart and soul, to another man—a man who'd always thought of her as his sister's best friend and nothing more. And what could any psychologist have done about that?

Money had been another ever-pressing problem. Ben had

spent money recklessly when he was drunk, and when she'd insisted on going to work herself, to help out, there had been terrible arguments. Finally she'd given up trying to offer her help and reconciled herself to living in poverty. The months had gone into years, and Ivy eventually withdrew completely into herself and avoided contact with everyone, especially Ryder. That had been necessary because of Ben's rage at seeing her speaking to him once at her mother's. That had been, she remembered, shivering, the first time he'd struck her.

A month shy of her twenty-fourth birthday, a piece of heavy equipment had fallen on him. A freak accident, they'd called it, but only to spare her feelings. She knew he'd been drunk when he'd gone to work. He'd handled the equipment haphazardly and paid the ultimate price. Just the morning of his death, he'd raged at her about Ryder again. He'd accused her of being unfaithful to him in her mind, of making his life hell. The words had haunted her ever since.

She and her mother were churchgoing people, and it was that bedrock of faith that had helped Ivy get through the agony of guilt that had followed the funeral. It was all that kept her going even now.

"When did Ryder call?" Ivy asked suddenly.

"About an hour ago," Jean said, yawning, because it was early and she'd had only one cup of coffee. It took her at least two to wake up, so she dragged back to the coffeepot and filled a cup for Ivy as well.

"Will he stay long?" she asked, her eyes haunted.

"Now, who knows what Ryder Calaway's plans are, except for the Almighty?" the older woman teased as she retied her loose brown chenille bathrobe before she sat down at the dainty little white kitchen table and creamed her coffee. "For all that we've known him for years, he's still a mystery."

"That's a fact." Ivy sat down, too, her burgundy velour robe exquisitely hugging her figure, highlighting her face. "This is an odd place for such a high-powered businessman, isn't it?" she added gently.

And it was. They lived in a small county in rural southwest Georgia, in a heavily agricultural area near Albany. Neighbors lived far apart, and even in town, the lots were large. Agriculture was big business here, with most of the small family farms a thing of the past, because big farming combines grabbed them up as more and more farmers went bankrupt. In fact, Ivy's parents had been a farm family until her father's death. Jean still lived on the farm, and she still had two enormous chicken houses. She employed a family to pick up eggs and feed the thousands of chicks until they were old enough for market. One of Ryder's contacts bought chickens from her for his chicken processing plant, and Jean made a comfortable living.

After she had graduated from high school, Ivy had gone to work for Ryder's construction company in Albany some years before and had found that her friend Ben Trent was also employed there. They'd been in school together, and as time passed, they began to date. In no time at all they were married. Ivy frowned, remembering Ryder's shock when he'd found out. He'd congratulated her and Ben on their wedding, but he had been reserved and distant, and just afterward he'd gone to Europe for several months to set up some new company.

As Jean had said, Ryder was mysterious. He owned acreage like some women owned shoes, and judging by his clothing and his private jet and the luxury car he drove, he was never short of money. But it wasn't for his money that Ivy loved him. It was because he was Ryder. He was as big as all outdoors, with an indomitable personality, and he conquered things and people with equal ease. She'd adored him since she was in school, palling around with his younger sister. The Calaways had always been well-off, not minding at all that the McKenzies weren't. Ivy was always welcome in the big redbrick house with its exquisite rose garden, just down the road from the McKenzie's house. And Ryder never minded including her when he took his sister to movies or picnicking with whichever girl he was dating at the time.

He'd gone off to college, and then to Albany to take over a small construction company that had gone bankrupt. He'd turned it into a mammoth conglomerate over the years, with offices in Atlanta and New York, and it seemed to keep him busy all the time. After his mother's death, his father had returned to New York to live, and with his sister's marriage to a Caribbean businessman, Ryder was all alone in the big redbrick house. Perhaps he was lonely, Ivy thought, and that was why he traveled so much. She wondered why Ryder had never married. He was thirty-four now, ten years her senior, and women loved him. Surely, with his money and vibrant masculinity, he'd had opportunities.

She stared into her coffee cup as Jean got up to take bacon off the stove and check on hot biscuits in the oven. She wondered what her own life would be like from now on, if she could ever stop blaming herself for failing Ben so tragically. She should never have married him, feeling as she did about Ryder. She lived with the fear that Ben didn't really mind dying. He'd wanted more than she could give him, especially in bed. She was frigid, of course, she reminded herself. Surely that had been part of the problem with their marriage. She'd carry the scars forever, along with her sense of failure. If she'd tried harder, maybe Ben wouldn't have spent so much time with his friends. Perhaps he wouldn't have drunk so much, or spent most of their time together trying to hurt her. He'd gone from a gentle, laughing boy to a vicious drunkard so quickly….

"Isn't that Ryder's car? My eyes are getting old," Jean muttered, pausing with a platter of bacon to peer through the kitchen window.

Ivy got up with a quick heartbeat, following her mother's gaze. "A black Jaguar." She nodded. "Did he say why he was coming?"

"Does he ever? Just to visit between world trips, I guess, as usual." Jean laughed. "He hasn't been home since the funeral."

"Well, I'm glad, whatever the reason," Ivy confessed. "It's been a long time. Ryder has a way of livening people up."

"And one of us needs that," Jean murmured under her breath.

Ivy wandered onto the porch in the concealing burgundy velour robe she wore over her thick flannel gown, her hands unconsciously fiddling with the knot that held it together, her long hair wisping around her patrician features as she watched the tall, dark-haired man untangle himself from the elegant vehicle. As always, her heart leaped at the sight of him, and she went warm all over with excitement. Only Ryder had ever had that effect on her.

He stared up at the porch, big and rough-looking, as formidable as a tank. He looked like a man who owned a construction company, from his craggy face to his huge hands. His face looked as if someone had chiseled it out of concrete. He was all hard angles, except for a body that would have made him a fortune in the movies. He had to be six foot three, and all muscle. He still liked to do construction work himself, frequently spending a Saturday helping his men catch up on jobs when he was in a town where they were working. His eyes were a steely gray color, deep-set and piercing, and his mouth was firm and faintly sensuous. He was wearing a charcoal pin-striped suit, and it clung to his muscular frame like silk.

"Not bad, honey," he drawled as he lifted his arrogant chin to give her a good going-over with his eyes. "But you could use a few pounds between your neck and your knees." He had a voice like dark velvet, smooth and silky.

Ivy felt her blood racing, as it always did when Ryder was around. He generated a wild kind of excitement that she'd felt ever since she'd known him and had never fully understood. Her full lips smiled involuntarily as he joined her on the porch, her black eyes laughing up at him.

"Hello, Ryder," she welcomed.

"Hello, yourself, tidbit," he murmured dryly. It was a long way down, despite her above-average height. He smiled faintly as his eyes made an intent and disturbing survey of her face.

"Don't I even get a kiss?" she asked, trying to call back the easy affection of her youth, so that he wouldn't guess at the depth of her lacerated feelings. "It's been months since I've seen you."

His face seemed to tighten for an instant as he responded to the gentle query. "I'm getting old, honey," he confessed, reaching out to lift her by her waist with careless ease so that her face was on a level with his lean, dark one. "Before long, I'll forget how to kiss girls at all."

"That'll be the day," she said with a smile. She smoothed the shoulders of his jacket as he held her, liking the rich feel of the fabric over all that imposing muscle. He looked different close up. Not the carefree man she remembered at all. He was a stranger these days, darkly observant, intense and very, very male. He smelled of expensive cologne and smoke, and his big fingers felt steely biting into her soft waistline. She felt shaky down to her toes in his grasp. "You look tired," she said softly.

"I am tired." He looked down at her lips. "You have a pretty mouth, did I ever tell you?" he asked with a faint grin. "Come on, come on, I don't have all day."

"Do I have to kiss you?" she asked, eyebrows lifting innocently.

"You'd better," he murmured. "If I kiss you, God knows where it might lead us."

"Promises, promises, you heartless tease," she chided. "Oh, Ryder, it's so good to see you!"

"You've been mooning around, haven't you, pretty girl?" he asked softly. "I'll have to take you in hand."

"I guess I need it," she sighed. She leaned forward and nuzzled her nose against his with warm affection. "Where have you been this time?"

"Germany." His voice sounded oddly strained. His eyes searched hers. "Ivy," he whispered.

He sounded strange. She frowned and felt his big hands contract, bringing her robed body closer.

"What is it?" she asked gently.

His mouth suddenly dropped to her neck and pressed against it hotly. She heard his breath shudder faintly, and her body tensed at the unexpected feel of his mouth on her skin. His lips opened; his tongue stroked the side of her neck. The sensation was suddenly, shockingly intimate. She actually gasped and her body went rigid.

"Shocked?" he murmured. His mouth moved up to her ear and his teeth took the lobe, gently biting. All the time his arms were closing around her slender body, until she was closer to him than she'd been in five years. Her hands clenched on the fine cloth of his suit as he wrapped her up against him and worried her earlobe with his teeth and tongue. Her body began to tremble, to burn. Her legs felt as if they might not support her at all. It had never felt this way with Ben. Even when they were most intimate, she'd never been on fire for him. Her eyes closed and she could have cried out with the anguished pleasure of his mouth on her skin. Dreams had sustained her for so long. The reality was shattering.

She moaned softly. Ben, she thought miserably. Ben, I'm sorry, I'm sorry…

She must have unconsciously said his name because Ryder went rigid all at once, deadly still. He set her roughly back on her feet and released her. Above her his face was like a granite carving, his eyes cold.

"Don't ever make that mistake," he said curtly. "I won't play substitute for you, Ivy."

Her face began to color. "But, Ryder…"

"Where's your mother?" he asked. "Inside, staring out to see what happens next?" The hardness left and he was Ryder again, lazily indifferent to her blushes as he took her by the arm. "How about breakfast? I'm starved. They only gave us a three-course meal on the damned airplane. I haven't had anything in hours."

He was impossible. A minute ago, she'd been vibrating with desire, seconds later she'd wanted to slap him soundly, now he had her laughing again. "You and your appetite," she burst out. "Your sister Eve used to go into gales of laughter telling about your midnight raids on the kitchen."

"I miss Eve," he sighed. "She and Curt live in Nassau, but I'm hardly ever in that neighborhood anymore."

"I had an email from her a few weeks ago," she replied.

At that moment Ivy's mother bounced into the hall. "Ryder, how wonderful to see you!"

Ryder made a grab for Jean, arched her over one arm and kissed her cheek with a theatrical flair. "Darling," he said with a stage leer, "come away with me."

"Alas," Jean sighed, holding her forearm over her eyes, "I cannot. The sink is full of dirty dishes."

"Cynic," he accused, raising her again. "You've broken my heart. It will take at least a platter of scrambled eggs to make it whole again. A couple of biscuits. A pot of coffee…" He was already on his way into the kitchen.

"Your stomach will do you in, one day," Ivy accused as she followed with her mother.

"Only if I marry a girl who can't cook," Ryder returned. He sat down at the table wearily. "God, what a long drive."

"Where did you come from?" Ivy asked as she set him a place at the table, which was already laden with food.

"The stork brought me…" he began.

"The stork couldn't have carried you," came the smug reply. "You were probably unloaded under a cabbage leaf by a backhoe…."

"Keep it up," he dared. "Come on. One more remark about my weight and you'll be wearing your scrambled eggs."

"Peasant," she said with mock arrogance.

"I have earthy leanings, all right," he mused, watching her with a predatory smile.

She went scarlet, grateful that her mother's back was turned. She couldn't meet his playful eyes. Remembering the feel of his mouth on her neck made her knees go weak. It was disloyal to go lusting after a man on the heels of her husband's death. Except that she'd lusted after Ryder since her fifteenth birthday, heart and soul. She'd managed to keep him from seeing it, but over the years her love had grown stronger. It was because of Ryder that she'd never been able to give herself fully to Ben. It had been Ryder whom she'd wanted, from the first day she'd seen him. But he'd been rich and she'd been poor and too young to catch his eyes. So she'd buried her hopeless longings and married Ben. She couldn't afford to try to go back to the past. She'd cheated Ben and now he was dead. She owed him loyalty if nothing less. Ryder didn't want her that way, anyway. He was only teasing. She was sure of it.

Ryder, watching her, could see the wall going up. He sighed as he creamed the coffee Jean had just poured him. "I drove down from the Atlanta airport," he volunteered. "The house is cold and there's no heat…" He contrived to look pitiful.

"You can stay with us," Jean said. "We have a spare bedroom."

"Of course," Ivy seconded, but she wouldn't look at him.

He hesitated, watching Ivy. "No, that's all right," he murmured. "I wouldn't want to impose. I can buy some thermal underwear and wrap up in a blanket."

Ivy burst out laughing at that picture. Ryder could have checked into the local motel. For goodness' sake, he could have bought the local motel. And here he sounded as if he'd freeze without them.

"You poor man," Ivy said, turning, vividly beautiful with her black eyes sparkling in her flushed, animated face.

"Poor, in some ways," he agreed, smiling faintly while he stared and stared, mesmerized by her beauty. "You're a nice girl, Ivy," he mused, and forced his eyes back onto his plate as they all sat down. "I'll stay at the house, but I appreciate being invited to breakfast. I was starved, and this is delicious," he added, savoring a bite of perfect scrambled eggs.

"Thank you," Jean said, grinning at him.

"Can Ivy cook like this?" he asked.

"Of course," Jean replied.

Ryder pursed his firm lips and grinned. "My stomach hears wedding bells."

Ivy went white. It was the shock, of course, the remembrance of grief, of what she'd lost. Ryder didn't feel things this deeply, she tried to tell herself, he wouldn't understand how much it hurt to joke about it, when she had Ben on her conscience. Ben. She'd killed Ben...!

He caught her just as she went sideways, lifting her gently in his hard arms. "For God's sake..." he ground out, his face betraying a flash of helpless shock.

"She'll get over it," Jean said. "She's hardly slept lately, or eaten very much. It's early days yet, and she loved him."

"Yes," Ryder bit off coldly. "I know."

Jean glanced at him and glanced quickly away, because what she'd glimpsed in his face was too private, too hellish, for words. "Here, put her on the sofa. I'll get a cold cloth."

He didn't reply. He carried his light burden into the living room and put her down gently on the big couch. He knelt beside her, brushing back the long, silky hair from her still face. Like a sleeping princess, he thought irrationally, his eyes lingering, his heart aching...

He watched those long, thick lashes slowly lift. Her eyes showed confusion and then she smiled at him. His hands in her hair tightened, clenched. It was all he could do not to bend his head that bare inch it would take to feel her soft, sweet lips under his. He was aware of Jean then, of her voice. He didn't hear what she said, but he got to his feet and moved back to let her put the cloth on Ivy's head. He felt as if he'd stopped breathing, but Ivy was all right. She was sitting up, now, and looking embarrassed.

"Sorry about that," she said. Her eyes went to Ryder, who looked like death walking. "Ryder, I'm so sorry," she said gently. "It was just…"

"I know what it was. I'm sorry, too," he replied tersely. "Perhaps I'd better go."

"Without your breakfast?" Ivy asked. "And what for?"

"I don't want to upset you any more," he said.

Jean mumbled something about putting away the cloth and left the room, but neither of them noticed.

"You won't," Ivy continued, puzzled by that coldness in his eyes.

"He's dead," he said curtly. "Nothing you can say or do or feel or think will bring him back. If the mention of the word wedding has that kind of effect on you…"

"It doesn't, normally," she shot back. "I haven't been eating properly and I'm just weak!"

"And touchy," he added. "After six months, still touchy and nervous and overwrought."

"I have a right to be," she said angrily. "I loved him!" she said. Maybe if she said it enough, she could make herself believe that she had, that she hadn't cheated her husband because of what she'd felt for Ryder.

He didn't say anything. He just stared at her, his face pasty under his tan, his eyes fierce and intent.

"I did!" she cried. "I did, I did!"

She put her face in her hands and the tears came, hot under her fingers. "I can't live like this," she whispered brokenly.

"You can, and you will." He lifted her off the sofa, holding her firmly with both hands. "This has got to stop. Six months is long enough to grieve. You're going to start living again."

"That sounds like a threat. What are you going to do, take me on as a new construction project?" she challenged tearfully. "Remodel me? Renovate me?"

"Something like that," he said absently. He whipped out a handkerchief and mopped her up, his fingers deft and sure on her pale face. "Now stop wailing. It upsets me."

"Nothing upsets you," she said, obediently blowing her red nose. "Well, maybe little things do," she corrected. She smiled faintly. "Like the day your car kept cutting off in traffic and you drove it back to the construction site and dropped a wrecking ball right through the windshield."

He chuckled. "Damn it, good enough for it. I'd had it in three different shops and nobody could fix it."

"I'd love to hear what you told the insurance company."

"I didn't call the insurance company, I just bought another car," he said. "From another manufacturer," he added, grinning.

"It must be lovely, to have that kind of money."

"I can't eat it," he said lazily. "Or drink it. Or snuggle up to it on a cold winter night. I could use it for wallpaper, of course, or make cigarettes out of it…"

"You're nuts."

"Thanks, I'm crazy about you, too. How about breakfast, before I starve to death? Carrying you in here used up my last few ounces of strength."

She laughed helplessly. "All right. Come on, bottomless pit." She frowned suddenly. "You said you ate on the plane…?"

"When it left Germany," he replied. "And I'm starving. My God, airlines need to consider hardworking men and pregnant women when they serve food!"

"You're obviously a hardworking man, since you'd hardly qualify as the other…hey!"

He made a vicious swipe at her posterior, and she jumped clear just in time with a shocked laugh.

"No fighting at the table, children," Jean said, wagging a finger at them, "or I'll hide the food."

A corner of Ryder's mouth tugged down as he glared at Ivy, who'd retreated to a strategic position behind her mother.

"All right. She's safe. For now." The way he said it, and the look in his pale eyes, made Ivy melt inside. But she had to pretend that she wasn't affected. She turned away, making a joke of it, and refused to take him seriously.

She had to forget what had happened out on the porch. It was disloyal to Ben. She didn't deserve to be happy. She wouldn't let herself have Ryder, even if he was finally within her reach, because she'd caused Ben to kill himself with her hopeless longing. It wouldn't be fair to expect happiness at such a price.

Chapter 2

Ryder answered Jean's teasing questions about his latest jaunt, but his eyes kept going to Ivy. She felt them on her, curious, searching, and she was more nervous with him than she'd ever been.

"I said, do you want some more bacon, darling?" Jean asked her daughter for the second time, smiling as Ryder grimaced—he hated bacon.

"What? Oh, no, thanks, I've had enough." Ivy smiled. She sipped her coffee slowly.

"You look as if you haven't eaten for weeks," Ryder observed, studying her over his empty plate. He was leaning back in his chair and he looked impossibly arrogant.

"She hardly eats anything," Jean muttered, getting up from the table. "Talk some sense into her, Ryder, will you?" she called as she disappeared.

Ryder toyed with his cup, glancing up at Ivy with suddenly piercing gray eyes. "I think what you need most is to get away from things that remind you of the past. Just for a little while."

She considered that. "That's a nice thought," she agreed. "But I have a total of twenty-eight dollars and thirty-five cents in my checking account…"

"Oh, hell, what do you think I'm suggesting, a tourist special with a sight-seeing jaunt by bus thrown in?" he grumbled. "Listen, honey, I've got a cabin in the north Georgia mountains, a villa in Nassau and a summer house in Jacksonville. Take your pick," he said. "I'll even fly you there myself."

She smiled at him. "You're a nice man, Ryder," she said. "But I couldn't."

"Why not? I won't try to seduce you," he said, and smiled faintly, although there was no humor in his eyes. Her breath caught and he saw her stir restlessly at the suggestive remark. "I'm just offering you a vacation."

"I'm not sure what I want to do, just yet," she said, faltering.

"You aren't afraid of me, are you?" he asked curiously. "Surely not, as long as we've know each other."

She stared at him then, her eyes faintly hunted. "Yes," she confessed. "I think I am, a little. Do you mind?"

His smile was gentle and puzzling. "As a matter of fact, Ivy, I don't mind in the least," he said. "I'm flattered."

Despite her marriage, she felt frankly naive in some respects. She stared at Ryder curiously and thought that he'd probably had more women than most men she'd been acquainted with. The thought of Ryder in bed with a woman shocked her, angered her. She was grateful that her mother came back in time to spare her any more embarrassing remarks.

"I wrapped you up some biscuits to take with you," Jean said, coming out of the pantry with a small sack in hand. She closed the door, picked up the coffeepot and returned to the table.

"You angel," Ryder said, grinning. "Come home and cook for me. Ivy can feed herself."

"Brute," Ivy said indignantly.

"You have Kim Sun," Jean reminded him as she refilled their cups. "By the way, where is he?"

"Shivering, I expect, and trying to make cherry crepes on an open hearth." He sighed. "He's making me a new dish for dinner." He looked hunted. "Wouldn't you like to invite me to dinner, and save me?"

"Kim Sun is a wonderful cook!" Jean burst out.

"When it comes to French pastry, maybe," he muttered. "He'd gone through two pounds of flour when I left the house. I just asked him to fix me some eggs and he muttered something in Korean that I know I'd have fired him for, if I could have translated it."

"He makes marvelous pastry," Ivy offered.

"I can't live on desserts. When I hired him, I didn't know about this one fatal flaw—I didn't know he could *only* cook desserts. He was a pastry chef, for God's sake, he can't even boil a damned potato!"

"He spoils you rotten," Jean reminded him.

He glared at her. "He also has the world's sharpest tongue and he treats me like dust under his shoes. I'm going to fire him!"

"Oh, is that why you sent for his parents and got them a house to live in and…" Ivy began, amused.

"You can shut up," he enunciated curtly. He finished his

coffee and got up. "I've got to go. He may have burned the house down by now."

"If you'd called us, we'd have had the gas company turn things on for you," Jean said.

"I thought about it, but I was in a big hurry to get home." He bent to kiss Jean's cheek. "Thanks for breakfast."

"Anytime."

His pale eyes shot to Ivy, lingering on her face. "Walk me to the door, Ivy," he invited.

She got up, too, sticking her hands into her pockets. "Poor soul, he can't find his own way out." She shook her head. "What do you do when you're in the city, hire a man to point?"

He glanced at her. "I got the distinct impression earlier that you'd be delighted to show me to the door," he said softly.

She flushed. "You…you do come on pretty strong," she said as they reached the hall, out of Jean's earshot.

"And if I didn't?" he asked carelessly.

"I like you just the way you are, Ryder," she said with unconscious warmth, looking up.

His jaw tautened at that softness in her lovely eyes. He had to drag his eyes away. "I worry about you," he said tersely. "You can't live in the past. You've got to start living again."

"I know. It's the way he died…" She swallowed, folding her arms around her. "It's going to take time to cope with it once and for all."

"I know that," he sighed. His eyes went over her in soft sketches. "If what happened out here disturbed you," he said suddenly, watching her color as he brought back his unorthodox greeting, "it's been a long dry spell."

That she could believe, since he hadn't noticed her in that way in years. She threw off the pain and managed a dry smile.

"Long dry spell, my foot," she scoffed. "What happened? Did your harem trip over their veils and break something?"

"I don't have a harem," he remarked as they reached the front door. His pale eyes wandered slowly down her exquisite figure. "I've gone hungry for a long, long time," he said in a different tone.

She flushed, because the statement seemed to have an intimate connotation, but when he looked up, his eyes were dancing.

"Beast!" she accused, hitting his broad chest playfully.

"Beauty," he replied.

She started to speak and gave up. He was always one step ahead. "I give up," she muttered. "It's like arguing with a broom!"

"I'm going down below Blakely to a farm equipment auction in the morning. Want to ride with me?"

Of course she did, but she knew he only asked out of pity. He was an old family friend and he felt sorry for her. It only made her unrequited love for him more painful. "I have things to do here," she hedged.

"Tomorrow is Saturday," he reminded her.

"I know that." She searched for excuses, but they ran through her mind like sand through a sieve. Her big black eyes lifted, dark with frustration.

"All right," he said. "No pressure. If you don't want to come, I won't hound you."

She relaxed visibly. "I'm sorry, Ryder…"

"Of course. Another time, then." He said it lightly, but he seemed brooding, preoccupied as he left.

Later, when she mentioned the invitation to her mother, Jean was puzzled.

"Why didn't you want to go with him?" she asked her daughter.

She didn't want to have to explain that. She turned away. "It's too soon," she said. "Ben's barely been dead six months."

"For heaven's sake, Ryder isn't asking you to sleep with him! He only wanted you to go for a ride. Honestly, Ivy, I don't understand you! Ryder's the best friend you have."

"Yes, I know," Ivy said in anguish. And she thought, that's the whole problem.

Even though she'd refused to go with him to the auction, Ryder came by the house on his way. He was driving the farm's four-wheel-drive this time, a big tan-and-brown pickup, and he was dressed in tan boots, tight jeans, and a chambray shirt that might have been tailor-made for him. A black Stetson was cocked over his pale eyes. Ivy stood at the back door and just stared at him, filling her empty heart with the sheer masculine perfection of him as he climbed out of the vehicle and strode lazily toward the porch.

She was wearing a denim skirt and a long-sleeved white blouse with a patterned scarf carelessly knotted at her throat. She had on her boots, too, because she'd planned to go for a walk so that she wouldn't brood over having turned down Ryder's invitation. If she'd left five minutes earlier, she'd have missed him. She didn't know whether to be sorry or glad.

She opened the door as he came up the steps, noticing the way his eyes narrowed and skimmed lightly over her figure before they found their way to her own.

"Ready?" he asked with a taunting smile.

"I was going for a walk," she began.

"Jean, we're gone!" he called to her mother.

"Have fun!" Jean called back from her bedroom.

"But, I'm not going with you," Ivy began weakly.

He swung her easily up in his hard arms, smiling at her consternation. "Yes, you are," he said softly.

He turned and walked out the door, his taut-muscled, fit body taking her weight as easily as if she were a sack of feathers.

His chest was warm and hard against her breast, and she smelled the tangy cologne he wore and the faint scent of shaving cream on his face. He had lines beside his silvery eyes, and thick black lashes over them. His nose was slightly dented from a few free-for-alls in his younger days. But his mouth…she almost groaned aloud just looking at it. Wide and sensual, chiseled, with a thin upper lip and slightly fuller lower one over perfect white teeth. She wanted so badly to lift her face the fraction of an inch necessary to put her open mouth to his.

The feverish need shocked her. She'd never wanted to kiss anyone else so badly, and she'd dreamed about it for years. But she had to remember that Ryder was only being kind. He didn't feel that way about her, and the sooner she realized it, the better.

Her convictions didn't help, though, when he balanced her on one knee to open the door and slid her onto the seat. She fell against him in the process and his mouth came so close that she could all but taste the coffee on his breath.

He hesitated, his eyes narrow and glittery, his body tense for just an instant. Then he smiled and let her go, and the moment passed.

He climbed in beside her to start the truck, lifting an eyebrow at her fumbling efforts to fasten her seat belt.

"Bulldozer," she accused.

He grinned. "Women are like machinery, you have to give them a push sometimes to get them going."

She laughed in spite of herself. She couldn't really picture another man with Ryder's boldness. He was in a class of his own.

"What do you need to buy at an auction that you couldn't afford at retail prices?" she asked curiously.

He draped his hand over the steering wheel as he sped down the driveway toward the main road. "Nothing in particular." He shrugged. "It was someplace to go. I don't like sitting at home. People know where to find me. And Kim Sun loves to put through people I don't want to talk to," he added, scowling. "Damn it, I ought to fire him!"

"What did you do to him?"

His eyebrows arched. "What?"

"You must have done something to irritate him," she persisted.

He glanced at her. "All I did was throw a plate of fish at him," he muttered. "Well, I hate most fish, anyway," he said defensively. "But this wasn't even cooked."

"Sushi." She nodded.

He glared at her. "No, not sushi," he muttered. "I had my heart set on salmon croquettes like your mother makes. He brought me balls of raw salmon with, ugh, onions cut up on them."

"Did you tell him how to make salmon croquettes?" she asked, trying not to laugh.

"Hell, I don't know how to cook! If I knew how to cook, would I cart that vicious renegade around with me?"

"Kim Sun can't read minds," she said. "If you'll send him down to us, mother can show him how to make the things you like."

He shifted his eyes back to the road. "You can cook. You might come up to the house and show him yourself."

She didn't answer. She stared at her hands in her lap. The temptation was overwhelming, but he wouldn't know that.

"We'd have a chaperone," he said softly.

She flushed, refusing to meet his eyes. "Ryder…!"

"So shy of me," he said on a heavy sigh. "I've stayed away too long. I guess I knew it wouldn't be long enough, at that, but a man can stand just so much," he added enigmatically. "I thought you'd be healed by now."

She swallowed. "Healed?"

"You can't climb into the grave with him," he said through his teeth.

"I'm not trying to do that," she said. She glanced at his strong profile and felt her heart jump. "I…missed you," she said huskily.

He seemed to shiver. His pale eyes cut sideways, narrow, dangerous. "I'd have come home anytime you told me that," he said roughly. "In the middle of the night, if you needed me."

She felt warm all over at the tenderness in his tone, and wanted to cry because it was just friendship. He cared about her, of course he did, but not in the way she wanted him to. She straightened her full skirt. "You had enough to do, without worrying about me," she said. "All I need is time, you know."

He pulled into a drive-in and cut off the engine. "Want coffee?" he asked.

"Yes. Black, please."

"I remember how you like it," he said. He got out of the truck and came back less than five minutes later with coffee and doughnuts. He handed hers to her and made room for the cups in the holder he'd installed on the dash.

She sipped coffee and ate the doughnut. "Delicious," she said with a smile. "I haven't had breakfast."

"Neither have I. Food bothers me if I eat too early." He let his eyes slide over her figure. "You're too thin, little one. You need to eat more."

"I haven't had much appetite lately."

He turned toward her, crossing his long legs as he dipped his doughnut into his coffee and nibbled it. "Talk about it. Maybe it will help."

She searched his pale eyes, finding nothing there to frighten her. "He was drunk," she blurted out. "He went to work drinking and pushed the wrong buttons."

His chiseled lips parted. "I see."

"Didn't you know? Don't pretend you haven't asked how it happened. The insurance company refused my claim, but the company stood for it, so that we could afford the funeral." Her big black eyes searched his. "You did it, didn't you? You made them pay it."

"Employees pay into the credit union," he said tersely. "Ben had accumulated a good bit, to which you were entitled. That's what paid the funeral expense."

"You knew he was drunk on the job," she repeated, her eyes huge and hurt.

He sighed. "Yes, Ivy, I knew," he replied, meeting her gaze. "I knew about the drinking." His face tautened. "It's why I stayed away as much as I did. Because Jean told me about the bruises, once, and if I'd seen them, I'd have killed him right in front of you."

She started as the words penetrated her brain. She couldn't even respond, because he looked and sounded violent.

He saw her reaction and cursed his tongue. He couldn't afford to let anything slip; not now. "I'd have done the same if Eve had been in a similar position," he added. "You girls mean a lot to me. I'm sure you know that."

"Yes. Of course." She couldn't afford to look disappointed. She managed a smile. "You always were protective."

"I needed to be, just occasionally." His eyes pierced into hers. "If I'd been around when Ben made his move on you, you'd never have married him. I couldn't have been more shocked than I was the day I came back and found you married to him."

"I'd gone to school with him, you know. We were good friends."

"Friends don't necessarily make good mates," he returned. He finished his coffee. "Ben was known for his drinking even before I hired him. He'd sworn off it and seemed to be on the wagon, so I told the personnel department to give him a chance."

She'd wondered suddenly why he'd done that. She knew that Ben's father had worked for the company, but it was curious that he should have hired a man who'd been known for his tendency toward alcohol. Perhaps it had been out of the goodness of his heart, but there was something in his face when he said it...

He looked at her suddenly and she averted her eyes. "Ben appreciated your giving him the job," she said.

"Hell! He hated my guts and you know it," he returned, glaring at her. "The longer you were married, the more he hated me."

She held her breath, hoping he wasn't going to start asking why. Surely he didn't suspect the reason?

"He hated mother, too," she said, trying to smooth it over, "although he never let her see it. He hated anyone I... cared about."

His face hardened. "And he hit you?"

She averted her gaze to the floorboard. "Not often," she said huskily.

"My God—" His voice broke. He sat up straight and began to bag up the refuse.

Ivy felt his pain even through the cold wall he was already putting up. Impulsively she touched his hard arm, feeling him stiffen at the light touch. His pale eyes met hers and she saw his breathing quicken.

"Please," she said softly. "I hurt him. I can't tell you all of it, but he was a gentle kind of man until he married me. He wanted something I couldn't give him."

His eyes held hers. "In bed?" he asked roughly.

She flushed and drew back, embarrassed. "I can't talk about that," she said huskily.

"Shades of my prim and proper spinster aunt," he murmured, watching her. "Three years of marriage and you can't talk about sex."

The color deepened. "It's a deeply personal subject."

"And you can't talk to me about it?" he persisted. "There was a time when you could ask me anything without feeling embarrassed."

"Not about…that," she amended tautly.

His eyes fell to her firm, high breasts and lingered there with appreciation before they ran back up over her full lips to her eyes. "So reserved," he murmured. "Such a ladylike appearance. But you have French blood, little one. There must be sensuality in you, even if your husband was never one to drag it out of you. Wasn't he man enough?" he taunted mockingly.

She actually gasped. He sounded as if he hated Ben, and it was in his eyes, in the way he spoke. He even looked rigid, as if his backbone were encased in plaster.

"I'm sorry," he said abruptly. "That was a question I had no right to ask. Here, give me that."

He took her cup and the paper that had held the doughnut and put them into the sack that had contained the food. He got out without another word to put it in the garbage container.

She sat almost vibrating with nerves. She'd never dreamed that the conversation would turn into an inquisition, and his attitude toward Ben was frightening. How much did he know? And if he'd been aware of Ben's drinking, why hadn't he fired him? Ryder was so particular about his work force. He knew intimate little things about almost all of them, and he had his secretary send get-well cards when they were sick and flowers if someone died. He wouldn't tolerate crooks or drunkards, but he'd tolerated Ben, whom he actively disliked. Why? For Ivy's sake? Because she was like a younger sister to him? She couldn't understand it.

He got back into the truck. "Well, I'm still starved, but that will have to do," he said, good humor apparently restored. "A few hamburgers at lunch will save me yet."

She laughed, their earlier harsh words already forgotten as he turned the pickup toward the highway.

The auction was fascinating. She walked along beside Ryder, looking at equipment she didn't even know the name of, listening while he expounded on its merits and flaws.

His pale eyes looked out over the flat horizon and narrowed. "Before too many more years, little one, land and water are going to be as rare as buffalo. The population keeps growing, and someday soon there isn't going to be enough for all the people."

"Land grows, too," she said, smiling up at him. "It comes up out of the ocean."

"Not around here, it doesn't," he mused, tapping her nose with a long forefinger. He smiled back, but his finger moved down to her mouth and began to trace, with apparent carelessness, the perfect outline of her lips.

The tracing made her feel shaky all over. Her breath jerked out against that maddening finger, and he seemed suddenly intent on her mouth, his jaw tensing, his eyes going glittery. His own lips parted and she could actually hear his heartbeat.

"How long have we known each other?" he asked huskily.

"Years," she whispered. "Since I was…in grammar school."

"All those years, and nothing but bitter memories for both of us," he said harshly. His voice had gone deeper, huskier, and his gaze was intent on her mouth. "Yes, you remember, don't you?" he asked, watching her cheeks flush. "It's still there between us, even now."

She could hardly breathe. She dropped her eyes to his chest. "I didn't realize the door was open," she said miserably.

"I know. But at the time I didn't. And for that, I'm sorry."

Her face did a slow burn. She remembered that night as if it were yesterday. She'd tormented herself with it for years. She'd been spending the night with Eve. She was only eighteen, and a very naive eighteen. Eve had gone with her mother to get a pizza, leaving Ivy alone in the house, or so she thought. Ryder had come home unexpectedly. Not knowing he was in the house, she hadn't thought to close her bedroom door.

She'd been on her way to the shower and had stripped off everything but the lovely cream-colored silk teddy that Eve had given her for Christmas. It was the most expensive piece of lingerie she'd ever owned, despite the fact that she never expected anyone—much less Ryder—to see her wearing it.

But that night he'd seen the open door, and Ivy in the lacy teddy, and he'd thought she was parading around in it deliberately, for his benefit.

Even now she could see the look on his face. He'd frozen in the doorway, his pale eyes narrowing, darkening. His lips had parted on a shocked breath, and instead of apologizing and going out, he'd closed the door and walked into the room, something in his face vaguely accusing and angry.

Ivy had been eighteen. Young, hopelessly naive, and in the throes of her first real crush. She'd looked up at him with all her helpless longing in her eyes, so innocently beautiful that it had taken all his willpower to keep his hands off her. His eyes had touched her, though, like caressing hands, lingering where the all-but-transparent lace of the bodice gave an explicit glimpse of the tight bud of her nipples, dark against the pale lace.

She'd stopped breathing. Ryder's eyes had met hers then and held them, his big body rigid.

It was a permissive world, and Eve made no secret of her liberated attitude toward the boys she dated. But Ivy was old-fashioned, and to let a man see her in her underwear was a shocking and embarrassing experience. Unfortunately for her, Ryder didn't know that. He'd always assumed that she shared Eve's modern outlook.

"Very nice," he'd said, his voice caressing while his eyes had feasted on her lace-and-silk-clad body, lingering where her breasts pushed against the bodice. "But then, you always were a beauty, Ivy."

"You shouldn't be in here," she faltered, torn between delight and fear.

"Why not?" His pale eyes had glittered. "You left the door open and waited for me, didn't you?"

Her eyes had dilated wildly even as he reached for her. "Ryder, you don't understand…!"

But the feverish protest had come too late. Ryder had been watching her, wanting her, for a long time. Despite his anger at what he thought was entrapment, her beauty was too much for his self-control.

His big, lean hands had framed her face and his eyes watched her as he bent his head. But it wasn't her mouth he touched. It was the hard, aching tip of her lace-covered breast.

Her hands had curled on his shoulders and she'd made a sound that she could barely recall making. The warm, moist suction of his hard mouth had caused the most abandoned sensations in her slender body, had made her ache and burn and shiver with needs she hadn't been aware of before. She'd been dazedly aware of his hands sliding the straps of the teddy down her arms, of his eyes suddenly, shockingly, on her bare, mauve-tipped breasts before he bent again. This time, he'd picked her up in his arms, lifting her, his mouth still covering her nipple.

Her fingers had been in his thick hair, holding his mouth to her body while she fought with pride and inhibitions and a certainty that he'd lost control of his own body.

"Ryder, you mustn't," she'd whispered weakly as he laid her on the twin bed across the room from Eve's, the bed she was sleeping in during her overnight visit. "You mustn't!"

He hadn't seemed to hear her. He'd followed her down onto the bed, his long, powerful legs trapping hers, his hands smoothing the satiny skin of her back while his mouth suddenly found hers and took it with deliberate intent.

It was the first real adult kiss Ivy had ever received, and so passionate that even the memory of it could make her blush.

It was a deep, sultry probing of her mouth that had left her shaking and helpless in his arms.

His mouth had smoothed over her body then, like fire, and she'd arched upward, her response so uninhibited that it had knocked any suspicion of her innocence right out of his whirling mind. Her arms had twined around him, her hands tangling in his thick hair, and tiny little moans had whispered into his mouth as he teased her nipples with strong, warm hands before he began to nuzzle them with his lips and bite at them gently.

Her trembling pleas had sent him over the edge. "Feel how hard you turn me on," he'd whispered roughly, his dark eyes looking down into hers as his hands contracted on her hips, bringing them into tight contact with his aroused body. He ground her against the hardness, watching her lips tremble, her eyes widen at the graphic evidence of his desire. "I want you so much, I can hardly bear it! Can you take care of yourself, baby?"

The husky question had brought her to her senses like a shower of cold water. "Take…care of myself?" she'd faltered, her body throbbing with pleasure from the warmth of his hands, the sweet brush of his mouth.

"Have you got something to use, or are you on the pill?" he'd demanded, his voice deeper, his eyes dark with passion as he fought to maintain control.

Her face had gone scarlet. "Ryder, I'm… I'm a virgin," she'd whispered. "I don't know how to…to…I mean, I'm not on the pill."

His dark brows had drawn together. "You're a what?"

She'd swallowed, because he looked frightening. "I've never done this before," she whispered.

He'd said something that she'd never heard from a man's lips before he dragged himself away from her and got to his feet, glaring down at her as if he hated her. "Damn you," he'd sworn huskily, the very softness of his voice more intimidating than shouting would have been. "You vicious little tease!" He'd added some other insults to that one, words she'd spent years trying to forget, explicit things that she couldn't have imagined Ryder saying to any woman. He'd left her, but she hadn't heard him go. She'd cried all night long, deceiving Eve when she returned with the pretence of a migraine. And she'd never again spent a night at the Calaway house, despite all Eve's invitations. Only she and Ryder knew why, and until now, they'd never mentioned the subject.

It had left scars on Ivy's emotions. The experience had made her feel cheap, somehow. Also, it had shown her how vulnerable she was, and how skillful Ryder was at seduction. Eve had talked occasionally about Ryder's women and his love of freedom, so she knew it had only been an impulse with him, a momentary yielding to desire.

But she'd given him her heart that night. Afterward, she'd found reasons not to go to the Calaway house overnight again. And, indeed, during those two years before Ben came into her life, Ryder had seemed to avoid Ivy as well. But about the time Ben started noticing her, Ryder had come back into her life and casually invited her to dinner one night. Frightened of herself, and of the look in his eyes when he watched her, she'd invented a date with Ben. When she'd confessed what she'd done to Ben, he'd made the date real. Weeks later, while Ryder was out of the country, she and Ben were quietly married.

"Yes, you remember, don't you?" he asked. "I made the mistake of my life that night. The next day I went to Toronto, and I avoided you like the plague after that, or didn't you notice?" he asked on a rueful laugh. "And from that day on, if you spent the night with Eve, it was at your house, not mine."

"It wasn't what you thought," she began. "I honestly didn't know you were in the house."

His face contorted and he looked away. "Oh, God, don't you think I finally realized that? But the damage was done. The only reparation I could make was to keep out of your way. I'd made you afraid of me. I didn't want to do any worse damage. But in the end it wasn't necessary. You ran straight to Ben the first time I asked you out on a date."

Her shoulders lifted and fell in a helpless little gesture. "I thought you might still think I was a…tease and…" She swallowed. Her fears sounded juvenile now. She wrapped her arms around her. "I couldn't be sure that you might not be in the mood for a little revenge. You seemed to hate me that night. You said…" She laughed brokenly. "You said I was too small-breasted to appeal to any real adult male, and that it was just proximity that had made you touch me at all."

His eyes closed on a heavy sigh. He turned toward the horizon again and rammed his hand into his pocket. "Men… say things when they're frustrated," he murmured uneasily. "I'm sure you know that now. I didn't mean any of the things I said to you that night. I was hurting pretty bad."

She stared at the ground. She'd managed to work that out, over the years. It didn't help very much. She'd loved him, and he'd savaged her fragile ego. "I'm sorry," she said helplessly.

"It wasn't your fault," he replied curtly. "I should have walked away, but I couldn't. I'd never seen anything so beautiful." He glanced at her, his face rigid when he read the doubt in her dark eyes.

She felt warm all over at the softness in his deep voice. She couldn't quite manage to meet his eyes, though, and it sounded more like an apology than praise. "Thank you, but you don't have to pretend," she said, her eyes staring blankly toward the distant trees. "Ben thought I was...too small, too—Ryder!"

He took her by the arms, his steely grip unconsciously bruising as he jerked her up against him. "I lied," he said huskily, eyes blazing. "Can't you get it through your head that I lied? I wanted you almost enough to force you, damn it! I had to get out of there, I had to hurt you so that you wouldn't reach out to me when I let you go!" His tall, powerful frame seemed to vibrate with passion. "Oh, God, Ivy, you don't know how that night has haunted me over the years. You don't know...!"

She recognized the unholy torment in his face without understanding what was causing it. Without thinking, she reached up to his lean cheek and touched it gently. He actually flinched, but when she started to draw her hand back, he pressed it, palm flat, to his jaw.

"It's all right," she faltered. "It was years ago."

"It was yesterday." He looked older suddenly. Bone-weary. His eyes darkened as they searched her face. "You ran from me," he said huskily.

Her eyes fell. "I didn't know what else to do. I could never talk to Mama about things like that."

He pulled her against him and held her gently, his eyes staring blankly toward the auction platform. "Maybe it was a good thing to get it out in the open, to talk about it."

"Yes." She closed her eyes. It was heaven to stand in his arms, to be close to him like this. She shivered with pleasure.

Ryder felt the trembling and went rigid. She was afraid of

him. He'd thought the fear was because she wanted him. But was he only deluding himself, again? His big hand slid slowly down her back, bringing her even closer. He could feel her breath sighing out quickly at his throat, an erotic little sigh that made him feel hot all over. He liked the feel of her so close. It brought back memories of that night long ago when he'd tasted her, when she'd been everything in the world to him. She still was, but over the years the feeling had grown and ripened, until now what he felt for her was a raging fever that all the oceans on earth couldn't have put out. He wanted her, but not just physically. He wanted her like a thirsting man wants water, all of her, just for him.

"I used to wonder what life would have been like if I hadn't lost my head with you," he said under his breath, folding her even closer. "We were friends. Over the years I hoped that we could regain that closeness."

"I…thought we had," she said, trying to make her voice steadier, to calm her screaming pulse. The feel of all that masculine strength so close to her was doing impossible things to her. She wanted to reach up and hold him, to bury her face against his bare skin and feel him wanting her….

"Not quite," he said huskily. He drew in a ragged sigh. "But maybe if we work at it, Ivy, we might manage friendship again. What do you think?"

She closed her eyes. "I think we might, too," she whispered.

His heart raced wildly in his chest. He lifted his head and tilted her face up to him. "So beautiful," he said deeply. "Every man's dream."

Except yours. She almost said the words aloud. She smiled a little sadly and pulled away. "Not quite," she replied, laughing nervously. "Shouldn't we get back?" she said evasively, noticing the crowd gathering around the auction platform. "I think they're starting."

"What?" He had to force his mind to work. The scent of her was in his nostrils, the feel of her... He glanced where she was staring. "Oh. The auction. Yes, we'd better get back."

Back to reality, that was. He took her arm and guided her through the crowd, still savoring his brief taste of heaven. Friendship, he told himself firmly, was better than nothing. And from there, he might build something much more lasting and satisfying. He was smiling by the time the auctioneer began rattling off items for sale.

Chapter 3

Ivy stood beside him, feeling his warmth, his strength while the auction went on and on. He didn't speak to her until the bidding was over and they were walking back to the truck.

"You've gone quiet," he remarked, his hands toying with his coffee cup.

She stared down at her own feet while she waited. "It hurts to think back," she confessed. "I'd pushed it to the back of my mind for so long...."

"So had I," he said shortly. He took a long drink from the cup. "I misread the whole damned situation. I should have known what an innocent you were."

"Considering the way I gave in, I couldn't blame you for thinking what you did," she said miserably.

"Couldn't you?" he asked angrily.

Her eyes dropped and embarrassment washed over her in

waves. "I didn't even try to stop you at first," she said in a subdued tone, because it would do no good to lie anymore. "I felt like a streetwalker."

"I'm sorry about that." He glanced toward her with bitter regret in his eyes. "You had no reason to feel ashamed."

"You avoided me afterward," she said, her face showing traces of remembered pain.

"I felt that I had to," he replied, his voice quiet. "I handled it badly. But that taste of you gave me some problems," he murmured, laughing bitterly.

"I learned my lesson," she mused, staring straight ahead as other people milled around in the darkness. "It cured me of any wanton tendencies."

He stiffened. "You weren't wanton," he said curtly. "You were young and curious, that's all."

"Do you think that makes it any less embarrassing?" she asked wearily.

He stopped and looked down at her, his eyes hidden under the shadow cast by the brim of his hat. "We should have talked about it years ago," he said. "I could have told you that I wanted you badly enough to forget your age, that I stayed away because you were a temptation I couldn't have resisted. Does that make it less painful?"

She hesitated. "You…wanted me?" she whispered.

"Oh, yes," he replied grimly. "I wanted you. But you were eighteen, Ivy, and I was twenty-eight."

She searched his eyes, her body still, waiting. "I wanted you, too," she confessed softly.

His jaw tautened. "Do you still?" he asked bluntly.

She averted her face, tightening her arms across her chest.

"I can't feel anything right now," she said evasively. "Not with Ben lying dead because of me."

"What do you mean, because of you?"

She closed her eyes. "I failed him," she whispered huskily. "I could never…" Her shoulders rose and fell jerkily, and she stared in anguish toward the horizon. "I wasn't a good wife."

He let out his breath in a long, slow rush. He'd never considered that she might feel guilt. He scowled as he looked down at her, wishing he knew more about her marriage, about her feelings for her husband.

She uncrossed her arms and shoved her hands into the deep pockets of her skirt. "It's all over now, anyway," she said. "As you said, I have to start living again."

"Yes." He had to drag his eyes away from her face. Looking at her was a taste of heaven. He lit a cigarette. Ivy strung out his nerves; just being near her made him vibrate like a taut cord. "Why don't you get a job?"

She laughed. "Here we go again."

"That's right. Sitting around brooding is not good for you." He stopped and turned toward her. "Come to work for me. My personal assistant quit last month and I haven't found anyone yet to replace her. I have to have someone who can travel with me, and most especially, someone I can trust not to gossip about company business. You and I have known each other for a long time. I think we could get along."

The thought tempted her. But the anguish of being that near him made her hesitate. She loved him. How would it be to work for him, knowing that all he felt was a casual affection with lingering traces of a long-buried desire?

"I don't know," she said hesitantly. "I don't know if I'd like trying to keep up with you all over the world."

"I think you might enjoy it," he replied. "You'd get to see a lot of exotic places. The pay's good. You've got a quick mind, and I think you'd find the work interesting."

There was no doubt about that. Ryder always had something exciting going on in his business, and he knew a surprising number of famous people. It would be a fascinating job.

"Can I think about it?" she asked finally.

He smiled. "For a couple of weeks. I can't go on like this indefinitely. I'm no good at keeping the office organized, and the secretarial pool isn't adequate."

"It would mean a lot of travel?"

His eyes began to glitter again. "Yes. But the offer is an honest one. I'm not offering you a job so that I can lure you away from Jean's protection and throw you onto the nearest bed. I'm not that hard up for women these days."

She drew in a painful breath. "That was uncalled for!"

"Was it?" He glared at her with something akin to dislike. "Maybe you think you're irresistible, is that it? If it will set your mind at ease, I can take along one of my usual companions…"

She walked away from him, her heart pounding, her eyes flashing. "Take your job and sit on it," she fired at him as they reached the truck. "I wouldn't work for you under any circumstances!"

The flash of temper amused and delighted him. Maybe the idea of another woman in his arms affected her. It was a heady thought.

"Oh, I think you will," he mused, watching her. "You'll get damned tired of all this inactivity sooner or later. Sitting around will drive you crazy."

"So would you," she retorted.

He shrugged. "Better crazy than buried alive," he said, and

all the amusement left his hard face. "The best way to get over a loss is to get your mind off yourself. Get it on other people."

"How would working for you accomplish that?" she demanded.

He smiled. "Do it and see. One of my newest projects is a retirement village in Arizona. I'm designing it with the future residents in mind, so I keep in close contact with a few of them. They're well into their seventies and eighties, and they'll make you want to live to get old."

Despite herself, she was interested. "I like elderly people," she began hesitantly.

"So do I. The wisdom of the world resides in those keen minds. You'll find yourself fascinated by them."

"I don't doubt it." She traced a pattern on the door handle, her thin brows drawn into a frown. "I think I might like it," she said after a long minute.

Ryder didn't realize he'd been holding his breath. He let it out slowly, so that she didn't notice. "You could start Monday. I have to fly to Phoenix."

She lifted her eyes to his. "Why do you want to do this for me?"

"You're too young to hide in a mausoleum," he said simply. "I'd do the same for Eve. Despite the scare I gave you when you were eighteen, I think you know that you can trust me. Don't you?"

She nodded. "Yes. I know." She managed a smile. "Okay. I'll polish up my rusty office skills and pack my bags."

He searched her dark eyes for a long, static moment. "Good girl," he said finally. "Get in."

"But aren't we going home?" she asked when he pulled up in front of his own big brick house.

"Not until you teach that damned devil how to cook salmon, we aren't," he said curtly, helping her out of the pickup. "I'll call Jean and tell her where we are."

She burst out laughing. He had to be the most unpredictable man she'd ever known.

"That sounds good," he murmured on the way up the steps. "I haven't heard you laugh, really laugh, in a long time."

"Poor Kim Sun," she began.

Just as she spoke, the front door flew open and a small man with almond eyes, a balding head and a golden complexion launched himself at Ryder, shouting in an unintelligible language, waving his arms.

"Calm down," Ryder said heavily. "Damn it, calm down!" he repeated.

Kim Sun glared up at him. It was a long way, too. "No milk," he raged. "No eggs. No flour. No shortening. No sugar. How do you expect me to cook under such primitive conditions?"

"The lights are on," Ryder said. "At least you have a stove that works."

"What good is a stove without food to cook?"

"You've got salmon," Ryder said with a poisonous smile.

"Two guesses where I put your salmon this time…?" Kim Sun fired right back.

"I brought you an instructor," he said, pushing Ivy forward. "She and her mother make the best salmon croquettes south of the Antarctic."

Kim Sun bowed elegantly. "Miss Ivy. So good to see you again. Tutoring in the art of salmon cookery would be much appreciated." He glared toward Ryder. "Some people too stupid to realize one must be educated in preparation of a desired new food."

"Call me stupid one more time, and I'll send you home in a cornflakes box!"

"No breeding," Kim Sun told Ivy, shaking his head. "This peasant knows nothing of proper social behavior. I shall undertake his enlightenment. Again," he said with practiced weariness.

"Who are you calling a peasant?" Ryder demanded. "Who the hell pays your salary?"

"That pittance?" The indignant man scoffed at his employer. "You pay me not one tenth of my true worth."

"Listen, buster, if you got what you were really worth, you'd owe *me* money!" Ryder ground out. "A pittance!" He threw up his hands and looked skyward. "He must be the only cook in Georgia who drives a Mercedes-Benz!"

"Now, now," Ivy said gently. "Remember your blood pressure. Come on, Kim Sun, let's retreat before he cuts loose another barrage."

"Good idea," he replied. He made a face at Ryder. "Tomorrow, I quit!"

"Tomorrow, I fire you!" came the gruff reply.

Kim Sun said something in his own language and strutted off to the kitchen with an amused Ivy behind him.

He was a quick study. It took no time at all for Ivy to teach him how to make the croquettes that Ryder liked.

"Is he really so horrible to work for?" she asked, nibbling at a celery stick while she watched Kim Sun fry the croquettes in vegetable oil.

"Not horrible. Impossible!" Kim Sun shook his head. "He stays up all hours, never eats properly—work, work, work. He has no time for women, and he seems not to sleep very much. At first, I thought he was wasting away for love of someone. But now I think it is an addiction to making money."

"He's always been a restless kind of man," Ivy mused, smiling with the memory. "He could never sit still. But I didn't think you'd have a problem getting him to eat. Heavens, his appetite is legendary around these parts."

"Only for things I cannot cook. I thought he knew I was a pastry chef. The first time he asked for beef stew, I had a nervous breakdown. From that day, everything went downhill."

"I can imagine," she said, laughing. She pushed back her long hair and got up from the table where she'd been sitting. "I'd better go and reassure my mother that he hasn't kidnapped me."

He stared at her curiously. "Were you ever engaged to Mr. Boss?" he asked unexpectedly.

"Oh…why, no," she faltered. "Why do you ask?"

He averted his eyes. "Please excuse my curiosity," he asked softly, and even smiled. "Someday perhaps you will understand the reason for the question. Are the croquettes done now?" he added to divert her, drawing her attention back to the frying pan.

She wondered what he knew that she didn't. Ryder's attitude was brotherly for the rest of the afternoon. He talked to her about Eve and her husband, showed her the wooden elephants he'd brought home from Sri Lanka, and coaxed her to stay and eat a small salad and some of the salmon croquettes. Kim Sun had done a great job, she had to admit.

"Next week, fried chicken," Ryder told her, leaning back in his chair after he'd polished off an exquisite Pavlova that Kim Sun had created from egg whites and fruit and whipped cream. "You can't stop now. We'll make a Southern chef out of him yet!"

"Not likely," Kim Sun muttered as he removed dishes. "One dish does not a chef make."

"Then we'll get her to give you weekly lessons," Ryder assured him. "She can consider it part of her job."

"Kim Sun might not like me for a role model," she began.

"He will," Ryder said, glaring at the fuming cook. "Or I'll let him polish the entire family silver service tonight."

A furious spate of Korean echoed from the direction of the kitchen after Kim Sun exploded out of the room and down the hall, both arms waving emphatically.

"He'll quit one day," Ivy assured Ryder.

"He wouldn't dare," he replied smugly. "Where else would he get a cushy job like this and a terrific boss like me?"

Ivy burst out laughing. "Poor Kim Sun."

"Poor me," he sighed. "The minute you leave, he'll hide my coffee."

"I don't really blame him," she said, but she smiled, her dark eyes lingering involuntarily on the strong lines of his face.

Her intent scrutiny made his pulse leap wildly. He returned the long, steady stare and saw the color seep into her cheeks before she jerked her eyes down. Her shyness made him feel protective.

He got up from his chair. "I'll run you home. Can you be ready to go by six Monday morning?" he added, all business in an instant. "We'll have to catch a commuter flight out of Albany so that we can make connections in Atlanta."

"Yes, I can be ready," she assured him. Mentally she was kicking herself for agreeing to work for him. It was probably going to be the worst mistake of her life.

Jean didn't think so. She was all smiles when Ivy told her. "You'll enjoy it, you know you will," she told her daughter. "And Ryder will take care of you."

"I suppose I'm doing the right thing," Ivy sighed.

"Just take it one day at a time, sweetheart," her mother said gently. "And don't worry. All right?"

Ivy smiled and hugged her. "All right."

Ryder picked her up at the house at 6:00 a.m. sharp the following Monday. He looked elegant in a dark blue vested pinstriped suit. A black Stetson and black boots completed his ensemble. She felt much less stylish in a two-year-old black suit with a simple white cotton blouse.

"Did it have to be black?" he muttered after they'd said goodbye to Jean and headed for the Albany airport.

"My suit, you mean?" she faltered. She smoothed a hand over her hair, which was pulled tight into a French twist at her nape. "It was the only one I had…."

"I could have advanced you enough to buy something less morose," he said tightly.

"It isn't morose," she returned. "Basic black is supposed to be very flattering."

His eyes stated his opinion of it. He shifted his gaze back to the road. "I'm sorry to toss you into the deep end like this. Ideally you'd have a few weeks in the office to get used to the routine. But I've got to do some work in Phoenix on site, and you might as well see what we're doing out there. It will help you to understand the work you'll be involved with."

"I've never been to Arizona," she confessed.

"You'll love it or hate it," he said. "Especially the part of it we're going to."

"Sand and rattlesnakes?" she suggested nervously.

He smiled. "Wait and see."

They flew into Phoenix several hours later, and Ivy, who had the window seat, gasped aloud at the height of the jagged mountain ranges they flew over before they landed at the airport.

"I thought it was flat!" she exclaimed.

Ryder chuckled softly. "Did you? This isn't the only surprise you'll get."

He was right. When they got off the plane, she saw mountains rising right off the desert floor. And as they drove out of Phoenix after he picked up the rental car he'd reserved, she realized that what looked like desert from the air was alive with vegetation. It wasn't the green mountains and valleys and abundant streams of Georgia, but the changing colors of the landscape and the variety of plant life were beautiful just the same.

The air was clean and clear away from the city, and the pace of life itself seemed to slow on the long, rolling highways that arrowed toward endless horizon.

Ryder was enjoying Ivy's fascination with her surroundings. She made it new to him, and he watched her face as he pointed out the various types of flora and fauna on the long drive to the town where his retirement complex was planned. He'd reserved rooms in a luxury resort nearby. One, he was careful to point out, that wouldn't be competition for *his* project.

"It's so much bigger than I thought it would be," she remarked as they drove toward Mesa del Sol, a small grouping of buildings in the distance.

"The land, you mean?" he asked, chuckling. "It's the lack of trees, honey," he explained. "The horizons seem bigger because there's nothing to hide them. If you think Arizona is big, you should see southeastern Montana."

"Are there any ghost towns around here?" she asked suddenly, all eyes.

"As a matter of fact, there are quite a few. I'll try to find time to escort you around one or two of them. Okay?"

She smiled broadly. "Okay!"

They settled in at the hotel, in adjoining rooms with a connecting door, and drove immediately out to the site, where a construction gang had already graded the area, laid the foundation and finished the ground floor of two buildings.

"It's beautiful, Ryder," Ivy commented, approving of the way the stucco design fitted in with the jagged mountains and the desert.

"I think so, too," he agreed. He escorted her to the main building, where the construction foreman—a redheaded giant of a man—was waiting for them.

"This is Hank Jordan," Ryder introduced the other man. "He's in charge of the project. Hank, this is my new assistant, Ivy."

"Nice to meet you," the foreman greeted cordially.

She nodded and smiled shyly.

"How's it going?" Ryder asked his foreman.

While they talked shop, Ivy wandered around what had to be the offices of the complex, enjoying the spaciousness and simple lines of it. She could imagine potted plants and modern furniture filling it, and mentally she approved Ryder's choice of architects.

"What do you think?" Ryder asked eventually, taking her arm to lead her back down the long corridor toward the car. "It will house approximately sixty couples, and include a doctor's building, a restaurant, a theater, a pharmacy, a small grocery store, clothing boutiques and even a hardware store. We'll have our own water and sewage system, not to mention built-in air filters and air conditioning."

"It sounds like something out of the future," she exclaimed.

He smiled down at her. "Hopefully it will be. Space is already at a premium most places. This complex will make

the most efficient use of its space, with emphasis on complementing the existing ecosystem around it."

"Greek," she informed him.

"By the time it's finished, you won't think of it as Greek."
He slid back his cuff to check the time. "Let's get something
to eat. Hungry?"

"I could eat sand," she said heartily.

"Tacos are better. In fact, fajitas are much better. Let's go."

They said goodbye to Hank, and Ryder drove back to Mesa
del Sol and the huge motel complex where they were staying.
The temperature was surprising. Ivy had dressed for winter,
but it was warm, and the heated swimming pool was a real
temptation. She wished she'd had the presence of mind to
pack a bathing suit.

She changed her suit for jeans and a pink striped shirt with
a bulky pink sweater and sneakers. She pinned her hair away
from her face but left it loose. When she met Ryder downstairs
in the dining room, she found him similarly dressed in casual
dark slacks and a burgundy pullover, but he was still wearing
the boots and the Stetson that were such a familiar part of his
usual dress.

"You look more comfortable," she remarked, smiling up
at him.

"So do you, honey. Tired?"

She shook her head. "I can't remember when I've had so
much fun," she said, laughing, and meant it. Being with Ryder
was an adventure in itself. "I feel dishonest. I should be taking
notes or typing or something."

"Plenty of time for that later," he assured her. "I'll feed you
and then we'll do some paperwork out by the pool if you like.
Did you bring a bathing suit?"

"There was frost back home," she pointed out.

"This is Arizona," he replied. His eyes slid over her body possessively, and a darkness lingered there just momentarily before he seated her at a window table and broke the spell.

They ate tacos and fajitas and refried beans and drank incredibly large glasses of soft drinks. Amazing how thirsty you get out here, Ivy mused. Perhaps it was the evaporation rate on the desert terrain that accounted for it.

Ryder was unusually quiet throughout the meal. When it was over, he excused himself and went to get his briefcase before he joined her at the pool. He seated them at a table with a sheltering umbrella and started pulling out documents. He pushed a pad and pen toward her.

"Time to pay the piper, then we can relax for a while," he said. "I need you to take down some figures for me. If I have a laptop sent up, can you transcribe them this evening?"

"Of course," she said. She couldn't protest. This was why he'd brought her with him. But he'd been tense since they'd arrived in Arizona, and she wondered what was bothering him.

She couldn't know that her proximity was working on him like a drug, making him vulnerable and restless and hungry. He was doing his best to keep it from her, but the way she looked in those tight jeans was making him crazy. Work at least kept his mind where it belonged. Having enticed her into working for him, he couldn't risk losing her again by being impatient.

His eyes fell to her hand on the table. She was still wearing the wedding band Ben had put on her finger. Ryder longed to rip if off and throw it as far as he was able, to purge her of Ben's mark of possession, to make her his own. But even as he thought it, he knew how impossible it would be. Despite Ben's faults, Ivy had loved him. How could he compete with that?

Perhaps in time, she might turn to him. He had to hope that she would. It was all that kept him sane.

Chapter 4

Ivy hardly had time to worry about being in a room adjoining Ryder's. He seemed to be deluged with paperwork and correspondence that had to be answered. The laptop was familiar to her, and it saved quite a lot of time, but it took the better part of her day to transcribe Ryder's terse dictation and produce emails that satisfied him. Often, he rewrote the same email three times before he allowed it to be mailed. He was on the run almost constantly and spent much of each day out at the site. When he was in his room, they were working.

The number of emails was incredible. There were the usual intercompany memos, notices of meetings, updates for his board of directors, problems to be solved overseas that required masses of documents, queries about sites and funding, replies to bank queries…enough to keep three assistants stoop-shouldered.

Ryder eventually noticed that Ivy was having trouble coping.

"It will get easier," he promised early on their third day at the motel. "Just do the best you can with it. When we get back to Albany, I'll commandeer someone from the typing pool to help you. It's been like this ever since Mary quit. She'd been with me for ten years, and she knew every facet of the business. It would be difficult for anyone to step into her shoes immediately, so don't feel threatened. Okay?"

She smiled with pure relief. "Okay. I was beginning to feel a little inadequate."

"You're not. Your typing is above average, and your short-hand is admirable, if unorthodox." He chuckled. "We'll get by. Want to go out and see a ghost town tomorrow?"

"Could we?" she exclaimed. "Will we have time?"

"As hard as you've worked, we'll make time." He checked his watch and grimaced. "God, I forgot, I've got a meeting at the bank. I'll have to rush. Have room service send something up for you, and stay by the phone. I've got a call in to a colleague in London. Take a message if he calls."

"I'll do that." She watched him leave, fascinated by his seemingly inexhaustible supply of energy. He left her breathless with his pace. All the same, it was an exciting, challenging job, and she knew she wouldn't tire of it soon.

The next afternoon, after lunch, he packed her and a cooler of soft drinks into the car and set off toward the north. Both of them were dressed in jeans and boots, and he'd insisted that she take a hat along because of the heat, even at this time of year. She sat next to him in the four-wheel-drive vehicle and smiled at the way they matched, he in his chambray shirt and she in hers, both pale blue. But she had a jaunty red scarf around her neck, and he'd forgone that touch of Western Americana. It was much too warm for jackets, and she knew that the long-sleeved shirts were to protect them from sunburn rather than cold.

"Where are we going?" she asked.

"Off the beaten path," he replied. "You won't find this place on any of the tourist maps. It's an old silver mine that belonged to one of Hank's ancestors. I told him that I was going to tour you through a few ghost towns, and he suggested I bring you here. He gave me the key to the gate."

"That was nice of him," she said, smiling.

"Hank's not immune to women," he remarked, glancing at her with a faint chuckle. "You charmed him."

Her dark eyes widened. "But, I hardly spoke to him," she protested.

"You don't know how potent you are, do you?" he asked, a faint edge on his deep voice. "I've never known a woman so unaware of her own gifts."

She could have told him that Ben had made her that way, finding fault eventually with everything about her. But she didn't say it.

"There were lots of mines in Arizona, weren't there?" she asked.

"Were, and still are," he agreed. "One of the most famous old ones is the Silver King near Superior."

"Wasn't Tombstone originally the site of a silver strike?"

He laughed. "That's right."

"I started reading up on Arizona when you said we were going to come here," she confessed. "But nothing I read prepared me for what I saw. It's like another world out here."

He followed her rapt gaze to the jagged mountains in the distance. "I felt the same way the first time I saw it," he said. "It's an unexpected country. Nothing like back East."

"But so beautiful," she said fervently.

"And deadly. When we get there, make sure you stick to me like glue. You can fall into a mine shaft out here so quickly it isn't funny."

Her eyes mirrored her fear. "You're joking, aren't you?"

"I am not. There are towns around here with buildings that have shifted over the years because of the number of tunnels under them. They have a habit of collapsing. And, yes, people have fallen into abandoned mine shafts."

She shivered, wrapping her thin arms around her body. "What a horrible fate."

"You'll be fine as long as you don't wander around indiscriminately." He glanced her way and smiled. "I'll take care of you, little one."

Her heart jumped. He sounded protective and tender all at once, and she felt herself melting inside. She had to be careful not to give in, not to show how she felt. But it wasn't going to be easy. Just sitting next to him made her tingle all over.

"There are rattlers around, too, so watch where you put your feet."

"Just like back home," she reminded him, tongue-in-cheek.

"Point taken."

A few miles down the highway, he pulled off onto a dirt road and drove to a locked gate. The key Hank had given him unlocked a big padlock that held together the ends of a heavy chain. He refastened it before he continued down the rutted road to a valley that fronted the site of a mine. Tunnels in the mountains told their own stories. There was a stone foundation and a few adobe walls, attesting to the former site of the main office, and the remnants of houses and a smelter.

The wind seemed to blow constantly. She walked beside

Ryder, feeling somehow insignificant in this vast nothingness. The ruins were like a reminder that nothing really lasted, least of all people. She took a deep breath of the air and closed her eyes. She could almost hear voices.

"Daydreaming?" he teased.

She shrugged, opening her eyes with a smile. "Just listening to the ghosts. I'll bet they could tell some stories."

"I don't doubt that."

"All those people who worked here, who lived here," she began, bypassing a row of unconnected stone steps to stare up at the mines, "they're dead now. It seems so useless somehow, Ryder. What was it all for?"

"They were prospecting for dreams, I imagine," he said, and for a moment, his eyes were dark with hunger as he looked at her profile. "God knows, some dreams are worth any price."

"Are they?" she murmured absently. She stretched lazily. "I'm starved!"

He chuckled. "That's my line. I'll get the basket."

He went back to the four-wheel-drive, and, minutes later, they were feasting on cold cuts and salad off of paper plates, washing it all down with cold soft drinks from the cooler.

"Paradise," she sighed, smiling across at him. They were sitting on the stone steps, using a wall of the foundation for a makeshift table. Around them, the sun shone brightly and the wind blew. "I'll bet people had picnics here back when the mine was worked. Children probably played on those big boulders," she gestured toward them, "and women walked up from the settlement to shop at the store."

"Store?" he asked, frowning.

"Oh, they had to have one," she said with conviction. "This far from any settlement, with the men at work in the mines, there had to be a store where women could buy cloth and flour and coffee and sugar. There were probably other kinds of places, too. Didn't Jerome have a brothel and several bars?" she added with a shy glance.

He laughed with pure delight. It had been so long since he'd felt so lighthearted, so at peace with himself and the world. Watching Ivy made him feel whole again. She was beautiful, he thought, from her long black hair to her gentle heart. He'd never wanted anything as much as he wanted her.

"Yes, Jerome had its entertainments," he agreed. "But a small settlement like this with close family ties probably wouldn't have tolerated a brothel."

"You mean, the wives wouldn't," she said, grinning at him.

"Absolutely." He pushed his hat back on his head and studied her blatantly. "You look more relaxed than I've seen you in months."

"You haven't seen me in months," she reminded him with gentle humor. She toyed with a long strand of her hair. "I think getting away from home has helped more than anything," she said, smiling at him. "You've been so good to me, Ryder…."

"I don't want gratitude," he said tersely, looking away toward the cliffs. "I needed an assistant, you needed a job. It was business."

Her heart fell. She'd hoped for something more than that, but she didn't dare let her disappointment show. What had she expected, anyway, she wondered, when the past had killed any hope of a future between them? Besides, there was Ben and her guilt still standing in the way.

She folded her hands in her lap and stared down at them. "It was still kind of you," she said doggedly. "Mama said I was wasting away. Maybe I was. After…after Ben died, I lost interest in everything."

He took off his wide-brimmed hat and pushed an impatient hand through his thick, dark hair. "I suppose that's natural enough," he said shortly. He glared at her. "But he's dead and you're not. You've wasted enough time trying to live in the past."

That was truer than he knew, but it wasn't because of Ben. It was because she wanted so desperately to go back to that night Ryder had first kissed her, to have a second chance with him. And that was impossible.

She sighed. "Have I?" she mused. She gathered up the refuse and put it into a plastic bag. He put that, and the hamper and cooler, back into the four-wheel-drive while Ivy sat at the bottom of the unattached stone steps and stared out over the beautiful emptiness of the plain that led to the mountain chain.

Ryder came up beside her, frowning slightly as he stared down at her. "No brooding," he chided.

"I wouldn't dare." She smiled gently. "Do we have to go right away?" she asked. "It's so nice here."

"No, we don't have to rush off." He moved to the step above hers and sat down. Then, abruptly, he slid behind her, so that his long legs enveloped hers, his lean hands folding below her breasts to hold her. "Don't panic," he said when he felt her stiffen. "We'll just sit and watch the wind blow. All right?"

She swallowed. The feel of all that warm strength behind her, around her, was intoxicating and she was afraid of what she might inadvertently reveal about her vulnerability. But it was too sweet to protest.

"All right," she said softly, and forced herself to relax, to let him hold her. Her eyes closed and she let her head rest naturally on his broad chest. Just this one little taste of heaven, she promised, and she'd go back to work without complaint.

She felt his arms contract around her, so that his broad chest and flat stomach were completely against her spine.

"Comfortable?" he asked at her ear, his voice deep and slow in the windy stillness of the valley. They might have been the only two people in the world.

"Oh, yes," she said, her voice hushed because she didn't want to break the spell.

His cheek nuzzled her hair. He felt at peace for the first time in years, without the fierce restlessness that had possessed him for the past few months. She smelled of roses, and he remembered long nights when he'd ached for the feel of her in his arms. Amazing, he thought, that she was letting him hold her. Perhaps she felt the closeness as he did, felt the need for touch in this desolate remnant of the past.

She glanced down at the darkly tanned hands holding her, at the paleness of her own fingers against them. His hands were enormous.

"Your hands are so big," she murmured, touching them delicately, tracing the flat, immaculate nails.

"Yours are elegant," he replied, his deep voice rumbling from the chest so close against her back. "You never studied music, did you?"

"No. I wanted to, but there was never much money. Dad died when I was very young, you know."

"I never knew him. We moved to Albany when you were in grammar school, but there was only you and your mother by then."

"Your family was so good to us," she recalled. "I loved your mother."

"Everyone did," he said quietly. "She was a lady. A real lady."

Her eyes opened and she stared at the changing shades of red and orange and yellow on the bare cliff face, still scarred from mining days past. "Your father always seemed remote, somehow," she said. "Was he?"

"He liked making money," he said, drawing her closer as the wind kicked up and grew cool. "He loved my mother, in his own way. But he hurt her. He was never an affectionate man. Even now, Eve and I are lucky to hear from him at Christmas. He isn't big on family."

She rested her hands on his. "Are you lonely, Ryder?" she asked softly.

His face tautened. He stared down at her long black hair, his blood surging as the feel of her warm body worked on him. "Yes, I'm lonely," he said tersely. "Aren't you? Isn't everybody?"

"I suppose so." She traced one of his deeply tanned fingers to the flat nail, unaware of how sensual a gesture it was until she heard Ryder's breath catch and felt his hands contract under her.

"Careful, honey," he murmured roughly at her ear. "I could misinterpret that."

Her heart skipped. That note in his deep voice was unmistakable. It made her knees weak, and she was glad she was sitting down.

"Could I ask you something?" she queried softly.

"What?"

"Why haven't you ever married?"

His long-fingered hands drew her closer before they slid down to her jean-clad thighs and rested there with easy familiarity. "Marriage is serious business," he said. "I don't believe in divorce."

"You must have…have thought about it," she faltered. She

really should protest that intimate touch, but it was intoxicating. Her body was alive as never before.

"Thought about what?" he whispered at her ear, just before his strong teeth caught the lobe and bit it gently.

She gasped audibly. "A…about…marriage," she managed.

"Once, perhaps," he whispered. His hands slid up her thighs and over her flat stomach to come to a hesitant rest underneath her breasts. "You're trembling."

"Well…what do you expect…when you touch me…like that?" she exclaimed hoarsely.

"Like this?" he murmured at her ear, and his fingers moved over her full breasts in a light, teasing touch that made her nipples go hard and sensitive.

"Ryder!" she cried.

"Surely it doesn't shock you?" he asked at her ear, his voice faintly mocking. "You're a widow, after all, not an innocent virgin."

She shivered as his hands pressed suddenly into her taut, swollen flesh, dragging her closer. "I was…that night," she said, burning with pleasure. "You pushed me away…!"

"Yes." That night. He could hear her soft voice pleading, taste her silky skin under his lips, and his body made a sudden involuntary movement. He bit off a curse and released her abruptly, getting to his feet before she had a chance to feel what had happened to him. He turned away, moving up two more steps so that the temptation of her was out of his vision until he could get hold of himself. He could have kicked himself for letting things get out of hand like that. It was too soon. He seemed to lose control the minute he touched her. He was going to have to keep his distance.

Ivy, watching him, didn't understand what was wrong.

She was shivering with reaction. She could hardly believe he'd actually touched her like that, except for the evidence of her tingling body. She crossed her arms over her sensitized breasts and felt the cold biting into her. She hadn't even noticed that it had grown cold because of the warmth of his body so close to hers.

"We'd better get back," he said curtly a minute later. He turned and started toward the Jeep, leaving her to follow. He opened the door for her, but he didn't touch her or even look at her as they got underway.

She felt too unsure of herself to speak, so there was a tense silence all the way back to the motel. Incredible, she thought, that things had gone wrong so quickly. But she was too shy to ask what she'd done or said that had made him so cold. When they reached the motel, he was courteous and polite, and all business. But it didn't escape her notice and he kept a stiff, formal distance between them for the rest of the day.

She knew, because he'd told her once, that he'd gone a long time without a woman. Perhaps it was just proximity, and any reasonably good-looking female would have done. She had to think about it that way and not go chasing rainbows. Ben was dead. She was responsible. She couldn't give in to her need for Ryder, so it was just as well that he hadn't let things go any farther. It wasn't, after all, as if he was in love with her or anything. It was just that same fierce, frightening desire that he'd felt for her when she was still in her teens, arousing an equal, shaming desire in her.

They went home the next day. Ryder dropped Ivy off at her house.

"Can you get in to the office all right tomorrow?" he asked quietly.

"Yes, thank you," she replied. "I'll be there at eight-thirty sharp. And thank you for the trip, too," she added formally, avoiding his gaze. "I enjoyed it."

"Until I spoiled things, you mean," he chided, his face hard, his eyes cold. "Well, it will be easier here. Plenty of people around, to keep me in line."

She stared at him curiously and started to speak.

"Let it go," he said, his whole look a challenge. "See you tomorrow."

"All right." He was obviously in a hurry to leave. She got out, and he deposited her bag on the front porch, barely staying long enough to exchange greetings with Jean before he got back into his car and drove off.

"Did you have fun?" Jean asked with a smile after she'd hugged her daughter warmly.

. "It was work, Mama," Ivy reminded her, "not a vacation. But, yes, I did have a good time."

Jean didn't ask any more questions, and Ivy didn't volunteer any more information. She didn't really want to talk about it.

Ryder had one of the women from the secretarial pool work with Ivy the next day to help her catch up, and he managed time himself to show her the more important aspects of her work. He was at least a little more approachable, for which she thanked her stars.

"I know it seems like a lot," he said when she had a good idea of what her duties would involve. "But you'll have help for a while, and you'll adapt."

"Of course I will," she agreed. She was wearing a simple business suit with a pink blouse, and her hair was in a neat French twist. She looked elegant and professional, all at once.

"I like the way you look in pink," he murmured absently,

letting his pale eyes wander over her exquisite complexion, the faint pink of her soft mouth. "Very, very pretty."

She colored, enhancing her complexion, and smiled up at him. He towered over her, big and strong and deliciously masculine. Her eyes went to his wide, chiseled mouth and she wanted to reach up and put hers against it. The fierce, unexpected need made her pulses race.

"Thank you," she said breathlessly.

He couldn't drag his eyes away. She made him helpless. At the same time, she made him ten feet tall and bear-strong. He sighed angrily at his own vulnerability.

"Did I do something wrong?" she faltered. That scowl made her uneasy, and the other people in the office were beginning to murmur a little at the tableau.

"What do you mean?" he asked absently.

"You're glaring at me."

"Am I?" He shrugged and averted his gaze. "Well, if you've got the hang of it, I've got a board meeting."

"I think I can cope," she said. Her dark eyes ate him for an instant before she quickly lowered them. "Thanks for the tour."

"My pleasure." He started past her and abruptly stopped, looking down straight into her eyes. He was wearing a dark vested suit, without a hat, and he looked every inch the businessman. The fabric was expensive enough to fit properly, and it molded the powerful lines of his body. Ivy almost groaned aloud at the sheer masculine perfection of him.

"I'd take you to lunch," he said softly, "but we'd raise eyebrows."

"Yes." She smiled shyly. "Thanks for the offer, anyway."

"You have to come over Saturday."

"Why?" she asked, stunned by the sudden change of subject.

"Salmon croquettes," he said simply.

"You mean, like in that Walt Disney movie? You got Kim Sun started and now you can't stop him?" she asked with a gleeful laugh.

"That's right. You have to teach him how to make something else before I sprout gill slits and scales."

"All right."

"No argument?" he murmured.

She shook her head. "Kim Sun is a very apt pupil. I like him."

"He likes you, too." He made a sound deep in his throat and smiled faintly. "See you later."

He walked away and she watched him go. He had to be the world's most puzzling man. He looked, she thought, so alone. Even in a crowd, even in the office, he was remote. She wondered if she was ever going to get close enough to really know him.

One of the other assistants called to her and she went to answer a question about the Arizona project, mentally consigning her worries about Ryder to the back of her mind.

After all, she was here to work, not daydream about the boss.

Chapter 5

It was a good thing that Ivy enjoyed traveling, because the very next week, Ryder had to fly down to Jacksonville. He took Ivy with him, checking them into a luxurious hotel right on the St. Johns River, in a suite this time. The bellboy came right out to the rental car Ryder had hired at the airport, got the luggage, and carried it up to the room for them. Ivy wasn't used to such grand treatment, but Ryder seemed to take it for granted. It was one of the many differences between her lifestyle and his.

They ate in a restaurant just down the street from the hotel, a fabulous place that looked as if the whole thing had been carved out of a gigantic tree. It featured some of the best seafood Ivy had ever tasted, and the service was wonderful. Afterward, Ryder walked with her beside the river on the way back to the hotel, silent and brooding, as he'd been ever since their arrival. They were both in casual clothes—dark slacks and a pale yellow pullover sweater for him, a simple oyster-white dress with a colorful burgundy patterned scarf for her. She wondered how many other women he'd been here with, because he seemed to know his way around very well. But she didn't dare ask him such a personal question.

A couple with three small children came toward them, and as they watched, a well-dressed little boy made a sudden dash toward the river. The mother screamed, but Ryder was quicker than the overweight father. He caught up with the boy and lifted him in big, secure arms, laughing as he carried him back to his horrified parents.

"He's quick," he told the couple, who were closer to Ivy's age than his.

"Quicker than you know!" the mother laughed with pure relief. "Thank you very much! We'd never have reached him in time."

"I guess I'll have to lose a few pounds," the father said as he added his gratitude to his wife's. He took the squirming child from Ryder. The little boy had blond hair and blue eyes and a purely mischievous smile. He squirmed trying to get down again.

"Fish," he told his father. "Mama says the river has fish. I want to see."

"You almost got a firsthand look, tiger," Ryder murmured, smiling gently at the child. "Better stick to aquariums for now."

"I'll see that he does," the boy's father promised. He greeted Ivy as she joined them, his eyes all too appreciative on her slender figure. He noticed Ryder's sudden rigidity and the set of his head in the nick of time and turned his attention back to the threatening taller man. "Are you and your wife here on vacation?" he asked with a nervous cough.

"A working vacation," Ryder replied tersely before Ivy could contradict the man. He slid an arm around her thin shoulders and drew her closer. "We'd better get to it. Good night."

"Good night," they echoed.

Ryder watched them walk away, and under the streetlight, Ivy saw something like anger on his lean, dark face.

"What is it?" she asked. "You look irritated."

"You didn't notice that he was undressing you with his eyes?" he asked, his tone mocking and faintly savage. His own eyes slid down her body with a look she couldn't make out in the sparse light from widely placed street lamps.

"Ryder, he had three children…" she protested.

"He was a man, wasn't he?" he demanded. He took a slow breath. This was getting out of hand. He couldn't afford to show that kind of jealousy, it might frighten her off.

He lifted his shoulders. "Nice little boy, though," he said, changing the subject. "A real character."

"You like children, don't you?" she asked, smiling up at him as they walked on. She didn't object to his arm around her shoulders, and he didn't offer to move it. She felt its warm weight with pleasure, measuring her steps to his as they walked along the wide sidewalk and traffic came and went on the street beside it.

"Yes, I like kids." He glanced down at her. "You don't really know much about me, do you?" he asked.

"Well, I know that you like to eat, that you make a lot of money, that you're always busy and that you have a big heart." She smiled self-consciously. "But, no, I guess I don't know a lot about you." Except that I love you, she could have added.

He stopped walking and turned her toward him, his big hands gentle on her shoulders, while around them Jacksonville's night lights shone colorfully and the noise of the traffic seemed to dim suddenly.

"Stop running," he said unexpectedly.

She couldn't see his eyes in the dim light. She wished that she could, because his voice sounded strange.

"I...I don't understand," she said.

"Yes, you do." His chest rose and fell heavily. "Ivy, I know that I hurt you, all those years ago. But now that you're older, maybe you understand a little better that men can be unreasonable when they're aroused and frustrated."

The feel of his warm, strong hands biting into her shoulders made her feel giddy. She stared up at him in the darkness, wanting to take that one step that would bring her body into close contact with his. She wanted him to hold her, so that she could deal with all the fierce emotions he aroused. Ben had never made her feel any of the confusion and delight that Ryder did.

"That was a long time ago," she said, choosing her words. She stared at the front of his sweater. "Ryder, it's still...early days."

"Ben again, is that it?" His hands tightened. "By God, I'll knock him out of your head...!"

He bent, finding her mouth with his. He was rough without meaning to be. The feel of her soft, warm body in his arms stirred him almost beyond bearing. He groaned harshly against her shocked mouth, lifting her higher, devouring her in a silence where the loudness of her heartbeats drowned out the traffic.

Ivy felt hot all over as he kissed her, and she wanted so desperately to give in to the sensations he was arousing. But he gave her no room to respond. And when she felt the faint tremor in his bruising arms, she pushed at his shoulders. His ardor frightened her because it was violent. Violent, like Ben...

Ryder heard her say the other man's name and drew back instantly, putting her back on her feet with a jerky movement. His face was suddenly hard. "Damn Ben!" he ground out.

He turned away, ramming his hands into his pockets. His heartbeat was choking him. He was on fire, and all she could manage was Ben's name, Ben's memory. He wanted to hit something.

Ivy realized belatedly what she'd done. She hadn't meant to blurt out her dead husband's name, it was just that Ryder's violent behavior brought back nightmarish memories.

She moved toward him, but he wouldn't face her. She reached out and gently touched his spine above his belt buckle. He stiffened at the light contact.

"I know what you think," she began softly. "But you're wrong. It wasn't because…"

A huge tractor trailer roared past, drowning out what she was trying to say. By then, Ryder was walking again, impersonally drawing her along by her elbow, back to the hotel.

"Ryder," she tried again when they were in the lobby.

He handed her the key to the suite. "You might as well go on up," he said tersely. "I've got a stop to make."

Before she could argue, he was gone, in the general direction of the hotel lounge, taking his misapprehensions with him. Ivy threw up her hands and went up to the suite.

Perhaps they were fated to be apart, she thought as she lay sleepless in bed. She wanted so badly to give in to Ryder, to get close to him, to love him. But she didn't understand his anger, his roughness with her. He couldn't know that when he was rough, he reminded her of Ben, and she couldn't tell him. As long as there were secrets between them, there was no hope of loving.

That night, the old nightmare came back. Ben was looming over her, shaking her, accusing her of cheating on him with Ryder. He stripped her, laughing drunkenly, and forced her down into the mattress with hands that hurt. He smelled of whiskey, and she began to scream.

"Ivy, wake up!"

She shuddered as the feel of real hands shaking her got through the fog of sleep. She jerked up, her eyes wide open and tear filled, her body sweaty in its white cotton gown.

"Are you all right?"

Not anymore, she could have said. He'd been in bed, judging from the navy-blue silk pajama bottoms clinging to his lean hips. His torso was bare, his dark, hair-roughened chest exposed to her fascinated eyes. His hair was tousled, his face hard as he stared down at her with glittery gray eyes.

"You were screaming like a banshee," he muttered, his gaze drawn involuntarily to the darkness of her nipples under the thin gown as he stood over her, both hands propped on his lean hips.

The wedge of black hair on his chest arrowed down toward his flat stomach, and that was sensually revealed by the low waist of pajamas. He looked big and sexy and dangerous, here in her bedroom, and the sight of him was making her mouth dry. Incredible how his half-nude body affected her, when she'd never liked looking at Ben when he was that way. But Ryder was different. It made her tingle all over to look at him. She frowned slightly. Would he know?

Nervously she raised her drowsy, fascinated eyes to his. "I had a nightmare," she said.

He nodded. "About Ben, I gather."

"Yes."

"It simply amazes me that you still care that much, after everything he did to you."

She lowered her eyes to his bare chest, involuntarily sketching the perfection of it. "He was my husband," she said huskily. "I owed him fidelity, if nothing else."

He started to speak, but the words choked him. "Even after death?" he bit off.

She closed her eyes. How could she tell him what her obsession for him had done to Ben, to her marriage? There was simply no way to put it into words.

"Get up," he said unexpectedly, running an irritated hand through his already ruffled dark hair. "I'll pour you a drink."

He'd had some brandy and snifters sent up earlier, she knew. But she didn't like liquor. It had caused her too much pain.

"You know I don't drink," she began.

He glared at her. "Well, I do when the occasion calls for it. And you can't tell me you don't need something to help you sleep. Come on."

She got up without wanting to. She didn't have a robe and she hesitated, standing nervously beside the bed in the thin white cotton gown that molded her breasts gently before falling to her ankles. With her long hair loose around her shoulders, bare save for the spaghetti straps of the gown, she looked like a fallen angel.

"I'll try not to stare," he said quietly. He turned away, leaving her to follow him into the suite's luxurious living room, complete with sofa, chairs and coffee table.

He poured brandy into two snifters and handed one to her before he joined her on the sofa. She was curled up in one corner of it, her legs under the gown.

"Still afraid of me?" he asked, sprawling back against the other end of the sofa. "I'm no more dangerous than any other man. But in my case, I'd need a blatant invitation. Does that reassure you?"

She stared down into the brandy snifter at the pale amber liquid. It was probably some rare, expensive vintage, but she wouldn't have known. When Ben had gone on binges, plain bourbon had suited him.

"I'm afraid of most men," she said after a minute. The nightmare had knocked the stuffing out of her, and she felt so tired of the pretense. "You try living with threats and violence for three years and see how it affects you."

His face hardened. "I know he hit you at least once," he said tersely. "Only a blind man could have missed the bruises. I told you, that's why I stayed away. Jean swore you were passionately in love with him. I know all too well how women can delude themselves about men they care for."

She didn't know how to handle it. He had a totally wrong idea about her loyalty to Ben, but there was no way she could correct it without telling him things she didn't dare. While she hesitated, she sipped the brandy and the silence between them began to lengthen. Across from her, Ryder sipped from his own snifter, his long legs stretched out over the coffee table. He looked worn. Probably he was, because he lived at twice the pace a normal man did.

Ivy sighed. The taste of the brandy wasn't unpleasant, but she wasn't used to alcohol and she didn't really like the effect. Her head started swimming in no time and she felt all too relaxed.

"What if you hadn't stayed away, Ryder?" she asked, lifting her eyes to his.

His face went taut. He emptied the brandy snifter. "If you think you can sleep now, we'd better call it a night," he said, rising.

She got up, too, weaving a little as the alcohol worked on her. He was much taller when she wasn't wearing shoes. She paused just in front of him and stared up, entranced by the sheer impact of his masculinity in his state of undress.

"Ben was all white without his clothes," she said dizzily.

His jaw tautened. "I spend a good deal of my time in the field."

"So did he," she pointed out.

"Ben was fair. I'm not. I tan easily. Ivy…"

She touched his chest, hesitantly. Her fingers were cool, but they burned his skin like a brand. He felt his body going rigid and his fingers went to her hand to pull it away from his aching body. But he couldn't quite manage to drag it loose. The scent of her drifted up into his nostrils, a clean, flowery scent that was hers alone.

"Don't," he said quietly. "Not like this, when you're three sheets in the wind."

She drew in a slow breath. "Just like old times," she said huskily. "You accuse me of trying to get away from you, when you're the one who pushes me away." She felt the pain of his rejection keenly in her intoxicated state, and tears choked her. She flattened her hand over his hair-covered breastbone, feeling the hard slam of his heart under the warm muscle of it. "Why?" she whispered.

"Because it's never the right time or the right place," he said angrily. He caught her hand and pushed it over one hard male nipple and a furious heartbeat, trapping it there. "Feel me," he whispered roughly, while his free hand grasped her long hair and pulled her head back so that her eyes met his. "Feel what you do to me. I've never known a woman who could knock me off balance the way you do."

"Is that all it is?" she asked sadly. "Just…desire?"

His eyes were blazing and he was rapidly losing control. He had to get her out of here while there was still time. "You know how I feel about commitment, don't you?" he hedged.

"You don't want it," she said. "You never have." She let her eyes fall and pulled her hand away from his body. "I'm sorry. I think I'm a little tipsy."

"You're a lot tipsy," he corrected. "And it's time you went to bed."

"Not as stoic as you look?" she chided gently.

His eyes darkened as he stared down at her. "Not stoic at all," he said. "But I won't take advantage of you."

"My legs feel funny," she murmured on a stifled giggle.

"No wonder."

She took a deep breath and felt the world vanish around her.

Ryder caught her before she fell and carried her into the bedroom. She was a soft weight in his arms and as he laid her down on the sheets he had to fight his conscience every step of the way. He put her under the sheet and coverlet and drew them up over her breasts. She looked like an angel lying there, her black hair haloed around her gentle face, her eyes closed and her long lashes resting on her creamy cheeks. She was the most beautiful woman he'd ever known, and he loved her desperately. But she was still hung up on her late husband, and he was no match for a ghost. With a vicious curse, he turned and left the room.

He overslept the next morning for the first time in years. He hadn't managed to get to sleep until late, aching with his need for Ivy. When he got into the suite's living room, she'd already ordered breakfast, which had apparently just been delivered because the coffee she'd poured into her cup was steaming.

"Oh," she said self-consciously. "I was just about to call you."

She'd hoped she wouldn't have to. She had embarrassing memories of the night before. Her hands went to smooth her oyster blouse down over her dark slacks in an unconsciously nervous gesture.

"Let's eat something," he said. "Then we might go sightseeing down to St. Augustine."

"To the Castillo de San Marcos?" she asked hopefully.

"There." He nodded. "And to the Ripley Believe it or Not Museum as well, if you like."

She poured him a cup of coffee and pushed it across the table to him, her eyes lingering on the blue checked open-neck shirt he was wearing with his slacks. The color complemented his pale eyes, and sexy glimpses of his chest were visible in the opening. She remembered touching him there, and felt self-conscious all over again. Would she never learn to stop throwing herself at him?

She sipped coffee slowly. "I'm sorry about last night."

"I'll bet you are," he replied, his voice deep and curt. "Head hurt?"

She grimaced. "A little. I took a couple of aspirin."

"The sea air may help some. Try to eat something."

She managed the toast, but nothing else. Eating wasn't easy with a hangover, as she was learning the hard way.

"I didn't mean I was sorry I got tipsy," she began.

"If you're going to start making apologies for anything else, forget it," he said, without looking at her. "Finish your coffee and we'll go."

That wasn't a promising start, but she supposed it was just as well not to dwell on her behavior.

He drove them down the long, seaside stretch of U.S. 1 to St. Augustine, the nation's oldest city. The magnificent old fort took Ivy's breath away. It was located on a stretch of land facing the Matanzas Bay, five miles from the Atlantic Ocean. Made of stone, the structure was gray and worn smooth with age. A moat surrounded it, with a wooden bridge that allowed tourists to enter.

It had a long and proud history, belonging alternately to Spain, France and Great Britain, and then to America. It was, in fact, the oldest fort in the United States, dating to 1672. Ivy had read a tourist brochure on the way down from Jacksonville and learned a little about the old city. Ponce de Leon had landed here in 1513. He claimed the land for Spain, but in 1564 the French claimed it and established a settlement there. That settlement was destroyed by Spain the following year, and they founded the city of St. Augustine.

The basic fortress of the present Castillo de San Marcos was completed in 1695, although the ground breaking for it was some twenty-three years earlier in 1672. Several protective earthworks were built as time passed. In 1825, however, the fort's name was changed to Fort Marion and remained so until 1942, when the original name was reinstated. The fort had withstood attack after attack. One siege against the Spanish fortress was launched by Carolinians in 1702. It lasted for fifty days and resulted in the destruction of the entire city—all of it, that is, except for the Castillo, which was the only structure still standing afterward.

One thing Ivy had discovered from some other reading was that back in the late 1800s, the proud Chiricahua Apache tribe had been housed here after Geronimo's disastrous defeat. As they walked around the ancient structure, Ivy tried to imagine how the desert-dwelling Apaches would have felt in its damp confines. Except for the small green courtyard, surrounded on all sides by the walls, there was only the sky above to look at. She closed her eyes, picturing Spaniards in their armor tramping to and fro, followed by the early Americans who'd defended this place. The sense of history was strong here, and if there were ghosts, then surely the fort had them. So many memories, she thought.

She shivered, both because of the atmosphere and the cool mist. She hadn't brought a coat, but Ryder suddenly shrugged out of his nylon jacket and gently put it around her shoulders, holding it there by the lapels.

"It's getting chilly," he remarked. "I hadn't thought it would be this cool."

"I'm all right," she said softly. "But you'll get chilled without your jacket," she protested, looking up at him with liquid dark eyes.

"My God, don't look at me like that when we're surrounded by people," he groaned. His hands were still on the lapels of the jacket, keeping it close around her, and behind them was a group of senior citizens following a tour guide over the gray stone fortifications.

Ivy was thrilled by the effect she had on him. The power to arouse him was heady and sweet, and she couldn't resist exercising it. She moved just enough to bring his knuckles against her breasts. She expected him to turn the jacket loose then.

But he didn't. His pale eyes held her dark ones in thrall while the wind blew and the fog misted and the tour guide's low voice droned on. Ryder's gaze fell to the jacket and his hands moved, deliberately caressing down to her taut nipples and back up again in a soft sensual tracing that made her knees go weak.

His eyes moved back to hers and searched them slowly

while his breath rasped deep in his chest and threatened to stop altogether.

"You…shouldn't be doing this," she whispered brokenly. "And I shouldn't be letting you."

"Then stop me," he challenged softly. He glanced over her shoulder. The tour guide was still holding forth, but the group was moving away from them, although they were on the same level, near one of the tiny guard stations fashioned of stone blocks.

She could hear her own heart beating. She trembled a little with reaction and moved forward to rest her head on his broad chest.

"Ryder," she whispered longingly.

He registered her capitulation with a sense of wonder. She was vulnerable and he shouldn't take advantage of it. God knew, he'd tried hard enough to keep his distance, especially while she was still grieving for Ben. But this was asking the impossible. The feel of her was like a narcotic. He couldn't stop.

"Stand still," he whispered. "If you cry out, we're going to have an audience."

She wondered at the wording until she felt his hands turn and slowly unfasten her blouse. She should protest, she knew she should, but it was too sweet. She felt the backs of his lean fingers against her bare skin and she stifled a gasp.

He lifted his head and looked down at her, darting a careful glance at the slowly departing senior citizens. He should never have started this. His blood was raging already, and this wasn't going to help things. But she was sweet and submissive, and he'd gone hungry for her too long already. His eyes feasted on the soft pink skin. He drew the fabric farther aside to reveal the high, taut rise of her mauve nipples and his face hardened.

"Ryder," she whispered shakily.

"Perfect," he breathed roughly. "I lie awake at night and dream of you like this, your breasts hard-tipped and swollen under my mouth…"

She bit back a cry at the word pictures he aroused, and she shivered.

"Yes, you'd like that, wouldn't you?" he whispered huskily. "So would I. But if I bend down and put my mouth on you like that, I'll lose my head completely. I think you might, too. And we're not here to become the tourist attraction."

Her lips parted as her breath rushed out jerkily. His pale eyes lingered on her exposed breasts and began to glitter. "I can almost taste you, Ivy," he groaned.

She moved feverishly against him, shivering again as his arms went around her and crushed her to his broad chest.

"Oh, Lord, what a time to want each other," he bit off at her ear. His hands flattened on her shoulder blades. The tourists were going slowly down the steps and he thanked God, because his body was giving him hell.

He moved her just enough to get his hands in between them. They eased under her blouse and began to caress her swollen breasts. His lips nuzzled her temple and her forehead, breathlessly gentle, while she stood yielding in his arms and enjoyed the tenderness of his seeking hands.

He could feel her trembling, but she was clinging, not resisting. It went to his head like the brandy he'd had the night before. "Look at me," he said softly. "I want to see your eyes while I'm touching you."

Her face lifted, and her misty eyes met his. She gasped a little as his hands grew bolder, his thumbs abrasive against the hard tips.

"Someone will see," she managed in a shaky whisper.

"No," he replied. "They're leaving now."

And they were. The senior citizens followed the tour guide down the steps, leaving Ryder and Ivy alone on the battlements overlooking the bay.

"Alone at last," he whispered, and bent his head.

She felt his lips brush lightly over her mouth. This time there was no violence at all. His mouth teased hers in the windy silence, coaxing it to follow him, to plead for a harder, deeper contact. He was her heart, and she wanted nothing more than to be close to him for as long as she could.

Her arms slid under his and around him and she pressed close. His hands moved abruptly to her hips and drew them to his in a slow, sensual rhythm that dragged a moan from the lips his were nibbling. He was fiercely aroused, and she could feel the evidence of it like a hot brand against her belly. But even that was welcome.

He wondered at the lack of resistance from her. His hands contracted and he lifted his head to look down into her eyes as he shifted her hips deliberately from one side to the other against him.

"Feel it?" he bit off.

"Yes." She searched his eyes, blushing a little at the sensual, faintly mocking smile she found on his hard face.

"Thank your lucky stars that we aren't in that suite alone. This is what you've been inviting for the past week, every time you turned those bedroom eyes on me."

That wasn't what she wanted to hear. Her face paled at the insinuation that she'd been teasing him. Could he really think her that callous?

"You started it," she accused helplessly.

"You started it," he corrected. He moved back, his eyes blatantly on her breasts. "No bra, either. Was that for my benefit, to make it easier for me to get to your skin?"

She flushed and dragged her blouse together, fastening it with hands that shook. He always seemed to find a way to blame her when things got out of control. Didn't he have any idea why it kept happening?

He moved away from her, staring out toward the bay. His body was still in anguish. Why did she keep letting him do that, he wondered. And then, all at once, a horrible suspicion grew in his mind.

"Are you missing sex?" he asked abruptly, turning fiercely accusing eyes on her.

Chapter 6

Ivy spared a moment to wonder at the density of the male mind before she reacted to the question. Had she missed sex, indeed, when it had been nothing more than a hated, frightening ordeal fraught with embarrassment and humiliation.

Her dark eyes searched his and trembling hands drew the nylon jacket closer around her shoulders. Why should he ask such a question, after the sweet intimacy they'd just shared? He lost his temper every time he touched her.

"I seem to be missing the boat, if you want to know," she said after a minute. She moved to the edge of the wall and leaned against it, staring out over the snaky outlines of the earthen breastworks with their smooth green cover of grass, beyond the moat.

He joined her, but he didn't quite look at her. His head was bare, and the dampness made his hair look even blacker than usual.

"You…disturb me," he said roughly.

"I've noticed." She smoothed her fingers over the rough, weathered stone, aware of the musty, dusty smell of it in the dampness around her. "Why do you lose your temper every time you touch me?"

He blew out a heavy breath, his eyes narrowing on the distant horizon. "I want you."

Her fingers bit into the stone. "Yes, I know," she said softly. "But that doesn't really explain it."

He glanced down at her. "It was a long time ago, but you surely remember that I damned near lost control with you that night when you were eighteen?"

"I remember." She closed her eyes. "All you do is push me away."

He turned to face her, his jaw tensing before he spoke, his eyes slow and bold on her body.

"I have to," he said, his voice curt. "My God, all it's going to take is one kiss that lasts five seconds too long, and we'll be lovers. Or are you going to pretend you don't know that?"

She couldn't deny it. She traced a pattern in the stone and tried to breathe normally.

"It's for your sake," he said roughly. "You and I both know that you aren't ready for a physical relationship with a man. Not when you're still having nightmares about betraying Ben."

She wanted more than that from him, although she was touched that he'd felt that way for so long. It was now or never, she thought. She was going to trust to luck and tell him the truth about her marriage. Perhaps if he understood why she felt the way she did, they might be able to start over.

She pushed back a strand of her long black hair hesitantly. "The nightmares aren't about betraying Ben," she said huskily.

He felt his breath catch. "Then what are they about?" he asked.

"He hurt me, physically," she said nervously. Her eyes fell to his throat.

It was the first time she'd ever confided in him, even if she was telling him something he already knew. That was a start, at least. But he had secrets of his own, that she didn't know about. Secrets that were involved with Ben's life and death. He was carrying around a lot of guilt that he hadn't tried to deal with. Every time he touched Ivy, the guilt came back, and that was half of what made him mad. The other half was the desire borne of his desperate love for her, so sweeping that it possessed him. He wanted the communion of love with her, the oneness, knowing already that it was going to be the most profound experience of his life. But only if Ivy loved him, too. He couldn't bear to make love to her completely unless he had her love. That was what stopped him every time. That was what tormented him.

Now she was admitting that her marriage hadn't been perfect. Her love for Ben had apparently sustained it, though, despite his cruelty to her. It hurt him, thinking that the other man could have been so unkind to her. She was a gentle, sweet woman. But for his own lack of vision when she was eighteen, he might have spared her the anguish Ben had given her. She might have loved him instead of Ben, but he'd drawn back, thinking her too young for marriage. He could hardly bear to think about it.

"I assume you had no idea that he drank when you married him," he said, choosing his words carefully.

"I felt sorry for him," she said. "He was a kind, gentle man and he'd stopped drinking, for good, he said. I thought I could help keep him straight." She laughed bitterly. "I had no idea what I was letting myself in for. I thought he'd get better, but he only got worse."

"I'm sorry about that," he said, his voice heavy with regret.

"So am I," she said. "Once I was in, I couldn't get out, I was trapped, as much as by my conscience as by his need. I just seemed to go cold." She hesitated. "I still am, in a lot of ways." She drew in a slow breath. "I couldn't have an affair with you, though, Ryder. Desire alone just isn't enough," she managed slowly, trying not to think how beautiful that ultimate expression of love would be with him, if he cared even just a little. She glanced at him, but his face gave nothing away.

He lifted an eyebrow. "It may surprise you to hear it, but it isn't enough for me, either," he pointed out. "That's why I'm trying to keep my distance," he added meaningfully.

"Oh." She didn't know why she was surprised. After all, he'd never mentioned love. At least he was an honorable man. He wasn't going to seduce her out of a purely physical need. That was reassuring, and she relaxed.

A reluctant smile touched his wide, chiseled mouth at her expression. "Did you think I notched my bedpost?" he murmured.

The teasing remark was more like the Ryder she used to know. She smiled back. "Don't you?"

He shook his head. "I told you in the beginning that it had been a long time. I wasn't joking. I've outgrown my curiosity about the opposite sex. Although," he mused with a slow appraisal of her body, "not about you, I suppose. God, I love looking at you without your clothes."

She went scarlet and averted her face. "I don't know what possessed me!" she burst out.

"Nothing so terrible, little one," he said quietly. "Loneliness gets to us all eventually. Don't worry about it. You're human, that's all. Just like me." He slid a big-brother arm around her. "We'll keep things on the old footing, okay? No pressure, no problems. We've been friends for a long time. Let's not lose that."

"I couldn't bear to," she confessed, savoring the nearness. She sighed contentedly. "The tour guide said they had an exhibit of arms and armor down below," she reminded him. "Want to go and see it?"

Her enthusiasm was contagious. He chuckled softly. "We might as well," he replied. "Then I'll treat you to some extraordinary seafood."

"Great!" She brightened as they went back down the steps. He seemed in a better mood altogether, and what he'd said, combined with his less threatening behavior, reassured her.

She wasn't paying attention to her footing and she missed a step. It was a long way to the stone floor below, and she would have had a bad fall. But Ryder threw himself toward her and caught her, spinning her into his hard arms.

"My God, watch what you're doing!" he exclaimed angrily.

She only heard the anger at first, but then she felt the faint tremor in his hands, and when she regained her balance and looked up, she saw that his face was pale.

"Thank you," she said softly.

He let go of her abruptly. "No sweat. Just pay attention from now on, will you? It's a long way to the ground."

"I will." She felt his hand under her elbow, and she smiled to herself. It made her feel warm all over that he cared whether or not she hurt herself.

That sense of jubilation lasted the rest of the day. They toured the Ripley Museum nearby and she shuddered at the

Iron Maiden exhibit and the Chinese man with two sets of eyes. They had fish and chips at a local restaurant and then went on to the small arcade, which featured a Christmas shop that stayed open year-round. Ivy found a whole roomful of teddy bears, and Ryder impulsively bought her one, a honey-colored bear with a lifelike face and a long nose. She hugged its plush softness against her as they walked along the sidewalk to the car.

"Thank you," she said, laughing up at him as she cuddled the huge toy. "I've wanted one of these most of my life. We were poor when I was little, so I did without a lot of toys."

"No one could call you spoiled," he murmured. It made him feel protective, watching her with the stuffed animal. He remembered how poor the McKenzies had been when he moved to south Georgia with his parents and sister. But Ivy, like her mother, had always been bright and cheerful despite their lack of material wealth. It was one of the things he admired about them.

"I'm beginning to feel spoiled," she murmured, hugging the bear. "Thank you, Ryder. I'll take good care of him."

"My pleasure." The look on her face was thanks enough. It amused him that she liked the toy so much. She had to be persuaded to put it in the back seat while he drove them back to Jacksonville.

He had to meet a businessman for supper, so Ivy ordered a chef's salad and watched a late-run movie on TV before she finally turned in. She lay on top of the covers with her precious bear next to her, praying that the nightmares wouldn't come back tonight. She'd wanted to tell Ryder about her marriage, about the way it had really been with Ben, in bed. She'd tried, but he'd changed the subject before she could. Perhaps it was a good thing. The last thing she wanted from him was pity.

Her mind went back to the way he'd kissed her at the Castillo, and the passionate way she'd responded to his ardor. Perhaps she wasn't completely frigid after all. It gave her a little hope. She closed her eyes and let the memories flow over her. She felt anew the impact of his eyes on her body, the warm, hard crush of his mouth on her own, the delicate caress of his warm, strong hands. She moved restlessly on the covers, her gown riding up around her thighs. She burned all over. The sensations she felt were new and delicious, and she watched the open door half hoping that Ryder would come in. But he didn't, and the fever her own memories aroused eventually exhausted her.

She pulled the covers over her, curled the bear closer and closed her eyes. Finally she slept, and without nightmares.

When Ryder came in, she was dead to the world. He paused at her open bedroom door, smiling as he saw her cuddling the bear. He moved to the bed, the smile fading as he looked down at her sleeping face. Her long black hair lay in disheveled ripples around her face. Long black eyelashes curled down on cheeks flushed with sleep. The cover was over her breasts, and he fought the need to pull it away, to bare her to his eyes. Every day brought a new struggle with himself to keep his distance. He loved her more than his own life. He didn't know how long he could hold out.

He bent and brushed his lips with breathless tenderness over her closed eyes. She stirred and smiled and whispered a name.

He stood up slowly, his heart pounding furiously in his chest. As he went out, closing the door behind him, he felt dazed. The name she'd whispered so huskily was his.

The next morning they headed home, but he stopped off in Savannah to buy her mother some pralines on River Street. They strolled along the cobblestone streets, made of ballast left off by visiting ships generations ago, past the statue of the Waving Girl. Ivy had never been to Savannah. The huge live oaks fascinated her, like the port itself. There were people milling around, and Ryder wanted privacy. He wanted to talk to Ivy, and not while he was trying to concentrate on driving. Privacy. Of course. Why hadn't he thought of it?

"How would you like to go to the beach?" he asked suddenly.

"It's winter!" she exclaimed.

"Sure it is. But it's plenty warm enough for us to sit on the dunes and watch the ocean."

She laughed. It was crazy. "All right. I'd love it!"

"Then let's go," he said, catching her hand warmly in his. He took her back to the car, where the bear was sitting regally in the back seat, and drove out of town to Savannah Beach. It was pretty deserted at this time of year, but they could still walk along the strand and watch the waves roll in.

He pulled her down beside him near a dune rippling with sea oats and fingered part of a shell he'd found. They were both wearing jeans today, but he had on a green polo shirt, and she was wearing a white blouse and gray sweater. Amazing, she mused, how they never clashed in their color choices.

"Tell me about Ben, Ivy," he said unexpectedly.

She hesitated. There were things still too painful to talk about, but she'd wanted to tell him. Now was as good a time as any.

"I failed him," she said simply. "He was a good man when he wasn't drinking. But toward the last, he drank almost constantly."

"That was when he hurt you," he murmured.

She nodded. "He was always sorry afterward," she said. The wind caught her hair and tousled it. "I couldn't be what he wanted me to be. I did try," she said, lifting her tormented eyes to his. "But I... Ryder, I think I'm frigid."

He picked up a shell from the sand, rubbing it absently. "Do you?" he murmured, and smiled gently, a momentary softening of his hard face. "After what we did together in St. Augustine?"

She realized immediately what he was saying, and her breath caught. "Yes...well, I wondered about that."

"Wondered?" he prompted gently.

She swallowed. "I never felt like that with Ben," she confessed.

The shell froze in his fingers as he stared at her. "Never?" He exploded.

Her thin shoulders rose and fell. "Never," she said. "He knew, of course. I tried at first to pretend, but..."

"Why in God's name did you marry him, feeling like that?" he demanded.

"I didn't think it was that important. He was gentle and kind and I didn't mind when he kissed me. It's just that I didn't really feel anything, either. And in bed...oh, my God," she groaned, putting her hands over her face. "Oh, my God, I've never hated anything so much in all my life as I hated...that!"

At last, they were getting somewhere. He turned the shell over and over in his hand and chose his words. "That," he said, emphasizing the word, as she had, "is a beautiful communion between two people who care for each other. But the chemistry has to be there."

"I found that out the hard way," she said. "Ben and I were good friends. I thought it would be enough."

"Not in bed," he mused, watching her.

"No. Not ever in bed." She twined her fingers together. "I was afraid, after that time with you. Not only of you," she said, when she saw his face harden, "but of what I felt and the way I acted. I thought that since Ben was so gentle, and I didn't get very excited, that everything would be wonderful. I wasn't afraid of him, you see. He was safe…." Her voice trailed away.

"But I wasn't," he said, staring at her.

She glanced up and then back down again. "No. You weren't. You turned me into someone else when you touched me, and I couldn't handle it." She stared out at the crashing whitecaps and her eyes dulled. "My wedding night toppled all my illusions. And his. He thought I knew what to do. Isn't that incredible—?" Her voice broke.

"I don't want to hear about it," he said through his teeth.

Ivy glanced at him, surprised. He wouldn't look at her, and his body was rigid. Why…it mattered to him!

"It wouldn't have been like that with you, would it, Ryder?" she asked gently. "The way I felt with you—that wildness, I mean—it would have made it easy, wouldn't it?"

"Yes," he said. His voice seemed to vibrate with the same dull roar as the waves hitting the beach. "That wildness would probably have spared you most of the pain, because you'd have gone with me every step of the way. It would have been the way it was at the Castillo, Ivy, when you threw back your head and arched toward my lips. Only much, much more violent and sweet."

"I never thought of violence in bed," she said hesitantly.

"I don't mean cruelty," he said. "There's a difference."

"Is there?" Her voice was sad. "Until I married, the only experience I ever had was with you, that night."

His body reacted feverishly to that statement. He stood up and kept his back to her, struggling for control. "It might have been better for both of us if I'd never touched you," he said bitterly.

She didn't look up. She'd thought of that, too—that if he'd never kissed her, she might have responded to Ben. Ben might still be alive, because she wouldn't have had anyone to compare him with. But even as she thought it, she knew it wasn't so. She'd been head over heels in love with Ryder long before Ben came into her life as a prospective husband. Ryder had been her life. He still was.

Ryder glanced at her brooding face for a long moment before he turned his attention back to the sea. He threw the shell as hard as he could into the ocean, walking absently down the beach with one lean hand shoved deep into his pocket. The wind lifted his hair, tousling it.

Ivy's eyes were drawn to him, and they lingered on his long, powerful body as he stood staring out to sea. He was a handsome man, and he had a physical presence that worked magic on women. But it was more than that. He had a kind, generous spirit that compensated for his quick temper and occasional melancholy. He was everything a man should be, and she wanted him so, in every way there was. She wondered what he might say if she told him that.

She got to her own feet, following along behind him. It was warm on the beach, but inside she was chilled to the bone.

"You always go away," she said sadly, joining him where the waves dampened the sand. "You do it without even moving."

He didn't look at her. He shoved both hands deep into his pockets and watched the water swirl in over the beach. "Do you know how much of my life I've spent alone?" he asked.

No, she didn't. She knew that he'd been alone since Eve married and his father moved to New York, but his early life was pretty much a blank for her. Eve, while fond of her brother, had never been really close to him because there was such a difference in their ages. Eve had never talked about Ryder's early life, and he himself was very reticent on the subject.

"I assumed you had the usual home life," she began.

"I grew up in an exclusive boarding school," he said. "When I was at home, my father tolerated me and not much more."

"Your mother loved you," she said.

"Yes, she did," he agreed absently. "But I needed my father, and he never gave a damn about me. I don't think he really wanted children at all. God knows, he never acted as if he did. Eventually, he made it all but impossible for me to spend any time with my mother. I wasn't allowed to come home for holidays after I was twelve. I was sent to military school in the eighth grade, and from there I went to college—ROTC— and into the Army. By then, Eve had come along and my mother adored her. Oddly enough, my father didn't seem to mind her affection for their daughter."

He sounded bitter, and probably he was, she thought, watching him. "Maybe he didn't think a daughter was the same kind of competition."

"Yes, I finally figured that out for myself. I grew up to be an overachiever, and probably I owe my father for it. But there were times when I'd gladly have traded it all for somebody to take me to ball games and play catch with me out in the backyard."

"At least you had a father, of sorts," she said with a smile. "I never knew mine. Mama said he was very special."

"Your mother is very special, too." He turned toward her, his pale eyes sliding warmly over her face in the sunlight. "Bright as a new penny," he murmured, watching her. "God, you're beautiful."

"Oh, no," she argued softly. "Not me."

"You. And not just the outward trappings." His lean hand touched her cheek, lightly caressing. "You're a little Dresden china doll with a heart like a marshmallow. I'd give you anything."

Her heart raced. He looked sad and sensual, a dangerous combination. He made her feel reckless.

"Anything?" she asked. She moved closer deliberately, her body singing with needs it was only just discovering. She wanted to kiss him, and it showed in her eyes, in her face.

"Yes," he said huskily. His breathing quickened. "What do you want?"

She lifted her face. "Your mouth," she whispered, her voice barely discernible above the waves.

His eyes flashed. "Are you sure?" he replied quietly. "At my age, kissing is serious business."

She touched his chest, liking the feel of the soft fabric over the warm, hard muscle. "I'm sure," she told him, her eyes as gentle as his were threatening.

"Then come here," he said softly, opening his arms.

She pressed against him, withholding nothing, making not even a pretence at modesty as she settled her body completely against his and raised her mouth.

He almost shivered with reaction at her unexpected compliance. He framed her face in his hands and searched her eyes for one long moment before he bent and began to bite tenderly at her mouth.

The whispery little kisses aroused, but didn't satisfy, which was apparently his intention all along. She began to feel a surge of heat that ran from her stomach down into her legs, making them trembly. She clung to his hard-muscled arms, her pose consciously inviting, her eyes slightly open, misty with longing and shocked delight.

Ryder was enjoying it every bit as much as she. He smiled lazily as he savored her soft lips, teasing them into parting. But he drew back when she lifted toward him, keeping her carefully at a distance while he skillfully built the tension between them to flashpoint.

Her teeth caught his lower lip and then his upper one as the pleasure grew. Her soft body pressed coaxingly against his, savoring the powerful muscularity of him until she felt the slow, fierce reaction of her provocation. And even then she didn't draw away. Her breath caught gently, because this was becoming familiar to her, this rigid set of his body. Familiar. Even welcome.

He felt her yielding and barely kept himself in check. Slowly, he thought. Slowly, so that I don't frighten her.

His lean hands began to slide down her back while his lips toyed with her. They moved to the very base of her spine and pressed tenderly. He felt her breath expel in a soft rush against his mouth and his heart skipped.

"Your legs…are trembling," she said against his mouth, her nails biting into his arms.

"Yes." His head tilted to give him better access to her lips. "I'm going to make yours tremble even more," he whispered. His hands contracted and began to move her lazily from side to side, so that her belly brushed the evidence of his fierce arousal. She felt her body contract with anguished pleasure, even as she stiffened and lifted to him.

"On a…public beach," she began in a wobbly voice.

"A deserted public beach," he whispered. "And we're only kissing."

"No," she said, shivering. "Oh, no, it's not…only kissing!"

"It isn't enough, either," he bit off against her mouth. "Hold on tight, little one. I have to have something more…"

Even as the last word was drowned out by the roar of the surf, she felt his mouth suddenly pushing her lips apart just before his tongue thrust insistently inside them.

The sensation was one she'd never felt with anyone except Ryder, and it was almost unbearably sweet. Fierce heat clenched in her belly and made her shudder rhythmically against his taut thighs. He gathered her up tight in his arms and his mouth became urgent. She felt her own heart beating and at that moment she'd have given herself to him in the sand without a thought of shame.

He knew it. Her reaction was impossible to miss. It gave him a sense of aching elation, increasing his ardor.

"I can't stand up much longer," she managed when his mouth released her swollen lips just briefly.

"If we lie down, there's going to be a whole new definition of the statement that we know each other," he said unsteadily.

"But we couldn't…here," she protested weakly.

"That's what you think," he said with rueful humor, pressing her hips against his to prove to her that they could, here.

"I mean, people," she faltered. Her eyes met his. "Someone might come down here."

"I know." His mouth touched her eyelids, her nose, her cheeks, her chin. "Letting you go is going to rank along with scaling Everest on ice skates."

"I'm sorry." She opened her eyes and looked up at him, with her arms still linked around his neck. "I wasn't teasing. If you need me that badly, I won't even try to stop you," she whispered shyly.

His jaw tautened. "I think I knew that. But I won't ask the supreme sacrifice. Not now." He began to let go of her, very slowly. His arms still had a faint tremor, and his body was painful.

"It hurts, doesn't it?" she asked gently, searching his darkening eyes.

"Yes." He put her away from him and took a deep breath, trying to get past the knifelike pain in his gut.

"I suppose I shouldn't have done what I did," she said hesitantly, watching him straighten his clothes with shaking hands.

He looked up, his fingers still on the buttons of his shirt. "Shouldn't you?" he asked and began to smile. The pain was easing, and now he could hardly believe that Ivy had actually come on to him. But unless he'd lost his mind, that was exactly what had just happened. "Why not?"

"It was, well, brazen," she said slowly.

He chuckled, but it wasn't a mocking kind of laugh. It was deep and pleasant and his eyes mirrored it. "As long as you confine your outbursts to me, we'll manage," he told her. He leaned toward her. "I enjoyed it," he whispered.

She blushed. "So did I."

His eyes twinkled. "In which case, you have my permission to do it again, whenever you like."

"Really?" she stammered.

His eyes were kind. Ben had hammered the impulsiveness out of her, the natural affection. But he was slowly bringing it back. He only hoped he was going to survive it. For the past few years, he'd been mourning Ivy, so there hadn't been a woman. Before that, he hadn't been accustomed to stifling his passions. Only now was he beginning to realize what an uphill battle it was going to be not to rush Ivy into a relationship she wasn't ready for.

"We'd better get on the road," he said after a minute. "We don't want Jean to worry."

"No, of course not."

He slid a protective arm around her shoulders. "You can show her your bear. Have you thought of a name for him?"

She smiled. "Bartholomew."

"What?"

"Well, he's a very uptown sort of bear," she said seriously. "You can't really expect me to give him a common name."

He shook his head, but he didn't make any more comments about her choice of names. He just smiled.

Chapter 7

Ryder found Kim Sun at Ivy's house, teaching Jean how to bake sponge cake.

"Don't fuss," Kim Sun challenged his boss. "You said *my* menu bored you, so I have learned beef stew, liver and onions, fried chicken and macaroni and cheese. Mrs. McKenzie taught me. In return, I taught Mrs. McKenzie to make Napoleons, crepes Suzette and sponge cake. Good trade, huh?"

"Good trade," Ryder had to admit. His pale eyes went to Ivy. She smiled at him, her eyes liquid, and for the first time, he felt nervous. She was going soft on him physically, and he was old enough to see dangers that she couldn't. He'd gone too fast, despite his good intentions. She wanted him, and apparently she was willing. But he didn't want her on the rebound. Even if she hadn't wanted her husband, she'd loved him. He wanted her heart much more than he wanted her exquisite body. But he wanted that enough to lose his head and take it, which would only complicate things. He had to keep the pace slow and steady, which meant, unfortunately, that he was going to have to draw back and put a rein on her impatient desire. He was going to have to manage that without turning her off completely or damaging her pride, and without going out of his mind because of his own frustrated desire. A tall order for a man violently in love.

Ivy saw the expression on his face and misunderstood it. Had she been too forward? Had she frightened him off?

"I'd better get up to the house. See you tomorrow, Ivy," Ryder said. "If you're through," he told Kim Sun, "you can drive me up to the house."

"I am through for now," the smaller man agreed. "Thank you, Mrs. McKenzie." He bowed his head to Jean.

"Thank you!" she replied heartily. "I'll fatten Ivy up yet with these new recipes!"

"She could use a little weight," Ryder said, his eyes sliding warmly over Ivy's slender body. "Not that there's anything wrong with the way she looks," he added gently.

"Flattery will get you supper," Ivy teased.

"Thanks, but I've got a lot of paperwork to get through," he said after a minute, hating the refusal when he saw her crestfallen look. But he couldn't handle being alone with Ivy much more today. His body was already giving him hell for what he'd refused it earlier.

"You still have to eat." Jean came to her aid.

"I'm taking your daughter to Paris next week," he pointed out, startling Ivy as much as her mother. "It's a business trip, but she'll have time to shop and do some sight-seeing. The condition is that I have all my work caught up first."

"In that case," Ivy said softly, "please go home, Ryder."

He laughed. "Heartless woman. First you offer to feed me, then you send me packing. At least I get to take the cook with me. Come on, Kim Sun. Let's see how you ruin fried chicken."

The little man glowered at him. "You wait and see how nice I make it, then there will be no more smart remarks!"

"Promises, promises," Ryder murmured.

They went out the door with a wave, still arguing.

"You look happy," Jean remarked when they were sitting down to their own supper.

"I am," Ivy said. She toyed with her fork. "I guess you know that I'm crazy about him."

"Yes."

"I hope it's not too soon," she began.

"Ivy, Ben's dead," her mother said quietly. "And I'm not as blind as you might think. I know that your marriage wasn't happy. I've pretended, because you seemed to want me to. But don't you think it's time we both stopped?"

Ivy gave in. "I guess so. No, it wasn't happy. I was running from Ryder and Ben knew it. I should never have taken the easy way out. I just hope it isn't too late to change course. Ryder is acting…well, strangely."

"How?"

"He can't seem to decide between growling at me and kissing me."

"That's promising." Jean grinned.

Ivy scowled at her. "I don't understand."

"Never mind. Take it one day at a time and don't rush your fences. I've discovered in my old age that if you simply let things happen without trying to make them happen, loose strings get tied up neatly. Try it."

"Have I got a choice?" Ivy murmured. She sighed heavily. "I wish I could go back. Ben might have been happy with someone else. He might still be alive."

Jean covered her hand gently. "Honey, you can't remake the past. You have to go ahead. Ben didn't have to marry you. Will you try to keep that in mind? If you made him unhappy or not, he had as much choice as you did about staying married. He could have asked for a divorce. He didn't."

"He knew how I felt about Ryder," Ivy confessed miserably.

"If he knew, he had even less reason for continuing a marriage that was going nowhere," Jean said sensibly. "You can't love to order."

"Ben drank because of me," Ivy whispered.

"He did not," came the terse reply. "You can't keep tormenting yourself like this! Ivy, pity is no basis for a marriage. And if you're honest, you'll admit that pity was why you married Ben. You didn't love him, you felt sorry for him!"

Ivy buried her face in her hands. It was the truth. Ben had showered her with attention at the same time Ryder was avoiding her. He'd cried on her shoulder, and she'd taken pity on him. That was all it was. She hadn't thought ahead. Part of her motive had been getting back at Ryder, showing him that someone wanted to marry her, even if he didn't. But her revenge had certainly backfired.

"My poor baby," Jean said gently, pulling the weeping younger woman into her arms. "It's all right. Facing problems is half the battle of solving them. You just cry it all out and you'll feel better."

She did, too. That night, she admitted for the first time just how much of a sham her marriage had been. Ben's problems had been largely of his own making, and her guilt and pity had probably contributed to them. But he'd made his choices, just as she'd made hers. She hadn't forced him to marry her. Now that she'd come to grips with the failure of her marriage, she could start putting it behind her. Now she could concentrate on Ryder for the first time, and rediscover her lost womanhood. She felt wonderful.

That feeling lasted until the next morning. When she got to work, she found Ryder pleasant and courteous, but as distant as he had been when they'd come home from Arizona. Every time she came close, he withdrew. He'd said it was because he wanted her so badly, but she felt there was much more to his odd attitude. She only wished she knew what it was.

They left for Paris on the following Monday. Ryder's brotherly attitude had left Ivy in the dumps, and only the excitement of the trip kept her buoyed. Seeing Paris had been one of the big dreams of her life. Even now, she could hardly believe that she was actually going there, and with Ryder. They said that anything was possible in Paris. Perhaps the City of Lights could melt even his hard heart and help her win it.

He checked them into one of the ritzier hotels downtown near the Champs-Élysées. She could walk out on the balcony and see all of Paris.

The smell of baking bread, and the faint, foreign smell of the city, drifted into her nostrils as she stared out over the wrought-iron rail toward the lighted Eiffel Tower. Far away, the silver ribbon of the Seine flowed lazily through the city with its barges and boats, and nearby were the spires of Notre Dame cathedral. It was magic. She closed her eyes and could almost hear peasants singing the Marseillaise in the streets, hear the excited cries of the crowds on those long-ago days when the monarchy in France had gone to the guillotine.

There was such history here, such a presence. It was all she'd hoped for and more.

"Quite a view, isn't it?"

She turned at the balcony door to see Ryder standing behind her. His coat and tie were off, his collar unbuttoned. He looked as tired as she felt.

"It's the most beautiful view I've ever seen," she agreed. "Ryder, you look so tired."

"Jet lag. Aren't you tired? Or is your age a point in your favor?" he added with faint sarcasm. "I'm ten years your senior, after all. My stamina is a little strained."

"Don't be like this," she asked gently. "We're in Paris." She started to move toward him, but he held up a big hand.

"No, you don't," he said shortly. "When you're back in one piece again emotionally, maybe. But not now. I don't want you on the rebound."

"What?" she stammered.

"You loved Ben. I don't want any leftover emotion from you. So keep it cool, honey." He turned and left the room before she could say a single word.

But if she hadn't got the message from what he said, his behavior would have punctuated it. He did everything but hold a knife in front of him to ward her off. He did it nicely, although there was a coldness in his manner that she'd thought was gone until they came home from Jacksonville. Now she didn't know what he wanted from her. She wondered if he knew himself. If only she could tell him how she felt about him. She had a feeling that it would clear up all the misunderstandings and misconceptions and pave the way toward the future. But she couldn't get up the nerve.

Ryder, meanwhile, was having problems of his own. He'd

held in his own guilt about Ben until it was tearing him apart. Ivy didn't know that an order of his had sent Ben's father to his death, or that it was the reason Ben had started drinking. He'd hired Ben out of guilt, and subconsciously maybe he'd even moved aside for him with Ivy out of that same sense of responsibility. If Ivy blamed herself for what Ben had become, he could imagine that she'd blame him more. She'd loved Ben, and he was responsible for what Ben was. Indirectly it was his action that had caused the chain reaction, that had given Ben a drinking problem and caused him to be cruel to Ivy. He hated knowing that. He hated even more the thought of having her find out one day.

Keeping his hands off her was hell. He couldn't stop watching her. She seemed so at home in Paris. Perhaps it was because of her French ancestry. She looked as if she belonged among the relaxed, happy citizenry, her dark hair and eyes and her exquisite complexion helping her to fit right in.

She seemed to glow, except when she looked at him. He knew she was puzzled and hurt by his attitude, but he hadn't been kidding about his loss of control when he was around her. He didn't want them to slip too soon into a physical relationship before Ivy had time to get over Ben.

His intentions, however, took a step backward on their second day in Paris. Unfortunately, a very handsome young French businessman attending the conference got a look at Ivy and complicated Ryder's life.

Ivy was flattered by the man's attention. After two days of alternate freezing cold and brotherly lukewarm behavior from Ryder, it was almost a relief to find a man with a raging interest in her, even if it was focused mostly on her looks. She responded to it without realizing what it would do to Ryder.

The Frenchman was Armand LeClair, and he spoke English almost as fluently as he spoke French.

"Ivy," he savored her name, sitting close beside her during a brief lull while the speaker prepared his notes. "It is a delightful name. Very pretty. Like you, *mademoiselle*."

"You're very kind," she replied, smiling shyly.

"I am honest," he corrected. "You are free for lunch, yes?"

She glanced toward Ryder and barely escaped blanching at the expression on his face. He looked murderous, and the way he was staring at her companion didn't bode well. He'd been talking to another businessman while everyone was being seated. Now he'd returned, to find himself supplanted by a younger, obviously smitten foreigner, and he didn't like it. He couldn't have made his disapproval more obvious if he'd fired a gun.

"You'll have to ask my boss about that," Ivy said evasively, and dropped her eyes, leaving Ryder to deal with the gentleman.

She didn't know what was said. But the young man actually flushed as he got quickly to his feet, murmuring something that sounded vaguely like an apology.

"*Pardonez-moi, mademoiselle,*" he said fervently, and perfunctorily kissed her hand before beating a hasty retreat with a wary glance at Ryder as he departed.

"Did you tell him you were a hit man or something?" Ivy asked, all eyes as he sat down in the chair the Frenchman had vacated.

He didn't answer her. He was obviously still smoldering. "You're here to work, not to get involved with amorous playboys," he said shortly.

"Was he a playboy?" she asked curiously, refusing to let him needle her.

He shifted restlessly and seemed to relax a little. "Yes," he replied. "His people are well-to-do. Titled, in fact."

"How flattering that he noticed me, then," she murmured demurely.

"Flattering, hell!" He glowered at her. "Unless you want to see him knocked senseless in front of your eyes, don't encourage him again."

Her eyebrows arched in sheer surprise. "Ryder!"

"You just don't understand, do you?" he bit off. "My God…!"

The speaker's voice blared out from the microphone, cutting off Ryder's heated reply. He crossed his long legs and glared straight ahead, but he was still bristling. She could almost feel him vibrating.

She didn't understand. Well, that was an understatement if she'd ever heard one. He was violent about her, and probably that violence should have frightened her, but it didn't. It was oddly flattering, that he didn't like other men flirting with her. It could, of course, be a purely physical jealousy…

Her mind dismissed the unpleasant thought. She had to start thinking positively. He was very protective of her, he loved kissing her, he wanted her madly and he was jealous. That had to add up to more than just desire. She was just going to have to work a little harder, that was all.

He didn't make it easy. After the workshop, he took her to lunch and translated the more useful remarks he'd memorized from the workshop. He did it rapid-fire, watching her scramble to get it all down on paper and apparently even enjoying her discomfiture.

"You're being vicious," she muttered between mouthfuls of a delicious chicken-and-rice entrée.

"Of course I'm being vicious! I bring you to Paris, and the first chance you get, you start appropriating natives!"

"I was not trying to appropriate him," she shot back, and her black eyes glittered in a face reddened with temper. She put her fork down. "He asked me to go to lunch with him. Just that. He was a nice, kind young man."

"He was a wolf looking for a woolly appetizer," he countered doggedly. "A man knows when another man's hunting, honey. It's an inborn instinct."

"I wasn't going to go out with him," she protested.

"Weren't you? I arrived in the nick of time to prevent it unless I'm blind."

"You sure might as well be blind," she raged. "You alternately freeze me out and turn on the heat. One day you're Mr. Cool, the next day you're Romeo, and the day after that you suddenly discover that you harbor brotherly feelings for me! It's like swimming in a blizzard!"

"You're shouting," he observed.

She took a deep breath and tried not to see the amused looks she was getting. With her long hair smoothed down her back, and the neat navy-blue dress with white collar she was wearing, she looked very young and very pretty. Not to mention very angry.

Ryder, his dark suit complementing his olive complexion, was watching her with mingled exasperation and amusement. In a temper, she was vivid—not the shy, biddable little creature he remembered from her girlhood. He very much liked her tempestuous outburst. Not that he was going to admit it to her.

"I don't know what you want from me," she muttered.

"I'll drink to that," he agreed, lifting his wineglass with a mocking smile.

She was having wine, too, although she was carefully sipping hers because she wasn't used to it. Everyone drank wine with lunch, except for an occasional diner sipping Perrier water. Ivy had no taste for what she thought of as plain seltzer, so she'd opted for a light, dry white wine. Now she was regretting it, because it made her temper worse and fractured her credibility.

"If I'm to be just the assistant, why can't I go out on a date?" she asked.

"You're the one who told me you were still in mourning for your husband," he said harshly. "Or was that because I'm too old to suit you?"

She wondered if she'd actually heard him say that. "Too old?" she parroted.

"Handy to flirt with, but not to get too close to, is that it?" he continued, fanning the flames of his temper. "Maybe the young Frenchman is more your style. After all, you married Ben, and he was barely a year older than you—not a jaded, aging workaholic like me."

He looked as if he meant it. Worried, she slid her soft hand over his big one. "Ryder, I've never thought of you as old or jaded."

His jaw clenched. "Haven't you?"

She looked down at the long fingers hers were caressing. Strong hands. No jewelry on them. Flat nails, immaculately clean. "You're the one with the doubts," she said quietly. "I think it's that I don't appeal to you."

His hand turned and clenched hers. "And that is a lie," he said.

"Physically, maybe I do," she said, refusing to look up. "But your world and mine are so different. I never felt—" She stopped, shocked at what she was about to admit.

But he wouldn't let it go. His hand contracted again. "You never felt *what*?" he demanded. "Tell me!"

She drew in a steadying breath. "I never felt that I was good enough for someone like you," she said miserably. "I was too young, too unsophisticated, and too poor to ever fit in your world."

He was quiet for so long that she looked up, surprising a glimpse of some horrible deep wounding in his lean face.

"You never told me that," he said after a minute.

"You must realize that you're rich," she chided softly. "Ryder, I barely knew which utensils to use in this very exclusive restaurant. If you hadn't ordered for me, I couldn't have read the menu. I don't drink wine as a rule, and I don't know how to act in high social circles. It embarrasses me and frightens me."

"Baby," he breathed huskily, "why didn't you tell me?"

Her spine tingled at the way he said it, at the way he was looking at her. "I didn't know how."

He sighed and brought her hand, palm up, to his warm lips. "I'm sorry. I didn't realize there was a difference between us socially. I've always accepted you as part of my own circle. Mine, and Eve's."

He meant it! Her eyes searched his curiously and were trapped by the same dark electricity that always held her in thrall when he was close. His mouth brushed sensually over her damp palm while he looked at her.

"That was partly why you ran from me, wasn't it?" he asked slowly.

She shrugged and lowered her eyes. "Well…yes."

"So many misunderstandings," he murmured. "Too many. Sometimes I wonder if we'll ever get it all straight."

"We won't…if you keep running away," she said boldly, and couldn't look up as she said it.

"When you can put Ben in the past, and start thinking ahead, then I might stand still. It depends," he added in a dry tone, "on what you have in mind. I'm not easy."

That shocked her into looking up, and when she saw his face, she laughed with pure delight.

"Are you sure?" she replied mischievously. "Eve used to say you had to beat women off with a stick."

"I was younger then," he reminded her, forcing himself to release her soft, warm hand. "Younger and much less discriminating."

"Meaning that you're discriminating now?" she asked.

"Oh, yes," he replied with a mocking smile. "One-night stands are out, for one thing."

"But then, so is marriage," she pressed delicately.

He schooled his face to show no emotion at all. "Marriage is forever," he said. "That's a long time to spend with one woman."

She felt her heart sinking. She touched the stem of her crystal wineglass and traced it. "Marriage should be forever, shouldn't it?" she asked pensively. She thought about Ben and what her life would be like even now if he was still alive, and she shivered.

Ryder's face closed up. Ben. Always Ben. He threw down the rest of his wine.

"I have a meeting this afternoon," he said abruptly, his tone pleasant, but all business. "Can you transcribe those notes for me and keep yourself occupied until I get back?"

She lifted her face, puzzled by the sudden mood change. Had it been the mention of marriage that had set him off? Probably so. She could hardly miss the contempt he had for it now, which meant that if she ever made love with him, all she could expect was a brief, casual affair. She knew deep in her heart that she could never live with that kind of lifestyle. She was too programmed by her upbringing to be sophisticated. On the other hand, she was too much in love with Ryder to refuse if he ever asked her. She could have groaned with frustration.

"Yes, I can keep busy," she murmured.

"Not with that damned Frenchman," he cautioned, his whole look dangerous. "I swear to God, Ivy, I wasn't kidding. If I see him within a country mile of you, I'll deck him!"

"Why do you care if I see someone?" she demanded, fighting tears as she stood up. "You don't want me!"

"Oh, hell, yes, I do," he said in a heated undertone.

"That…way, maybe," she said in a wobbly tone, her huge dark eyes brimming with tears. "But that's not enough!"

He glanced around irritably, remembering where they were. "We can't talk about it here," he said tersely.

"We don't need to talk about it at all," she returned. "You be the boss and I'll be the assistant. Let's leave it at that. You say I'm not ready for anything else. Maybe you aren't, either, Ryder." She picked up her purse, assuming a dignity she hardly felt. "I'll go back up the suite and get to work, if you don't mind."

"Go ahead." He watched a particularly lovely French woman walk past. She was giving him the eye very obviously and, just to irritate Ivy, he smiled back. The girl smiled and then walked on slowly. "If I'm late, don't wait up," he told Ivy meaningfully, with a coldly mocking smile.

She glanced toward the woman, who was waiting around the counter with her eyes on Ryder. "I can't but you can, is that how it goes?" she asked, hurt.

"I'm a man," he returned. "What did you expect, that I'd turn down an obvious invitation?"

Tears stung her eyes. "I hate you!" she whispered violently.

He drew in a furious breath. "Oh, God!" he ground out. "Go on, will you? I'm here to work, not to pick up women, although I swear I could almost be driven to it sometimes because of you! Get to work!"

She started to leave, hesitated, and turned back toward him, all her longings and fears evident in her lovely face. "Ryder, you won't...?" she asked softly, glancing toward the woman.

"Would it matter?" he replied, his voice equally soft.

"Oh, yes," she whispered, her face briefly anguished. "It would matter...very much."

He took a long breath and his fingers reached out to touch her soft mouth, devoid of lipstick just at the moment. "I don't know if I'm sorry or glad about that," he murmured. "But at least you understand about the Frenchman now, don't you?" he added pointedly.

She tried to speak, but she couldn't. She had no defenses left. She turned and left the restaurant, trying not to see the lovely French woman who watched her go and then moved toward Ryder.

He sent her packing in a very nice way, although Ivy wasn't around to see it. He had to find something to keep him occupied tonight, or he was going to do something stupid. But another woman wasn't the answer. He wanted only her. That was his whole problem. He muttered a curse and went off to his business meeting, hoping it would take his mind off Ivy and give him a few minutes' peace. With any luck at all, she'd be asleep when he got back to the suite.

Chapter 8

Ivy had a salad for supper and drank a pot of black coffee in the suite. Midnight came and went, and still Ryder hadn't come in. She tormented herself with the thought of him and that French woman. He'd said he wouldn't, but what if he needed a woman so desperately that he couldn't help himself? She couldn't bear to think about it—Ryder's hard, powerful body against that French woman's soft sensuality.

She put on her gown and lay down, but she couldn't sleep. It was a long time before she finally heard the suite door open. But if Ryder went to his own bedroom immediately, he didn't go to sleep.

He hadn't looked in on Ivy. Tonight, he was too raw to take the risk. He'd thought of nothing but her all day, and despite the taunt he'd made about the French woman, he wanted nothing to do with any woman except Ivy. He undressed and climbed under the sheet, trying to drive the memories of her out of his mind. He could see her the way she'd been at the Castillo in St. Augustine, feel her response on the beach in Savannah. And the more he thought about it, the more aroused he got until his body had him on the rack. He moved restlessly, stifling a groan. He had to get his mind off her!

Ivy heard his restless movements in the other bedroom, despite her closed door. His temper was so short lately that it was almost triggered by breathing. He went from bad to worse, and she didn't know what to do. She had felt him watching her, as if he were waiting for something, but she couldn't decide what. All she knew was that he was hurting in some terrible way, and she wanted to help him.

With the lights out, the noises seemed magnified. She heard what sounded like an agonized groan and, without stopping to think, she got out of bed and turned on the light.

She moved toward his door, all too aware of the dangers of walking into a man's bedroom dressed in a practically see-through blue gown with a bodice cut low in front and back. But this was Ryder, not some stranger, and he was her friend.

She opened the door quietly. The small lamp by his bed was on, but he wasn't reading. He was lying sprawled under part of the sheet, one muscular forearm thrown across his eyes.

Her bare feet made no noise as she walked across the carpet and paused, fascinated, by his bedside. The sheet only covered his hips. The rest of him, from his broad muscular chest with the thick black hair curling down below his lean waist, to his long, powerful bronzed legs with their feathering of hair, was bare to her curious eyes.

She'd never really cared to see Ben without his clothes, but Ryder was another matter. She looked at him with eyes that widened with a shock of pleasure, delighting in his masculinity, in the perfection of his body.

He moved, moaning again, and his forearm slid away from his eyes, revealing Ivy standing by the bed.

He stiffened. "I must be drunk," he said absently.

"I heard you," she said softly. "Are you all right, Ryder?"

His jaw tautened as his eyes slid over her body, lingering on the thrust of her breasts, their creamy rise visible in the deep neckline. Her black eyes were soft, her long black hair falling gently around her creamy shoulders, and he wanted her with such an anguish of longing that it almost choked him. "Get out of here, Ivy," he said huskily. "Quick!"

He sounded dangerous, and for once, she didn't care. She felt alive as never before. She tingled all over, just looking at him.

"Why?" she asked. "Can't you tell me what's wrong?"

"Do you really want to know?" he asked in a goaded tone, frustration and desire so hotly mingled that his body was in agony. "All right, why not? You're a big girl now. This is what's wrong with me, Ivy."

He threw off the sheet.

Her lips parted on words she couldn't speak. He was totally aroused, so blatantly that even a virgin couldn't have missed it. He was trembling faintly, too, and his eyes were gray and glittery in his drawn, dark face.

"Oh, Ryder," she whispered helplessly, and the dark, soft eyes that looked at him were openly worshiping, not afraid or even embarrassed. It was, she thought dazedly, impossible to be embarrassed at the sight of so beautiful a man.

"God!" He sat up, turning away from her with his head in his hands. "God, I must be mad! I'm sorry. Go away, honey, will you?"

She moved forward, unbearably touched by his pain. She sat down beside him, her cool fingers hesitant as they touched his arm.

His head jerked around and he looked at her as if he didn't believe she was still there.

"Lie down, Ryder," she whispered, her voice unsteady. She didn't know exactly what to do, but she had a pretty good idea. She couldn't walk away and leave him like this, even if he hated her for it when he was himself again.

"What?" he burst out, disbelieving.

She pushed at his shoulders, coaxing him onto his back, his silvery eyes astonished. She didn't meet them. Her head bent and she touched her mouth hesitantly to his hair-roughened chest while her other hand slid down his flat belly.

He cried out harshly, his voice throbbing, and his hands caught her hair. "Ivy...for God's sake...no!"

She didn't stop, though. Her trembling fingers found him, touched him, a little intimidated by the sheer power of his body. Her lips drifted over his taut skin, the hair at his waist tickling her face, while her hand stroked.

"No..." he groaned, shivering.

"Teach me how," she whispered without looking at him, and she kept on. He was vulnerable, and she'd never been less frightened in her life than she was right now.

"Ivy!" His voice broke, but her touch had an inevitable effect on his reserve. His hand guided hers, his body reacting with shattering need, the shudders racking him now. She felt him tremble under her mouth, heard his tortured breathing as he tutored her.

When he convulsed, crying out in ecstasy, she forced her embarrassed eyes to lift, to look at him. It was incredible.

Even in their most intimate moments, Ben had never looked like...*that!* She might have thought he was dying if she hadn't known better. He pulsed in her grasp, helpless, blind, deaf, to anything but the pleasure that almost made him pass out.

When the spasms passed, she left him to find a damp cloth and a towel. He lay just as she'd left him while she drew the warm cloth over him with exquisite tenderness, her heart beating fiercely in the aftermath of what she'd shared with him.

His dark eyes opened, faintly accusing, almost incredulous. He was still trembling.

"Are you all right?" she whispered softly.

"Yes." He caught her free hand and drew its palm hungrily to his mouth. "Thank you!" he whispered feverishly, his voice still husky with pleasure.

"I'm sorry I was so clumsy," she said hesitantly. "I've... well, I've never..."

His eyes searched hers. "Not even for him?"

She knew he meant Ben. She shook her head shyly. Her eyes glanced off the curiosity in his and down to his broad, bare chest with its thicket of hair. "Ryder, could I ask you something...well, something personal?"

"What do you want to know?" he asked softly.

"What happened to you, just now..." she began hesitantly, her wide eyes meeting his. "What does it feel like?" she asked in a subdued whisper.

He scowled. "You were married. Don't you know?"

She paused, then with a sigh, she shook her head.

He sat up, his dark eyes holding hers at an unnerving proximity. What he asked then was blunt and to the point.

She blushed. Even Ben had never asked her something so intimate. "No."

"Did he know?'"

"Oh, yes," she replied. "He said that I was frigid." She moved restlessly. "It was so uncomfortable," she murmured, wincing. "And sometimes, it hurt awfully!"

His lean, beautiful hands framed her face and made her look at him. "Did he never do to you what you just did to me, to make it easier for you?"

"I don't understand," she said.

He couldn't believe what she was saying. All that beauty, all that innocent sensuality, and it had never been tapped. In every real respect, she was untouched. His hungry eyes went over her soft oval face with its big black eyes dominating it, her silky black hair falling around her bare shoulders, around the firm thrust of her beautiful breasts. He had to drag his mind back.

"How long did it take him?" he asked bluntly.

"Ryder!"

"I have to know," he said softly. "Trust me."

She averted her eyes. "I don't know. Not long. He was always in a hurry…."

"Less than five minutes?" he asked through his teeth, his face rigid.

"Well…" She swallowed. "Yes."

He sighed heavily. "My God," he said.

"I thought I loved him," she said. "But I didn't want him," she said miserably. "I had no idea how it would be to live with him, feeling that way."

He tilted her face up to his. "I want to give you what you gave me," he said quietly. "Will you let me?"

She colored. "You don't have to…"

"You asked me how it felt," he said, his voice deep and slow. He drew her onto the bed and eased her down on the sheet, her dark hair waving around her flushed face like a halo. "I'm going to show you."

"Ryder…" she protested nervously, pushing both hands against his hard, bare chest, feeling the thick hair crisp under her fingers.

"It's all right," he coaxed. "I don't have anything to use, so intercourse is out of the question. It won't hurt you, either."

She felt his breath on her parted lips as he bent. "Don't men usually have…something to use?" she asked nervously.

He smiled against her trembling mouth. "Ivy, I haven't had a woman for almost two years," he whispered. "Why should I bother to keep anything?"

"You haven't…?"

He took the muffled question into his mouth. She smelled of roses, and he thought that he'd never been so close to heaven in all his life as he was tonight. The touch of her, the taste of her was exquisite. His body still throbbed warmly from the peace she'd given him so generously, and so unexpectedly. Now he wanted her to have it, too. To experience the unbearable sweetness of belonging to someone who cared deeply, who loved her more than his own life. He couldn't tell her that. She wouldn't want to hear it, just yet. But knowing it added another dimension to his soft kisses, to the delicate caress of his fingers on one soft, bare arm as he gentled her, made her receptive to his advances.

"Relax," he whispered. His hard lips touched her softly rounded chin, moved down to the quick pulse in her throat, to her collarbone. "Relax, little one. I won't hurt."

She caught her breath as his mouth moved again, nuzzling aside the gown to find the soft curve of her breast. Her hand went involuntarily to his thick, dark hair. But instead of pushing him away, it lingered in the cool strands. Something was happening to her. She quivered as his lips brushed and lifted, brushed and nipped, brushed and nibbled ever closer to the hard, sensitive peak of her breast. She couldn't fathom the sudden hardness of it, or the throbbing warmth that began to build in her lower belly.

Ryder felt her heartbeat building, heard her breathing change. She was aroused already, and he'd barely begun. He slid his open mouth fully over her nipple and created a faint, warm suction, tasting the nipple with his tongue as he built the pressure.

She cried out. Her fingers trembled and she arched up to him, her body shuddering.

He felt his own swift arousal, triggered by hers, and fought to keep his head. It was her satisfaction he wanted now, not his own.

His free hand moved down, bunching the gown slowly up her silken thighs until he found his way under it, to the soft bareness of her inner thigh. She tensed, and when he touched her delicately, she caught his hand and gasped.

He lifted his head, looking down into her wide, frightened eyes. "Yes, it's very intimate, isn't it?" he asked softly. "But I let you touch me like this."

That was true. And despite the faint embarrassment she felt, his fingers were creating some feverish sensations as they moved deliberately. Her grip on his wrist relaxed and she let her hand fall back to the bed, watching his face as he touched her more and more intimately.

A flash of pleasure caught her unawares and she jumped, shivering.

"Yes," he said quietly, his eyes steady on hers. He touched

her again, watching her reactions, and increased the slow rhythmic movement until she was gasping, faintly writhing on the sheet.

She arched, hating the fabric that concealed her body from him, because quite suddenly she wanted him to look at her. Sensuality was killing her shyness, desire burned in her body like white heat.

"Look…at me," she whispered brokenly.

"I am," he breathed huskily.

"No. At all…of me," she managed.

His breath caught. "God!" he ground out. He moved long enough to strip her hungrily out of the gown before his hand found her again, keeping her in a sensual daze. His eyes lingered on her exquisite nudity, the sight of her hurting him. He forced his eyes back up her long, shapely legs to full hips and a small waist and taut breasts. His gaze held on the dark nipples so tight and swollen, and he bent to suckle them, enjoying the noises she was beginning to make. She had pretty breasts, and she seemed to enjoy having them touched and kissed. His teeth drew gently over a nipple, making her catch his head and gasp fearfully.

He lifted his head, feeling her legs part even more as she began to arch up to his hand. "I won't hurt your nipples," he whispered. "I like to bite," he added, bending his head to nibble hungrily at her bare shoulder, her waist, and back up again. "Is it all right?"

"Yes…!" She was trembling now, shivering all over as he increased the smooth rhythm of his hand. "Ryder!"

He lifted his head so that he could watch her. In a very real sense, this was her first time, and he didn't want to miss a gasp, a grimace, a single expression on her face. He leaned closer, filling her vision.

"When you feel it," he whispered sensuously, "try not to close your eyes. I want to watch you."

Watch you…watch you…watch you. The deep, sexy voice echoed in her mind as the pleasure bit into her body. He blurred in her wide, shocked eyes as she convulsed. She heard a helpless, high-pitched cry that seemed to go on and on as the sensations piled on themselves and racked her helpless body. She'd never imagined anything as exquisite, pleasure so hot and intense that it was almost pain. She didn't know how she was going to bear it, and she felt tears wet on her face as the spasms reached a crescendo and then, finally, began to recede to uncontrollable trembling. Silver threads of pleasure wound down her spine and she collapsed, her helpless, shocked eyes meeting his and understanding the triumph and savage pleasure she read in them.

He smoothed his lean hand up her body, pressing down hard on her belly, sliding boldly over one soft, swollen breast and lingering on its silky heat.

"Is making love fully like this?" she whispered shakily.

He nodded slowly. "More complicated, of course," he whispered. "And much more dangerous."

"Why?"

His eyes slid to her belly and lingered there with an almost desperate hunger that she couldn't see. "Because I could make you pregnant," he said gruffly.

Her heart leaped, but all too soon it came back to earth. Her smile was sad and regretful. "No, you couldn't," she said gently. "Ryder…I can't have a baby."

His breath caught. He lifted his head and winced as he looked down at her. "Oh, God, Ivy!" he groaned hoarsely.

She couldn't understand why he looked as if he needed comforting. Her own pain was familiar. Even though she'd had a rocky time with Ben, she wouldn't have minded a baby. Involuntarily her mind went back to Jacksonville, to the little boy Ryder had rescued from the river, and the way he'd been with the child. He loved children. He would want them, and now he knew that she couldn't have them. But another woman probably could… She pushed the thought away and touched his cheek tenderly. "I'm sorry," she said, forcing back tears. "I wanted children, so much!"

He bent and put his mouth gently over hers, moving so that his hair-covered chest brushed over her swollen breasts in a lazy, teasing seduction.

"It's all right," he whispered at her lips. "It doesn't affect who you are, what you are. It doesn't make you less a woman. I think I've already shown you that." He lifted his head and looked down at her flushed face, levering up on his forearms so that he could see her breasts.

She shifted nervously at that bold, intent appraisal.

His eyes met hers. "Are you going to go shy on me, now that we've eased the need in each other?" he asked gently, smiling.

"I'm afraid so," she said. She shivered a little. "I could never even let Ben look at me…like this." Her eyes widened. "And I let you look at me when…when…"

His face hardened. "Shall I tell you how you looked?" he asked huskily. "Or is it easier to picture if you just remember my face when you brought me to fulfillment?"

She went red, but she didn't look away. "I never dreamed I could do that to a man."

"For the record, why did you?" he asked.

"You were hurting," she whispered. Her fingers touched his hard mouth gently. "Oh, Ryder, you were hurting, and I had to do something!"

He shivered. So there was still hope. She cared that much, so it was possible that she might one day care even more. It gave him hope.

He caught her fingers and nibbled them one by one. His pale eyes kindled. "In that case, I'll tell you a secret," he said, his voice deep and slow in the quiet room. "I've never let a woman, any woman, do that."

She brightened visibly and smiled at him. "You let me," she whispered.

"I didn't stop you," he murmured dryly. "I didn't have much choice by that time. My God, who'd have thought it? Shy, gentle little Ivy, pushing me back onto the bed and having her way with me. Your mother would be shocked speechless."

She sat up, her body exquisitely positioned above him. "You wouldn't tell my mother?" she protested.

"For God's sake, she'd kill us both!" he reminded her. "Come down here." He pulled her into his arms again and loomed over her, his face relaxed, his eyes and soft and possessive. "I want to sleep with you."

She wasn't in the throes of passion now, and she hesitated. It was hard to consider doing that in cold blood, even after the intimacy they'd just shared. "I...I don't know," she said hesitantly, frowning.

He smoothed out the frown with a forefinger. "Not that way," he said softly. "I mean that I want to hold you all night."

"Oh." She wanted it, but she felt oddly shy with him now, even though her blood was surging through her veins.

"Ivy, we're both consenting adults," he said quietly, as if he read the thought in her mind. "I was in agony tonight and you gave me peace. I hope I did the same for you. But it was a need I wouldn't have wanted anyone else to satisfy. Do you understand, honey?" he added, as if it mattered. "I'd have gone hungry before I'd have permitted any other woman that kind of freedom with my body."

She searched his soft eyes, feeling that he was trying to tell her something that she couldn't seem to hear.

"Such big eyes," he murmured, smiling. "Turn it around. Would you lie nude in the arms of any other man and let him do to you what I did?"

She gasped. It had only just occurred to her that she was nude!

He stopped her frantic grasp for the sheet. "Your body belongs to me, now," he said softly. "You gave it to me, remember? I won't shame it, or use it selfishly, or put it at risk, so there's no reason to hide it from my eyes. I could live on the sight of you like that," he said tautly, studying her with bold, possessive eyes.

She was half sitting, and his eyes told her that it was true. They touched her with something bordering on reverence. She couldn't seem to move. At the same time, her gaze lowered to his own body, and it dawned on her that she felt the same way. She'd never seen anyone who could compare with him.

He took a slow, shuddering breath, aware as she must be now of the helpless reaction of his body to her. He turned and stretched out on the bed with a long sigh. "God, what you do to me!" he laughed ruefully. "Turn out the light, sweetheart, and come here."

"You won't…?" She hesitated.

He shook his head. "Your mother would strangle us both for what we've already done. We'd better go to sleep before we get in over our heads. Okay?"

She smiled gently. "Okay."

There were, of course, fifty good reasons why she should have put her gown back on and gone back to her own room. But she slid into his arms, feeling with awe the delicate sensation of soft skin against hair-roughened skin as he enfolded her in his arms and drew her cheek to his chest.

"Nobody will just walk in, will they?" she asked nervously, because they were lying on top of the bedclothes.

He kissed her closed eyelids. "No one will see us like this," he whispered. "Go to sleep, my darling."

She wasn't sure that he'd said that, but it sounded like it. And if she liked believing that he had, well, it didn't hurt anyone.

He had said it, of course. He waited until he was certain she was asleep. Then he lifted himself and looked at her sleeping face. She cared for him. Probably more than she even knew, just yet. He could have danced on the bed. Right now it was only physical, but that didn't mean it wouldn't grow. He lay back down eventually, drunk on the sight and sound and feel of her. He curled her into his body, aroused all over at the warm softness so trusting in his arms. But he did, finally, sleep, at peace for the first time in years.

When Ivy woke up the next morning, he was fully dressed, standing beside the bed looking at her hungrily. Her body was sprawled across the sheets in a pose that was frankly inviting, and he shivered as his eyes slid back up to hers.

She'd been dreaming. She didn't remember what, but he'd been in it, and her body, attuned now to the wonder of fulfillment, knew what he could give it. She wanted him. She arched her hips delicately, her eyes half-closed, and her nipples suddenly went hard.

"My God," he ground out in a tormented voice.

His sudden paleness, the tautening of his body, brought her

completely awake. "Ryder?" she faltered, levering herself up on her elbows.

He had to force himself to speak. Everything male in him ached to throw off his clothes and take her in a savage fury of hunger. She was fire, and he wanted to fall into it, be consumed by it. But he couldn't. He could lose control very easily right now. It was too risky.

"I'm on my way to the conference," he said through his teeth. "I should be back by one."

"All right." She flushed at his bold gaze, and the night before seemed suddenly unreal and embarrassing. She reached for the sheet and shyly covered herself with it. "I'll…I'll get the conference notes checked and corrected. I was too tired last night." A blatant lie. She was simply too hurt and miserable after Ryder had left her in the restaurant.

His jaw tautened. "You do that," he said.

He turned and stormed out of the room without a backward glance, cursing his own vulnerability, his helplessness. He'd had women on his terms all his life, but not until Ivy had come into it had he known this depth of vulnerability. She had him on his knees, and all they'd done was some very heavy petting. God, if he ever made love to her completely, he wouldn't be in possession of his own soul anymore! He'd looked down at her and knew that he was lost, that he'd do anything she asked, that he'd be helpless for the rest of his life because he loved her so much.

He went blindly out of the suite, and the outer door slammed behind him furiously.

Ivy agonized all day over what had set him off. Was he regretting, as she was, their uncharacteristic encounter? Perhaps she shouldn't have gone near him. But what he'd given her starved body had been worth the embarrassment. She groaned silently remembering the hot, fierce sensations that had carried her away at the last. And he'd watched. She'd let him look at her, in that intimacy…!

She couldn't look at herself in the mirror without blushing. Imagine shy little Ivy pushing him back onto the bed, he'd said. He couldn't believe it, and she certainly couldn't. Ryder had been, up until this morning, the best friend she had. Now she wasn't sure what he was—a friend or a future lover or something caught in between.

She wondered if he'd even speak to her again. Perhaps he was embarrassed, too. Surely he didn't make a habit of telling his women how long he'd gone without sex, or letting himself get into that helpless state of need.

But he'd had women, she realized suddenly. He'd known exactly how to reduce her to a mindless wanton. His touch had been skilled and expert, like the hard mouth that had seduced hers.

She hated them all. She hated every woman who'd ever lain in his arms and admitted the fierce possession of his body. His body…

She shivered. Such power and strength, such masculine perfection. He'd let her see him helpless, he'd let her make him helpless. She remembered the way he'd looked, his fists clenched at the headboard, his powerful body arched and convulsing, his face contorted while he cried out in the ecstasy of satisfaction.

She went hot all over. He'd said that making love fully was like that. But it wasn't. She knew making love fully hurt. It was quick and uncomfortable.

On the other hand, Ryder had been very slow and thorough

with her, and she'd felt a staggering pleasure. Wouldn't he be just like that if she allowed him to…

She swallowed, feeling feverish. What would it be like to lie under that powerful body and feel the expert control of his hands and mouth? Her eyes closed and she could picture it: her body arching, his lean hands jerking her hips up against his, his face hard and damp, his breathing jerky and quick as he increased the rhythm of his hard thrusts, her own delighted cries of pleasure…

"Oh, God!" she burst out, shuddering.

She went into the bathroom and turned the shower on full. Stripping off her gown, she climbed under the cold spray, welcoming the shock of it. Life had suddenly become very complicated.

Chapter 9

It was the worst day of Ivy's entire life. Ryder was the soul of courtesy for the rest of the day, and he didn't refer once to what had happened or even to his own inexplicable temper when he'd left the suite. He was remote, as he'd been before so many times. Only this was worse, because something was simmering under it.

She didn't know why, either. If he'd regretted their night together, wouldn't he have said so? Or was he saying so, with his rigid manner and businesslike demeanor?

She only knew that her frustration was killing her. A short month ago she hadn't known what desire or fulfillment really were. Now she did, and she wanted Ryder in every way that a woman was capable of wanting a man. She dreamed of him, ached for him, would have died for him. But he apparently didn't notice her waking fever, even though she trembled when he came close, even though her eyes must have been eloquent when she looked at him.

He'd announced over a brief working lunch, that they were going home tomorrow, and she didn't know how she was going to live. Maybe it would be for the best, of course. Out of sight, out of mind, and he didn't spend that much time in the office these days. But thinking about the future didn't help the present.

She'd already told him a stiff, impersonal good-night and gone to her room. But even the touch of her light gown on her burning skin was painful. She threw it off and sprawled on the cool coverlet, arching helplessly as she thought about Ryder. Her long hair framed her flushed, hungry face like a black halo. She could only imagine how she looked. Wanton, probably, and she didn't care. Her body ached as if with a killing fever. At least the coverlet cooled her a little. She should get up and turn off the light, but she was too miserable to care.

The door opened unexpectedly, and Ryder walked in. His taut face went even harder at the sight of her. He was wearing a black toweling robe and nothing else, and his straight black hair was damp from the shower that hadn't taken his mind off Ivy. Now, looking at her, it was easy to see why. He'd tried, God knew he'd tried, to keep away from her. But he couldn't bear it any longer. He'd heard her restless movements, her quick breathing, just as she'd heard his the night before. Or maybe he'd sensed it, because he seemed to be perfectly attuned to her lately.

He slammed the door behind him with fierce purpose and threw off his robe as he approached the bed.

Ivy didn't move. He was unashamedly aroused and not bothering to hide his body from her rapt gaze. She saw the intent in his eyes even before he lay down beside her, arching over her to let his eyes feast on her delicate contours, on her flawless pink skin.

She moved hungrily, her eyes glazed with desire, her blood on fire. "I want you," she whispered helplessly. "I'm sorry, but I can't help it. I want you so badly, Ryder! I can't bear the ache!"

"Yes, I know how it feels. It's all right. I want you just as much." He bent to brush his mouth lovingly over her parted lips, his brows drawing together with pure ecstasy as he felt her lips eagerly opening under his. "We'll make a little love, and then maybe we can both sleep," he breathed into her mouth.

But as his hand slid down her warm, soft belly, she caught it.

He lifted his head to meet her feverish eyes.

"No," she whispered, her voice shaking. "I want *you*. All of you."

His face clenched. "Ivy…"

She saw the protest in his eyes. He was an old-fashioned man and he'd known her and her mother for years. He was having protective second thoughts. But she didn't want his conscience. Not now.

She slid one of her silky legs under his and moved so that she lay in the curve of his hips. She drew her other arm under his, so that her soft breast pressed up against his chest, and with her free hand she touched him delicately and felt him shudder uncontrollably.

"Please," she whispered at his lips, pushing forward so that she was guiding him into an intimacy she hadn't shared with a man since her tragic marriage. She felt the touch of him with shivering awe and pressed closer, trembling at the incredible throbbing strength under her hand.

"All right," he ground out, catching her hair to jerk her away from him. "But not like that. Not…like that. Let me arouse you first. If we're going to make love, I'm going to satisfy you completely. It isn't going to be a two-minute interlude."

She stared up at him curiously, but his mouth bent to hers, and she felt the warm furry weight of his chest over her breasts, the slide of his lean hand lazily down her belly to her thigh and back up again.

For all the urgency she could feel and see in his taut body, he was the soul of patience. He kissed her with teasing, unhurried warmth, nibbling her lips, probing them delicately with his tongue. And all the while that maddening hand played around her breasts until he made them swell, and even then he avoided the taut, aching nipples.

"Oh, please," she whimpered.

He laughed softly, wickedly. "Already?" he whispered. "And we've barely started."

"I'll die," she protested, her big black eyes opening, accusing.

He straddled her hips, the proof of his own need blatantly warm on her belly as he bent to her lips and nibbled them. "That's what the French call a climax," he whispered. "A little death. Did you know?"

"No." She blushed.

He felt the heat in her cheeks as he nuzzled her face. His legs extended, cradling hers in their muscular warmth, and he shifted so that he could bend his head to take her nipple in his mouth and torment it.

"You like this, don't you, little one?" he whispered, and tugged softly at the hard tip. "I like it, too. Your breasts are soft and firm and I love the way they feel against my naked chest."

"Ryder," she moaned, shivering.

His mouth slid down to her belly, pressing there, then to her thighs and her hips, nibbling softly, making her burn. His hands slid between her thighs, caressing them apart, creating sensations that she'd never felt.

He turned her, pulling one leg over his so that he could slide between them. His nose rubbed softly against hers and he smiled as he touched his lips to her closed eyelids. His lean hands smoothed over her hips, back to the base of her spine, bringing her intimately close. One hand shifted, sliding down her belly, and he lifted his head to seek her eyes with his as he touched her, once, with intimate purpose.

"Yes," he whispered softly. "You're ready. More than ready."

She didn't understand. She was trembling, her mouth swollen from his long, hard kisses, her fingers cool at the back of his head. "Ready?" she managed weakly.

"To accept my body," he whispered. He held her eyes. "To become part of me. Envelope me, Ivy," he breathed, and his hips moved.

It was incredibly erotic. She gasped as she felt him, trembled as the formidable threat of his warm body began to penetrate. She stiffened, because for an instant, there was pain.

His pale eyes looked into hers. "Well, well," he whispered tenderly, and smiled as he paused. "Slowly, little one. Try not to tense up. You can take me. Relax now. That's it." He pushed then, and there was an odd, glittery triumph in his dark eyes. "Yes. Yes!"

She looked into his eyes and felt him complete his possession of her with smooth, exquisite ease.

He didn't move, or even seem to breathe. There was a flush of color over his high cheekbones and he shuddered, his face rigid, his eyes blazing into hers.

"My God," he whispered reverently, his deep voice shaking. "Oh, my God, Ivy, I'm part of you!"

She shivered, too. Lips parting incredulously, she drew away and looked down, coloring as she saw how intimately they were joined. She caught her breath, and felt him looking, too.

"I feel like a virgin," she whispered.

"You don't know how true that is," he said huskily. "You make me feel like one, too, sweetheart." He tilted her face back up to his, his fingers faintly unsteady. "Ivy. Ivy," he whispered, and as he said her name, he moved slowly, his hips advancing and withdrawing in a slow, tender rhythm that very quickly kindled exquisite sensations in her young body. She gasped and shifted a little, to make them more intense.

He watched her face, his own tautening. "That's it," he breathed. "Fit yourself to me. Show me where it feels good. Yes. Yes, Ivy, yes!" he bit off as the sensations jumped to him.

She felt him begin to shudder helplessly with each hard thrust, and she moved her hands to his hips, and then, looking into his eyes, she shifted them to his flat belly.

He groaned in anguish and she did it again, tracing him, her lips parting as she felt him intimately and shivered at her own daring.

"God, Ivy," he whispered hoarsely. "Oh, God, I can't hold it…!"

She could feel that in his feverish roughness, but it didn't matter, because she was already going over the edge. Her nails bit into his hips with unintentional cruelty and she clenched her teeth and gasped. She moved against him with blind fury, driving for her own fulfillment even as she felt him matching her mindless thrashing with a similar lack of control.

She began to cry because it was unbearable. She wanted

more of him, more, more, and there was an aching emptiness that he had to fill…now!

She went over into shuddering, exquisite convulsions. She cried out, her head thrown back, her body racked as his lean hands gripped her hips with helpless bruising strength and ground her into him.

He was murmuring something that she only dimly heard, his deep voice shattering, and then he threw back his own head and cried out harshly. She felt him go into the first convulsion, and it was followed by another and another that, incredibly, fed her own fulfillment until it was unbearable.

She felt his damp skin against hers. Beads of sweat had run down his hair onto her breasts, where his lips were buried hungrily. He was shaking in her arms, trembling helplessly, just as she was, fighting for every gasping breath he drew.

Her heartbeat was impossibly loud. Or was it his? She touched his damp hair to make sure she was still alive. Her body ached as if it had been beaten. But a furious warmth was stealing through her body and every silvery tremble of it prolonged the pleasure.

She moved and felt him. He was still part of her.

He started to lift away, but her trembling hands caught his hips and protested.

He brought his head up to look into her wide, fascinated eyes.

"Your body is capable of endless fulfillment," he whispered with a tender, weary smile. "But mine has to rest first, little one. I need a few minutes before we love again."

She tingled all over at the phrasing. Before we love again. Yes. It had felt like that, like loving. She touched his face and traced his thick, dark eyebrows.

"That wasn't why," she whispered.

"Why, then?" he asked softly.

She met his eyes shyly. "I…like the way it feels."

His body reacted impossibly and he gasped, astounded.

She searched his face curiously. "You said you couldn't," she began.

He shivered. "Did I?" He shifted her so that he was above her. His hips moved in a slow, tender thrust and she shivered, too. "Last time damned near killed me," he breathed, bending to her mouth. "I don't know if I can bear another one like that."

"It hurt?" She frowned, not understanding.

He laughed even through his building desire. "Ecstasy," he whispered, holding her eyes. "The little death. God, you sounded as if I were killing you. Wild little sobs, tears…"

"It was good," she whispered, watching him. She lifted rhythmically, helping him, feeling the tremors start again down her spine. "It was good, so good…! Oh, Ryder, Ryder… please…make me feel it again!"

He couldn't wait this time, and he didn't try. Her hunger was as sweeping as his. He pushed down against her with fierce, almost savage, movements and she clung with her last ounce of strength as the exquisite pleasure lifted them convulsively back into the throes of completion.

It was morning. Ivy's last memory was of Ryder folding her against him and drawing the sheet over them, his arms still faintly trembling from exertion, cradling her as her eyes closed.

She rolled over, but the bed was empty. She sighed. It seemed that she was never going to wake up in time to see Ryder leave.

She swung her long legs out of bed and stood up, stretching. Her eyes went to the sheet and she frowned at the stain there. Her lips parted on a puzzled intake of breath.

"Now do you see why it was like the first time?" came a quiet voice from behind her.

Her shocked eyes went to Ryder. Her mind wasn't working.

"Can't you work it out, little one?" Ryder asked from the doorway, sensual appreciation in his smile. He was already fully dressed, again, and apparently on the point of leaving.

"Work what out?" she faltered, reaching shyly for the robe he'd left behind and easing into it.

He moved closer, pulling her gently against him. "Why it hurt at first."

She searched his eyes and suddenly the puzzle fell into place. She blushed scarlet.

"That's right," he murmured. "You were still partially intact. I removed the rest of the barrier," he breathed, his lips teasing her mouth. "So in a sense, little one, I had part of your virginity last night."

She moaned against his mouth and clung to him, feeling his ardor with a sense of pure wonder.

"Does it please you, knowing that?" he whispered, reeling from her headlong response.

"Yes!" Her eyes opened, worshiping him. "I wanted you to be the first. Oh, I wanted you, for so long," she whispered, letting it all out. "When I was only fifteen, I used to watch you and dream about how it would be if you came to me in the night and made love to me!"

"What?" he asked hoarsely.

His expression made her self-conscious. She faltered. "I thought you knew," she said. "I told you that I never felt that way about Ben. It was because…because I only felt it with you, and he knew it."

"Ivy, do you realize what you're saying?" he asked unsteadily. "I didn't know! I never knew you'd wanted me like that, for a long time!"

"But I was sure you did. You avoided me after that night…" she reminded him.

"It was mutual. You avoided me like the plague and went running to Ben."

"Because I knew I couldn't have you," she whispered huskily. "You didn't want me because I was too young; more like a sister than a lover. I thought that was what you were telling me without words when you stayed away from me. Even when you asked me for a date, that time, I thought it was just out of pity, because you knew how I felt about you. So when Ben asked me out, I went."

He stopped breathing. "God!" he said hoarsely.

"What is it?"

He couldn't speak. He couldn't breathe. She'd wanted him. She hadn't known how he felt, because he'd thought she was too young. So he'd walked away and she thought it was rejection, so she'd married damned Ben. Ben had known that she wanted Ryder instead of him, and that was why he'd been cruel to her. His head whirled. He couldn't bear it.

"I've got to go and check on our plane reservations and wind up a few things," he said roughly. "I'll see you later."

He went without looking back, preoccupied and solemn. And Ivy stared after him with her heart breaking, because she'd just told him how she felt and he'd walked away as if she had disgusted him.

Had he felt only desire, and now that it was satisfied, he didn't want the complication of her love for him? Was that it? Tears stung her eyes. Now what was she going to do?

Ryder deliberately didn't come back to the hotel until

almost lunchtime. He'd said goodbye to his colleagues, double-checked the reservations, and then gone walking in the rain, trying to come to grips with what he'd done. Why hadn't he known how Ivy felt? Why hadn't he seen her hunger?

But he finally realized that hunger was all it was, perhaps mixed with affection and infatuation. Hunger was all she'd felt the night before. Ben had never fulfilled her, and now she knew what it was to be a whole woman. Ryder had given her that, and she was his because of it. But it wasn't love. It was more affection, infatuation and desire. And he wanted her love.

He felt guilty when he saw her puzzled unhappiness as he entered the room. He didn't know what to say to her now, to make things right again. He should never have touched her. Now she was aroused and whole, and she was going to want a full sexual relationship that he couldn't give her. He cared too much to let what they'd shared turn into a casual affair.

He took off his hat and laid it on the table. "Ivy," he began quietly, his pale eyes searching her wounded black ones, "we need to talk."

"There's no necessity," she said with what pride she could muster after his rejection that morning. She'd brooded on it all day, until she'd decided that the best way, the only way, was to pretend sophistication and let him off the hook. He didn't want marriage and she didn't want an affair, so this was the best way out for both of them. She could always blame her behavior on the madness of being in Paris.

"You don't have to explain anything," she continued. She didn't try to understand the odd look on his face. She just plunged in. "You were hungry and so was I. We…we satisfied a mutual need, that's all. You don't have to worry that I'll make things difficult for you."

He sighed wearily. How could she put it like that? The satisfaction of a mutual need, when it had been so much more to him.

Her casual dismissal of their lovemaking angered him. Well, if it had meant so little to her, he sure as hell wasn't going to tell her what it had meant to him. Two could play at that game. He lifted his chin and studied her wan face. She was wearing a simple black dress that made her look ever more pale, but it gave her a regal kind of elegance. How beautiful she was, he thought in anguish. And now for the rest of his life he had to remember her nude body sprawled over his bed, her mouth welcoming him, her long, soft legs sliding against his, her cries of pleasure echoing in his ears. He could have groaned out loud.

"I'm glad you understand," he said tersely.

"I'm a grown woman, not a child," she said, avoiding his eyes. "It will be business as usual from now on. We'll just be friends, I…won't embarrass you."

"As if you could," he muttered. "But we've forfeited friendship, Ivy," he said heavily.

She hesitated, because she didn't want to hear that. "Have we?"

He laughed bitterly and poured a drink from the bar, something he couldn't seem to stop lately. "You don't know." He emptied the glass in one shot, his eyes dangerous. "Then let me enlighten you. Every time you look at me for the rest of your life, you'll see me naked in your arms. And I'll see you the same way."

She flushed and her hands clenched in her lap. "It might be a good idea if I get another job."

"That won't be necessary," he said curtly. "I'll be out of the country a good bit in the next few weeks, so it's more than likely you won't even have to see me."

She lifted her wounded eyes to his. "Ryder," she whispered miserably.

Her turned away, his face unreadable. "We'd better get to the airport, Ivy," he said in a voice that was almost normal.

"I've already packed," she said. "I'll just check one last time."

Not for one second would she admit that she was disappointed that they were leaving so soon. She'd wanted to see Paris, to visit the Eiffel Tower at least, but all they'd done was work. She colored as she checked the dresser drawers. No, that wasn't quite all they'd done, she thought, averting her eyes from the bed.

Her breath caught as her body reacted to the memory, making her tingle all over and long for Ryder. If only he'd come in and tell her that it was a mistake, that they were staying another week, that he wanted her again, that he loved her. She stared around the room one last time with a heartfelt sigh. Paris was a city for lovers, they said. Well, she and Ryder had been lovers, but only once really and if their lovemaking meant anything special to Ryder, it didn't show. He seemed much the same as usual, if a little more abrasive.

What had she expected, she wondered miserably, professions of undying love and eternal commitment? It was just as well that she hadn't, because it was obvious that she wasn't going to get them.

In the days that followed their return from Paris, Ivy often wondered if she worked for a ghost. Ryder took off for parts unknown the day after he and Ivy arrived home. She went into the office in Albany a little nervously, but her anxieties were for nothing, because Ryder left word with his vice president's assistant that he'd be out of the office for a month and for Ivy to take care of the mail, the filing and the phone until he got back. Other than that, there was no message. None at all.

Ivy wished that Eve was in the country, so that she could sit down and cry on her shoulder. It would be pretty difficult, of course, since the root of her problems was kin to Eve. She couldn't talk to her mother about what had happened in Paris. It wouldn't do at all to admit to that kind of madness. She loved her mother, but Jean was very straitlaced and not at all modern. She wouldn't understand.

With a long sigh, Ivy sat down to go through the mail and wondered how she was going to manage the rest of her life with her heart in a sling.

The sad thing was that Ryder had been her friend before they became involved physically. Removing him from her life was going to be impossible unless she moved to Mars. Even then, her mother would find a way to get messages to her and tell her all the latest news about him. There was no place to run.

Her appetite dwindled until she was living on toast and black coffee and salads. She had no interest in the world around her and she grew weaker and less energetic by the day. Depression was taking a terrible toll on her.

Jean inevitably noticed her condition. "Don't you think you'd better see a doctor?" she asked worriedly one night.

"I'm just tired," Ivy protested. It was barely seven o'clock, and her eyelids were drooping.

"Tired! My goodness, you're always tired. You go to sleep sitting up, you won't eat…oh, honey, I'm so worried about you," Jean wailed.

"If you want to know the truth, I guess I'm depressed," Ivy said after a minute, lowering her sad eyes. "I do miss Ryder so much."

Jean relaxed. "So that's it."

Ivy nodded. "He's been away almost a month, and he hasn't even phoned me," she said, revealing the most hurtful part. "He sends messages through Mr. Wood's assistant about what he wants done, and he sends emails about contracts, but he never actually talks to me."

"Did anything happen in Paris?" the older woman asked softly.

Ivy turned away before her mother could see her scarlet face. Jean was nobody's fool, and Ivy didn't want to discuss such a personal subject with her mother.

"The only thing that happened was that he said he didn't want to get married," Ivy replied.

"My poor baby," Jean sighed, taking the remark for the whole truth. She hugged her daughter warmly. "Do keep one thing in mind, though. Most men don't want to be married. Sometimes it just takes a little time for them to come around to it." She laughed softly. "You know, your father was one of those. But he decided that marriage wasn't so bad, and once you came along, he was the happiest husband you ever saw. He did adore you."

"I wish I could have known him," Ivy said with a sigh.

"So do I. He was very special." She let go. "Do you think you could eat something now?"

"I'll try. I just haven't had much appetite," Ivy replied, sitting down at the table. "And the oddest thing, the smell of bacon makes me sick. Do you suppose there might be something wrong with my stomach?"

"Maybe a little indigestion," Jean agreed with a smile, thinking privately that it couldn't be anything else, since Ben had been dead for over six months. She moved to the stove and began dishing up supper.

Three more weeks passed before Ryder came back. Ivy had gotten over much of her nausea, but the weariness in the evenings seemed to get worse. Her appetite was still sketchy, but she stopped worrying because her waistline was growing. That, she decided, had to be proof that she was healthy.

Ryder walked into the office unexpectedly early one Monday morning. Ivy looked up from her desk and saw him, and her dull eyes brightened in her thin face.

She couldn't know how different she looked to Ryder, who hadn't seen her in almost seven weeks. He remembered a healthy, bright woman with an exquisite complexion and sparkling eyes. Now that same woman was rail-thin with lackluster hair and skin, looking as though she'd been desperately ill. The smile she'd been hoping for from him didn't materialize. If anything, he looked positively grim as he stood frozen in the doorway looking at her.

"My God!" he burst out, staggered at what he saw. "What's happened to you?"

"Why, nothing," she stammered. She got up from her chair and walked around to the front of the desk, forcing a wan smile to her mouth. "It's good to see you again, Ryder."

He didn't budge. He was carrying an attaché case, and he did put that down on the floor. But he looked worried.

Seconds later, there seemed to be reason for his concern. Ivy blinked, felt her head begin swimming suddenly, and with a tiny cry of protest, she felt the floor coming up to meet her in a nauseating whirl.

Chapter 10

Ryder caught her up in his arms and frowned as she rallied almost at once.

"I'm all right," she assured him, smiling gently. He was home. Everything would be all right now. She looked up at him with her heart in her eyes, while she clung to him with delight. "Don't I get a kiss?" she teased in the old familiar way, even though her voice was strained and her eyes pleading rather than afraid.

"You'd get one, if I was certain I could stop," he murmured, wary of passersby even though the door was partially closed. He searched her big, dark eyes. "You don't weigh anything at all. Aren't you eating?"

She loved the concerned note in his soft, deep voice. "I had a virus, I guess," she murmured drowsily. "I stayed sick forever, and now I just don't have much appetite. The oddest things turn my stomach when I'm cooking."

He could hardly believe that she didn't realize what she was describing. She'd told him she couldn't get pregnant, so apparently she hadn't made the connection. But what she was describing certainly sounded like morning sickness to him. He should know, having heard in detail about his sister's three pregnancies. His head spun with the delicious possibility.

"Have you seen a doctor?" he asked softly, standing very still while he waited for an answer.

"You sound like Mama," she said, laughing. "No, I haven't. I don't need to, Ryder. I'm all right now, even if I do still tire easily. I expect it was something like flu."

"You don't look all right."

"If we're going to trade insults, you look sort of drained yourself," she remarked, seeing new lines in that hard, lean face and dark circles under his pale eyes. He smelled of expensive cologne and soap, and the scent of him was very sensual. "Too many long nights with pretty girls?" she murmured dryly, but with an underlying curiosity.

He glared down at her. "As if I could ever touch another woman after that night with you," he said quietly.

Her heart felt as if it might try to jump right out of her chest. "Really?" she asked huskily.

"Really." He bent his head and brushed his mouth softly over hers, feeling her lips part, accepting him without reservation. It felt as it had that night in Paris. He groaned softly and pulled her closer as his mouth grew gently insistent. He was still carrying her, and instead of carrying her into his office, he sat down on the edge of her desk and held her across his thighs and kissed her until he had to stop to draw breath. She was almost certainly pregnant, and it amused and delighted him that she apparently didn't suspect it. Jean might, but he doubted that Ivy had mentioned that wild night to her mother. She would have been too shy. He was astonished at the force of his own feeling, at the pleasure that washed over him at the thought of Ivy pregnant with his child. He could have danced a jig.

But as he lifted his head and looked at her shyly welcoming face, it occurred to him that he couldn't tell her he knew. Not yet. She didn't think she could get pregnant, so he was going to have to steer her toward a doctor. Then he was going to have to watch her very carefully to make sure she didn't go off the deep end. After that, he'd have to act surprised when she told him, because if he let on that he knew, she'd think he only wanted her because of the baby. It was a sticky proposition all around, and he only hoped he could handle it properly.

The first step, he decided, was to court her. No rushed loving, no intimacy. He had to prove to her that he was loyal and trustworthy and desperately in love. He should have done all that before he took her to bed, he realized, but he'd been too far gone to think it through. Thank God, there was still time, if he was careful.

He nuzzled his nose against hers and smiled. "That was a nice welcome. Can I come to supper?"

Her breath caught. "Yes, of course! Kim Sun can come, too," she began.

"Kim Sun is visiting his parents for a much-needed vacation. He won't be back for two weeks. Lucky me," he chuckled wickedly.

"You know you miss him," she chided.

"Not nearly like I missed you," he whispered. His mouth touched hers again, with breathless tenderness while he cradled her against his hard chest. "All the color went out of the world."

"Just like here, without you," she whispered back. Her arms tightened around his neck and she moaned as she kissed him hungrily. "Can we go to bed together?" she asked boldly.

He stiffened. His cheek slid against hers as he rocked her. "I want to. You don't know how much! But you and I need to start again, at the very beginning. Holding hands, going to movies, out on dates…that sort of thing."

She jerked in his arms. He couldn't be saying… But she lifted her head and looked at him, and it was very apparent that he was saying it. He was talking about a commitment. What kind she couldn't guess, but she didn't care. Having him home again, having him want to be with her, that was all that mattered.

She said so. He looked as rapt and wondering as she felt, as if her feet wouldn't even touch the floor when she walked.

"I used to dream about going on a date with you," she confessed.

"I had some dreams of my own. You made most of them come true in Paris," he murmured and kissed her flushed face. "Don't be embarrassed about it. It was the sweetest loving I've ever known."

"Yes, but you've known a lot," she worried.

"Neither of us has known that kind," he emphasized. His eyes kindled. "And in several ways, you were virginal. Remember?"

She did. Her body trembled in his arms as the memories came back full force.

"I hate myself for bringing that up," he groaned when the words aroused him. He got up quickly and put her down. "I'm sorry, but I've got a problem."

She leaned back against the desk, delighted that he did, because it was proof of how easily she could stir him. Her eyes were dreamy as they watched him. "But we can't do it again?"

He shook his head. "Not yet."

"Eventually?" she persisted.

He chuckled. "Eventually neither of us will have a choice. But we've got a lot to learn about each other."

"Can you spare the time?" she asked mischievously.

"I'll make the time," he assured her. His pale eyes narrowed. "I'm going to take very good care of you, Miss McKenzie."

"You make it sound as if I need to be looked after," she mused.

"Don't you? Honest to God, you're as thin as a spaghetti strand—vermicelli, at that."

"I was pining away because you were gone," she said, making a joke of it when it was the truth.

He figured that out easily enough, and smiled faintly. "I'm back now, and I'm not going away again. So you don't have any excuse to starve yourself."

"Just don't offer me bacon. Yuuuck!" She made a face. "God knows why, but it makes me sick."

He thought about the tiny thing that didn't like bacon, and his heart swelled. He couldn't tell her just yet that he hated bacon, too. His son or daughter had obviously inherited his taste already.

She didn't cook him bacon that night. Instead she baked a ham and made potato salad and homemade rolls to go with it, rounding off the meal with pecan pie, which was his favorite. Jean teased her about it, but Ivy didn't protest this time. She was so happy that she seemed to glow.

Ryder ate seconds of everything, the first food he'd really wanted or tasted in weeks. He'd lost a couple of pounds himself. His eyes swept over Ivy's radiant face with pure possession, lingering on her soft mouth. She was wearing a simple, oyster-white dress with a colorful burgundy patterned scarf—one he'd seen before—and it did something for her. He loved the way she looked in it.

She approved of him, too. He had on a white shirt with a tweed sports coat and dark slacks, and looked handsome enough to make her heart turn over.

After dessert, Jean—sensing new undercurrents—volunteered to do the dishes and chased Ivy and Ryder into the living room, tactfully closing the door between the two rooms with a grin.

"Cupid in a cotton apron," Ryder murmured his approval.

"Except for lack of a bow and arrows," Ivy agreed shyly.

"Good thing she doesn't know about Paris, or she'd probably break it over our heads, honey," he said. His pale eyes smiled down at her, liking her shyness. He reached out and drew her gently to him. "No heavy stuff," he promised as he bent his dark head and his breath whispered against her parting lips. "Just kisses this time, little one. We don't want things to get out of hand."

"Yes, we do," she whispered, moving closer to him.

He chuckled and kept her hips away from his with insistent hands. "Yes, we do," he agreed reluctantly. "But not here. Not tonight."

She slid her arms under his and pressed her cheek to his thin white shirt, feeling his heart beat hard and heavy under her ear. His body was warm and strong, and it was pure delight to hold him. "I haven't slept," she said involuntarily as she stared at the fireplace across his chest. There was a fire in it, because the electric heaters weren't enough to keep the old-fashioned house warm. The fireplace wasn't very efficient, but it did warm the small living room. And the fire was beautiful to look at.

"I haven't slept well, either," he confessed. "It wasn't other women. It was missing you in my arms at night. I got used to holding you until dawn."

"Shh," she cautioned, glancing worriedly toward the kitchen door. "Mama might hear you, and we don't want her to beat us."

"Dead right, we don't," he chuckled against the top of her head. His arms contracted. "But you missed sleeping with me, too, didn't you?"

She nodded. Her eyes closed and she sighed. He made her feel so feminine. It was nice to be able to lean on a man for a change. Ben had leaned on her, almost constantly.

"You've gone quiet. Why?" he asked.

"I was thinking about Ben. About the way he depended on me. I was thinking," she added when she felt him stiffen, "how nice it is to lean on you."

He relaxed again. "There's something you don't know about Ben," he said. "Here, sit next to me, Ivy. Before we go any farther together, you've got to know it all."

She moved off his lap, because he looked, and sounded, worried. He sat down next to her on the worn couch and clasped his hands behind his head as he spoke.

"Ben's father was killed in a wreck, because I sent orders for him to go out to a construction site and bring back some paperwork for me. He found a bottle of Scotch I kept in my desk drawer, and he was heavily intoxicated when they cut him out of the car." He didn't look at her. Not yet. "That was when Ben's life fell apart. It was why he started drinking. So you see," he finished heavily, "I'm partially responsible for every problem you had in your marriage."

She sat very still for a minute, thinking about her own guilt and the way her mother had made her face it. Ryder hadn't faced his own. She had to help him do that. She could, now, because she was finally free of her past.

Her hand reached out and touched his, stroking it gently. "Nobody is responsible for anybody else's problems," she said quietly. "Ben drank supposedly because of his father's death, but he had a choice, Ryder. We all have choices, and sometimes we make the wrong ones. Ben did. I did. Now I have to go on living, and so do you. Looking back won't help. All the regrets in the world won't change one single second of what happened."

He scowled, staring pointedly at her.

"Mama helped me sort out my own guilt," she explained simply. "I got through it. I failed Ben, but he didn't have to stay with me and he didn't have to drink. Those were his choices."

He twined her fingers around his. "I've carried that around for a long time. It's been between us." He studied her hand. "I thought you might blame me."

She smiled. "No. I don't blame you for anything. Except dragging me home from Paris before I got to see the Eiffel Tower," she clarified, grimacing at him.

He laughed softly, feeling free. "My God, I did, didn't I? I'm sorry, honey. I wasn't thinking too clearly about then."

"Why did we leave so suddenly?" she asked, confident enough now to ask the question.

"Don't you know?" He lifted her across his lap and let her head fall back into the crook of his elbow. "We wouldn't have been able to stop. We'd have had each other all day, every day, from then on, for as long as we stayed there. We had Jean when we came home, to save us from ourselves. We still do."

"Yes, but with Kim Sun gone, there's no one in your house," she said slowly.

He smiled at her. "I won't take you home with me. Jean wouldn't like that, with her sense of propriety, and I won't have your reputation threatened."

"How old-fashioned," she whispered.

"That's the way I am, except when gorgeous black-eyed brunettes make me lose my head." He kissed her softly, so that when he spoke, his lips were just touching hers. "I wish I could make you pregnant, Ivy," he whispered sensually, with a secret smile, and waited for her reply.

She trembled. A tiny sound purred out of her throat as she reacted to the words. She reached up and pulled his face closer so that her mouth could grind hungrily into his. "So do I," she whimpered. "Ryder, so do I!"

His arms contracted and the kiss went on and on, building feverishly in the silence as the magic spun between them. His tongue thrust softly into her open mouth, stirring her so deeply that she caught one of his big, lean hands, and carried it hungrily to her breast.

He tried to draw back, but her nails bit into the back of his hand and held it there.

"This isn't a good idea," he managed huskily.

"Oh, yes, it is," she whispered against his mouth. Her arms slid up and around his neck, lifting her breast closer into his hot palm. "I want to take off my clothes," she moaned. "I want to make love with you right here on the floor!"

"God Almighty, I'll die!" he groaned. His mouth burned down into hers and his hand dropped to her stocking-clad legs, sliding under the hem of the dress to find her soft, warm thigh. "Ivy…!"

The furious rattle of pots and pans alerted them to the approach of Jean.

Ryder lifted his head and moved his hand back to her waist
with flattering reluctance. His breath was jerky, like her own,
and his heartbeat was shaking him.

"I guess you'll really think I'm wanton now," she whispered unsteadily. "I don't care. I'll never be able to feel this
with anyone else."

"I should hope not," he murmured gently and smiled through
his fierce desire. Especially in your condition, he could have
added. He pushed back her long hair. "And for the record, I don't
think you're wanton. I think you're a normal woman with a very
healthy attitude toward intimacy. I'm glad you trust me enough
to give me that kind of freedom with your body."

"Do you want me that badly?" she asked softly.

He nodded. "Oh, yes." His voice was quiet, but there was
a breathless hunger in it.

She leaned against him, letting her cheek rest on the rough
tweed of his jacket. Her eyes closed. "I don't want to get up.
Do I have to?"

"Your mother might get the wrong idea, sweetheart," he
said at her temple. "We'd better be circumspect for a while."

"All right." She let him lift her onto the sofa and only just
in time, because Jean came in with a tray of coffee seconds
later. She beamed at them, sitting close together on the sofa,
her approval in her face.

But approvals didn't keep her from her self-appointed role
of chaperone when Ryder came to supper or just to watch
movies he brought for, he said, his own pleasure. He brought
first-run movies, too, and sat with his arm around Ivy while
they watched them.

He never suggested that they go to his house, and he made
sure that he and Ivy didn't spend too much time alone. Mean-

while, he sent her flowers and called her up late at night just to talk, and gloried in his secret knowledge about her condition. Sometimes it was all he could do not to run down the street telling everybody he met. She was carrying his child, and she didn't know it. That had to be a first. He smiled to himself, sometimes, just watching her, delighted with her beauty, her poise, her evident pleasure in his company. It was like a taste of heaven.

All the while, she kept on working for him, and it was hard for him to keep his mind on the job. He couldn't take his eyes off her.

With secret joy, she caught him watching her at her desk after a visiting architect had left the office.

He lifted an eyebrow, smiling as he propped his shoulder against the door between her office and his and stared openly. "You're a dish," he murmured. "The color's starting to come back into your face now."

"I feel better," she agreed. "Well, except for being sleepy all the time."

He was fighting with himself, wanting to carry her into a doctor's office and insist that she be checked, so that he could be sure she was all right. It had only been a short time since he came home, though, and he had to approach her in the right way. Their whole lives hinged on what he did now. He couldn't afford to rush their relationship, but he couldn't wait much longer, either.

"Do I have any more appointments for the day?" he asked.

She checked the calendar. "Nothing until tomorrow," she said. "Are you leaving?"

"We both are." He shouldered away from the wall and called his vice president, informing Mr. Wood that he and Ivy were leaving for the day and to please have one of the assistants answer the phone in his office.

"But where are we going?" she asked as they drove off in Ryder's car.

"Over to Kolomoki Mounds," he told her, naming a site where the forerunners of the Lower Creek Indians had lived. The mounds were huge and deserted most of the winter. In summer they drew tourists and archaeology students in equal numbers.

"Isn't it the wrong time of year?" she faltered.

"Not for what we're going to do. Are you up to climbing the Temple Mound?" he added with a quiet glance.

It was almost fifty-two feet up to the grassy top of the mound, and while there were concrete steps and metal rails to hold on to, it was still a hard climb.

"I think so," she said. "Why there?"

"Now that Kim Sun is back, where else can we be completely alone together?" he asked without looking at her.

She flushed. There was a note in his voice that thrilled her, and her body tingled. She was wearing a long wool plaid skirt with a white blouse and blue sweater. Fortunately she'd worn flat black shoes and not the high heels she usually favored. She could climb. Her eyes darted to him. He was in a dark blue suit, matching her color scheme as usual.

"We really aren't dressed for climbing mounds," she began.

"We aren't dressed for rolling around in the grass, either, but that's what's going to happen when I get you up there," he said matter-of-factly, and with a rueful smile in her direction. "Or do you think we're going to be able to sit and talk without touching each other?"

She leaned her head back against the seat and stared at him hungrily. "I don't think that's even possible."

"Neither do I, little one." He reached for her hand and tangled his fingers sensuously with hers. "If it gets out of hand, I'll be exquisitely tender with you."

"Would you let it…get out of hand?" she whispered huskily, because until now, he'd been the one holding back.

He turned off onto the road that led to the mound site, his eyes briefly touching hers. "If you want me to."

That thought tantalized her all the way there. The mounds were impressive, located on red dirt roads. There were smaller mounds, but the temple mound towered over the flat plain, dominating its tree-lined surroundings. Trees dripped Spanish moss and thistles abounded in the unspoiled land. Ivy hoped that the area around the park never deteriorated into the kind of overbuilt tourist trap so common in other parts of the state. It was like walking back a thousand years into the past to come here, to hear the stillness, the bird songs in spring and summer, the wildflowers that bloomed in warmer weather. Now, with the trees bare and the grass dead, it was ghostly. There wasn't a soul around, although they had passed a government vehicle farther back.

Ryder held Ivy's hand, moving slowly up the steps with her, careful not to let her trip. She didn't understand the reason for his concern, so it struck her as wonderfully overprotective and she delighted in it.

When they were on top of the mound, still breathless from the climb, he put a protective arm around her and they looked out over the landscape.

"You can see forever from up here," she sighed.

"Not quite. Too many trees in the way. Out west you could climb this high and see for miles, because there's nothing to obstruct the horizon."

She looked up at him. "I enjoyed Arizona," she said.

"So did I." He turned her in his arms and looked down into her rapt face. "I love you, Ivy," he said softly. And he kissed her.

Tears spilled from her eyes while she clung to him. The words ricocheted through her trembling body, a beloved echo that went on and on and on.

"You didn't say that." She wept against his hungry mouth. "You didn't, did you? I must have dreamed it!"

"I said it," he breathed. His mouth touched her eyelids, closing them over the salty tears trickling from her eyes. "You didn't dream it. I sometimes think I dreamed you. I loved you when you were eighteen, but I thought you were too young and I overreacted the first time I kissed you. I waited a few years and thought I'd try again, but I'd frightened you too badly and you ran to Ben." He lifted his head and sighed bitterly as he searched her face. "I thought you loved him," he said somberly. "That's why I stayed away after the funeral. I gave you a job, just so I could be near you, and spent night after lonely night trying to find ways to tell you how I felt."

"Oh…Ryder!" Her voice broke and the tears rained down her face. "I loved you…wanted you…lived for you. Ben knew and hated you, hated me, hated us both…!"

His eyes flashed wildly and his mouth was on hers, drowning out the words. He lifted her, too hungry to think about her condition as he fitted her body to his and kissed her with all the stored-up passion of years. She loved him. She'd said she loved him!

"Didn't you know?" she moaned when he stopped long enough to let them draw shaky breaths.

"No," he said unsteadily. His eyes searched her face with such love that she felt humble. "I never dreamed you might care for me that way. In Paris, I knew I could make you want me, but it wasn't enough. I never meant to let it go that far, but it had been so long and I wanted you desperately. So desperately," he breathed at her lips. "I'm not sorry for it, but I wish we'd both known at the time what we felt for each other was mutual."

"We know now," she said achingly. "Please marry me. I won't ever be able to say no to you again, and it will be such a scandal for mother to live through if we're just living together."

Shock waves trembled through his body. He'd been tormenting himself with ways to ask her, and she'd beat him to the punch. He almost laughed out loud.

"Do you want that?" he whispered, gently teasing her. "To be my wife. To live with me, always?"

"Yes," she said fervently. "I'll take such wonderful care of you, Ryder. I'll cook—well, Kim Sun and I will cook," she amended, thinking how much she'd enjoy that, because she and Kim Sun got along so well together. "And I'll look after you when you're sick and love you so sweetly at night."

His heart ran wild. He searched her soft eyes and bent to kiss her with aching tenderness, shaking all over with the newness of loving and being loved, belonging to someone.

"I'll love you just as sweetly," he breathed. His lips hardened insistently on hers and he held her closer, letting her feel his aching arousal. "I'd hoped it would be warmer here," he ground out, feeling the cold wind whip around them—a wind much too cold for the lovemaking he'd wanted to share with her.

"So had I," she whispered. "Ryder…we could park the car somewhere," she began.

He lifted his head, smoldering inside, and looked into her lovely face. He wanted her beyond bearing, especially now, but he didn't want to spoil what they had. "No," he said after a minute. "Not ever like that. I love you far too much to reduce what we share to a feverish interlude in the back seat of a car." He eased her hips away from his with a rueful smile at her knowing look. "And yes, I'm tempted. You can feel how bad it is for me."

"It was that bad in Paris," she recalled, coloring prettily.

"You don't really know why, do you?" he asked gently. He framed her face in his lean hands and nuzzled his cheek against hers. "Ivy, since the day I realized I loved you, there hasn't been a woman."

She drew back a little. "Two years, you said," she whispered.

"I lied." He linked his hands behind her and swung her lazily from side to side. "It's been five."

"Oh, my goodness," she burst out. "No wonder…!"

"Yes. No wonder I couldn't hold it back." He smiled slowly, with sinful delight. "And you still don't know all of it."

"I don't?"

"Ivy, why did you tell me you couldn't get pregnant?"

"Because I can't," she said sadly, her dark eyes searching his. "I never did with Ben. There's something, well, something wrong. Does it matter so much?" she asked plaintively. "You said it didn't, but…"

He stopped swinging her and took her hands, gently pressing them to her flat abdomen. The look in his pale eyes was overwhelmingly tender. "Feel," he whispered.

She didn't understand. Her expression said so.

"The nausea," he said gently. "The drowsiness. Feeling tired. Hating the smell of bacon." He smiled tenderly. "I hate bacon. So does he." His hands pressed hers closer to her body. "We made a baby together in Paris, Ivy," he said softly, watching her eyes begin to dilate, her lips part on an astonished breath.

Joy welled up in her like fire. She burst into tears and pushed herself close against him, shuddering all over as she clung to him, blind with ecstatic realization.

"You really didn't know, did you, little one?" he asked at her ear, laughing with utter delight. His arms contracted. "So, yes, I'll marry you, Miss McKenzie. And it had better be quick, before you start showing."

"I can't believe it," she moaned. "It's too wonderful. I never dreamed…" She drew back, her face worried. "But what if I'm not?"

"What about that normal thing that women have once a month?" he asked, to test his suspicions.

Her jaw fell. "Oh, my goodness. I thought it was all the excitement."

His eyes had a devilish twinkle. "It *was* all the excitement," he said knowingly.

She hit his chest gently. "I'll never live it down, if I am, and you knew before I did!"

He chuckled. "No, you won't, that's for sure." He kissed her gently. "See a doctor. Get an appointment today," he said. "But whether you are or not—and I'm damned near positive you are—we're getting married. God, I love you!" he whispered fervently, and it was in his eyes, his face, in the arms that held her.

"I love you, too," she whispered, drawing his mouth down to hers. "But, oh, I hope there's a baby."

Chapter 11

And there was a baby. Ryder drove her to the doctor's—his company doctor's office—and waited with her until they were worked in. It was really amazing to watch him invent excuses to get a quick appointment, she thought breathlessly. In less than an hour, the doctor had all but confirmed their suspicions and ordered tests to substantiate them.

"I gather this is a wanted child," he murmured dryly when they were in his office waiting for the results of his examination, Ivy sitting and Ryder kneeling beside her, holding her slender hand tightly.

"You don't know the half of it," Ryder said, his voice husky with feeling as he looked at Ivy, smiling when she blushed.

"Well, I'll give you the name of a good obstetrician. You'll be needing prenatal care from now on. The tests are only going to confirm what I know from the examination, so we'll go ahead and set up the appointment." He looked at them over his glasses. "I gather this is one of those modern arrangements?"

"Oh, we're not at all modern," Ivy assured him. "We're getting married."

"You might explain to her what five years of abstinence does to a man." Ryder grinned. "That's why she's pregnant before the ceremony."

"Have you been away at war or something?" the doctor asked, chuckling.

"In love with her, and she was out of my reach," he said, his expression poignant. "I've got her now, though. She'll never get away."

"She'll never want to," Ivy assured him, oblivious to the doctor's very amused scrutiny.

They waited until the next day, until the tests came back positive, as the doctor had said they would, to tell Jean.

Ryder drove Ivy home from the office and led her into the living room, where one of Jean's soap operas was just going off.

"We've got something to tell you," Ivy said.

"I gathered that from all the nervous looks and evasions last night when I asked her why she was so restless," Jean said with amusement. "But I've already guessed, you know, and I'm sorry to steal your thunder. You're getting married, so congratulations are in order."

"It's…a little more complicated than that, I'm afraid," Ryder said, and actually looked sheepish. He sat down beside Jean on the sofa and took her hand, so much like Ivy's, in his. "We're going to have a baby," he said, the awe and delight of the statement in his pale eyes, in his smile.

"She can't," Jean explained. "Have babies, I mean."

"She's pregnant, all the same," Ryder grinned. "We just got the test results from Dr. Jameson."

Jean grabbed her chest. "Glory!" she burst out. "Oh, Ivy!" Her smile was astonished, radiant.

Ivy joined them on the sofa, hugging her mother tearfully. "Isn't it incredible? All those years, and I never, and then the first time with Ryder…" She realized what she was saying and went scarlet.

Jean looked from Ivy's red face to Ryder's red face and pursed her lips. "Paris?"

"Paris," they sighed together.

"You're not married!"

"We got a license on the way home. We'll be married tomorrow. Okay?" he asked.

Jean glowered at him. "I ought to smack both of you."

"I love her," he said, glancing warmly at Ivy. "I waited five years to show her how much." He shrugged. "I showed her a little more graphically than I meant to."

Jean didn't have an argument left. "If you waited five years, I can understand how it happened. My gosh, she walked around here turning green every morning at breakfast and I never even suspected, not even when she started going to bed with the chickens."

"None of us suspected, me least of all," Ivy laughed. "Ryder told me I was pregnant. I had no idea what was wrong with me."

Jean whistled. "You'll never live that one down. I can see you now, trying to explain it to your children."

"One of my aunts had twins," Ryder murmured speculatively. "Are there any twins in your family?"

"My grandmother had twins," Jean recalled. "Your great-uncle Harry and your great-uncle Todd," she reminded Ivy. "They aren't identical, but they're twins."

"Twins would be lovely," Ivy sighed, smiling at Ryder.

"Twins, triplets, whatever," he murmured. "I hope we don't die of it," he said slowly, searching her eyes on a soft sigh.

"Die of what?" Ivy asked, smiling dreamily.

"Happiness," he said.

Jean laughed and hugged him. "I know exactly how you feel. Welcome to the family, son."

They were married the following afternoon, and that night as Ivy lay in Ryder's arms in his own bedroom, she snuggled close and reflected on the wedding.

"It was so lovely," she said. "All those flowers, and Eve for a bridesmaid and her children for flower girls."

"And the most beautiful bride in the world." He bent and kissed her very gently. They were wearing nightclothes, tucked up together, but he hadn't made love to her and she was curious as to why.

"You're very distant for a new bridegroom," she pointed out, smiling at him in the soft lamplight. "Aren't you the same man who was going to seduce me on an Indian mound just three days ago?"

"Two," he corrected. "And, yes, I was. But you were tired after the ceremony and seeing Eve and Curt and the boys off at the airport."

She turned and slid closer to him, one soft hand finding his flat belly and teasing the thick hair.

He shivered and caught his breath.

"I thought it was all an act," she breathed, and brought her mouth down on his bare chest.

He guided her hand to his body and turned, sliding one

long, powerful leg between both of hers. "Gently," he whispered through an anguish of need. "Gently. We have to remember our baby."

"Yes." She kissed him back, adoring him, showing her love with all the tenderness she felt as he stroked her body and laced kisses over her taut, swollen breasts.

She'd never known that lovemaking could be so tender, or so profound. He measured his body to hers and aroused her softly, until she was trembling and clinging to him, and only then did he bring her hips to his and tenderly begin the sweet, slow process of loving.

She felt the warm hardness of his body filling her, and she opened her eyes and looked into his, shivering with the achingly poignant hunger he'd aroused.

His hand went to the base of her spine and he smiled through his own need as he began to bring her closer. She absorbed him with ease, and there was none of the discomfort he'd had to subject her to during their first time.

"It doesn't hurt," she managed shakily.

"It isn't supposed to." His mouth touched hers. "You were like a virgin in Paris. Now you're my woman completely. We fit together like a hand and a glove."

Her breath caught at the analogy. He held her eyes and pushed softly, deeply, until he was as close to her as he could get. Only then did he pause and catch his breath before he began to move.

It was unbelievable. She stared straight into his eyes the whole time, feeling his body brushing hers in a slow, tender rhythm, his hair-roughened chest and stomach a sweet abrasion against her soft skin. She touched his chest and felt the hardness of a flat male nipple wonderingly as the pleasure caught her unaware and suddenly jerked her in his arms.

Her mouth opened on a low moan, her eyes clouded. He watched her with pure masculine triumph, feeling the pleasure build in her even as it built in him. He increased the rhythm and the pressure, holding her body where he wanted it with both hands at her hips, his voice coaxing, praising as she matched his urgent movements.

The room swam around her. She heard the sound of flesh against fabric under them, the rough sigh of his breath as he moved harder, closer, the building groan that emanated from his broad chest as he started up the swift climb to fulfillment.

She went with him, her own body lifted with pleasure as his deep movements suddenly unlocked her body and gave him total, absolute access to some hidden dark ecstasy. They seemed to throb as it culminated, clinging to each other in blind oblivion as heat burst in them and echoed in a feverish aching rhythm of pleasure.

It was gone so soon, almost as soon as they reached it. She buried her face in his damp, shuddering chest and wept.

"Why can't it last?" she moaned shakily.

He understood. His mouth touched her hair, her damp forehead. "How could we live through it, if it did?" he whispered. "No, don't move," he breathed when she shifted. "Here."

He rolled over onto his back, but without separating them. His hand at the base of her spine held her where they were locked together and his arms contracted, cradling her on his body.

"All right?" he asked above her head.

"Yes." She smiled against his chest and kissed it gently, the damp hairs tickling her nose. He was trembling faintly from the exertion, just as she was. "It's different, every time," she said.

"It's supposed to be. After the baby comes, and you've recovered, I'll teach you some other ways to do this." His hands caressed her smooth, bare back. "A few of them are pretty rough and demanding, so we'll save those until you aren't in this sweet condition."

She lifted her head and looked into his pale, loving eyes. "Passion can be violent, they say. That's what I was always afraid of. But now it isn't scary anymore." She smiled and he relaxed, as if he'd been holding his breath. "I love loving you," she whispered. "Can we do it again?"

He smiled slowly, wickedly. "I don't know. Can we?"

She was learning things already. Secrets. She moved very delicately, first one way, then the other. Then she bent her head and bit him gently. Seconds later, his breath expelled in a rush and she smiled.

"Yes," she whispered back, her eyes bright with feminine triumph. "Oh, yes, we can…!"

The baby came a little over seven months later, and he wasn't twins, but as Ryder remarked, he sounded like them. They brought him home from the hospital and were immediately pounced upon by a radiant new grandmother who stared down at him in her arms and spent several long minutes trying to decide who he favored.

"She'll come to the conclusion that he looks like her," Ryder whispered as they watched Jean with little Clellan Donald Calaway.

"Yes, I know," she murmured, resting her head on his shoulder with a contented sigh. "We're rather superfluous, you know. We only had him for Mama."

"I see what you mean." He looked down at her, searching her weary eyes. "I'll carry you up in a minute and put you to bed. It's been a long three days."

"A wonderful three days," she replied, her heart in the eyes that adored him. "Are you really happy with me?"

He touched her face with a hand that very nearly trembled. "You're everything," he said huskily. "The world."

Love like that was a responsibility, she thought, watching him. But one she was willing to assume. She felt the same way about him. It wasn't until she'd seen his bedroom for the first time that she'd known how he felt. Once they were married, all the photographs of her came out of hiding. Those, and the painting that now hung over the mantel.

Her eyes went past him to the fireplace, up to the beautiful oil painting of a young girl in a flowing pink dress, sitting in a patch of wildflowers, her long black hair windblown, her black eyes, like her pink mouth, smiling sweetly. He'd had it done secretly when she was eighteen, and if she needed any proof of how he felt about her, seeing that painting gave it to her. It was still overwhelming when she realized just how deeply, how desperately, he loved her.

"It was my solace all those years we were apart," he said, following her gaze to the painting. "A very private memory of a day I took you and Eve walking, and you wore that dress. I fell in love with you then."

"I fell in love with you about the same time. I'm sorry I was such a coward. I wasted years of our lives."

"No. You used them, to grow up, to become mature, to learn what love really was. I'm sorry for the pain you suffered, but then, it's the bad times that make us the people we are, Ivy. No character ever got shaped by sun and smooth sailing all the time."

She smiled. "I guess not. The main thing is that we're together now." She glanced toward Jean, who still held their son in her arms. "All this, and a baby, too. Talk about counting your blessings."

"I couldn't begin to count mine." He pressed her cheek back against his chest and closed his eyes.

"Nor I," she agreed softly.

Across from them young Clellan opened his eyes and looked up at his cooing grandmother with wide blue eyes.

"Why, I've decided who he favours," Jean exclaimed with a radiant smile. "He looks just like me!"

The other two occupants of the room burst out laughing, and a puzzled grandmother shrugged with faint curiosity and ignored them. She was much too happy comparing her eyes to the baby's to wonder what they found so amusing, anyway.

* * * * *

MATERNITY BRIDE

USA TODAY Bestselling Author

Maureen Child

MAUREEN CHILD

is a California native who loves to travel. Every chance they get, she and her husband are taking off on another research trip. An author of more than sixty books, Maureen loves a happy ending and still swears that she has the best job in the world. She lives in Southern California with her husband, two children and a golden retriever with delusions of grandeur.

Chapter 1

"Just stick it in, dummy," Denise Torrance whispered to herself and scraped the key across the doorknob plate again. The darkness in the hallway pushed at her. She glanced uneasily over her shoulder and wondered why a simple power outage could make her feel as if she were stuck in a fifties horror movie. For heaven's sake. She knew these offices better than she knew her own apartment. There were no monsters lurking in the shadows waiting to pounce.

"Ah." She sighed in satisfaction as the stubborn key finally slipped into the lock. Pushing her purse strap higher on her shoulder, she shoved the oversize bag out of her way, turned the key and stepped into the darkened office.

Automatically, her right hand went to the switch plate. She tried each of the two switches with no success. "Perfect," she said into the black stillness. "Apparently, no one is in a hurry to get the power turned back on."

But then, if she had collected the files from Patrick's office a bit earlier, she'd have been gone long before the lights went out and she wouldn't be standing there in the dark talking to herself.

"Ten o'clock at night," she muttered. "What kind of idiot works until ten o'clock when they could be home in a hot bath?"

"Just you and me, I guess." A deep voice rumbled out of the darkness.

Her heart shot into her throat.

"And honey," the voice added, "that bath sounds real good."

She choked her heart back into her chest and whirled around, her gaze sweeping across the shadowy corners of the room. Instinctively, Denise backed up, and wished she was wearing her running shoes instead of the three-inch heels wobbling beneath her. Her sharp eyes strained to find the intruder at the same time her mind screamed at her to run like hell.

Then he stepped closer, passing across a splash of moonlight shining through a window before disappearing into the darkness again. Still, she'd been able to see him. Not his face of course, but enough to know he was big.

And standing between her and the door.

Okay fine, she told herself. No escape there. They were on the third floor, so jumping out the window was quickly dismissed, as well. Think, Denise, think. Frantically, she tried to remember the self-defense lessons she'd taken the year before. Something about step into the attacker and throw him over your shoulder?

Yeah, right.

She took another step back, bumped into a chair and staggered. One of her heels snapped off and she dropped into a tilted stance. "Stay back," she warned, in her best I-am-a-trained-killer voice. "I'm warning you…."

"Take it easy, lady," that voice came again as the man took a step closer.

"I'll scream." An empty threat. Her mouth and throat were so dry, it was a wonder she could issue these whispery warnings, let alone scream.

"Oh, for…" He sounded disgusted.

She hobbled backward, listing dangerously to one side. Why couldn't she think? Why couldn't she remember *something* that she'd learned from that overpriced instructor? It was just as she'd always feared. When faced with a *real* attacker, her mind had gone blank.

Her purse swung around with her jerky movements and slapped her in the abdomen. She grunted with the impact.

"You okay?"

"Hah!" A concerned maniac! Oh God, she was hyperventilating.

"Look lady, if you'd only stand still for a second…"

"I won't make it easy on you," she countered and went into a wild series of bobs and weaves. Her broken heel actually helped in the endeavor. She banged her hip on the corner of Patrick's desk and promised herself that if this madman killed her, she would haunt Patrick Ryan for the rest of his life.

Some friend *he* is, she thought hysterically. Taking a vacation so that she would be forced to go into his office and get the files her father wanted for tomorrow afternoon's meeting. If she survived this, maybe she would have her father fire good ol' Patrick.

"Dammit, woman!" The huge man in black sounded angry. Swell.

She started singing to herself. Well, not really singing, more of a low-pitched keening, really. Anything to make enough noise that she didn't have to hear the man's voice as he taunted her. Denise took another few steps, then stopped cold as her purse strap snagged on the corner of the desk. Her breath caught, she leaned forward to free herself and at the same time…miraculously, an actual *thought* occurred to her.

Hurriedly, she dug into her purse. She couldn't see well in the dark. She had to depend on her fingers finding just what she needed. Blindly, she began tossing item after item out of her bag and onto the floor.

"Come on now," he urged and came much too close. "If you'll just relax, we can straighten all of this out."

Oh, sure. Relax. *There's* an idea!

Her breath staggering, her heart beating wildly enough to explode from her chest, Denise's fingers closed around the can she had been fumbling for. Triumphantly, she yanked it free of the leather purse, held it up and pointed it—hopefully—at the intruder. Just in case though, she closed her eyes and turned her head away as she pushed the aerosol button.

"Damn it!" he shouted and lunged at her.

A squeak of protest squeezed past her throat.

He slapped the can out of her grip and his momentum carried her down to the floor with him. They hit hard, but he had twisted them both around until he took most of the jarring blow. Immediately then, he rolled her beneath him. He lay across her, pinning her down with his imposing size and weight.

Helplessly, Denise heard her can of pepper spray hit the plank floor and roll into the far corner. She inhaled sharply, hoping for a good, long scream, then felt a large, very strong hand clamp down hard on her mouth.

The mingled scents of Old Spice, tobacco and what smelled like motor oil surrounded her.

"Take it easy, will ya?" he said angrily.

Yeah, that's what she would do, she thought frantically as she fought to draw a shallow breath into her straining lungs. Take it easy. Simple enough for *him* to say. His body lay full-length atop hers. She felt his belt buckle digging into her stomach and the hard muscular strength of his thighs pressing her legs down.

Why hadn't she gone home when everyone else in the building had?

Her mind raced with questions she didn't really want the answers to. What was he doing in Patrick's office? This was an *accounting* firm for heaven's sake. There was no money to steal. And what was he going to do to her? God, she suddenly remembered every horrifying newspaper article she'd ever read about the rising crime rate.

And now she was going to end up as nothing more than a grainy photograph beside a short sad story on page five.

Even as she thought it, her captor eased slightly to one side of her. Still keeping one of his legs tossed across hers, he captured both of her hands in one of his and held them tightly. As he shifted position, he moved into a patch of moonlight.

Denise closed her eyes and told herself not to look. If she couldn't identify him, maybe he would leave her alone. But somehow, her eyes opened into slits and her gaze drifted to his features anyway.

She gasped and felt a bit of her fear slip away.

He had the nerve to grin at her.

Surprise battled with temper. What was going on here, anyway? Except for his too long hair, a week's worth of stubble on his cheeks and the black leather jacket he was wearing, her intruder looked an awful lot like Patrick Ryan. In fact, she thought with a growing sense of disgust, enough like him to be his…twin.

"Finally," he said and nodded at her. "If you hadn't been so damned eager to spray pepper into my face, I could have introduced myself a while ago."

"You're—"

"Mike Ryan."

"Patrick's twin," she said and tried to twist out of his steely grasp.

"Actually," he countered with a crooked smile, "I prefer to think of Patrick as *my* twin."

Dammit, she thought. Why was Patrick's brother loitering around his office?

"How did you get in here?" she demanded.

"Security let me in."

"Great. Why were you standing around in a pitch dark office?"

He snorted a laugh. "The power went out. Remember?"

"Well, you might have *said* something," she snapped and tried once more to yank free of him. Again, she failed. For some reason, he seemed reluctant to let her go just yet.

"You didn't give me much of a chance."

"There was plenty of time to yell, 'Don't have a heart attack, I'm Patrick's brother'," she countered. Her heartbeat slowed from its trip-hammer pace as she added, "Or do you *enjoy* scaring women?"

He scowled briefly. "There are lots of things I enjoy doing with women," he told her in a voice so deep and rough it scraped along her spine. "Fear has nothing to do with any of them."

She swallowed and found her mouth dry again.

"So," he went on and dragged the palm of one hand over the curve of her hip. "We both know who I am. Who the hell are you? Does Patrick have a girlfriend I don't know about?"

Denise fought to ignore the sensation of wicked heat that trailed in the wake of his hand.

"Maybe," she countered thickly. "But if he does, it isn't me."

"Glad to hear it," he murmured.

She shifted slightly, trying to move away from his disconcerting touch. He followed her.

"Name?" he asked.

"Denise Torrance." She gritted her teeth and redoubled her efforts to get at least one of her hands free. "This is the Torrance Accounting firm. Patrick works for my father. I needed to pick up some of his files.... Why am I explaining any of this to you?"

He shrugged. "Beats me. Am I supposed to believe any of it?"

She drew her head back and glared at him. "Frankly, I don't care if you believe me or not. But, why would I lie?"

He shrugged again and let that wandering palm of his slide across her abdomen. Her stomach muscles clenched. Deep inside her, a curl of something dangerous began to unwind.

As if he could read her mind, a deep-throated chuckle rumbled up from his chest.

She felt the flush of embarrassment stain her cheeks and for the first time since entering Patrick's office, was grateful the power was out.

"I don't see a thing funny in any of this," Denise said through her teeth. Especially, she added silently, her body's reaction to him.

"No," he agreed. "I don't suppose you do." As he finished

speaking, his hand moved up her rib cage, slipped beneath her sensible linen blazer and strayed dangerously close to her breast.

"Okay, that's it," she muttered, wrenching violently to one side. She wasn't about to lie on the floor being mauled by a virtual stranger…no matter how much her body seemed to enjoy it.

"You son of a—" Denise gave a furious heave and wrenched one hand free of his grasp. Curling her fingers, she drew her arm back and then let it fly. A fist too small to do any damage clipped him across the chin.

Immediately, he released her and Denise rolled far away from him. Scrambling to her feet, she tugged at her wrinkled, pin-striped business suit until she felt back in control. Then she lifted her gaze to his and glared at him.

The bastard had the nerve to *laugh* at her?

Rubbing his chin with one hand, he nodded at her slowly. "Not a bad right, for a girl."

"I'm not a girl. I'm a woman."

"Oh yeah, honey." His gaze swept over her. "I noticed."

The overhead lights flared back into life and Denise blinked, momentarily blinded by the unexpected brightness. When her vision had cleared again, she looked at the man standing so casually just a foot or two away from her.

A relaxed, half smile curved his well-shaped mouth as he watched her. His nose looked as though it had been broken more than once—no doubt by some furious female, she told herself. The whisker stubble on his face gave him a wicked, untamed look, which she was somehow sure he cultivated purposely. His too long black hair hung down on either side of his face and lay across the collar of his jacket. As she looked at him, he reached up with both hands and slowly pushed the mass back out of his way.

Tall and muscular, he wore a spotless white T-shirt beneath the leather jacket that seemed to suit him so well. His worn, faded jeans rode low on his narrow hips and hugged his long legs with an almost indecent grip. Scuffed, square-toed black boots completed the picture of modern-day pirate.

She lifted her gaze back to his face and saw sharp green eyes assessing her. It was as if he knew what she was thinking. Amusement flickered in those eyes and she wanted to smack him. Again.

No one should be that sure of himself.

In an instant, his gaze swept over her, mimicking the inspection she'd just given him. Instinctively, she pulled the edges of her navy blazer together and balanced herself carefully on her one good heel.

When his gaze lingered a bit longer than necessary on the fullness of her breasts, Denise shifted uncomfortably. She could almost *feel* his touch on her body. Her traitorous mind wandered down a dangerous path and imagined what it would feel like to have his fingers caressing her bare flesh. At that thought, another onslaught of heat raced through her, leaving her unexpectedly shaky.

"Well," Mike said as he eased down to perch on the edge of his brother's desk. "I've got to say, I've never been hit by anyone as pretty as you."

"I find *that* hard to believe."

He chuckled again and folded his arms across that magnificent chest.

Good Lord, she groaned silently. Magnificent?

"Most women don't find me as…distasteful, as you do, Denise."

The sound of her name, spoken in that voice, made her knees weak. Instantly, she wished heartily that she was already in the elevator on the way to the parking lot.

"What do you say we try it again?" he asked.

"What?"

"Oh," he nodded congenially at her. "I'll let you hit me again too, if it makes you feel better about enjoying my touch."

"I can't believe you!" Another flush rose up in her cheeks, but this time, she was sure it was just as much anger as embarrassment.

"You can believe me, honey. I never lie to my women."

"I am *not* one of your women."

His gaze raked over her slowly, deliberately, before coming back to stare deeply into her eyes.

"Yet," he said simply.

"You're incredible!" She gasped and fought to ignore the surge of heat flooding her. Something flashed in his eyes and was so quickly gone, she couldn't identify it. But it had almost looked like a teasing glint.

"So I've been told." He pushed away from the desk and took a step toward her. "What do you say, honey?" He rubbed his chin with two fingers and said softly, "That little punch of yours was worth it, you know. To touch you again, I just might be willing to put up with anything."

Her stomach dropped to her feet and her heartbeat hurtled into high gear. She limped backward a step, never taking her eyes from him. She wasn't frightened. At least not of him.

Whether he was teasing her or not, she knew she wasn't in any physical danger from him. He hadn't *had* to let her go.

She knew as well as he did that her fist hadn't done the slightest bit of damage to him.

The only thing worrying her now was her reaction to him. Mike and Patrick Ryan were more different than she had at first thought. Oh, they looked alike, there was no denying that.

But she had never experienced this sizzling rush of desire for Patrick. Not once had she imagined rolling around on the floor of his office with him…burying her fingers in his hair…feeling the scrape of his whiskers against her skin.

As those images rocketed around in what was left of her brain, she took another uneven step back in self-defense. What in the world was happening to her? Only moments ago, she had been fighting him, sure that he was some maniac out to destroy her. Now, she trembled at the thought of being kissed senseless by that same maniac?

Oh, she was in big trouble.

Mike smiled. A slow, seductive smile that told her he knew where her thoughts were going.

And that he approved.

Short, shallow breaths shot in and out of her lungs.

She grabbed at the remaining bulk of her shoulder bag and clutched it in front of her as though it were a magic shield, designed to keep lechers at bay. Her fingers worked the leather, locating her wallet and car keys. One corner of her mind realized just how much of her stuff she'd thrown onto the floor. Her purse only weighed about half as much as usual.

The hell with it, she thought, keeping one eye on the man opposite her. She could get the rest of her things later.

"I'm leaving now," she said and took another hobbling step. "I assume, since you're Patrick's brother, you're not here to rob the place?"

"Good assumption," he countered and moved a bit closer.

"Then why are you here, anyway?"

"How about we go get a drink and get acquainted?" Mike asked and took another step toward her. "I'll tell you everything you want to know about me."

All she wanted to know was why he had such a strange affect on her. But she wasn't about to ask him *that*.

He smiled at her again.

Run, her brain screamed. Run now, before it's too late.

It was the rational thing to do.

It was the only thing that made sense.

So why did a part of her want to stay?

"What do you say?" he repeated. "A drink?"

He reached out one hand toward her.

Denise looked from that hand to his eyes and shook her head, more disgusted with herself than she was him. She mentally shoved her raging hormones aside. "Ryan," she said slowly and distinctly, "if this was the Sahara and you had the only map to the last Oasis in existence, I *still* wouldn't have a drink with you."

Then she turned and clomped inelegantly from the room and down the hall with as much dignity as she could muster under the circumstances.

As the elevator doors slid soundlessly closed behind her, she heard him laughing.

Chapter 2

Mike stood in the doorway looking after her for a long moment, then turned around to stare at the mess strewn across his brother's office. In her hurry to find her pepper spray, Denise Torrance had thrown the contents of that huge purse of hers all over the room.

He snorted another laugh and shook his head. Next time he volunteered to fix his twin's air conditioner, he'd make sure to find out if there was going to be a pint-size tornado dropping by.

Of course, if the tornado happened to have short blond hair, wide blue eyes and a dusting of freckles across her nose, he wouldn't work too hard to avoid her.

From down the hall, he heard the discreet hum of the elevator as it carried her farther away. He'd thought about chasing after her, but then realized that he didn't have to.

He'd see her again.

As he bent and scooped up some of her belongings to stack them neatly on the desk, he muttered, "She has to come back. Hell, she left half of her life behind."

Quickly, he went around the room, snatching up the items she'd tossed. As he grabbed the can of pepper spray, he winced and told himself it was a damn good thing he was quicker than she was. He almost set the can with everything else, to be returned to her, then thought better of it and stuffed it into his jacket pocket instead. No sense in arming the woman, he told himself.

He placed the last of her things on the desk and took a long look at them. Everything from a hairbrush to a tube of toothpaste and a neatly capped toothbrush sat atop the mahogany surface. Shaking his head, he noted the foil-wrapped sandwich, a package of Ding Dongs, a screwdriver set and a package of bandages. But then his gaze fell on the jumbo-size bottles of aspirin and antacid tablets, two black eyebrows lifted high on his forehead.

Ms. Denise Torrance apparently led a *very* stressful life.

Even as he wondered why, he told himself that it was none of his business. He made it a point never to know too much about anyone. With knowledge, came caring. With caring, came pain.

A small, shiny object on the floor caught his eye and he leaned over to pick it up. His long fingers turned the key over and over as he studied it. A smile crept up his features and he glanced at the wall of file cabinets across the room from him.

The only way she was going to get back into this office was with a key. And she'd left hers with him.

Folding the key into his palm, he pocketed it, then walked back to the faulty air-conditioning unit in the corner.

Whistling softly, he told himself that just because he wasn't going to get involved, that didn't mean he had to avoid her completely. Besides, anyone so stressed out that they carried enough medication to dose a battalion was desperately in need of some relaxation.

As he pried the metal cover off the unit, he smiled. It would be his distinct pleasure to introduce Denise Torrance to a little fun.

In the soft morning light, Denise stood outside the brick-and-glass building and stared at the foot-high letters painted on the front window.

Ryan's Custom Cycles.

That unsettled feeling leapt back into life in the pit of her stomach and she sucked in a gulp of air, hoping to quiet it. It didn't work.

Her fingers clenched and unclenched on the soft, brown leather of her shoulder bag. It hadn't been hard to locate Mike. Patrick had once mentioned his twin's motorcycle shop, so a quick glance through the yellow pages had been all the help she had needed.

Denise's stomach lurched and she laid one palm against her abdomen in response. "Stop it," she muttered. "He's just a man." And, her mind quietly jabbed, the Statue of Liberty is a cute little knickknack.

"Oh, for heaven's sake!" she admonished herself as she started across the parking lot. She didn't have all day. Her first meeting of the morning started in less than forty minutes. Her father, as president of the firm, would be there and he wasn't the kind of man to accept excuses for tardiness.

Denise groaned. Just thinking about having to face her

irate father this early in the morning was enough to churn up the acid in her stomach. Rummaging in her purse, she yanked out a small roll of colored tablets and popped two of them into her mouth.

As she chewed, she told herself that she didn't have much choice in this. She *had* to see Mike again. "Of course," she said under her breath, "if I hadn't let him bully me into running for cover last night, this wouldn't be happening."

But she *had* allowed it. Not until she was halfway home had she remembered that she'd left behind Patrick's spare key and the files she had needed. She had also forgotten about the things she'd thrown out of her purse in her wild search for pepper spray.

"Pepper spray, self-defense classes," she grumbled in disgust. "A fat lot of good they did me."

Too late to worry about that, though. She stopped in front of the sparkling-clean glass door and took a deep, calming breath. Then she pushed the door open and stepped into another world. A world where she obviously didn't belong.

The showroom was immense.

Her gaze flew about the room, trying to take it all in at once. Blond pine paneling covered the long wall behind the room-length counter. On the side wall, glass-fronted shelves displayed everything from helmets to gauntlet-style black gloves to black leather pants and boots. The opposite wall appeared to have been designated an art gallery. Against the soft, cream paint were bright splashes of colored signs, proclaiming the name, Harley-Davidson. Beneath those signs stood racks of clothing. T-shirts, jackets, chaps, even ladies' nightgowns, all with the same Harley-Davidson logo.

But the most impressive displays were the motorcycles

themselves. Gleaming wood floors mirrored the chrome surfaces of the almost elegant-looking machines parked atop it. Sunshine filtered through the front and side windows, sparkling off the metal, glinting against the shining paint jobs.

Denise shook her head, dazzled in spite of herself. Somehow, she had expected to find a dirty, oil-encrusted garage where beer-swilling mechanics scratched their potbellies and traded dirty jokes.

A long, low whistle caught her attention and her head snapped around.

"How did *you* slip in here, honey? Are you lost?"

The big man in worn jeans and a flannel shirt scratched at his full beard and grinned at her.

She tugged at the front of her sea green blazer and tightened her grip on her purse. All right, so maybe she *did* look out of place. She glanced around the room again, noting the sprinkling of customers for the first time.

Only a handful of people were in the store and *none* of them were in a green silk business suit. Except of course, Denise. And, they were all staring at her as though she'd just been beamed down from the planet Stuffy.

Apparently, she thought, as the people went back to what they had been doing when she entered, jeans and black leather were the preferred costume of motorcycle enthusiasts. Even for the women, she told herself as she spotted the only other female in the room.

A pang of envy rattled around inside her as she noted the tall blond woman's long, straight hair and skintight jeans. Without benefit of a shirt, her black leather vest looked provocative. Dismally, Denise acknowledged that even were she to wear the same outfit, the results would be very different.

A quick glance down at her own, less than impressive bustline confirmed the thought.

"Looking for a bike, lady?"

She turned toward the first man again. "No." She cleared her throat and told herself to remember why she was there. It didn't matter if she would look terrible in a leather vest, since she had no plans to acquire one. "Actually, I'm looking for Mike Ryan."

He nodded, then said wistfully, "Too bad." Jerking his head toward the door behind the counter, he added, "Mike's in the service bay. He'll be back in a minute."

"Thank you."

A moment later, that door opened and Mike stepped into the room. Denise's stomach jumped. She ignored it and walked toward him.

"Nice wheels," the bearded man said.

She stopped and looked at him. "What?"

"Your legs, Denise," Mike spoke up and shot a telling look at the other man. "He said you have nice legs."

"Oh." Flustered a bit, she nodded and said, "Thank you very much."

Hell, Mike thought, what did he care if Tom Jenkins looked at her legs or not? He ignored the skitter in his gut, slapped both hands down on the countertop and leaned forward as Denise came closer.

Dammit, he'd been hoping that he had imagined most of the instant attraction he had felt for her the night before. His gaze raked over her quickly, thoroughly, as she marched determinedly across his shop.

Just his luck, he thought. Even in a boxy, green suit jacket and too long skirt, she did things to him he would have thought impossible at this time yesterday. From the sound system overhead came the muted strains of the Eagles. But over that familiar music, came the sharp click of her high heels against the floorboards. They seemed to be tapping out a rhythm that screamed silently in his head, "Take her, she's yours. Take her, she's yours."

His body tightened and he gritted his teeth in an effort to ignore the voices and concentrate on the woman. Even though he'd been expecting to see her again, he hadn't expected to feel such a rush of pleasure.

It's nothing, he told himself. At least nothing more than a very healthy response to a pretty woman. It had been a long time since he'd confused hormones with something deeper.

"Morning," he said as she came to a stop opposite him.

"Good morning."

He watched her nervous fingers playing with the strap of her bag. Good. That gave him the upper hand in whatever was going to be between them. And he knew already that there would definitely be *something*.

"What can I do for you, Denise?" he asked, despite the fact that he knew damned well why she was there.

She inhaled sharply, glanced to either side of her to make sure no one was near, then said, "When I left Patrick's office last night, I forgot to take the spare key with me."

"And the files you needed," he added.

"Yes…"

"Oh, and all that junk from your purse."

She frowned. "That, too."

"I know." He smiled at her and saw temper flare in her eyes before she battled it down again.

"You're not going to make this easy," she said quietly. "Are you?"

"Nope."

Her lips thinned a bit, the only sign of her agitation. "Why not?"

"What would be the fun in that?" he asked.

"Does *everything* have to be fun?"

He gave her a long, slow smile. "If we're lucky."

She sucked in a gulp of air and laid her palms flat on the counter, just an inch or so from his. He thought about touching her, but decided to wait.

"Look, Mike. I just want to retrieve that key, get back into Patrick's office and pick up my things." She looked him dead in the eye, hoping, no doubt, to convince him with her calm appeal to his better nature.

Too bad he didn't have one.

He should do what she wanted, he told himself. Just give her back her stuff and let her disappear from his life. He didn't want any entanglements. He wasn't interested in love or long-term relationships. Mike had learned the hard way that love was an invitation to pain and he wanted no part of it. Besides, Lord knew, he had no business getting any closer to a woman who practically had *conventional* stamped on her forehead.

Still, something inside him just couldn't seem to let go. To let it…whatever *it* was between them…end just yet.

"I'll make you a deal," he said instead.

"What kind of deal?" Her head cocked to one side and she looked at him through the corners of *very* cautious eyes.

"Here's the key for Patrick's office and the files, but to get the rest of your stuff you have to go to dinner with me tonight." Even as he said it though, he knew dinner wouldn't be enough. He wanted to be alone with her again. Somewhere quiet and dark, where he could kiss her, touch her. And discover if the sensations that had tormented him long after she had stormed away from him the night before were real…or just a product of the unusual situation they had found themselves in.

"Dinner?"

"Yeah."

"Where?"

"My choice."

Her toe tapped against the floor. He watched her as she mentally went over the possibilities. She threw him a worried glance and he knew she was thinking the same thing he was. That here was their chance to prove that absolutely *nothing* had happened between them the night before.

Then she surprised him.

"You know," she said thoughtfully, "Patrick never mentioned this ruthless streak of yours."

He widened his stance and folded both arms across his chest. "I'm not ruthless, honey. I just live my life on my terms."

"Which are?"

She wouldn't understand his terms, he told himself. To understand, she would have had to have been sitting in the desert sun, listening to gunfire. She would have had to watch friends die. She would have had to experience the one inescapable fact that life is short. Too damned short.

Since it was pointless to try to explain all of that, he said only, "The terms vary from day to day."

"Now, why doesn't that surprise me?"

He gave her points. Irritated and frustrated, she still gave as good as she got.

"So," Mike said. "What about dinner?"

"Can't you just give me my stuff?"

"I could…but I won't."

Her lips thinned and that toe of hers started tapping even faster. Finally, after she checked her narrow-banded gold watch, she spoke.

"All right, dinner. Here's my address." She dug into that saddle bag she called a purse and came up with a business card. She set it down and took a step back from the counter. "Of course, it's not like I have a choice, is it?" she asked. "To get my things back, I have to go."

"True," he agreed and ignored the small stab of conscience.

"Do you always use extortion to get a woman to have dinner with you?"

"Only when I have to. Like I said, the terms vary. Seven-thirty."

"Seven-thirty."

"You don't have to go, Denise," he heard himself say. "You *could* call Patrick and whine until he agrees to rescue you from me."

One pale blond brow lifted. "First, I don't whine. Second, I don't need anyone to rescue me from you, Mike Ryan. I can take care of myself."

She really was something else. He rubbed his chin thoughtfully and grinned at her. "I remember."

"Good," she said as she turned for the door. "It'll be better for both of us if you keep on remembering."

What do you wear to have dinner with a man who dresses like a B movie from the fifties and has far more self-confidence than any three people deserve?

Denise stood in the foyer of her condo and checked her appearance in the full-length mirror one more time. Her navy blue dress looked perfect, she thought and swayed to watch the full skirt swirl around her legs.

Nodding to herself, she said aloud, "You wear something that gives *you* confidence, naturally."

She smoothed her fingertips along the modestly cut neckline. Revealing just a glimpse of her collarbone, the long-sleeved dress looked demure, almost prudish, until one saw the back. Smiling to herself, Denise half turned and looked into the mirror over her shoulder. The deeply scooped back dipped sensuously low, coming to a stop just below her waist. The smooth expanse of flesh it displayed was evenly tanned a warm, golden brown.

Denise fluffed her hair one last time, checked the hooks of her sapphire drop earrings, then reached into her tiny evening bag for her lipstick. Though the small, black leather envelope on a slim gold shoulder chain looked lovely, she did miss having her day purse.

Leaning toward the mirror, she carefully lined her lips in a dark rose color, then dropped the tube back into the bag.

"Well, I'm ready," she told herself. "Where is he?"

A quick glance at the clock behind her and she smiled ruefully. Only 7:20. Whatever was wrong with her? She hadn't *wanted* to go on this... She refused to call it a date, even to herself. "So why am I ready and waiting ten minutes early?"

She caught her own eye in the mirror and looked away again quickly. Denise wasn't sure she wanted to know the answer to that question.

A rumble of thunder sounded outside and she winced. Looking heavenward, she muttered, "Give me a break, okay? No rain tonight?"

But the thunder continued grumbling until it rolled up in front of her house and stopped.

Frowning, she opened the door.

"Good God."

Chapter 3

Denise stepped onto the porch, pulling the front door closed behind her. She twisted the knob, making sure the lock had set, then started down the pansy-lined walk to the street.

In the hazy, yellowish glow of a streetlight, Mike sat, straddling the biggest motorcycle she had ever seen. Painted bloodred and black, it would have looked intimidating had it been parked and silent. As it was, its engine rumbled like a growl coming from the chest of some jungle beast waiting to pounce.

The word *intimidating* didn't even come close to describing it.

Mike pulled his shining black helmet off and set it on the seat in front of him and Denise took a moment to study him. Dressed entirely in black, he looked even more like a pirate than he had the night before. And was, if possible, even more dangerously attractive.

His hair was pulled back into a ponytail at the base of his neck and, she noted nervously, he had shaved for the occasion. When he turned to look at her, his pale green eyes widened in appreciation, then narrowed thoughtfully.

"It looks great," he admitted. "But it's not what you usually wear on a bike."

"I didn't expect to be riding a bike," she said, although why she hadn't considered it, she didn't know. "We could take my car," she suggested.

"No, thanks. I don't do cars." He reached behind him to the tall bar rising up at the end of the narrow seat. Quickly, he undid the elastic ropes, freeing a silver-and-black helmet, then turned around to hand it to her. "Here. You have to wear this."

"Mike, I…" Sighing, she pushed the helmet back at him. So much for her spectacular dress. "I'll go change."

"No time," he said. "We're going to be late as it is."

"I can't ride that—" she waved one hand at the motorcycle, then at her dress "—in *this*."

His lips twitched in what might have been a smile if given half a chance. But it was gone in the blink of an eye.

"It'll be all right," he said. "Just stuff the skirt between your legs and mine. Keep it out of the spokes."

This was a first. She had never had a man tell her to stuff her skirt between her legs before. Lovely.

"Can't you just give me three minutes to change?" she asked.

He snorted a muffled laugh. "There isn't a female alive who can change clothes in three minutes, honey. And like I said, we're already late."

His expression told her there was no sense debating the issue a minute longer.

"For heaven's sake," she muttered and threw one last, longing glance at her condo, behind her.

"Come on, honey," he told her and pulled his own helmet on. "Just swing one of those gorgeous legs over the saddle and plop down."

Gorgeous?

He released the kickstand and stood up, balancing the bike between his thighs. His hands twisted the grips on the handlebars and the powerful engine grumbled in response.

She couldn't help wondering what her neighbors were thinking at that moment. She could almost feel their interested gazes peering at her from behind the draperies. Well, what did she expect, going to dinner with a man who looked like he'd be back later that night to burgle houses?

He revved the engine again to get her attention.

Then something else occurred to her.

"Hey," Denise shouted over the rumbling engine, "wait a minute."

He looked up at her. "What?"

"Where's my stuff?" She wasn't about to go through with this little deal of theirs if he hadn't brought her things with him.

Mike scowled, reached back and patted a dark red compartment hanging off the left rear fender. "It's all there," he assured her. "Now, get on."

Gamely, Denise balanced on her right foot and swung her left leg across the motorcycle. Scooting around until she was comfortable, she braced the toes of her Ferragamo pumps on the foot pedals provided and bunched her skirt into the V between her legs. Muttering under her breath, she pulled the helmet on, winced at just how heavy it felt, then secured the chin strap. She didn't even want to think about what her hair was going to look like later.

Then Mike sat down in front of her, easing her thighs farther apart with his black-denim-covered behind. She stuffed her skirt between them, hoping the pooled fabric would dull the heat arcing between their bodies.

The engine beneath her shuddered and throbbed, and something deep in her core began to shake in response.

"Hang on to my waist," he said over his shoulder.

She nodded before realizing he wasn't looking at her. Rather than try to talk over the noise of the engine though, Denise wound her arms around his waist, pressing herself close to his back.

He tossed a glance at her, then reached around and snapped her visor down. "You ready?" he shouted.

She nodded again, but as they pulled away from the curb, she told herself she wasn't ready.

Not for him.

When he shut down the engine, the silence was soul shattering.

Denise climbed off the motorcycle and staggered unsteadily for a moment. Her legs felt as if they were still shuddering in time with the engine of the beast that had brought her here. Undoing the strap, she pulled her helmet off and handed it to Mike. Her head felt twenty pounds lighter as she fluffed her hair, hoping to revive it.

She shivered as a sharp, cold ocean wind swept across Pacific Coast Highway and swirled around her like icy fingers tugging at her. The hum of traffic on the busy highway faded away as she studied the restaurant Mike had chosen.

She'd seen it before, of course. No one living in Sunrise Beach could have overlooked it. Denise had even heard that the city fathers were talking about making it an official landmark.

It looked as though it had been standing in the same spot for a hundred years. The wooden walls looked shaky, the hot pink neon sign across the door, a couple of spots either dimmed with age or broken, spelled out, O'D ul s. Five or six pickup trucks were parked in the gravel lot, but there were more than twenty motorcycles huddled in a tight group near the front of the building.

As she watched, Mike pushed his own bike into their midst.

She had managed to avoid entering O'Doul's Tavern and Restaurant all of her life. Even though she had been tempted to go inside once or twice since turning twenty-one eight years ago, the thought of her father finding out she'd been there had been enough to dissuade her of the notion.

"Ridiculous," she muttered, "a grown woman afraid to stand up to her father."

Unfortunate, but true. All Richard Torrance had to do was look at her with disappointment and she felt eleven years old again. An eleven-year-old girl whose mother had just died, leaving Denise alone with a father who expected perfection from a child too frightened to deliver anything less.

Denise supposed there was some kind of logic in the fact that it would be Mike Ryan to first take her to O'Doul's. Because Richard Torrance would never approve of him, either.

While she waited for Mike, she studied the old tavern-restaurant's claim to fame. Their mascot. Good luck charm.

On the rooftop was a fifteen-foot-tall, one-eyed seagull, holding an artificial dead fish in its beak.

"Oh yeah, your dress will fit right in here," she muttered under her breath.

"You know," Mike said as he walked up beside her, "I've noticed you do that a lot."

"Do what?"

"Talk to yourself."

An old habit, born of loneliness. But he didn't need to know that. "It's when you argue with yourself that you're in trouble, Ryan."

"If you say so."

She nodded at the huge bird. "Now I understand why you were in such a hurry to get here," she said. "Reservations must be hard to come by."

"Obviously, you've never eaten here before."

"No, I generally make it a practice only to eat at restaurants where the giant bird has both eyes intact."

His lips quirked. "Vandals. Some kids with rocks and no values mutilate poor old Herman and you blame the bird?"

"Herman?" She smiled, in spite of her best efforts.

With a perfectly straight face, he said, "Herman Stanley Seagull. Jonathon Livingston's big brother."

"Very big."

He grinned.

A moment later, she nodded. "I get it. Stanley…Livingston."

"And I thought you had no sense of humor."

"I'm here, aren't I?"

His eyebrows arched. "A bit touchy, are we?"

"Not touchy," she countered. "Just…cautious."

He laughed shortly. "An accountant? Cautious? There's a shock."

She had heard any accountant joke he could possibly come

up with. Personally, she thought that the members of her profession were as unfairly maligned as lawyers. More so, since lawyers usually *deserved* the ribbing they took.

"Well," she said, with another look at Herman, "I hope the food's better than the ambience."

He chuckled. "Don't be a snob, honey. O'Doul's serves the best pizza in town. And if you don't get here early, it's all gone."

"Gone?" Denise stared up at him. "What kind of way is *that* to run a business? Won't he make more food if his customers demand it?"

Mike shrugged. "He could, but then he wouldn't have time to play pool with his friends."

"Of course," she said, nodding slowly. "A man has to have his priorities, after all."

This time, he laughed outright.

But when she started walking toward the restaurant, Mike's laughter died. He had thought it was torturous, with Denise sitting behind him on the bike. Every turn he had made, her thighs pressed harder against his. He'd felt the swell of her breasts pushing into his back and the surprisingly strong grip of her slender arms around his waist. Never had the ten-mile drive to O'Doul's seemed so long.

But all of that was nothing compared to what he felt now. As if a fist had slammed into his belly, his breath left him in a powerful rush the moment his gaze locked on the smooth, tanned surface of her back.

His gaze followed the column of her spine and rested on the curve of her bottom. His palms itched to stroke that expanse of flesh and then to explore further, beyond the boundaries of that incredible dress.

Mike's groin tightened uncomfortably, and he had to muffle a groan as he gripped the chin straps of their helmets in one hand. He took three long strides and caught up to her easily. Taking Denise's arm with his free hand, he said, "You should have warned me about that dress."

She stopped and looked up at him. A knowing smile curved her lips, but she asked anyway, "What do you mean?"

What could he say? He wasn't about to admit to her what that dress did to him. Nor, he thought with a glance at O'Doul's front door, did he want to think about the impact that dress would have on the men inside. His gaze shifted to her again and Mike found himself staring into those deep blue eyes. After a long moment, she looked away and he took the opportunity to bring himself back under control.

"Let's just say, I like a good tan. Especially when there aren't any suit lines."

She only smiled and Mike's racing brain took care of the rest. Immediately, he imagined her nude, lying under the hot sun. And in his mind, he was right beside her, smoothing lotion onto her warmed skin. He could almost feel her soft, pliant flesh beneath his fingertips.

Great. Now he had *that* mental image to drive him nuts all night.

Steering her toward the door, he grumbled through gritted teeth, "C'mon. I'm hungry."

The fact that he was hungrier for tanned, smooth skin than he was for pizza, had nothing to do with anything.

She should have gone to O'Doul's years ago.

If she had guessed just how much fun the game of pool could be, she might have risked her father's ire. Of course, she wasn't sure if it was the game, or her teacher that she was enjoying so much.

She bent at the waist, set her left hand on the worn, green felt and laid the tip of her cue stick between her curled fingers. Behind her, Mike stood close and leaned over her, his right hand on hers, his chest pressed to her naked back.

Warmth seeped through him down to her bones and she felt the unmistakable, hard bulge of his groin against her behind. She swallowed and tried desperately to listen to what he was saying.

"Take your time, honey," Mike whispered near her ear. "We've got all night to line this shot up."

All night. She inhaled the scent of Old Spice and wondered why more men didn't wear the old-fashioned cologne. Spicy and cool and sexy, it seemed to be everywhere, drawing her deeper into fantasies she had no business indulging and even less of a chance of experiencing.

He worked the pool cue back and forth between her fingers and instead of pool, her mind was caught on another mental image created with that smooth, in-and-out motion.

Glancing to one side, she noticed a biker Mike had called Bear, watching her with knowing eyes. Like the other men in the place, he wore jeans and leather and a leering expression that would have worried her if not for Mike's presence. She turned her gaze back to the pool table in time to see her stick make contact with the cue ball.

Laughter rose up around the table as the white ball missed its mark by inches. Mike straightened up and Denise, suddenly so warm she could hardly breathe, took a step away from him.

"Hey Mike," one of the men called over the pounding, pulsing beat of the music, "losin' your touch?"

"Doesn't look like it to me," a woman in the crowd

answered for him. More laughter and Denise was grateful for
the smokiness of the room. Hopefully, it was enough to hide
the flush she felt staining her cheeks.

The other man in the game, someone called Stoner, took
his shot and missed.

"Our turn," Mike said over the music and waved her back
to the table.

"I think I'll just watch for a while," she said with a shake
of her head. "You finish the game."

"Sure?"

She nodded, knowing damn well the only reason she was
quitting was because she didn't know if she could take being
that close to him again.

Denise held her pool cue and watched Mike pick up
another stick and work his way around the green felt table.
He paused every other step or so to exchange some comment
with one of his friends and each time he smiled, the knot in
her stomach tightened.

She swayed a bit unsteadily and tightened her grip on the
stick in her hands, using it more for balance than anything
else. Apparently, the beer she'd had with her pizza—the best
pizza she'd ever tasted—had gone right to her head. Fog
nestled in her brain and Denise struggled to clear it. Of course,
the loud rock music blasting over the speakers, the crowded
press of bodies in the place and the heavy cloud of blue-gray
cigarette smoke wasn't helping things any.

A huge man with tattooed forearms the size of ham shanks
slapped Mike on the back in a friendly gesture that would have
sent any other man sprawling to the sawdust-covered floor.

Not Mike.

The black T-shirt he wore hugged his shoulders and upper

arms, defining muscles that seemed to have a life of their own. They rippled and shifted whenever he took a shot and Denise caught herself holding her breath to watch the show in admiration.

Foggy brain or not, she knew enough to realize that she was in deep trouble.

A moment later, the pool game ended when Mike sank the eight ball in a corner pocket. Cheers erupted and a dark-haired woman in jeans tight enough to cut off her circulation wrapped herself around Mike like a child's grubby fist around a Popsicle stick.

Except that there was nothing childlike about the voluptuous brunette.

When the woman grabbed Mike's face between her palms and planted her lips on his in a long, lusty kiss, Denise gritted her teeth and fought down the roiling in her stomach. She told herself that she had no claim on him. That it didn't matter *who* he kissed. Or when. Logically, she knew that this wasn't even a real date.

But logic had nothing to do with what she was feeling.

Mike pulled his head back, patted Celeste's shoulder and peeled her off him. He shot a quick look at Denise's tight features and felt…guilty, for God's sake. Stupid. He didn't owe her anything. He wasn't her boyfriend—or God forbid, her husband. And the knowledge that he had no intention of getting involved didn't do anything to quiet the storm inside him.

While he gave Celeste a gentle push toward her date for the night and walked toward his own, he told himself that Denise had no claim on him. He was as free as old Herman, up on the roof.

The fact that Herman was not real and permanently attached to the wooden building was beside the point.

When he reached Denise's side, he took the pool cue from her and passed it off to another player.

"I don't want to interrupt your *fun,*" she said loudly, to be heard over the music.

Sure you do, he thought. The look in her eye would have sliced Celeste to ribbons if the other woman had been aware of it. But he didn't say that. Instead, as he heard the music change, he grabbed her hand and headed for the postcard-size dance floor.

She dragged behind him as he wended his way through the Friday night crowd. Once, she even tried to slip away, but he tightened his hold on her and kept walking. When he reached the small area where two other couples were already swaying in time to the music, he stopped and turned around to face her.

Her expression was mutinous, but he didn't give a damn. He'd put up with the other men in the place ogling her all night and now, he wanted the chance to put his arms around her and hold her close. He wanted to show the rest of them that Denise was his.

At least for tonight.

He tugged her closer and she moved slowly, reluctantly.

"Dance with me," he said into her ear and inhaled the delicate, flowery scent of her perfume.

She pulled her head back and looked up at him.

Their gazes met and locked together. A heartbeat of time passed and in that instant, something flashed in her eyes. Mike couldn't identify it and at the moment, didn't want to. All he wanted was this one dance.

For now.

The old song smoothed over the crowd and here and there, a voice picked up the words and sang along. The melody was sad, the lyrics lonely and most of the regulars at O'Doul's could identify with it all too easily. Every desperado in the room felt as though the song were meant especially for him.

Then Denise stepped into his arms and followed as he led her around the floor. Mike bent his head close to hers, relishing the softness of her hair on his cheek. The summery scent of her. The smooth, warm flesh of her back beneath his hand.

The music surrounded them, caressing them as they moved in tandem, as if they had danced together hundreds of times.

She laid her head on his chest. His palm slid across her back, caressing, with strokes as gentle as the song they danced to. She sighed against him and he cradled her closer.

As the Eagles song swelled to its finish, Denise tipped her head back to look at him. He stared into the depths of her eyes as the last line of the song swirled around them.

Caught in the midst of fantasies he decided long ago had no place in his life, Mike only half heard the musical warning of letting someone love him before it was too late.

Chapter 4

His fingers moved lightly up and down her spine like a classical musician teasing notes from a grand piano. Denise stared up into his eyes. Green clashed with blue in a silent challenge. One dark eyebrow lifted as his right hand skimmed over her flesh. She shivered. He noticed. In her own best interests, she knew she should move away. End this so-called dance now. While she still had the strength to stand. But she didn't. Even when the last of the song had faded away, they stood locked together on the dance floor, each of them somehow reluctant to step back. Away.

But the spell was broken in the next instant when a swell of pounding, driving rock music poured over the crowd. Someone bumped into her from behind, sending her crashing into Mike's chest. He stiffened, grabbed her shoulders to steady her, then immediately released her again.

A shutter dropped over those brilliant green eyes, hiding whatever he was thinking. Feeling. Denise staggered backward a step or two. She winced at the assault of sound blasting into the room. Her head began to pound in time with the pulsing drumbeat.

Looking up at Mike again, she found him glaring at her. What did *he* have to be mad about?

"Come on," he said abruptly, over the music. "I'll take you home."

Home. Yes, she needed to be home. In the quiet safety of her condo, where she could forget all about this night and the almost overpowering sensations she had experienced in Mike's arms.

She turned blindly toward the table where she had left her bag. She felt, rather than heard Mike following close behind. Without a word, she grabbed her purse. Mike snatched up their helmets and with his free hand, steered her to the front door.

The short ride back to her condo was torture.

Denise did everything she could to avoid leaning into Mike's back. She held herself stiffly, her thighs ached with the effort to keep from aligning themselves along his legs. The powerful engine beneath her vibrated with each grumbling roar it sent into the night and every nerve in her body throbbed in response.

Mike guided the bike to a stop in front of her building, then cut the engine. Silence dropped on them like a heavy, uncomfortable blanket. Denise scooted back on the seat. Mike stood up, allowing her to get off the motorcycle with one quick, clumsy move.

She took off the helmet and handed it to him. "Thanks," she said in what she hoped was a light, casual tone. "It was an interesting evening."

He shot her a long, thoughtful look before swinging his left leg over the bike.

"Interesting," he repeated as he pulled his helmet off and set it down on the bike's seat. "That's a good word for it, I guess." He reached down, unhooked a compartment at the back of the motorcycle and reached inside. Pulling out a grocery bag, he stuffed it under his arm, slammed the compartment closed again, then turned to face her. His expression was ferocious.

"Are those my things?" she asked, glancing at the bag.

"Yeah." He took her elbow in a firm grip, turned her around and started for the front door.

"You know, you don't have to walk me to my porch." She glanced at the front of the condo. The light she had left burning sifted through the bougainvillea vines stretched across the trellis that shadowed her porch. "I'm perfectly safe." At least, she thought, she *would* be safe as soon as he left.

"Humor me," he said, and kept walking.

Short of digging in her heels and screaming for help, she really didn't have much choice.

On the porch, he turned and handed her the rolled-up grocery bag. She glanced down at it, then lifted her gaze to his. Green eyes glittered in the glow of the porch light. A muscle in his jaw twitched. Not exactly the picture of a happy man.

Well, the evening hadn't been a picnic for her, either. But he didn't have to be so obvious about his displeasure. A little polite lying never hurt anybody. Refusing to be intimidated by his biker scowl, Denise forced a smile and said, "Thanks again."

His jaw muscle twitched again and she deliberately looked away to fish in her purse for her key. When she had it, Mike took it from her, opened the door, then gave the key back to her.

Curling her fingers around it, Denise took a step toward safety. "It was a lovely evening," she lied in as convincing a manner as she could manage.

"Don't do that."

She stopped cold and looked up at him. "What?"

"Don't give me the standard good-night speech. It wasn't a lovely evening and you damn well know it."

He glared at her, daring her to contradict him.

"Fine. It wasn't lovely." She nodded abruptly. "Like I said before, it was interesting."

"Oh," he countered quickly, "it was more than that."

She looked at him. "What do you mean?"

"You know what I'm talking about, Denise." He placed one hand on the doorjamb and leaned in close to her.

Too close. She could hardly draw a breath. Yes, she knew what he was talking about, but she would be blasted if she was going to stand there and admit that every time he touched her, her body lit up like a nuclear power plant. "Look Mike, let's just call it a night, all right?"

"Not yet."

Her back flat against the wall, she looked up into eyes that seemed to devour her. A white-hot thread of awareness began to uncoil in the pit of her stomach. Her mouth dry, she muttered thickly, "This is crazy."

"Crazy?" He nodded slowly. "Maybe. But before I go, I intend to do something I've been thinking about all night."

Her heartbeat staggered, stopped, then started again. Slower. Harder. She held her breath as he bent his head toward hers. One kiss. How much trouble could one kiss cause?

The moment his lips met hers though, she knew. This wasn't just a kiss. This was an invasion.

His mouth came down on hers with a raw hunger she had never experienced before. Brilliant light exploded within her in a sunburst of color and sensation. He parted her lips with his tongue, sweeping into her warmth with a plundering confidence that stole her breath and urged her to surrender to the wildness building between them.

Pulling her to him, Mike's hands moved up and down her bare back. Not with the gentle, teasing caresses he had shown her at O'Doul's, but with urgent, desperate strokes.

Mike arched into her. Need shimmered through her. In one dark corner of her mind, she realized that she was spinning out of control, but she didn't care. She wanted to be closer to him. To feel his lean, muscular form pressed to her.

His belt buckle dug into her abdomen. He widened his stance. Pulled her tightly to him and tore his lips from her mouth to follow the line of her throat. One big hand cupped her behind, holding her hips to his. She felt the hard strength of him and an answering need spiraled to her center.

Tilting her head back, she stared blindly at the light overhead as Mike's mouth and hands tormented her. Her fingers curled into the black leather of his jacket and she felt his muscles tighten and bunch beneath her hands.

Insane. This whole situation was insane. A man she barely knew, causing such passion and desire to swirl through her bloodstream?

From somewhere down the street, the high-pitched yapping of Mrs. Olsen's Yorkie drifted to her.

Gasping for air, Denise realized that she was standing on her front porch, under the telling glow of a seventy-five-watt bulb, letting a man make violent love to her in full view of her neighbors. Any minute now, Mrs. Olsen would be walking past her condo and who knew how many others of her neighbors were glued to their front windows peering out from behind their draperies? She had to stop him, she knew. This couldn't happen. She couldn't allow either of them to take this one step further.

Then he slipped one hand beneath the fabric of her dress and smoothed his fingertips over the curve of her behind. A harsh moan erupted from the back of her throat and her thoughts dissolved under the onslaught of fiery emotions.

As if her sigh of surrender had been a bucket of cold water tossed at his head, Mike stopped suddenly and lifted his head. Trembling, she met his gaze and knew the confusion she saw there was mirrored in her own.

Viciously, he rubbed the back of his neck with one hand, took a step back from her and drew a long, shaky breath.

"Denise…"

She held one hand up for silence. Shaking her head like a sleepwalker finally waking up, she said, "Let it go, all right? I'm not up to a discussion right now."

"Yeah, me either."

Breathe in, breathe out. Simple really, once you got the hang of it. After practicing a few more times, Denise forced herself to move for the door. Once over the threshold, half hidden behind the safety of her solid oak door, she looked at him and said simply, "Good night, Mike."

He nodded, then turned, hurrying down the flower-lined walk toward the street. A moment later, the Harley roared into life and carried him away.

Usually, working on motorcycles brought him peace. With his hands and mind busy, he didn't have the time or energy to worry about anything else. Sometimes, it was enough just to walk into the service bay behind his shop. The rock music playing on the radio, the easy conversation between the mechanics, even the cool ocean breeze that blew through the two open ends of the workshop, all worked together to make Mike Ryan a happy man.

Until today.

For the third time in as many minutes, Mike tried to fit the wrench head around a stubborn nut. He swore disgustedly as the wrench slipped off target for the third time, this time skinning his knuckles.

"Damn!"

"Bad day, Mike?"

He didn't even bother to look at his chief mechanic, Bob Dolan. The nosy man had been hinting for information all day. "Butt out, Bob."

"Nothin' to me, of course," the other man said from the workbench on the far side of the service bay. "But if I was in a foul mood because of some woman, I'd just forget about her and move on."

Mike smiled to himself. "So speaks the man married for twenty-seven years."

Bob laughed. "True, but only because she hasn't made me mad, yet. For instance, you don't see me grumbling at everyone who comes near me, do ya?"

Mike set the wrench down, put both hands at the small of his back and stretched. Every muscle in his body ached with fatigue. No sleep and a day of frustration was liable to do that to a man. He shouldn't even have bothered going in to work today, he told himself. It wasn't like anyone there needed his help. He had the best bike mechanics in the state working for him. And Bob's wife Tina handled the customers in the showroom better than he ever had.

But it had been a matter of principle. He didn't want to admit that thoughts of Denise Torrance would ruin his day as effectively as they had ruined his night.

His plan hadn't worked. Instead, he had spent the last eight hours grumbling, complaining and pushing his employees until it was a wonder they all hadn't quit in protest.

"So," Bob asked gently, "you feel like talking about it now?"

He glanced at the other man and shrugged. "Nothing to talk about."

Shaking his head, Bob set the carburetor he was rebuilding down on the bench, then walked across the room to stand beside his boss. He tossed a quick look over his shoulder at the two other mechanics working thirty feet away before saying, "Spit it out, Mike. Something's been eating at you all day."

Mike wiped his greasy hands on an even greasier rag. He never should have hired a man who knew him as well as Bob Dolan did. Ever since they were in the service together, Bob had had the unnerving ability to read Mike's mind.

"It'd be different if you were the kind to suffer in silence," the man continued. "But whatever it is that's bothering you keeps spilling over onto the rest of us."

Pointless to argue. Giving him a rueful smile Mike said, "Sorry. I guess I have been taking it out on you guys."

Two bushy eyebrows arched high on the other man's forehead. Bob scratched his salt-and-pepper beard, then folded massive arms across a barrel chest. "So, Ryan, what's her name?"

Mike shot him a look. "Who says it's a woman?"

The mechanic snorted a laugh. "What else *could* it be?"

Disgusted with himself, Mike nodded. "True." He looked at his oldest friend, silently debating whether or not to ask for advice. It wasn't as if he were going to be seeing Denise again. So technically, he didn't really *need* advice. On the other hand, it might be good to talk about this woman and the effect she had had on him.

Besides, he and Bob had served in the marines together. They'd been in and out of more rough spots than most people dream about. And Bob Dolan was the one friend Mike had allowed himself to keep when he finally decided to leave the corps.

Knowing it was inevitable anyway, he said, "Her name's Denise."

"Ah…" Bob grinned, wiggled his eyebrows and waited.

"There is no 'Ah' here, Dolan," Mike warned him.

"Hell, it's high time you found an Ah, Ryan."

"I'm not interested in an Ah, Dolan. Besides, I didn't find her," Mike argued. "I kind of…stumbled onto her."

"Even better."

Mike scowled at his best friend. Not many people would guess that behind Bob's hard, dangerous-looking biker exterior beat the heart of a true romantic. For years, Dolan had been trying to convince Mike to find a woman and settle down. "I knew it was a mistake to talk to you about her."

"All right, all right," Bob said, wiping any trace of interest from his features. "I won't say another word about how you need someone. Not even about how you're not getting any younger—despite the ponytail."

Mike's teeth ground together.

"Go ahead, tell me," his friend urged, not even bothering to disguise his curiosity.

"There's not much to tell." Mike squinted at the late afternoon sunshine filling the far end of the service bay. Actually, there was plenty to tell. But he had never been the locker-room storyteller kind of guy.

"She's an accountant," he finally said.

"Oh." Bob sounded disappointed.

Mike laughed and the two other mechanics turned to look at him before going back to their work.

"I know what you're thinking," he told his friend. "But she doesn't look like any accountant you've ever seen."

"Oh?" Interested again.

"She's smart, she's funny. Independent as hell." He shot his friend a quick look. "She punched me on the chin."

"She *is* smart."

"Funny." Mike shook his head slowly. "I don't know what it is about her, but something…"

"Good, good," Bob grinned. "A woman you don't have figured out from the first minute you meet her."

"Maybe that's it," he muttered, more to himself than his friend. "Well, that and a good old-fashioned case of lust."

"You think so, huh?" Bob asked. "Sounds to me like something more."

"Well, it isn't." Mike turned his back on the other man and picked up the wrench again. All right, he was willing to admit that kissing her had been like nothing he had ever felt before. He was even willing to admit that he admired her. She had climbed on board his motorcycle despite her reluctance. And she played a surprisingly good game of pool. For a novice. Immediately, the memory of leaning over her, his body pressed to hers while he helped her line up a shot came to him. He smothered a groan and closed his eyes. Her image remained in the front of his mind and his body tightened uncomfortably.

No good, he told himself. She was no one-night stand and he wasn't interested in anything else. Abruptly, Mike slammed the wrench down onto the workbench and turned for the rear of the service bay where he kept his bike parked.

Only one way to handle this, he told himself. He and Denise had to talk. He had to let her know that whatever it was between them wasn't going to get the chance to grow. He wouldn't allow it.

"Where you goin'?" Bob called out.

"To set a few things straight," Mike answered.

As the Harley roared off into the late afternoon, Bob Dolan rubbed his palms together gleefully. Then he walked to the showroom to tell his wife about the woman who was going to bring down Mike Ryan.

Chapter 5

Denise stepped into her father's office and waited while he finished his phone conversation. He glanced at her briefly, waved her inside, then turned his gaze to the sheaf of papers on his desk.

Through the bank of floor-to-ceiling windows behind him, she watched the afternoon sun dipping toward the ocean. Streaks of clouds along the horizon gleamed with pale, rich color.

Color that was lacking in the large office's decor. Soft, cream walls surrounded what looked like an acre of sand-colored carpeting. Richard Torrance's mammoth mahogany desk sat squarely in the center of the room, facing the door. He kept his back to a spectacular view in favor of keeping his mind on the sheets of facts and figures that were always in front of him.

Four guest chairs sat clustered on the visitor's side of the desk and on one wall was a small, tasteful bar and two maroon leather sofas. No filing cabinets, adding machines or computers could be found in the roomy office. Those were relegated to an anteroom behind a narrow door to one side of the bar.

No clutter. In his office or his life. Richard Torrance preferred order. Indeed, insisted on it.

When he hung up the receiver, he didn't look up, but went on making notations in the file before him.

"I'm going home now," Denise said softly, not really expecting a response, but waiting for it anyway.

He finished scribbling notes to himself as she watched him. A tall man, even seated he was—an imposing figure. Light brown hair dusted with gray at the temples, he had a narrow, thoughtful face and sharp, pale blue eyes that rarely missed a thing.

"Hmmm?" Richard Torrance looked up from the file he was scanning. He glanced at the clock mounted on the wall opposite his desk, then frowned at his daughter. "Early, isn't it?"

"Only fifteen minutes or so," she said. Digging into her purse, she rummaged in its depths for her antacid bottle. When she had it, she pulled it out, took two of the tablets and popped them into her mouth. Slowly, she chewed and the familiar, chalky fruit flavor filled her mouth. Dropping the bottle back into her purse, she waited.

"Is there a problem?" her father asked.

A problem? she thought. Yes, but nothing he would care to hear about. She could just imagine her father's reaction to the knowledge that she had actually gone to O'Doul's—with a biker, no less.

Visions of Mike Ryan leapt to mind as they had all last

night. She had tossed and turned restlessly, her body still humming with the sexual fire he had stoked and then abandoned. And while her body burned, her mind had raged at her. How could she have let herself be swept away by something as unpredictable as *hormones?*

She looked at her father and not for the first time, wished that she could talk to him. *Really* talk to him.

"Well?" Richard prompted. "Something here at work? Something I should know about?" She didn't answer right away, so he went on. "Did you finish the Smithson file? He'll be here at eight o'clock sharp tomorrow morning."

She wasn't even surprised that her father assumed whatever was bothering her concerned work. To Richard Torrance, his accounting firm was the most important thing in the world. In dedicating himself to its success, he had neglected his wife and overlooked his daughter—until that daughter was of an age to take her rightful place in the firm.

"Denise?" he repeated. "The Smithson file?"

"It's finished."

He gave her one of his rare smiles. "If your work is up to date, what could be the problem?"

What indeed? She couldn't tell him the truth. He would never understand her fascination with Mike. Even *she* didn't understand it.

As she mentally groped for something to say, the telephone on his desk rang and saved her.

Her father lifted the receiver. "Hello? Hello, Thomas," he said, dismissing Denise with an absent nod. He swiveled his chair around so that he could stare out the window behind his desk at the ocean beyond while he talked.

Denise waited another moment or two before quietly

slipping out. She wasn't sure if she should be relieved or hurt that he had already forgotten about her.

Mike felt it again. The sense that worried eyes were watching him as he steered the motorcycle up to Denise's condo. Nudging the kickstand into place, he stood up, swung his leg over the bike and pulled off his helmet.

Glancing around the quiet, moneyed street, he noted the immaculate lawns, the well-cared-for homes and shuddered in response. What the hell was *he* doing in a tidy, self-satisfied neighborhood like this? He had spent most of his life avoiding little splotches of domesticity and yet here he was, riding up to a neat little condo to talk to a woman who could mean nothing but trouble for him.

The woman who had, with one kiss, made him forget everything but her. All of his rules, all of his plans had come to nothing once he had tasted Denise Torrance's mouth.

Which brought him to why he was back, now.

He had to face her. Tell her in no uncertain terms that it would be best if they just stayed away from each other. He had thought it all out. There was no other answer. Denise was the house-in-the-suburbs kind of woman—and Mike got cold chills just *thinking* about settling down.

Great chemistry or not—this was going nowhere.

Leaving his bike parked on the street, he carried his helmet with him as he marched up the front walk.

Denise watched him approach the house and every nerve in her body went on red alert. Why had he come back? Why hadn't he just stayed away?

She glanced down at herself and groaned. Faded, baggy

gym shorts and an old, oversize T-shirt with a picture of Tweety Bird on it did *not* make for an impressive outfit.

The doorbell rang and her stomach pitched.

She took a moment to collect herself, then turned the knob and opened the door.

Her gaze locked with his. All day she had been telling herself that whatever she had felt for him had been a momentary aberration. A lightninglike flash of desire caused by the excitement of the moment.

Lies. All lies.

Instantly the same, illogical, overpowering stirrings of desire rose inside her again. Her gaze slipped over him quickly, thoroughly. The tight black T-shirt, straining over his muscular shoulders and chest. The worn Levi's that hugged his long legs in a soft, faded grip.

"We have to talk," he said, his voice rough.

Talk. Denise drew in a long, shaky breath and told herself to get a grip. There was nothing sexual about *talking*. Besides, she was twenty-nine years old. Too darned old to let her hormones be her guide. She could do this. She was an *accountant* for Pete's sake. Accountants were not the stuff of wild, sexy fantasies starring muscular, dangerous-looking bikers.

To prove to herself that there was nothing to be worried about, she pulled the door wider and said, "Come in."

He stepped past her in the narrow entryway and a whiff of Old Spice staggered her. Frantically, she started to mentally recite the multiplication tables. Starting at the two's. Numbers. Numbers she was comfortable with. Numbers she understood. Numbers were her only hope.

Closing the front door, Denise moved around him in as

wide a circle as she could manage and led the way into the living room. Her gaze moved quickly over the familiar, spartan room. White walls, blue carpet. A sofa and two wing chairs upholstered in a dark blue fabric with bright red-and-yellow throw pillows for splashes of color.

On the low coffee table were a stack of files from the office and a rapidly cooling cup of herbal tea. The TV was on, turned to the news, but the sound was so low as to be only a small hum of voices in the background.

Curling her toes into the thick carpet, she turned to face him. Mentally, she was up to the five's. He looked out of place. Uncomfortable.

"Denise," he began, "what happened last night…"

Multiplication abandoned, she broke in hurriedly.

"Can't happen again. For heaven's sake, Mike. We have nothing in common."

"Agreed," he said, exhaling on a rush of relieved breath. Half smiling, he added, "You're not exactly my type."

"And you're not the kind of man I would feel comfortable taking to a company dinner."

He shuddered at the thought.

Good, she told herself. They were making progress now. Obviously, he had been doing a lot of thinking about this, too. And apparently, he had reached the very same conclusions. No matter how exciting…how *tempting* a relationship with him might be, it simply couldn't happen.

There was no future in it and she refused to set herself up for a broken heart.

"So we understand each other?" Mike said and took a step closer.

"Of course," her mouth went dry as she moved toward

him. Her heart pounded against her rib cage and her blood thundered in her ears.

"You and I have no business even *thinking* about being together."

"Absolutely not." The whole idea was ridiculous.

"I'm not interested in love or anything else that comes tied up in a neat little package," Mike grumbled. His gaze moved over her hotly and she shivered in response.

"I don't believe in quick little affairs." She wanted what she had always wanted. Someone to love. Someone to love her.

"Exactly," he muttered thickly and reached out to smooth her hair back from her face. "It doesn't matter a damn what you do to me."

"Or what you do to me." She inhaled sharply as his finger-tips brushed across her cheek. Jagged streaks of heat shot through her body. "Hormones," she whispered.

"Lust," he said softly, urgently.

"Pure and simple. That's all it *could* be." She tilted her head back to keep her gaze locked with his. "Right?"

"Right. Good, old-fashioned lust."

She took a deep, unsteady breath and dragged the scent of Old Spice deep into her lungs.

"Oh," she said on a sigh, "we're in trouble, aren't we?"

"Damn straight," he said and brought his mouth down on hers.

She wrapped her arms around his neck, pulling him closer. Her lips parted for him and her tongue met his stroke for stroke. In a wild, desperate joining, their mouths mated, breath mingling, tongues exploring, caressing.

Denise arched into him, brushing her rigid nipples across his broad chest. She sucked in a gasp of air that shot from her lungs as one of Mike's hands slipped beneath the waistband of her shorts. His fingertips lifted the band of her bikini panties and his hand dipped lower, to caress her bare behind. She moved into him and felt his body, already hard and eager.

Desperately, hungrily, his tongue moved in and out of her mouth, touching, tasting. This was no tender, romantic coupling. This was need. A deep, instinctive need that demanded completion. He held her mouth with his as if trying to claim her breath for his own. She met his urgency with a wild, overwhelming passion that threatened to leave her puddled on the floor. When he finally tore his mouth from hers, Denise almost moaned at the loss.

But a moment later, he was tugging her T-shirt up and over her head and she was helping him. His palms cupped her breasts and his thumbs gently stroked the hard, sensitive tips of her nipples. She groaned in the back of her throat and began tearing at his shirt, pulling it free of his jeans.

In as frantic a state as she was, Mike released her long enough to yank the shirt off and throw it to the floor. Then he grabbed her again and pulled her tight against him. Flesh to flesh, heat to heat, the fire already raging between them burst into an inferno of passion.

With his knee, Mike shoved the coffee table out of the way. Absently, Denise heard the crash as the table tilted and fell on its side. Her teacup clattered quietly but she didn't care. He sank to the rug, dragging her with him, all the while touching and teasing every inch of her body.

She reached for him and held on to his shoulders, reveling in the feel of his muscled flesh beneath her hands. Warm, strong, his tanned chest lightly sprinkled with dark, curly hair, he looked wonderful.

"Denise," he whispered before bending his head to take one

of her nipples into his mouth. His lips and teeth worked the tender flesh until she was writhing beneath him, helplessly caught in the net of desire they had blindly stumbled into.

Denise pulled the rubber band from his ponytail and tangled her fingers in this thick, black hair. She felt his right hand sweep down her body to drag her shorts and panties off and she lifted her hips to assist him.

"Now, Mike," she pleaded in an agonized whisper. "Hurry. I have to feel you inside me, Mike. I need..." Her voice faded into silence. How could she possibly explain what she needed when she hardly understood it herself? This was more than desire. More than lust. Something within her was clamoring to be a part of him. To feel him slide his body into hers. She had never known such hunger, such mindless need before.

It both excited and terrified her.

"Soon, honey," he promised and moved away from her, despite the groan erupting from her chest. In seconds he had disposed of not only her clothes, but his. Then he was back, kneeling between her thighs, kneading the flesh of her behind with his strong hands. She twisted in his grip, reaching for him.

"Mike," she whispered. "Please Mike, now."

"Now," he promised in a hushed voice and lifted her hips for his entry.

Mike looked down at her as he pushed himself deeply inside her tight, hot body. She arched into him and a broken cry tore from her throat as he filled her. He clenched his teeth tight to bite back a groan of satisfaction building in his own chest. He held perfectly still, buried inside her, fighting for control. An explosive climax was only a breath away and he would be damned if he would give in to the pleasure before she was ready to take that leap with him.

In the space of a few heartbeats, he was able to move within her again. And then there was nothing but the overpowering, driving urge to brand her as his. To fill her so deeply, so completely, that even when they weren't together, he would still be a part of her.

She lifted her legs and locked them around his hips, drawing him tighter, closer.

Mike looked down into her blue eyes and saw the stunned wonder he knew was written on his own features. He pressed his mouth to hers and their bodies raced toward completion. He swallowed her cries when they were at last swept over the edge of passion and fell tumbling into peace.

When it was over, they lay locked together, neither of them willing—or able—to move, to separate. Heart pounding, Mike rolled over onto his back, keeping her with him, cradling her close. Her head on his chest, he felt her breath brush across his skin and tried to get feeling back into his limbs.

Now that his body had found rest though, his mind finally kicked into gear. As one, undeniable fact presented itself, he had to bite back a groan of disgust. He had acted like some dumb teenager. For the first time in years, he had acted without thinking. As a result, the two of them might now be in deeper trouble than either of them had thought.

She lifted her head and looked down at him. Giving him a rueful smile, Denise said, "Well, so much for talking."

Reluctantly, he smiled back at her. Damn. Now what? Obviously, the realization that had occurred to him hadn't popped into her mind yet.

"Denise," he said, then paused, hoping for inspiration.

"I know," she mumbled.

"What the hell happened?" Stupid question, he told himself.

He knew damn well what had happened. For the first time in years, he had allowed his body to make his decisions for him.

"*That* I don't know," she said, snuggling against him.

He ran the flat of his hand down her spine, wondering just how he should say what he had to say.

Across the room from them, the telephone rang. Neither of them glanced at it. On the second ring, the answering machine picked up. Seconds later, Denise heard her father's commanding voice. "Denise? Apparently, you're not at home."

She lifted her head and shot a covert, almost guilty look at the phone.

Mike watched her expression shift and change as she quickly scooted off and away from him. He frowned thoughtfully as the voice on the machine continued.

"I hope that means you're thoroughly prepared for the Smithson meeting tomorrow. And don't forget you're having lunch with Pete Donahue from Donahue's Delights. My secretary's made an appointment for you at the Tidewater for twelve o'clock. Since he's a new client, I'll expect you to impress on him just what Torrance Accounting can do for his business."

Denise groped around on the floor for her shirt and shorts. Still keeping one eye on her, Mike snatched up his own clothes and got dressed. Amazing, he thought as he looked at her. A moment ago, she had been cuddled naked against him and now she was acting as though nothing had happened.

"So," her father continued, apparently unconcerned about the machine cutting him off. "What was this problem, you said you had?"

She shot a surprised look at the machine.

Mike's eyebrows lifted. Problem?

"Well," Richard said and sighed heavily. "No point in

asking this infernal machine what's going on. You can tell me tomorrow…I'll pencil you in for 3:10 in the afternoon. Goodbye."

Real friendly guy, he thought. The man talked to his own daughter as if she were a client.

"You need an appointment to talk to your father?" Mike asked.

"He's a busy man." She stood up and bent to right the table. Mike helped her, then gathered the fallen file papers while she picked up the broken teacup.

Her features were tight. There was no sign of the wild, passionate woman of a few moments before. Odd, how just the sound of her father's voice could do that to her.

Odder still, that it mattered to him.

"Lunch with Donahue's Delights, huh?" He tried a smile on her, but there was no reaction. "They make great frozen burritos."

She nodded and folded her arms across her chest in an unconscious symbol of self-defense. What the hell was going on here? And why had she just clammed up on him when a while ago she had nearly burned his skin off?

But maybe it was better this way. Once he said what he had to say, the atmosphere in the room was certain to get a little chilly, anyway.

"Denise, about what just happened…"

"Let's not *talk* again, okay?"

"Dammit, we have to talk." Now was not the time to shut herself off from him. Fifteen minutes ago, maybe. But not now.

"It was stupid. What else is there to say?"

"Plenty." He reached up and pushed his hair back from his face with both hands. "It wasn't just stupid. It was irresponsible. We didn't use any protection, Denise."

Chapter 6

Was the world spinning? Or was it just this one room?

Suddenly sick to her stomach, Denise blinked furiously, trying to get her vision to clear. It wasn't working.

She clapped one hand to her mouth and looked at him through wide eyes. Protection. Birth control. Good heavens. This kind of thing only happened in bad movies. How could they have forgotten something so basic? Because, she admitted silently, they had been too busy dealing with something far more basic.

"Oh, Lord."

Plopping down onto the couch, she propped her elbows on her knees and cupped her face in her hands.

He paced back and forth in front of the couch in long, hurried strides. "As far as one worry goes," he said in a self-disgusted tone, "I can tell you that I'm healthy."

She was even more stupid than she had at first thought.

She hadn't even *considered* that particular aspect of life in modern times.

"Me, too," she said when she noticed that he had stopped pacing to look at her questioningly. Why wouldn't she be? At twenty-nine, she had had exactly two lovers. Including Mike. No wonder she had messed things up so badly. She didn't have nearly enough experience to be able to deal with a man like Mike Ryan.

She swallowed a groan and tried to quiet her mind so she could hear him.

"As far as a pregnancy goes, though…" He stopped pacing again suddenly and she felt him looking at her. Slowly, she lifted her head to meet his gaze. "Please tell me you're on the Pill," Mike said grimly.

"All right," Denise obliged him wearily. "I'm on the Pill."

"No, you're not."

"No," she said, and this time her groan wouldn't be silenced. "I'm not."

"Perfect."

She glared at him. Was he trying to lay the blame for this…incident entirely at *her* feet? Well, he could forget that idea right now. It took two people to do what they had just done.

Two very stupid people.

"I'm very sorry I wasn't more prepared," she snapped and tried to ignore the curl of worry already taking shape in the pit of her stomach. She only hoped that was *all* that was taking shape.

"That's not what I meant."

"Of course it is." She jumped to her feet and walked past him, heading for the kitchen. It didn't surprise her in the least to hear him following her.

She marched straight to the refrigerator and opened it. Reaching inside for a bottle of water, she grabbed two automatically and handed him one as she closed the door again.

The perfect hostess, her mind laughed at her.

Mike twisted the top off, lifted the bottle and drained half of it immediately.

Denise settled for a long sip before saying hotly, "This must be a new world's record. Not just for you, personally. But for *all* men."

"What are you talking about?"

She shook her head at him. "The sheets, so to speak, have hardly cooled off and already you're trying to weasle your way out of any responsibility for possibly conceiving a child."

"Hold on a minute," he said and stood up straight.

"You were there too, Mike. You could have stopped. You could have used something. Don't try to turn everything around and make this all *my* fault."

"That's not what I said," he argued. "And honey, I don't weasle out of responsibility. All I said was, I wish you had been taking the Pill." He leaned one hip against the slate blue countertop and looked at her.

"Well, so do I," she countered. "And stop calling me honey."

He drained the rest of his ice water, set the bottle on the countertop behind him and said deliberately, "So *honey,* why *aren't* you on the Pill?"

She scowled at him. "Not that it's any of your business, but I'm allergic—they make me sick."

"What?"

"Birth control pills. They make me sick."

"Wonderful."

She stiffened, took another drink and said, "I don't do this sort of thing every day, you know." No, she thought. More like once in the last six years. "There hasn't been a real big need for regular birth control in my life."

Mike folded his arms across his broad chest defensively and looked at her for a long minute. "This isn't getting us anywhere. What's done is done. But isn't there something you can do—after the fact?"

A short, strangled laugh shot from her throat before she could stop it. "Sure," she said, sarcasm dripping off every word. "I could take the morning-after pill and have an allergic reaction that sends me to the emergency room—or worse. Or, I could bury the warts of a toad under an oak tree by the light of a full moon."

He frowned at her, but she went on, warming to her theme. "Or, how about I boil up a little eye of newt and drink it down while balancing on one foot?"

"Denise…"

Patience gone, she slammed her half-full water bottle down onto the counter. Liquid sloshed up the neck and spilled onto her hand. She wiped it dry on her shorts and snapped, "Just go, Mike. Get out." Storming through the kitchen back to the living room, she felt her own fears fade away in the face of her anger.

It was as though she were stuck in a bad soap opera with a lousy script. Bad boy takes advantage of good girl, then accuses her of trying to trap him. Even as she thought it though, she had to admit that he hadn't taken advantage of her. It had been a mutual seduction. Incredibly careless, but mutual.

Unfortunately, *she* would be the only one to pay the price if Mother Nature presented a bill.

"Dammit, Denise," he shouted and grabbed her arm to turn her around to face him. "Stop treating me like I'm public enemy number one just because I don't want you to be pregnant."

She yanked free of him. "I'm not mad about that," she told him. "I'm angry because you only bothered to be concerned about it *afterward*."

"Neither one of us was doing much thinking." He moved in close to her.

She didn't want to be reminded. She didn't want to have to think about why she had reacted to him—responded to him as she had. It had never happened before. She had never known such an all-consuming need to be with a man. Until she had met Mike Ryan, Denise's love life had been as boring as the rest of her life.

Boring, her mind chided her. But safe.

"Denise," he went on, "if we made a mistake, we made it together."

Mistake. What they had done was foolish. Irresponsible. But a mistake? Instantly, she remembered the sense of completion she had experienced when he entered her. When his body and hers were joined.

Was finding that magic a mistake?

And if they had conceived a child—would the child be a mistake as well? She flinched from that notion.

"How long until we know?" he asked, his voice quiet.

For a moment, she wasn't sure what he was talking about. Then it dawned on her. She glanced up at him. "*I'll* know for sure one way or the other in about ten days."

He nodded. "Okay. So let's not make ourselves crazy about this yet."

That seemed reasonable, she thought and felt some of the tension drain from her.

"If there *is* a baby…" He paused. "Hell, we'll have plenty of time to figure out what's next."

"We?" She looked up at him.

"Yeah. *We.*" His green eyes locked with hers. She couldn't have looked away if she had tried "I told you already, Denise. I don't weasle out of my responsibilities."

A speech designed to warm any girl's heart.

"I think you'd better leave now," she said quietly.

Seconds ticked past.

She sat down on the couch, drew her knees up to her chest and wrapped her arms around them. She kept her gaze determinedly away from his.

"Fine," he said after a while, just as quietly. "I'll go. For now. But I'll be back."

She listened to the sounds of his footsteps as he moved through the condo. After the front door had closed behind him, she let her head fall backward against the couch. She closed her eyes and told herself that he had been right about one thing. It was too early to worry. She would find out soon enough if there was a need for it. And then, she would have nine long months to do all the worrying she wanted.

By the time her lunch appointment rolled around the next day, Denise had convinced herself that everything would be fine. After all, most couples had to try for years before conceiving a child. What were the odds she and Mike Ryan could accomplish such a feat with one, mind-boggling love-making session?

Astronomical.

In numbers, she told herself, there was comfort.

Pete Donahue sent her a smile as she signed the check for lunch and slipped her Visa card back into her purse. A widower, Pete was nice, fairly attractive and financially secure. And a week ago, she might have been flattered by his obvious interest in her.

Unfortunately today, she looked at his thinning blond hair and saw it as thick and black. His calm gray eyes were no substitute for the memory of the deep green eyes that had haunted her sleep. And, she admitted, blue suits just didn't have the same fascination for her as tight black T-shirts.

"You can tell your father that I'm happy with Torrance Accounting," Pete said, smiling. "Maybe then he can relax."

"My father? Relax?" Denise grabbed her purse and stood up. She maneuvered her way through the maze of tables in the crowded restaurant, then turned and waited for him to join her in the entryway.

Pete chuckled as he stepped past her to open the front door for her. "I used to be like him, you know. So wrapped up in business that I couldn't see beyond my own nose."

"What happened?" she asked idly and walked into brilliant afternoon sunshine.

"My wife died."

Denise looked at him quickly, lifting one hand to shade her eyes. "I'm sorry."

"It was several years ago," he said, holding one hand up to assure her that he wasn't wounded. "But her death did make me realize that life was too short to miss it all because of business appointments."

Her father, unfortunately, had never learned that lesson. When her mother died, Denise was only eleven. Unlike Pete Donahue, Richard Torrance had buried himself even deeper in his work once there was no one around to demand a slice of his time.

No one but a little girl.

And that girl had spent the past eighteen years trying to make Daddy proud of her. Was he? she wondered. Had any of her accomplishments been enough to get Richard Torrance's attention?

"Thanks for lunch, Denise."

"Hmmm? Oh," she said, as he walked her to her car. "My pleasure."

The hot summer sun bounced off the asphalt and tossed heat at them like heavy stones.

"I don't suppose I could interest you in the ballet Friday night?"

Caught off guard, she stalled, searching for something to say. "Uh…" She couldn't afford to offend her father's newest client. On the other hand, the only man she was interested in at the moment was someone she was working hard to forget.

"Maybe not," Pete said for her. "Somehow, I think he'd object."

She looked up at him and he jerked his head in the direction of her car.

There, propped casually against the right front fender, was Mike Ryan.

Despite her best efforts, her heartbeat accelerated. Her gaze swept over him, taking in the blue jeans, the white T-shirt and the huge Harley parked alongside her car.

He looked like every mother's nightmare.

And every daughter's fantasy.

Even as her blood rushed through her veins, she realized that she would have a much better chance at forgetting all about him if he would just stay away.

As they approached, Mike pushed up from the car and stood, long legs planted in a wide, almost belligerent stance. He looked every inch the dangerous male.

"Hello, Mike," she said.

He nodded abruptly and shifted his gaze to the man beside her.

"Pete Donahue, Mike Ryan," she said. "Mike, Pete Donahue."

Mike took the man's extended hand and gave it a brief, hard shake. "Good burritos."

"Thanks," Pete nodded, flashed Denise a quick smile and asked, "I'll speak to you at the end of the month?"

"That's fine," she told him, grateful that he was leaving so quickly. With Mike still in his Tarzan stance, it was probably a good idea. "I'll call your secretary."

He lifted one hand in a halfhearted wave and walked off to his own car.

A heartbeat later, she whirled around to face Mike Ryan. "What are you doing here?" she demanded, squinting up at him.

"I needed to see you," he said.

"So you show up at my business lunch?"

"Your lunch was over."

"That's not the point."

"No," he muttered thickly, "the point is, that I can't get you out of my mind."

She sucked in a gulp of air and told herself that it didn't mean anything. Obviously, they were both being plagued with some weird sort of attraction that they were just going to have to deal with sensibly.

"This is nuts," she whispered.

"Among other things," he agreed.

Mike looked down at her and felt something inside him shift, soften. Damn, this was playing with fire. For years, he had managed to avoid feeling anything more than a passing fondness for any woman.

He didn't want love. He didn't want to *need* anyone.

Yet, here he was, chasing after the one woman who could be real trouble for him. Denise touched him in ways he didn't even understand. Despite her strength, there was a vulnerability to her that brought all of his protective instincts rushing to the surface.

A moment ago, he had wanted to slam his fist into Pete Donahue's face simply because the man had been able to make Denise smile. He had the insane desire to stake a claim on her. To fight off any intruding males.

Blast it, around her, he wanted to go find some dragons he could slay and lay at her feet. He wasn't sure he liked this feeling, but it was too big to ignore.

Not to mention, he thought with a glimmer of panic, the possibility of a baby.

"Mike," she said, shaking her head.

"I know what you're going to say," he interrupted. "Jeez, I said it myself all last night. We're too different. We have nothing in common."

"Exactly." She took a step closer.

"And it doesn't matter." He moved toward her. "Look, you said we've got about ten days before we know for sure about…"

"Yes," she interrupted.

He swallowed hard past the knot of fear that had been stuck in his throat since the moment he had realized that there *might* be a baby. "All I'm saying is, why don't we spend those ten days together? Give us a chance to get to know each other a little."

She was already shaking her head, so he started talking faster. "If there's a decision to be made, wouldn't it be easier if we could face it together? As friends?"

"Friends?" Denise asked.

"All right," he conceded with a half smile. "Maybe friends is asking too much of either one of us." He rested both hands on her shoulders. Gently, his thumbs kneaded her muscles through the fabric of her red cotton suit. "I'm not talking about forever here, Denise," he said, his voice tight and low. "I'm talking about two grown-ups who share something…incredible."

She stiffened and shot him a quick look. Hell, he knew she would rather hear about hearts and flowers. Declarations of love and promises he had sworn never to make. But if they were going to be together, even if it was only for ten days, then she had to know that he wasn't going to fall in love.

He had seen close up just how love could destroy people.

"I told you before," she said quietly. "I don't do little affairs."

"I'm not asking you to."

"Aren't you?"

He scowled, released her and said, "I don't know what I'm asking for. All I know is that something happened last night." He didn't understand it any better than she did. Could hardly define it. But somehow, when he and Denise had made love, he had felt a sense of *rightness* that he had never known before. It was more than great sex. How *much* more scared the hell out of him. But not enough to make him keep his distance. "There's something between us, Denise."

She shivered.

"I'm not willing to give that up yet," he said flatly. "Are you?"

She looked away from him, staring blindly across the parking lot. He waited what seemed forever for her to finally shift her gaze back to his.

Mike wasn't sure what he would do if she turned him down and sent him away. He held his breath until his chest hurt with the effort.

"No," she admitted. "I want to be, but no. I'm not."

Air rushed from his lungs. He felt himself grinning like a fool as he reached for her hand. "Come with me."

"Where?"

"Just for a ride." He drew her toward his motorcycle.

"I have to get back to work," she said as she dragged her feet.

Mike flicked a quick glance at her and felt his pulse speed up. What was it about this woman? "It's your father's business. Take an extra hour."

At the mention of her father, Denise's expression tightened slightly. "No, I really can't."

He pulled her to him, slipped one arm around her waist and tugged her tight up against his side. Staring down into the wide blue eyes that had kept him awake most of the previous night, he whispered, "One hour. Tell him your lunch went long."

The tip of her tongue smoothed across her bottom lip and Mike's gaze tracked it. A familiar hunger rippled through him.

"All right," she finally said. "But just an hour."

He smiled and Denise's stomach flipped over. Telling herself that she was being a fool where Mike was concerned didn't seem to be helping. She hitched her suit skirt up to midthigh, climbed aboard the narrow seat and pulled on the helmet he handed her.

Mike got on the bike and sat down in front of her. Plopping her purse down onto her lap, she leaned forward and wrapped her arms around his middle.

"Ready?" he called loudly as he fired the engine.

No, she thought, but nodded against his back anyway. The powerful bike lunged forward and in seconds, they were roaring down the Coast Highway.

* * *

Four hours later, Mike took her back to her car.

"You're a pretty good pool player," he said.

"I distinctly hear, 'For a girl', in that statement," Denise countered and handed him her helmet.

"Are you accusing me of being a sexist?" He gave her a slow, lopsided grin that set off firecrackers in her bloodstream.

Denise tugged at the lapels of her suit jacket and straightened her short red skirt. "Sexist? Of course not. Male? Definitely."

He chuckled softly. "I'll pick you up at your place at eight."

She checked her wristwatch. Five o'clock. Only three hours to go before she climbed back onto that bike of his and… "Five o'clock!"

"What's the matter?" he asked as she hurried around to the driver's side of her car.

Denise hardly spared him a glance. She fumbled in her purse for the keys. Pulling them free, she opened the car door and threw her purse onto the passenger seat.

"Denise?" he said, louder this time. "What's gong on? What's the big hurry?"

"I had an appointment with my father at 3:10," she reminded him and slid behind the wheel. She fired up the engine, pulled out of the parking lot and sped down the street toward her office.

Most of the cars were gone by the time she arrived. Naturally, her father's was still there. The man never left work before seven at night.

Hurrying into the building, she grabbed the first elevator and rode it impatiently to the third floor. She bolted through the slowly opening doors and hustled down the long, quiet hall to Richard Torrance's office.

She knocked gently and walked in.

He looked up from his desk, gave her a vague smile, then returned his gaze to his work.

"Father, I'm—"

"Going home now?"

"Uh…"

"Fine, fine," her father muttered and began scribbling on the paper in front of him. "See you tomorrow then."

Denise stared at him for a long, thoughtful moment. He didn't remember. Obviously he had forgotten all about their appointment. He must not have written it down after all. Apparently something more important than his daughter had cropped up, wiping all thought of an appointment with her out of his mind. She wondered if he had noticed at all that she hadn't been in the office for most of the day.

The only sound in the room was that of his pen, scratching against paper. A humorless laugh caught in her chest, but she managed to squelch it.

As she walked back to the elevators, Denise told herself that it was a good thing that he had forgotten about her. At least, she wasn't in trouble for skipping out on work. She should be happy at the way things had turned out.

Chapter 7

It was as if she were a comic book superhero.

Like Clark Kent, Denise was leading a double life. By day, she was a mild-mannered, stuck-in-a-rut accountant. She said the right things, wore the right clothes and danced attendance on her father. In short, she did everything she was expected to do.

By night though, she had become someone quite different.

Someone she was enjoying.

Denise glanced at her reflection and smiled in amazement. If someone had told her three weeks ago that she would be wearing black leather pants, black boots and a red sweatshirt with the Harley-Davidson logo on it, she would have laughed at them.

She shoved two silver clips in her hair at either side of her head, then grimaced slightly. No matter how much fun her secret identity had become, she didn't think she would ever get used to flat "helmet" hair.

But that was a small price to pay for discovering this new Denise Torrance.

"And," she told herself, "Mike was right about the leather pants being warmer." When she wore jeans on their nightly rides, the icy sea air seemed to cut right through the denim.

She sat down on the edge of her quilt-covered bed and reached for her boots. As she yanked them on and stomped into them, she wondered where Mike was taking her tonight.

Over the last week or so, the two of them had hopped onto his motorcycle every night to ride off in search of another adventure. Besides a few return visits to O'Doul's, there had been quiet dinners in tiny, out-of-the-way restaurants, and even once, a trip to Tijuana.

At that thought, she looked up at her mirror again. Tucked into the frame was a photo of she and Mike, wearing sombreros, sitting astride two stuffed donkeys.

Silly, but she had never had so much fun.

A curl of excitement spiraled in her stomach. He would be here any minute, she knew. Denise felt as giddy as a high school kid on prom night. But then, she admitted silently, she had felt that way almost every night since meeting him. She deliberately ignored a niggling thread of worry. They hadn't done anything foolish again. There had been no more wild, out-of-control lovemaking sessions.

Instead, they spent time together. Talked. Laughed. And the desire between them grew hotter, stronger.

Yet in its own way, that was just as dangerous. She stared at that photo again, her gaze locking onto Mike's image. Over the past few days, the feelings she had for him had changed, gone beyond that initial attraction.

Denise drew one long, shaky breath and jumped to her feet. Her head swam and the room spun around her in dizzying circles. Closing her eyes, she carefully sat back down and waited for the odd sensations to pass.

Her mind raced with more questions than she had answers. The period she had expected to arrive that morning hadn't. But it was too early to start worrying, wasn't it?

In seconds, she was fine again. When the doorbell rang, she stood up slowly. Once she was sure she wouldn't fall over, she went to answer it.

He cut the engine, set the kickstand into place then climbed off the bike and stood waiting on the driveway. Denise pulled her helmet off, looked at him, then shifted her gaze to the small house just a few feet away.

One light shone from behind the curtains at the front window, spilling onto a tiny lawn banked by a riot of flowers, their colors muted now by summer moonlight.

"Who lives here?" she asked, wondering if they were visiting some of his friends.

"I do."

Denise swiveled her head to look up at him from her perch on the bike. Interesting. Somehow she hadn't imagined him living in a tidy Cape Cod. He seemed more the efficiency apartment type. No ties, no sentiment. Beige walls and communal hot tubs.

Curious, she let her gaze sweep across the small, well-kept yard to the three-foot-tall picket fence surrounding the property. Unlike most neighborhoods in beach cities, the old houses on this street weren't jammed too close together. At least fifty years old, they had been built before land in California became so valuable that contractors now shoved twenty houses onto lots meant for fifteen.

This house had character. A personality.

"I like it," she said.

"Thanks." Mike's defensive posture relaxed. It was almost as if he had been prepared for her to hate the place. He glanced at the house and said, "It used to belong to my grandparents. They moved in right after their wedding."

"No honeymoon?" she teased

Mike winked at her. "Grandpa Ryan always claimed that this was the best honeymoon cottage in the world."

A wistful pang erupted in her chest as she turned back to look at the little house again. In her mind's eye, she saw that long-ago young couple, coming to this house to start their life together. In a flash, she saw the years pass, children grow, grandchildren born and still that once young couple were together. Loving each other.

How nice it must have been she thought, to grow up seeing that kind of love.

Her own memories were less pleasant.

"Are they still—" She stopped, unsure of how best to ask that particular question. Yet she wanted to know. She somehow *needed* to know that his grandparents' love continued.

"Alive?" he finished for her. "Yeah."

Denise smiled, relieved.

"They moved to Phoenix a few years ago," Mike explained. "Grandpa said the ocean damp was bothering Gran, but I think he just wanted to live right on top of a golf course."

Ridiculous, she knew, to be so pleased that two people she

didn't even know were still healthy and together. Her gaze slid across the wooden shutters at the windows, the shake roof and the flowering vines creeping along a trellis attached to a side wall of the house.

"I know you and Patrick are twins," she said softly as she realized that Mike had told her almost nothing about his family. "Are there any other Ryans I should know about?"

He helped her off the bike, flicked up the kickstand again and pushed the motorcycle down the short drive to the garage beyond the house. "Besides Patrick and me, there's Sean and Dennis. Sean's the oldest, then Dennis."

Denise followed him, listening. "Didn't any of them want this house?"

"Get one of the doors for me?" he asked and waited while she opened one side of the double doors to the too-small-for-a-car garage. "Sean's stationed in South Carolina. Dennis has a houseboat moored south of here and you couldn't blast Patrick out of his apartment," Mike said with a laugh.

"He's gone now," she reminded him.

"Only on vacation."

She leaned against the garage wall and watched him as he set the kickstand again and stepped away from the bike. "You said Sean is stationed up north?"

"Yeah." Mike reached up, yanked the cord on a bare light-bulb, then turned to look at her in the dim glow. He shoved both hands into the back pockets of his jeans. "Career marine."

His features tightened and a muscle in his jaw twitched. He suddenly looked more like he had that first night in Patrick's office than he had in more than a week. Why? "You have something against the marines?" she asked.

"Not for Sean, I guess. He likes it. I didn't."

"You were in the service?"

"Eight years. Got out a few years back."

His answers were getting shorter. Sharper. Maybe she should have left it alone and backed away from what was apparently a tender subject. But she didn't.

"Why did you leave?"

He dragged a deep breath into his lungs and even in the indistinct light of that low wattage bulb, Denise saw the strain in his features. "Let's just say I saw enough of the desert to last me a lifetime."

Desert?

A cold chill ran down the length of her spine and she shivered. A marine in the desert. His grim expression. He had to have been in Iraq. She looked at him, trying to see behind the shutters he had erected over his eyes. Trying to see what that experience had done to him. But she couldn't. He was much too good at hiding his feelings behind a hard-as-nails mask.

At the same time, she realized that but for good fortune, he might have died in that desert war and she would never have met him. Never have known what it felt like to be held by him. Never have gotten to know the woman she had become since meeting him.

She couldn't imagine not knowing Mike. Her gaze settled on his features and she realized just how much he had come to mean to her. How much she looked forward to seeing him. Talking to him. How much she felt for him, despite her best intentions. What if they had never met? she wondered.

Another, deeper chill touched her and this time, he reacted when she shivered. He yanked the light cord again, plunging the tiny garage into darkness. "Come on," he said tightly. "You're cold."

She had caused this tension in him, by unintentionally stirring up old memories and now she wanted to dispel it. Denise wanted the real Mike back. The man she knew and cared for. As he came close, she said abruptly, "It must have been fun. Growing up with three brothers, I mean."

He walked to her side and as his features became clearer in the darkness, she saw a wry smile lifting one corner of his mouth. Apparently, he was relieved with the change of subject.

"Oh, yeah." He set one hand on the plank wall beside her head and leaned in close. "It was a blast. Yelling, fighting. Every day was Disneyland."

"You enjoyed it," she guessed.

"Every minute." He lifted his left hand to stroke her cheek. "What about you? Brothers? Sisters?"

Her breath caught at his touch. "No. None."

"Must have been lonely."

"And quiet." Maybe she wouldn't have been so lonely if she and her father hadn't been so far apart. Maybe… She cut short that line of thinking. It did no good to keep raking over the past. Denise sucked in a gulp of air and tried to keep the conversation moving.

The tiny garage suddenly seemed claustrophobic and it had everything to do with the fact that Mike was standing way too close to allow coherent thought.

"What about your parents?" she asked.

He chuckled, as if he knew exactly what she was thinking, before taking a step back from her. Then, leading the way out of the garage he said over his shoulder, "Both retired."

"From what?" she asked as he shut the door behind them and headed for the back porch of the house.

"Ever hear of Wave Cutters?"

"Of course. It's one of the biggest surfboard companies in southern California."

"That's the one." He unlocked the back door, opened it and ushered Denise in ahead of him.

She blinked at the brightness when he flicked the kitchen light on. A scrubbed pine pedestal table sat in the center of the big, square room and in the middle of the table was a huge, wicker picnic basket. As Mike moved to the refrigerator, she said, "Wave Cutters makes surfboards, wet suits, beach wear…just about everything."

"That's them."

"Them who?" she asked as he pulled a bottle of wine and a plate of sandwiches from the fridge and set them on the table.

"My parents. *They're* Wave Cutters." He stopped, shrugged. "Well, they were. Now, it's Dennis's headache."

"Headache?" Denise pulled one of the captain's chairs out and plopped down onto it. "You didn't want to be a part of your family's business?"

"Nope." He looked over the edge of the door and winked at her. "Well, all four of us are actually on the board, but Dennis is in charge. The rest of us just collect dividends."

"Why?" Wasn't he proud of what his parents had accomplished? Wave Cutters was one of the fastest growing companies in the country. "How could you not want to be a part of it? Your parents must have been furious."

"Furious?" Mike laughed out loud at that one. "My dad believes in doing what you want to do. *His* dad had wanted him to go into business with him—TV repair. Said that surfing and being a beach bum would never support a family." He shook his head. "Tell my dad 'No' and it's like issuing a direct challenge."

Like father like son, she thought.

"Anyway, when Wave Cutters took off, Grandpa sold his business and went to work for his son." Mike stood up, shut the fridge and leaned back against the door, smiling at her. "Together, they built it up so well, they both retired to do what they love best."

"Golfing."

"For Grandpa," Mike agreed. "My folks, though, bought a place in Hawaii." His black eyebrows wiggled and his eyes sparkled in amusement. "They're looking for the perfect wave."

Denise shook her head. Her own father seldom left his office. And Mike's father walked out on a hugely successful company to be a full-time surfer? She could just imagine what Richard Torrance would think of that.

"What's the matter?" Mike walked to her side and squatted down beside the chair. "Disappointed to find out that I've got money? That I'm not the dangerous desperado you thought I was?"

She looked into his green eyes and saw that he was actually worried about what she was thinking. Not dangerous? she thought. One look into his eyes and her toes curled and sparks skittered down her backbone. She drew a series of shallow breaths and forced her heart into a regular beat again. "Oh, you're dangerous all right, Ryan."

He grinned at her and her pulse jumped into jackhammer time again. "Good," he said. "I prefer dangerous to successful businessman."

Denise didn't understand that at all, but didn't bother to say so. At the moment, she was less interested in what he did for a living than in what he did to her. She stood up when he pulled her from the chair. Her vision blurred slightly at the quick movement and she leaned her forehead against his chest briefly.

"Hey," he asked, "are you all right?"

She pulled in a long breath, drawing the scent of Old Spice deep into her lungs. As the dizziness passed, she nodded. "Fine. I just got up too fast."

Mike looked at her warily. "You're sure that's all it is?"

Not entirely, Denise thought with a pang, but said only, "I'm sure."

He nodded abruptly. "In that case, let's get going."

"To where?" she asked.

Mike picked up the now full basket and gave her a slow smile. "A picnic."

High, craggy cliff walls surrounded him on three sides. Mike glanced skyward and sighed heavily. Maybe this hadn't been such a good idea, he told himself. Moonlight, an empty beach, a sheltered cove and Denise. Through hooded eyes, he watched her, standing only inches from the incoming tide.

Soft light from the full moon fell on her in iridescent patterns of shimmering silver. She lifted her wineglass to take a long drink and his gaze locked on the elegant column of her throat. Ocean air lifted her hair and teased the curls into a tangled mess that only served to make her more beautiful. The leather pants he'd given her for riding hugged her legs with a lover's grasp.

His hands itched to touch her. His body ached with a pain that had tormented him for the past ten days. She never left his mind. And that fact terrified him almost as much as the thought of never seeing her again.

But this couldn't go on and he knew it. Once they found out if she was pregnant or not, a decision would have to be made.

If she *was* pregnant… Instantly, his mind conjured an image of her lithe body rounded with the swell of his child. He groaned quietly as he realized she would be even more beautiful to him pregnant than she was now. He rubbed one hand over his eyes and told himself not to think about that yet. There was a good possibility that she *wasn't* going to have a baby. And if not, she would probably want him out of her life. Though that was most likely for the best, it bothered him to realize just how much he had come to count on seeing her every day.

To know how much she meant to him.

"Hey!"

He let go of his thoughts and looked at her.

"Are you going to hog all that grape juice to yourself?" She held out her empty wineglass toward him.

"You've had enough," he said, and wondered how anyone could get tipsy off of grape juice.

"Half a glass more," she called back over the roar of the ocean.

He shook his head, got up and walked to her side. Taking her glass, he filled it a quarter of the way and handed it back to her.

She nodded a thank you then reached up to push her wind-blown hair out of her face. So different from the woman who had tried to attack him with pepper spray. She looked relaxed. Happy.

And way too tempting.

"It's beautiful out here, Mike." She grinned at him. "I've never been to a picnic on the beach."

"In a couple of more weeks, this place will be so crowded, you wouldn't find a spot to throw a blanket down."

"I like it like this," she told him and leaned closer. "Empty. Private."

He told himself that she was drunk off the ocean air. That there were rules about things like this. You just didn't take advantage of a woman when her defenses were down. No matter how tantalizing the invitation.

"I know what you're thinking," she said and pressed herself against him. "You think I'm feeling reckless."

"A little."

"Not even a little," Denise said and met his gaze squarely, soberly. The wind brushed a lock of hair across her eyes again and she reached up to push it out of the way.

He set his hands at her waist to steady her as she leaned her slight weight into him. Every spot where her body met his was suddenly alive. His fingers tightened on her narrow waist. He looked down into her eyes and called himself a fool.

Only a couple of hours ago, his memories of desert warfare had been all too close to the surface. For one brief moment there in the garage, he had been able to feel the blazing heat of the sun. The scent of fear and sweat had surrounded him.

And with those memories had come another. The memory of a promise he had made to himself. To steer clear of love. To avoid giving anyone the power to hurt him as his friends and their families had been hurt.

Yet here he was, coming dangerously close to caring for a woman who even now might be carrying his child.

"Denise," he said abruptly, "when will we know about—"

She reached up and laid her fingertips over his mouth, effectively silencing him. "I'll buy a test tomorrow."

Tomorrow. A thousand differing emotions battled within him for dominance. He had never planned on being a father. Had figured on leaving all of that to his brothers. But, now that he was actually faced with the prospect of a child, it was different. Surprising as it was to admit, he had caught himself almost hoping there *would* be a baby. A girl maybe, with Denise's blue eyes and blond hair.

Something inside him shifted painfully. Was it the child he wanted…or was it *her* child that had suddenly become so important?

"We'll know for sure tomorrow," she said, "one way or the other."

He nodded.

"But tonight, Mike," she continued and her soft voice was almost lost in the pulsing rush of the ocean, "let's forget about everything but us. I want one more night with you before we know. Before things change forever."

Mike bit back a groan as an invisible hand tightened around his heart and squeezed. Her quiet words tore at him, leaving his insides open and unguarded.

"Kiss me, Mike."

A deep, throbbing ache settled low in his gut and his hands fisted at his sides to keep from reaching for her. He looked down into her face, brushed by moonglow, and silently admitted that he had also been hoping this would happen. He had counted on the moon and the stars and the seductive scent and sound of the ocean to urge her into his arms.

Why bother pretending now that he wasn't interested?

Mike groaned again as he grabbed her and pulled her into the circle of his arms. He lowered his mouth to hers like a dying man seeking salvation and dismissed the last of his guilt in the rush of need swamping him. No point in denying the truth to himself. He had to have her.

Chapter 8

She dropped the glass to the sand and when he tore his mouth from hers to lavish long, slow, wet kisses along her throat, her moan of pleasure heightened his every sense.

Mike couldn't wait any longer. He had already lived through the longest ten days of his life. Quickly, he scooped her up into his arms and practically ran back to their blanket. Setting her on her feet again, he yanked her sweatshirt off. As she unhooked her bra, he tore off his own shirt and threw it to the sand.

He grabbed her again, pulling her flush against him. He wanted to feel all of her. Touch all of her. The cold air blowing in off the water couldn't dampen the heat devouring them. Moonlight made her skin gleam like fine porcelain and he ran his hands up and down her back, relishing the smoothness of her skin. Denise's hands clutched at his shoulders and every one of her fingertips acted as a brand, searing him with tiny darts of fire that reached down into a soul too long untouched.

Anxious fingers fumbled with snaps and zippers. Her breath came in short, sharp pants, brushing his skin with warmth. Flames erupted inside him. His heart pounded fiercely and breathing became secondary. All he wanted, all he *needed* was her. Her touch. Her kiss. The silky grip of her body on his. He bent his head to take one of her nipples into his mouth. She arched against him, her fingernails digging into his shoulders.

"Mike," she whispered on a moan. He heard his own torment and need echoed in her strained voice.

Deliberately, he ran the edges of his teeth over her rigid nipple. Denise gasped and moved one hand to the back of his head, holding him in place. She needn't have worried that he would stop. If it had meant his life, he couldn't have left her. Drawing on that sensitive bud, he suckled her, tugging on her flesh with a steadily increasing pressure that pushed her forward, toward the edge of a precipice they had both dangled from for days.

As he gave first one breast, then the other, his devoted attention, his hands smoothed her underwear and those black leather pants down her legs. He lowered his head farther, trailing kisses along her rib cage, across her abdomen and finally, on the triangle of curls guarding her secrets.

Denise swayed unsteadily on her feet and he tightened his hold on her. With him bracing her, she stepped out of her clothes and stood before him, wearing only the glimmer of moonlight.

"You're so beautiful," he murmured as his fingers traveled up her inner thighs. "More beautiful than I remembered."

Her breath caught and she grabbed at his shoulders again

for balance. "Mike," she whispered, "don't make me wait. Make love to me again."

"I will, honey," he promised and gently nudged her thighs farther apart. "Nothing can keep us apart tonight." Holding on to her hips, Mike slowly leaned close and dragged a line of kisses along her belly. Her legs trembled. His grip on her hips tightened and he dipped his head to taste the heart of her.

"Mike!" she gasped his name and dug her fingernails deeper into his shoulder muscles.

Tremors rippled through her, leaving him shaken. He ran the tip of his tongue across one small, hard bud and felt her body quiver in response. Damp heat welcomed him and Mike gave himself over to the pleasure of loving her. Each gasp of delight that shot from her throat only fed the raging desire burning inside him.

"It feels so…good," she managed to say softly, brokenly.

Her legs stiffened, her hips rocked against his mouth as she tried to open herself even further to him.

He smoothed his tongue across that so tender spot and as he did, his right hand slipped to the valley between her thighs. His lips and tongue stroked her velvety softness and Mike gently dipped two fingers into the tight, hot sheath of her body.

She tensed, every muscle suddenly going rigid.

He redoubled his attentions. His fingers slid in and out of her damp heat and his mouth tantalized her.

She widened her stance, welcoming him, silently demanding the release that he knew was rushing toward her. A soft, broken cry issued from her throat when the first ripples of satisfaction shuddered through her. She held the back of his head to her and Mike groaned along with her as if her release were his own.

Staggering and limp, Denise leaned against him and he eased her gently down onto the blanket. She gave him a wan smile.

"Mike, I never knew that I could feel something like that. So…" Her eyes slid shut briefly and she paused to take a long, shuddering breath. When she opened her eyes again, she reached for him, lifting still trembling arms.

Quickly, unwilling to wait another moment to be joined with her, he shucked his boots and jeans. He paused only long enough to fumble through his wallet, before tossing it atop his clothes. Then he turned back to her, already tearing open a small foil packet.

She looked up at him and smiled. Lazily, she asked, "Isn't that like locking the barn door after the horse is out and running?"

Mike slid the sheath on, then moved to kneel between legs she parted in invitation. Grinning down at her, he said, "This time lady, we do things *right*."

"My hero."

"Damn straight."

Denise lifted her hips as he entered her. Though the flush of release still warmed her, she was immediately roused again. As his strong, hard body moved in and out of hers, she felt another driving need building inside.

Tension streaked through her body. She held her breath, sure that this time, the climax would kill her. She held him tighter, anchoring herself to his strength. Fireworks exploded within her. Her hips moved in time with his. Hands caressed. Lips met in hungry kisses that left them gasping for air. One last thrust and her body convulsed around his. He called her name as he fell into her arms and Denise used the last of her energy to catch him and hold him tightly.

The solid, heavy weight of him pressed down on her and

beneath the blanket they lay on, she felt the hills and valleys of sand digging into her back. Still, she didn't want to move. She wanted time to stop. She wanted this moment to last forever.

Tomorrow, they would know if they had created a baby and everything between them would change. A sheen of tears pricked at her eyes and Denise blinked them back as she held Mike even tighter.

They had no future. From the beginning, she had known that Mike Ryan was the wrong man for her. They were too different. They had nothing in common. Except perhaps, she thought, a child.

But she knew better than anyone that a child wasn't enough to keep two people happy. Her own parents had failed miserably and she refused to relive their mistakes.

Not even for Mike.

God help her, she loved him. She didn't know how it had happened, or even when and it didn't really matter. All that mattered was that she loved a man she couldn't have. Her eyes slid closed as she wondered how she would ever get through the rest of her life without him.

Her deep, even breathing told him she was asleep. Mike tightened his arms around her, drawing her even closer against his side. Her breath puffed on his naked chest, she mumbled something incoherent and slid one of her hands across his abdomen to rest on his hip.

Mike glanced at the window on the far wall and saw the first stirrings of dawn beginning to lighten the sky. Soon, it would be morning. Soon, he would find out if he was about to become a father or not.

His eyes squeezed shut briefly. Then he opened them again

to stare up at the ceiling. How the hell could she sleep? he wondered. In just a few short hours now, their lives might be changed forever.

He lifted one hand to smooth across her hair, loving the feel of the soft silky curls against his palm. She muttered again and shifted at his side. Mike took a long, deep breath and smiled into the darkness. Strange how right it felt, her body aligned with his, lying together in the big bed his grandparents had founded a family in.

"Mike?" she whispered and he bent his head to look into her face. Asleep, he told himself. Asleep and talking. He wondered if she knew about this little habit of hers.

Easing his head back down onto the pillows, he stroked her back gently and said quietly, "Shh, Denise. It's all right."

"Mmm…" She sighed and cuddled in closer.

His body immediately hardened. Desire and a deep-seated need to protect swelled up within him, fighting for precedence. Protection won.

"Sleep, baby," he crooned gently as he continued to stroke her skin reassuringly.

"I love you, Mike," Denise mumbled.

He held his breath.

She muttered something more, but he didn't quite catch it. It didn't matter, though. He had heard enough.

Snatches of emotions raced through him. Fear, wonder, pleasure. Love. She loved him.

In her sleep, he thought. Wide awake, he doubted very much that she would have said those three words. But did that make a difference? No. And how did *he* feel? Was this strange, unsettled feeling in the pit of his stomach love? And if it was, what should he do about it? He wasn't husband material, was he? As for being a father… God, he pitied the kid who was stuck with *him* for a parent.

A kid deserved someone who was good at all of the things parents were supposed to be good at. Right? What did he know abut PTAs and bingo nights and booster clubs? Wasn't that stuff important?

But his own childhood had been a good one, he told himself, and as far as he could remember, his old man had never gone to a single parent-teacher conference. Maybe, he thought, it was enough just to love your kid.

Wrapping both arms around Denise, he rested his chin on the top of her head. He didn't have any answers and Lord knew, the thought of parenthood still scared the hell out of him. But despite all of that, he silently promised the woman in his arms that everything would be all right.

"How much longer?" Mike asked again.

Denise checked the kitchen timer sitting on the bathroom sink. "About another minute."

"Are you sure you set that thing for three minutes?"

"Yes, I'm sure." She couldn't really blame him for growling. Three minutes had never felt so long to her, either. And Mike's tiny bathroom seemed to be shrinking. The two of them had been standing there, just a foot apart for two full minutes, waiting for an answer to the question that had been in the backs of their minds for ten days.

She glanced at him briefly, but couldn't bear to look into those shuttered eyes of his. Whatever he was thinking, he was keeping to himself.

Unable to stand still a moment longer, she snatched up the pregnancy kit's instruction sheet, stuffed it into the empty box then tossed it into the trash. Trying to keep busy, she also tried not to stare at the test stick. She looked at Mike again, standing in the open doorway to his house's one and only bathroom. She saw him watching that stick as if expecting it to blow up any second.

She wished she was home. In her own house. Denise rubbed her upper arms nervously. Somehow, this whole test thing would have been easier to handle if she had been in familiar surroundings. Alone.

Blast it, she had planned to buy a kit herself, take the darn test in private and then inform Mike of the results. It would have given her time to adjust to whatever those results were. But she was beginning to understand that *nothing* worked out as planned. When they had finally left the beach the night before, they were both too tired to take a step beyond his house.

She had fallen asleep in Mike's arms and awakened to find him already up and gone. He returned armed with a box of donuts and an early pregnancy test kit. Now all that was left to do was wait.

Denise studied his expression covertly. Tense, grim, he was no doubt silently muttering every prayer he had ever known in the hopes of keeping that stick from turning pink.

The only real question here was, why wasn't she doing the same thing?

A shrill bell rang out suddenly and Denise jumped. Mike took one long step into the room and shut off the timer. Looking at her, he asked unnecessarily, "One pink stripe, negative, two stripes positive, right?"

She nodded, knowing as well as he did that neither of them was likely to forget how to read the stick. Too much was riding on the answers. She took a deep breath and swallowed hard past an unexpected lump of emotion clogging her throat.

"You want to look," Mike prompted, "or do you want me to?"

"Go ahead." She closed her eyes and waited. It didn't matter who looked, she told herself. The answer would be the same. And her hope for privacy had already been shattered.

A long moment passed in silence, then Mike said flatly, "That's it then."

"What?" she asked, even though she knew what he meant.

"Congratulations, Ms. Torrance," he said. "It's a baby."

Did the room spin or was it just her mind racing, whirling with a sudden overload?

"Ohmigod," she said as air rushed from her lungs. "Let me see it."

"I know pink when I see it," his voice rumbled into the small room. "And even I can count to two."

Still, she held her hand out for the slender white wand. She needed to see it herself. She needed to look down at the bright pink stripes that had just thrown her life a serious curve. He slapped it into her palm. She stared down at the test square and then the control square. Each of them held a distinct pink line.

Pregnant.

"I need to sit down," she muttered and turned toward the door, still clutching that stick.

She walked down the short hall to the living room and practically fell onto the old, overstuffed sofa. She wasn't surprised. Stunned maybe, but not surprised. Somehow it only made sense that the one time she stepped out of her usual world…the one time she had acted before thinking…would end in a baby.

Fathered by the one man she should never have loved.

"You okay?" he asked.

Denise looked up at him, standing in front of the sofa, arms crossed over his chest. My, he looked delighted.

"Yes. I think so," she said, leaning back into the cushions. She reached up and rubbed her forehead, hoping to ease the headache that had just erupted behind her eyes. "A little… confused at the moment, but okay."

"Well," he countered, "I'm not."

Her eyebrows lifted. Not real surprising, she thought. He had made his feelings more than clear on the night this child had been conceived. It might have been nice if he didn't look as though he were about to face a firing squad. On the other hand, at least she knew exactly where he stood. Which should make living without him a bit easier to deal with.

After all, what kind of future could she have had anyway with a man who so clearly had no desire to be a father?

She didn't want to examine too closely the wrench of disappointment that tugged at her. She had no right to be let down or hurt at his reaction. Logically, she knew that. Unfortunately, logic didn't have a lot to do with what she was feeing at the time.

The thing to do, she told herself, was to go home. Get back to her own place where she could sit and think, out from under Mike Ryan's glare.

"Thanks for being honest," she said stiffly and started to get up.

"You didn't let me finish," Mike said sharply.

"Oh, I think you were fairly clear."

"Dammit, will you listen for a minute?"

"Why should I? Just by looking at you I can tell what you want to say." Her voice sounded more strained than she would have wanted ordinarily. But under the circumstances, she felt as though she was doing pretty well.

"Is that right?" he said, his own voice harsh and scratchy.

"It's perfectly obvious, Mike. You're upset about our...*news*. Well, that's understandable." She tried to get up, but he laid one hand on her shoulder, holding her down gently. She stared at that hand until he pulled it away. "But it should be just as understandable to you that I need to be alone for a while. To think."

"Thinking can wait another minute or two, all right?"

One minute. All right, she would give him one minute to tell her that he wasn't going to be trapped into being a father. Then she would let him know that she had no intention of springing that trap, either. Easing back into the sofa cushions, she drew her knees close to her chest and wrapped her arms around her legs. "Fine. I'll listen."

He reached up and used both hands to smooth his hair back from his face. When he was finished, he tucked his palms into the back pockets of his jeans. Staring down at her, the familiar shutters over his eyes, he said, "I didn't mean that I'm not okay. I meant, I'm not confused."

Now, *she* was more confused than ever.

"We've got some decisions to make, Denise."

"I'm not ready to make any decisions yet, Mike." This life-altering news was only about two minutes old. She needed a tad more time to be able to think rationally.

"It's not like you haven't known this moment might be coming."

"I knew the chance was there," she countered, "but I didn't really think it would happen." Her head dropped back to rest on the top edge of the sofa. On a groan, she added, "It was just the one time."

A half smile crossed his features briefly. "I wonder how many couples have used that particular phrase over the last thousand years?"

She didn't know and she didn't care. Denise had all she could do at the moment to concentrate on her. On this baby and what it meant in her life. Good God. *Her?* A *mother?*

Her gaze flicked to Mike. In his usual biker outfit, he didn't look like anyone's ideal of a father. Oh Lord, father. *Her* father. How would she tell her father this?

What would he say when…*if* he met Mike?

The headache became a driving, pounding force that drummed inside her head in time with her heartbeat. Every aching pulse screeched at her.

Suddenly too tightly wound to sit still, she jumped up from the couch. A wave of dizziness crashed down on her and she wobbled a bit before falling backward onto the sofa.

Instantly, Mike was there, kneeling in front of her. "Are you all right?"

"I'm fine. Just a little dizzy." And how long would this be happening to her? Lord, her entire world was sliding out of control and she was helpless to stop it.

"Again?" Mike demanded. "Is that normal?"

Patience suddenly gone, she glared directly into his green eyes and snapped, "How would I know? I've never been pregnant before." Her stomach pitched violently. Funny how just saying the word out loud made it so *real.* And so terrifying. "Oh, God," she whispered and clamped one hand over her mouth as she pushed past him and raced back to the bathroom.

Mike held her head and she was too miserable to care that he was seeing her in such a disgusting state. When her stomach was finally empty, he soaked a cloth in cold water, wrung it out and gently wiped her face. Then he lifted her from the floor and carried her to his bedroom. Laying her down on the mattress, he straightened up and started pacing.

Wrapped in her own misery, Denise didn't even notice when he came to a sudden stop.

"This pregnancy changes things," he said.

She opened one eye to look at him. "What things?" she muttered. "Besides the obvious, I mean?"

"Things between us."

There it was. It hadn't taken him long to recover fully enough to let her know he wanted their friendship to end. Well, she had known the moment she had agreed to go out with him that their time together would be short.

She was hardly the sort of woman he usually spent time with. And as for her, a man in black was so far removed from the usual ambitious, driven business-suit types she normally dated, it would have been laughable. If it all wasn't so damn sad.

Why had she fallen in love with him? Why hadn't she stopped this relationship before it started? She knew what could happen if a woman fell in love with the wrong man. Her own mother had been miserable.

The woman had loved Richard Torrance to distraction. And Richard had had time only for his business. He was a man who should never have married.

A man like Mike.

Oh, not that the two men were really alike in any way except one. Neither of them were interested in marriage. Somehow her mother had convinced Richard to take a chance. Denise wasn't going to make the same mistake.

"Don't worry about it, Mike," she said and pushed herself up onto one elbow. Pausing, she waited a moment to see if her stomach was going to rebel. When she was sure she was safe, she went on, forcing herself to look at him calmly. "I don't expect anything from you. I'll take care of—everything myself."

"Oh, thanks so much." Sarcasm dripped from every word.

She blinked. He sounded angry.

Furious, Mike simply stared at her. Did she really think so little of him? Did she just assume that he would do a quick fade-out the minute they found out she was pregnant? With *his* baby?

Of course she did. What else could she think? He had told her himself that he wasn't interested in love and marriage. He shoved one hand through his hair, then viciously rubbed the back of his neck. Looking at her again, he stared into wide blue eyes filled with confusion, and he *knew* what had to be done.

"There's no reason for you to take care of anything all by yourself."

"Mike…"

"Marry me."

"What?" She sat bolt upright on the bed.

He inhaled sharply, cleared his throat and forced the words out again. Barely. "Marry me, Denise."

"You're out of your mind."

"No, I'm not. I'm trying to find a way out of this for both— all *three* of us," he corrected himself.

"That's not a way out Mike," she said, with a slow shake of her head. "That's the way in. To deeper trouble."

"No, it's not." Talking fast now, he sat down on the end of the mattress and held her gaze. "It could work. We get along well. Neither one of us is a kid, we'd be able to work together. And you have to admit that two parents are better than one."

"Not if they don't want to be together."

"Fine, I admit that I never thought I'd get married."

Two blond eyebrows lifted.

"But I didn't have a reason before."

"You don't *now,* either."

"There's the baby."

"Mike, this is the twenty-first century. There are all sorts of solutions to this kind of problem besides the one you're suggesting."

"Problem?" he repeated. "This isn't a problem, Denise. It's a baby. *My* baby."

She looked at him for a long moment, then scooted to the edge of the bed and stood up. "It's *my* baby too, Ryan. And I'm not going to be pushed into doing something I think is wrong just because you've decided to play storybook hero."

"What?"

"This knight in shining armor thing." Color flushed her pale cheeks. "I don't need to be rescued, Mike. I'm a big girl and I can take care of myself."

She turned quickly and started for the hall. He caught her in two steps. Grabbing her arm, he turned her around to look at him. "You're not going to shut me out of this, Denise. It's my child and I deserve a say in what happens to him."

"We didn't even *know* about her until fifteen minutes ago," she said quietly, but firmly. "I think she deserves better than her parents making a decision without even bothering to think about it."

"Now isn't the time to think," he snapped. "It's a time to *feel.* Sometimes you have to go with your gut, Denise. You can't think everything to death."

"*Feelings* are exactly what brought us to this point, Mike. If we had stopped to think two weeks ago, neither of us would be standing here having this conversation."

She was right. He didn't like it, but she was right. Oh, not about two weeks ago. Nothing could make him regret that night with her. Not even this surprise pregnancy. But she did deserve a little more time to come to the conclusion that his was the only possible solution.

So maybe he wouldn't have proposed if there hadn't been a baby. But there *is* a baby. And that tiny life meant the rules had just changed on the game they had been playing. She could take all the time she wanted, but Mike wasn't going anywhere.

"All right," he said and released her. The battle gleam in her eyes faded a bit as she took a step back. "Take some time. Do some thinking. So will I."

"Good."

"I'll come by your place tonight and we'll talk again."

"Tonight?"

"Yeah. We can talk this whole thing out then."

She stepped into the hall, keeping her gaze locked with his. "Not tonight. I need a few days to myself, Mike. I'll call you, okay?"

"You're not planning on doing something and telling me about it later, are you?" he muttered thickly.

Realization dawned in her eyes and she shook her head. "No. No, I promise I won't do anything until I've told you what my decision is."

"Your decision?"

"It's your baby too, Mike, but it's inside *me*. The final decision will be mine."

Chapter 9

Five days later, she was no closer to a decision. True to his word, Mike had kept his distance. But now, Denise couldn't help wondering if he was staying away because she had asked him to—or because he had realized that his marriage proposal was a mistake.

She was still rational enough to know that she wasn't being fair. But emotional enough not to care.

And Lord, how she missed him.

"Denise?" Richard Torrance walked into his daughter's office, a sheaf of papers clenched tightly in one hand.

"Hmmm?" She turned her back on the view of the ocean to face the man's slowly purpling features. "Father, what's wrong?"

"Wrong?" he echoed. "Oh nothing, except that I almost had heart failure a moment ago."

"What are you talking about?"

"These figures, Denise," he said and waved the papers in his fist. "On the Steenberg account? According to your calculations, their company lost several hundred thousand dollars last month."

"I don't under—"

"You transposed the numbers, Denise. If I hadn't caught your error, Mr. Steenberg probably *would* have had a heart attack!"

"I'm sorry," she said and sat back in her chair. Propping her elbows on the polished wooden arms, she briefly cupped her face in her hands. There went her last safety net. She couldn't even count on numbers anymore.

"You've been sorry for nearly a week." He dropped the papers onto her desk, flattened his palms on the maroon leather blotter and demanded, "Where has your mind gone, girl?"

She lifted her head to stare at him. "I'm not a girl, Father."

"You're certainly behaving like one," he countered hotly. "Canceling appointments, coming in late, leaving early. If you weren't my own flesh and blood, I would have fired you days ago."

She jumped to her feet, waited for the now familiar touch of dizziness to pass, then met her father's glare with one of her own. If he had been more interested in his daughter's welfare rather than his employee's performance, he would know what the problem was. She would have been able to talk to him. Ask his advice.

Instead, they were further apart than ever, whether he knew it or not. And today, she was too tired to put up with it. Too exhausted to worry about saying just the right thing, she said flatly, "Fine. Fire me."

Richard jerked his head back, clearly as surprised as he would have been to have a lamp jump off the desk and bite him.

Reaching down into her bottom desk drawer, Denise pulled her huge purse out and slung the strap over her shoulder. Digging into the bag, she pulled out her bottle of antacids and shook two of them into the center of her palm. Before she popped them into her mouth though, she stopped and wondered if antacids were safe for the baby. She didn't know. Lately, she felt as though she didn't know *anything*. Carefully, she scooped the tablets back into the bottle, then dropped the container into her purse. Better to be safe than sorry.

"What do you mean, fire you?" Richard asked, his tone demanding an answer. "What has gotten into you?"

Briefly, she considered blurting out, "A baby." But thought better of it. One thing she didn't need at the moment was her father's opinion on her impending motherhood.

Instead, she said, "I mean, Father, if you're that unhappy with my work, fire me as you would any other employee. I won't have trouble finding a job. Any accounting firm in this town would be *glad* to hire me."

"I didn't say—"

"Yes, you did, Father. And you know what? I don't care." As she said the words, she realized the truth in them and felt her tension level drop just a little. Inhaling sharply, she came out from behind her desk and marched past him, toward the door. Before she left though, she looked over her shoulder at him. "I'll probably be late again tomorrow. I haven't been feeling well."

He opened his mouth to speak, but she cut him off cleanly.

"If I'm not working here any longer, leave word with my secretary. I'll pack up my things and be out by tomorrow afternoon." She turned on her heel and stormed past the secretaries in the main room, each of them staring at her as if she had sprouted another head.

Denise rode the wave of her anger all the way to the bank of elevators on the far wall. She stabbed the Down button with her index finger and tried to calm the roiling in her stomach while she waited what seemed forever for the car to arrive.

Finally, a bell chimed and the doors soundlessly slid open. As she stepped into the elevator, she saw her father striding out of her office. Every secretary in the room stared at him, but he didn't even notice their curiosity.

Looking after her, he shouted, "Denise!"

But the elevator doors closed before she was forced to acknowledge him.

"It's the accountant again, isn't it?" Bob Dolan asked as he watched Mike storm around the service bay. The other two mechanics on duty had opted for an early lunch, not that Bob blamed them any. In the space of a few weeks, their easygoing boss had turned into Godzilla. The last few days had been especially rough.

Mike's angry strides slowed long enough for him to throw an icy glare at his friend. "Stay out of it, Bob."

"Love to, Ryan," the other man said and leaned one beefy forearm on a workbench. "But you keep draggin' it in to work every day. You know your mechanics are set to quit?"

Mike gritted his teeth to keep from shouting.

Bob went on. "Even Tina's about ready to run you down with one of your own bikes."

He knew he had been making everyone around him miserable. But he was just too mad to care at the moment.

"Let 'em quit," Mike snapped. "As for Tina, if she can put up with you for twenty some years, she can damn sure put up with me."

"Maybe, but you're not as good lookin' as me, either."

Mike snorted a laugh, despite his foul temper.

"What's goin' on, buddy?"

He pulled a deep breath into his lungs, exhaled on a rush and shook his head. "I really loused things up this time."

"The accountant?"

"Denise."

"Right." Bob nodded. "What about her?"

Mike looked at him. "She's pregnant."

A few seconds ticked by before Bob pushed away from the bench and grinned. "That's great, Ryan."

Mike scowled

"Isn't it?" Bob asked.

"I don't know," he admitted, disgusted with himself, Denise, the situation, everything. He had done as she asked. He had stayed away. Given her time to think. But it had been five long days and there still was no word from her.

Was he supposed to just stand on the sidelines forever while she decided what she was going to do with *his* kid?

He didn't even sleep anymore. Every night, he ended up lying in a bed where he could still feel her presence, staring at a silent phone. Nothing was being solved this way, couldn't she see that?

"She won't talk to me, Bob. Says she needs time to think. Well dammit, how *much* time?"

"Have *you* been thinking?"

He snorted again. Hard to think when you're so exhausted you can barely see straight. "Trying to."

"Come up with anything yet?"

"I asked her to marry me."

A long, low whistle was Bob's only comment.

"She said no," Mike added, surprised that he could admit that humiliating fact even to his best friend.

Bob ducked his head to hide a small smile, but Mike saw it anyway.

"There's nothin' funny about any of this."

"I guess not," the other man conceded. "But I seem to remember a fella standing in the hot desert sand, swearing to anybody who would listen that *he* was never getting married."

Mike smiled briefly and shook his head. "Yeah, I remember him too. But that fella didn't have a baby coming. And that fella hadn't met Denise Torrance yet, either."

"So, did you tell her you love her?"

He shot a wild look at his friend. Love? Who the hell said anything about *love?* Love didn't have to come into any of this. It hadn't been love that had created that baby. It had been pure, old-fashioned, need. "I never said I loved her."

"So you *don't* love her?"

Instantly, images of Denise filled his mind. They were each so clear, he could almost smell her perfume, feel her hand in his. He recalled the feel of her sitting behind him on the bike, her thighs aligned with his. He saw her again as she had been that night in his kitchen, before they went to the beach. She had looked so right there. It had all felt so natural, talking to her there in his house where usually the silence was enough to drive him out onto the highway for a fast ride on his Harley. In memory, he heard her sighs, tasted her lips and felt her arms slide around his waist as they set off on an adventure. His breathing quickened and his throat was suddenly dry and tight. Was that love?

"I didn't say I don't love her, either."

"Hell, Ryan, what *are* you saying?"

"I'm saying…" Mike paused and searched for the right words. Words he could live with. Words to describe the only truth he really knew so far. "I'm saying I *want* her. And I want that baby. Isn't that enough?"

Bob scratched his beard and squinted at him. "I'm not the one you should be asking."

Mike kicked at a stack of tires, smiling grimly when the black rubber tower swayed unsteadily. "Aren't you listening? I can't ask her anything. She won't talk to me."

Just like always, Bob ignored Mike's temper and asked thoughtfully, "Since when do you take no for an answer?"

"Lately, I guess." This being fair and gentlemanly was for the birds. What he should have done was pushed his way into her house and demanded that she listen to him. He reached up to yank the rubber band from his ponytail. When his hair fell free, he stabbed his fingers through the mass and rubbed his skull, in an effort to stop the pounding going on inside.

"Mike," Bob said softly, "I never thought you were a stupid man, until now."

Mike's head snapped up. His gaze locked with Bob's. "Back off," he grumbled.

"Not this time," his friend said. "Now, I know you decided a few years back that you weren't going to love anybody."

"Dammit, Bob."

"You can't make those kinds of rules for yourself, man. They don't work. Hell, they *can't* work. Life happens, Mike." Bob looked at him long and hard. "Somehow, this woman got past that wall you built around yourself and there's no getting her out now."

He could argue with him, but what would be the point? The

man was right, whether Mike wanted to admit it or not. Denise had sneaked up on him. She had slipped beneath all of his defenses until she had reached the heart of him. The heart he would have bet money hadn't existed anymore.

He shifted his gaze to stare blankly out the open end of the service bay. "How do I make her see that?" he whispered.

"How?" Bob snorted and turned back to the workbench, his duty to his friend done. "Man, you were a marine. Storm her beaches, buddy."

Mike nodded to himself. Enough of this waiting around. She'd had it her way for five long days. Now, they were going to play by *his* rules. Blast it, he wasn't about to lose this war. Not when winning it meant the difference between a lifetime with Denise and a lifetime of loneliness.

The battle was about to begin.

Sitting on the floor in the middle of her living room, Denise reached for the closest stack of books and picked up the one on top.

"The Perfect Baby Through Visualization," she read out loud, then set the book down with a muffled chuckle. How had she ended up with *that* one?

Easy, she told herself. Go into a bookstore and ask for every book they have on pregnancy. One of the clerks had had to carry the bags to her car for her and it had taken her three trips to drag them all into the house.

"What Every Expecting Mother Should Know," she muttered, then flipped through the rest of the first pile. *"The ABC's of Babies, Pregnancy 101."* She shook her head and reached for the glass of milk she had set on the coffee table.

Glancing down at her flat stomach, Denise slid one palm across it protectively. "I'm even willing to drink *milk* for you, kiddo. I hope you appreciate it."

She took a long sip and smiled to herself. Somehow, after that fight with her father, some things had become clear to her. Oh, not *everything*. She still didn't know what to do about Mike and the feelings she had for him. But she had accepted one very important fact.

This baby was coming.

However it had happened, she had been blessed with the gift of a child. She couldn't get rid of it. Erase it as though it had never been.

Giving it up for adoption was just as impossible. Besides, there was no need for that these days. Like she had told Mike, it was the twenty-first century. Single women had babies all the time. No one batted an eye at it anymore.

Too, she was creeping up on thirty years old. Though she hated the expression, there was something to be said for that old "biological clock" argument.

She had a job, she could support her baby and herself.

Maybe she had a job, her brain corrected. She still couldn't believe she had actually stood up to her father. A small, tentative smile curved her lips. For the first time in her life, she had shouted right back at Richard Torrance.

"And you know what?" she asked the baby. "Nothing happened. The Earth didn't open up and swallow me whole. The world didn't stop. He didn't disinherit me or have me thrown out of the office."

Amazing.

Of course, she told herself, she might very well turn up at work tomorrow to find out he *had* fired her. "But don't worry," she said and grimaced as she took a sip of milk, "we'll be okay anyway."

A deep, rumbling roar thundered along the street and Denise looked up, toward the front windows. She knew that sound too well not to recognize it. When the powerful engine sliced off, silence fell over the room.

"Daddy's here," she muttered and pushed herself to her feet.

Walking to the door, she reached for the brass knob and paused before turning it. Was she ready to talk to him? Was she ready to tell him that she would be keeping their child and raising it alone?

Well, why not? she asked herself. She had already faced down her father for the first time ever and survived it. How much harder could it be to talk to Mike?

"Come on, Denise," he said from the other side of the door. "I know you're there. I went by your office. Your secretary told me you went home."

He had gone to the office? She tried to imagine it—an angry biker facing down a room full of secretaries and accountants.

"Dammit, Denise," he continued, his voice deepening. "I have to see you."

Her heartbeat jumped into triple time. Deliberately, she tried to regain control of herself as she turned the knob and pulled the door open. "Hello, Mike."

He didn't wait for an invitation. He stepped into the house, closed the door behind him and faced her.

"When were you going to call me?" he asked. "It's been five days."

"I know," she said and turned her back on him to walk into the living room. As she hurried to the couch, she tried not to look at the floor. The floor where they had made love so passionately that they had created a new life. "I'm sorry, but I needed some time."

He stopped just inside the room. His gaze drifted across the carpet and she felt a flush of heat rise up inside her. He was doing it deliberately. Trying to remind her of that incredible night. It was working.

"What happened to our original agreement?" he asked quietly.

"What agreement?"

"To make decisions *together?* As *friends?*"

She did remember that agreement. But things had changed. They weren't friends. They weren't lovers anymore, either. So, what did that leave? Parents?

"I've already made a decision," she said and took a deep breath to steady her racing pulse.

"Really?" He folded his arms over his chest, braced his feet wide apart and asked, "Do I get to know what it is?"

"I'm keeping the baby."

A heartbeat of time passed and she thought she saw a flicker of relief cross his face, but it was gone so quickly, she couldn't be sure.

"Good," he said.

"You approve?"

"Hell, yes. I approve. It's *my* kid we're talking about, here."

A shiver raced through Denise. Whatever he felt about her, he clearly cared about his child. Would he eventually fight her for it?

He glanced down at the stack of books on the floor and one black eyebrow lifted as he noted a particular title. With a few quick steps, Mike crossed the room, bent down and picked up the book in question. *"Being a Single Parent?"* he asked.

She heard the ice in his voice and fought it with some coolness of her own. "I thought I should start studying."

"On how to raise my baby alone?"

"Mike…"

"No, Denise, it's my turn to talk now." He dropped the book onto the fallen pile and walked to the sofa. Standing in front of her, he continued. "I'm not going to let you walk out of my life without a backward glance."

"Don't do this, Mike. We both know that getting married isn't the answer."

"How do we know that?" he shouted, frustration straining his voice. "You won't talk to me about it. What the hell is so awful about marrying me?"

She scooted farther down the couch, then stood up, a good three feet away from him. She couldn't seem to think straight when he was close to her and if she ever needed to be able to think, now was the time.

"Mike…" she began, and tried to sound reasonable. "We have nothing in common. You said so yourself on that very first night. You said you didn't want anything that came tied up in a neat little package."

"Quit throwing my own words back at me."

"But they're good words, Mike. They make more sense than what you're saying now."

"Things have changed, Denise."

"What? The baby?"

"Of *course* the baby."

"That's not a good enough reason to get married, Mike. In fact, it's a lousy reason to do it."

"Ordinarily," he hedged, "maybe I'd agree with that. But not now."

"Why?"

Couldn't he see how hard he was making everything? Why couldn't he just go away and let her find a way to live without him?

"Because I care for you, dammit!"

Her gaze locked with his. "Me?" She squeezed the words past a tight throat. "Or your baby?"

"Both of you." He took a long step toward her, but she moved back, staying out of his reach. "Why is that so hard to believe?"

"Because," she said softly, "before we knew about the baby, there was no talk about forever. In fact, I think you said something about 'just two grown-ups who share something incredible.'"

"Was I lying?"

She paused and gave him a sad smile. "No, you weren't. But that's not enough, either."

"Denise, I know you love me."

She inhaled sharply and felt the sting of tears in her eyes. "I never said that."

"Yeah, you did," he said quietly. "Once. In your sleep. The night before we found out about the baby."

One tear escaped from the corner of her eye and rolled along her cheek. She reached up and brushed it away. "Sleep talking doesn't count."

"Fine," he whispered. "Say it now. Or deny it."

Chapter 10

Mike held his breath. If she *did* deny it, he didn't have a clue what his next move would be. Odd, that a man who had never wanted love, now found himself hoping to God that he would hear those three words.

"Fine," she said and her voice cracked. "I love you."

Relief crashed over him like a tidal wave.

"But it doesn't matter," she said quickly, shattering the fragile sense of hope building in his chest.

"Of course it matters." He took another step toward her, but she shook her head, warding him off. "When you come down to it, that's *all* that matters."

She laughed shortly. A small, grim chuckle that sent a chill of foreboding up Mike's spine.

"No, it's not, Mike," she said in a strangled tone.

"What are you talking about?"

"I won't make the mistake my mother did," she blurted. "I won't marry the wrong man."

"The wrong man? What's that supposed to mean?"

Pacing now, she marched back and forth across the room and Mike's gaze followed her every step. He noted the tension in her body and wanted to go to her. But first he had to know what he was fighting against.

"My parents," she muttered. "They were miserable together. Oh, my mother loved him, but that wasn't enough to make either of them happy. He should never have gotten married. My father wasn't *meant* to marry and have a family." She turned her head to look at him. "Just like you."

"Wait a minute." It was one thing to be hanged for your own sins...but he wasn't about to be strung up because her father was an ass.

"No. You said from the beginning that you didn't want love. Or a family." She took a deep, shuddering breath.

Damn, he had said way too much that was now coming back to haunt him. "I was wrong."

She shook her head. "No, you were honest. Which is more than you're being now."

That stung. He was being as truthful with her as he knew how to be. Fine, maybe he wouldn't have leapt at marriage before he had known about the baby. But situations change. People change—if they wanted to badly enough.

"You're talking about love and marriage and the only reason you're proposing is because of the baby."

Her features tight, her eyes sparkled with a sheen of tears he knew she had no intention of surrendering to.

"Fine, maybe that's true. Maybe I did propose because of

the baby. But dammit, Denise, that's not saying I would never have proposed."

"Like I said," she whispered. "You're not being honest now. Not with me. Not with yourself."

Honesty wasn't always what it was cracked up to be. He had seen a lot of people destroyed by truths that should have stayed dead and buried. But blast it, if she wanted it, she would have it.

"Honest?" he snapped. "You want honest? All right, honey, here's honest." He knew he should shut up now, but he couldn't. Words he had kept locked away inside him for almost ten years came pouring out in a flood of frustration. "Back when Uncle Sam deployed me and a few hundred thousand of my closest friends to the desert, I had a chance to see love work. Up close and personal. In fact, I saw enough to convince me that loving *anybody* was a one-way ticket to pain."

"What are you talking about?"

"I'm talking about watching kids risking their lives, never knowing when they lay down to sleep if they'd get up in the morning." He rubbed one hand across his jaw as memories tumbled into his mind. Memories he had worked hard at forgetting. "Those same kids lived from mail call to mail call. Grabbing at letters from their *loved ones* like they were the last life raft leaving the *Titanic*."

"Mike…"

He ignored her and started pacing himself, unable to hold still under the barrage of images rushing through his brain. "You wanted to hear this," he said angrily and wasn't sure if his anger was directed at her or himself. Either way, it was too late to stop the flood of memories and way past time that he dealt with them. "After mail call, I watched those same kids—*soldiers,* dammit—break down and cry because somebody back home decided that their *love* wasn't as strong as they had thought. Wives, husbands, sweethearts, it didn't matter." He snapped her a look and wasn't assuaged by the glitter of pain in her eyes. "Love destroyed all of them more completely than any enemy's bullet could have."

His features tight and pale, he said brokenly, "Love isn't only a gift, Denise. It can be the most powerful weapon in the world."

"Mike…"

He shook his head and spoke quickly to cut her off. "It wasn't just the Dear John or Dear Jane letters. Hell, a soldier practically *expects* those damn things." A bitter smile lifted one corner of his mouth briefly. "Amazing how quickly *love* fades when it has to cross a few thousand miles."

She took a step closer and one tear escaped to roll slowly down her cheek.

Mike kept talking. "The worst was seeing young men and women die and knowing that somewhere back home, someone they loved would die, too. Not a nice, clean death in battle. But a long, slow death from a wound too deep to heal."

"So," she said softly, "you vowed to never love anyone."

"Yeah." He pulled in a long breath, surprised that now that he had actually voiced his fears out loud, they were a lot less intimidating. Looking into her blue eyes, he added, "Then I met you."

"Don't, Mike."

"Denise, people can change their minds, you know."

"Their minds, but not their souls."

"What's that supposed to mean?"

"It means that my parents had things in common. They liked the same things. Knew the same people. Shared the same world and they couldn't make it work!" She faced him, her fingers plucking at the material of her gray gym shorts. "What chance would you and I have?"

Before he could speak, she rushed on, tears raining down her face. "Look at us, Mike. *Really* look. I'm an accountant. You're a biker. I like my life neat and orderly. You don't even get *haircuts!* What chance would our *baby* have? I won't bring a child up in the kind of home where I was raised." She shook her head fiercely. "I won't do it."

Wounded by her outburst, he realized that he did love her. Desperately. It was the only explanation for the pain blossoming inside him.

Still, he tried to be calm. "Your own arguments are working against you here, Denise."

"Huh?"

"You said your folks had things in common and their marriage didn't work. Well, just maybe people need to bring a few differences into a marriage."

She shook her head, stubbornly unconvinced. He couldn't believe that he was going to lose her, not because of something *he* did, but because of the mess her parents had made out of their lives.

"You know, lady?" he said and started for her. "Maybe it's time you realized your parents made their mistakes. You can't go back and change them by refitting your life. Instead, maybe it's time you thought about being adult enough to risk making your own mistakes."

She glared at him through her tears, but he refused to be swayed by the bruised look in her eyes. He was fighting for both of them here and it looked as though he would be fighting alone.

"You and I could build something together, Denise. Something special for us *and* our kids. But you won't even give us a chance."

"Mike, you would hate living in my world."

He put his hands on her shoulders and felt her trembling.

"You're just not a suit and tie kind of guy," she went on, "and there are functions that we would have to attend. Can't you see that I'm trying to do us both a favor?"

"So you're willing to walk away from us over a suit?"

"It's not the suit itself," she whispered, looking up into his eyes. "It's everything. I like being a part of your world, Mike. The motorcycle, O'Doul's, everything. But I can't stay there. I have a life, too. One you would hate."

"Let me be the judge of that, okay?"

She sighed.

"At least give us a chance, Denise." As an idea blossomed in his mind, he started talking even faster. "Just because your mother fell in love with the wrong man, that doesn't mean that you have, too."

She sniffed and let her head drop to his chest. Wrapping his arms around her, he held her tight, loving the feel of having her close against him again. Dammit, he wasn't going to lose her. Not now.

Not when he had finally realized that what had started as a wild, intense flirtation had become good old-fashioned *love*.

"Go out with me tonight," he said softly.

"Mike…"

"I'll take care of everything," he said. "Just wear your best dress." He pulled his head back and looked down at her. One black eyebrow lifted as he added, "I'm partial to that blue number you wore the first night we went to O'Doul's."

She sniffed again, this time on a half smile. "You are, huh?"

"Yeah," he said and just the thought of seeing her in that dress again was enough to get his body up and ready. "That night, I thought I might have to kill a couple of my oldest pals just for staring."

It was a watery smile, but a smile.

"All right," she agreed. "Tonight."

"Six o'clock," he said and bent to plant a quick kiss on her lips. He tasted her tears and vowed right then to never let her cry again. "Be ready."

The phone rang moments before six.

"Denise?"

She tensed at the sound of Richard Torrance's voice at the other end of the line. "Hello, Father."

"I…" He cleared his throat brusquely. "About this afternoon," he said.

Denise's fingers tightened on the receiver. Had he called to fire her personally?

"You said you hadn't been well lately and I wanted you to know that if you need to take a few days to regain your strength, I'll have someone cover for you."

Denise pulled the receiver back and stared at it blankly for a moment. Then she tucked it against her ear again. "Thank you, Father, but that won't be necessary."

"Fine, fine…" After another long pause he began again. "As for the other nonsense about you leaving the firm—"

"It wasn't nonsense, Father." She squared her shoulders hoping for courage.

"Certainly it was. This is the *Torrance* Accounting firm. You are a Torrance. I'll hear no more about it."

Surprised, she held her tongue, wondering what might be next.

"Now," he said, "as to the annual cocktail party for our clients…"

Denise smiled ruefully. Back to business. "Everything is arranged for next Saturday night."

"No loose ends?"

"None."

"Very well," Richard said, then paused. "I was going to suggest that you have Patrick Ryan escort you."

Denise gasped, more from surprise than the outrage that took a moment to build.

In that moment, her father continued. "His vacation ends this week, he has a good future with the firm…."

"No, Father."

"I beg your pardon?"

"No." She stiffened slightly, readying herself for battle. Amazing that her father was even concerning himself with her escort, she thought. "I'm going alone."

"I just thought…"

"I appreciate it," she interrupted. Strangely enough, she *did*. As far as she knew, it was the first time her father had ever taken an interest in her life. "But frankly I'd prefer to be alone."

True. If she couldn't have Mike, she didn't want a replacement. Not even an identical one.

"Of course it's entirely up to you," he conceded and Denise could hardly believe it. "As to the other, will you be coming in to work tomorrow?"

"Yes. But as I said earlier, I might be a bit late."

"Take all the time you need," he said and hung up without a goodbye.

Denise held the receiver limply in her hand. She heard the hum of the dial tone as she stared at the phone. With her free hand, she reached up and rubbed her forehead. What was happening? Everything was changing so fast, she could hardly keep up.

Mike, talking about love and marriage.

Even *more* mind-boggling, her father, calling to inquire about her health? Trying to set her up on a date?

The doorbell rang and she jumped to her feet. Setting the phone down on its cradle, she snatched up her purse and walked to the front door. She had been so preoccupied with her father's peculiar behavior, she hadn't even noticed the sound of Mike's motorcycle.

A moment later, she knew why.

"A car?" she said, mentally cataloging yet another change in the universe. Denise looked up into Mike's face and saw him grin.

"Not *just* a car," he said. "*My* car."

"But you said you didn't do cars."

"I also said people can change."

"When did you…?"

"This afternoon," he interrupted and stroked the tip of one finger down the line of her jaw. "It's a BMW," he said unnecessarily. "Good family car. Safe. Practical."

Family. Safe. *Practical?* Mike?

She stepped out onto the porch and he reached behind her to close and lock her front door. Taking her elbow in a firm grip, he guided her down the front steps and along the walk to where the shiny new, candy apple red Beemer waited.

As he opened the car door for her, he said, "Safe and practical was for you. The racing red was for me."

"Mike, I don't know what to say."

"Good."

She glanced up at him and noted for the first time that he wasn't wearing a T-shirt, either. Not exactly a suit and tie, the white linen shirt with a banded collar and sharply pleated black slacks looked wonderful on him. His hair was pulled neatly into his ever present ponytail and the smile on his face sent her heartbeat into overdrive.

"Now," he told her, "slide in and buckle up."

Dinner was a blur, though she did recall the five-star restaurant on a cliff overlooking Dana Point. If it had meant her life however, she wouldn't have been able to testify to what she had eaten.

Now, she sat in a balcony box at the Orange County Performing Arts Center, watching their production of *Carousel*. The stylishly built hall was thrown into shadows, but for the brightly lit stage illuminating the performers. Beside her in the darkness, Mike lifted one hand and ran his index finger around the inside of his collar. When he caught her eye on him, he shrugged, gave her a smile, then returned his gaze to the stage.

Denise's mind was whirling with too much information. Too many changes had happened too quickly for her to take it all in. Her father's odd behavior. Her surprise pregnancy and the apparent redemption of the bad boy she loved.

She threw a sideways glance at Mike and found herself wondering if it could work between them. Just looking at him made her toes curl. But was that enough? Was it even enough that he cared for her, too?

Love alone couldn't make a relationship, could it? She rubbed her forehead again as the familiar music from the play swelled up into the darkened balconies. Her stomach in knots, Denise tightly folded her hands together in her lap and told herself to stop thinking. At least for the moment.

Mike had asked for this one night and she would give it to him. In the morning, she could face the same unanswerable questions again.

Decision made, she turned her attention back to the play. Silently, she watched the sad story of bad boy Billy Bigelow and the good girl who should never have married him.

"Why are we back here?" she asked as Mike pulled the BMW into his driveway.

He glanced at her, shrugged and smiled. "Thought you might like to take another bike ride with me."

Ever since the end of the play, she had been way too quiet for his peace of mind. He had hoped to prove to her that their worlds could meet. So what if he didn't use the Wave Cutter box at the Arts Center often? He would if it was important to her.

Hell, he could even get used to driving a car.

But he couldn't get used to the fact that she was so ready to walk away from him. A ride on his bike, where they would be forced into close contact, could be just what he needed.

He opened the car door, went around to her side and offered her his hand. She took it and stood up beside him.

"Mike," she said.

He didn't like the tone of her voice. It already carried the hint of goodbye in it.

"Come on," he said quickly and started for the garage. They walked up the dark, narrow drive and he released her hand to open one half of the double doors. Automatically, he stepped inside and yanked the chain that brought the lone, dim light bulb to life.

He dug into his pocket for the key, straddled the bike, then turned the powerful engine on. Looking at her, standing to one side of him, his heart began to thud painfully against his ribs.

How had this happened? How had love caught him so unaware? And so quickly? But more importantly, how could he convince her to take the risk that he was only now ready to take himself?

The rumble and vibration of the bike's engine trembled up his legs and back. She stepped closer to him and in the vague light of the overhead bulb, he watched her features tighten with a sadness that made him want to scream his frustration.

Instead, he reached out for her, grabbed her hand and pulled her in close. Dragging her head down to his, he planted his mouth on hers and gave her a kiss that demanded a response. She didn't fail him.

Returning his kiss with a desperate passion, her arms slid around his neck even as she pressed herself against him. Lifting her easily, Mike pulled her onto the bike in front of him. Perched half on his lap, half on the narrow seat, Denise moved in closer, holding him as tightly as she would have a life preserver thrown into choppy seas.

Beneath them, the engine grumbled loudly, sending vibrations bouncing along their spines. Mike's hands moved up and down her back in long caresses designed to drive her body into a fever pitch. His own body, hard and ready, pushed heavily against the fly of his trousers and Mike groaned from the back of his throat as she scooted around on his lap.

His hands dropped to her hips where he lifted the hem of that incredible dress. Bunching the fabric beneath his hands, his palms slid across the tops of her thigh-high stockings to the narrow band of her silk bikini panties.

The feel of her bare skin inflamed him and his already rock hard body tightened another notch.

"Denise," he whispered when he tore his mouth from hers.

Her head fell back on her neck as one of his hands moved between her legs to stroke that most sensitive piece of flesh. Through the sheer, silk fabric of her panties, he felt her heat and knew that he had to have her.

Now.

Chapter 11

He kissed the pulse point at the base of her throat and Denise arched into him, tilting her head to one side, welcoming his kiss.

His fingers moved again at her center and her thigh muscles tightened. The rumbling vibrations of the motorcycle's engine added their own trembling torture.

Denise pushed herself against his hand, letting him know silently that she wanted him as badly as he did her. It didn't matter that they were in his garage. Perched precariously on a motorcycle. All that mattered now was him and this moment when she felt so alive.

"I need you, Mike," she said on a sigh.

He groaned heavily and almost immediately, she felt the lace of her navy blue panties rip. Mike tore the fragile material from her body and Denise's hips rocked gently in an age-old invitation.

"Hold on, baby," he said and she felt him move to open the zipper of his slacks. Then his hands were on her hips, lifting her, guiding her to his hard, ready strength.

She gasped as he slowly lowered her body onto his. Denise braced herself with her hands on his shoulders and opened her eyes to stare into the shadowy green depths of Mike's gaze.

Squirming in his grasp, she tried to take more of his length inside her. He filled her so completely, she wasn't sure anymore that they could ever be separated. Her knees on his thighs, his hands at her hips, she moved on him, raising and lowering herself again and again, abandoning then reclaiming him as her own.

Her hips twisted, sending new spasms of delight spiraling within her. Mike's strong fingers kneaded her bottom. Her legs trembled and her hands tightened on his shoulders. He moved within her again and Denise smiled in the dim light. She watched his eyes slide shut as her hips rocked in a slow, rhythmic motion.

When the first tingling sensation started, low and deep, Denise's breath caught and held. Tension built slowly, creeping from her body into his as completion neared.

The heavy rasp of his breath sounded in her ear and she felt her own lungs straining for the cool night air whispering into the garage through the open door. An incredible tightness grabbed at her. Denise's eyes squeezed shut as she concentrated on the sensations, willing them to come faster, harder.

As the first convulsive climax ripped through her, she ground her hips against him. Wrapping her arms tightly around his neck, she muffled a shout by burying her head in the curve of his shoulder.

Seconds later, she felt Mike shudder, heard him whisper her name as he emptied himself into her.

The hard, physical release left them both breathless, locked together, clinging only to each other.

Thirty minutes later, they were standing on her front porch. He took the key she gave him, opened her door and pushed it wide.

"Can I come in?" he asked.

"Sure," Denise said softly. She led the way inside, dropping her purse on a small table in the entryway before continuing on into the living room. She hit the switch plate on the wall as she went in and instantly small puddles of light erupted all around the room.

Denise walked to the sofa and plopped onto the cushions. Mike, she noticed, didn't sit down.

She looked up at him. "Mike, what happened a little while ago doesn't change anything."

"What do you mean?" His jaw tightened.

"I mean," she said and leaned back into the overstuffed fabric behind her, "sex isn't the issue here. We already know that we get along fine on that score." Absently, she smoothed the skirt of her dress across her knees. "But we have to think about the baby. What's best for her."

"What's best for the baby is having two parents."

"I agree with you."

"You do?" Both eyebrows lifted in surprise.

"Of course. Two loving parents are always preferable to one."

His gaze narrowed, sharpened on her. "Then what's the problem?"

"The problem is, you want us to be *married* and parents."

"You don't." It wasn't a question.

She shook her head and chewed at her bottom lip for a moment before speaking again. "I've been thinking about this all night…well, since the end of the play, anyway."

"Thinking about what?"

"What to do. How to handle this." She pushed up from the couch, kicked her heels off and started walking aimlessly around the room. "I don't want to keep you from your child."

"Oh, thanks."

She ignored the sarcasm and said what she felt she had to say. "And I don't want to stop seeing you, either."

"So, what's your plan?"

Denise turned around to look at him from across the room. "That we keep things as they are. Like you said when we first went out. We're two people who share something incredible…I'm not ready to give that up."

"Perfect," he muttered. "Do you remember *everything* I say so that you can throw it at me at some later date?"

"Mike."

"Dammit, Denise," he shouted, "I don't want to be a visitor in my child's *or* your life." Shoving both hands into his pockets, he glared at her. "I never thought I would say this to anyone—in fact, I had *planned* to never say it. But I *love* you."

She sucked in a gulp of air past the knot in her throat.

"I want us to be together. A family."

Shaking her head at him, she said, "If we're unhappy, the baby will be, too."

"Who says we'll be unhappy?" he demanded, pulling his hands from his pockets to throw them wide, helplessly.

"I told you about my parents."

"Forget about your folks and the stupid mistakes they

made, will you?" His voice sounded raw with pain she knew she was causing.

"How can I forget? I grew up in a house where unhappiness was a way of life. *No* child should have to live like that. Especially not *my* child."

"Denise," he said through gritted teeth, "we make our own happiness. *Or* misery." Moving quickly, he walked toward her. He kept talking as he went, clearly trying to control a rapidly rising temper. "Maybe your father *was* a jerk. And maybe your mom let him get away with it."

"What?"

He snorted a choked laugh that held no humor. "If my dad tried to ignore my mother, she'd get in his face and shout until she had his attention. Same goes for him." As he got closer, she took a step backward, but bumped into the sliding glass doors and knew she couldn't go any farther. Mike stopped right beside her. Looking down into her eyes, he said, "Happiness doesn't just *happen*."

"I know that," she snapped, looking for a way past him and coming up empty. "But there's no point in stacking the deck against yourself, is there?"

"How is loving each other a *bad* thing?" he asked tightly.

"It's not bad, necessarily," Denise muttered and took the direct approach. She shoved at his chest until he backed up. Stepping past him, she walked to the far wall and stopped to look at him from a safe distance. "It's just not enough."

"There are no guarantees, Denise. Not for anybody."

She reached up and pushed her hair back from her face.

In seconds, he had crossed the room. His hands warm and strong on her shoulders, he waited until she met his gaze to speak again. "Who are you scared of, Denise? Me? Or you?"

She pulled away from him and shifted her gaze from his. Unwilling to admit to fear and unable to deny it, she said, "I'm not afraid. I'm just trying to think with more than my hormones."

"That's it." He grabbed her elbow and turned her around to face him again. "This is all bull, Denise. All of it. If you remember everything I said, remember this, too. Sometimes you have to stop thinking and just *feel.*"

She laughed and winced at the raw, scraping sound of her own voice. "Feel? Didn't you watch the same play I did tonight?"

"What are you talking about *now?*"

"*Carousel.* Weren't you paying attention?"

He released her, shook his head and stared at her, waiting.

She had felt it all through the play's production. It had been almost like a sign. Fate, reminding her just what could happen if the wrong two people fell in love. She had tried to ignore it, but she couldn't. Denise was only surprised that Mike hadn't drawn the same conclusions.

"It was right there on the stage, Mike. It was as if someone were trying to tell us something." She wrapped her arms about herself and hung on tight. "Billy Bigelow was the wrong man for her. But she married him anyway. She let her feelings get in the way. And look what happened? He died and she mourned him forever!"

"I don't believe this, Denise." He looked up at the ceiling for a moment, then shifted his gaze back to hers. "It was a play! Fiction."

She shook her head firmly. "No, it was a sign. Don't you get it, Mike? We're just like the players in *Carousel.*"

"You're way overreacting."

"No, I'm not. You just don't want to see the similarities between us and the couple in the play."

"I am *not* Billy Bigelow, dammit! And this is real life! Our decisions aren't based on whatever some fool playwright jots down on a sleepless night." He grabbed her arms again and yanked her to him. His hands held her firmly but gently. She sensed the leashed power in him and heard his anger in his voice. She looked up into fierce green eyes. "We're real people, Denise. With real feelings and real brains to sort out our problems. We can love and be loved without a script."

"Mike, I know the difference between reality and fantasy, but you have to admit—"

"No! I don't have to admit anything beyond the fact that you're driving me out of my mind. You seem determined to push me away no matter what I say or do. I've listened to your theories and your fears and tried to be patient." He sucked in a gulp of air and exhaled just as quickly. "God, Denise, don't you think all of this scares the hell out of me, too? I've faced down bullets and screaming, heavily armed enemies with more confidence…but I'm standing here telling you that I love you. I love our baby and now *you* have to choose."

"How can I?"

Mike looked down into those wide blue eyes and saw the fear and confusion written there. He didn't know how to reach her. How to get past the years of hurt she had experienced as a child.

Maybe though, he wasn't supposed to. Maybe, he suddenly thought, it had to come from her. Denise had to be the one to put her past behind her and come to him on her own. If he pushed her into it, leaving her no way out, she would never *really* be with him.

It would take every ounce of his strength to walk out of there. But he wasn't going to spend the rest of his life paying for the crimes of her father.

Lifting his hands, he cupped her face, letting his thumbs stroke her cheekbones as his gaze drifted over her features slowly, lovingly. He was taking a huge chance here and he knew it. But sometimes in war, you had to let the other guy think you were out of the battle. Make your opponent come to you.

"I'm not going to go along with your little plan, Denise."

She blinked a sheen of moisture from her eyes and his gaze locked on a solitary tear tracking down her cheek. His heart felt as though a giant fist were squeezing it.

"I won't be a visitor in my child's life and I won't be *just* the man who shares your bed."

Her bottom lip quivered and he felt her trembling. Fiercely, he steeled himself against surrendering to the urge to hold her, comfort her.

"I want it all. I want you and the baby and me, living in my grandparents' house at the beach." He paused to take a breath and smiled gently at her, despite the tears swimming in her eyes. "I want us to have the kind of life they had. I want to fall asleep every night with you in my arms and then wake up to your kiss." His fingers smoothed her hair back from her face and he felt, more than saw, her turn her head into his touch. "I love you," he said again and realized that it was getting easier to say all the time. In fact, he enjoyed saying it. Wanted to spend the rest of his life saying it to her.

"But what happens to us is up to you now. You have to decide if you're going to keep running your life according to other people's mistakes."

He bent down and pressed a soft, gentle kiss to her still trembling lips. Before he straightened up again, he added, "We deserve a life together, Denise. You, me and our child. You can give us that life."

"Mike—"

"Shh…" His thumb stroked across her mouth, effectively silencing her. "It all comes down to love, baby. Love and trust. I know you love me. But do you trust me?"

"I—"

"It's up to you, baby," he said, cutting her off because he couldn't risk hearing her decision now, before she had had her time to *think*. He sealed his last words with a kiss that left him aching for all the things she was denying him.

Before his courage could desert him, Mike turned and left the condo. He closed the door behind him and took the pansy-lined walkway in several long strides. Climbing aboard the motorcycle he had brought her home on, he jammed the key in the ignition then pulled his helmet on.

When the engine leapt into life, he twisted the accelerator on the handlebars, shattering the quiet on the street with an angry roar. Tossing a last glance at the condo, he told himself that this was all his fault. If he hadn't been trying to impress her, he never would have taken her to the Performing Arts Center and she never would have thought about *Carousel*.

"*Carousel,* for God's sake," he muttered in disgust. "First time I've used that box in years and they're playing *Carousel*." He flicked the kickstand up into place and tried to ignore the memory of making love with Denise on that very bike only an hour or so ago. "Damn plays. Why couldn't it have been *The King and I*?"

Four days later, Denise walked down the hall of the Torrance Accounting firm, trying desperately to think of anything else but Mike. It wasn't working. He hadn't called. He hadn't come by.

And she missed him so much it hurt.

"Mr. Ryan called," her secretary said as Denise walked past her desk.

She stopped dead.

Hope rushed into her heart.

She had tried to keep busy. Working on the firm's upcoming cocktail party had given her enough details to worry about that her brain was constantly active. But in those occasional moments of peace, Mike's image instantly leapt into her mind. As it did every time she tried to sleep.

Haunted by thoughts of what could be as much as by her memories, Denise hardly knew which way to turn anymore. The only certain thing in her life was that she had a baby coming. A baby it was up to her to protect and provide for.

And soon, everyone would know it.

The dizziness had passed but she was just beginning to experience the thrills of morning sickness. In another few months, the baby would be showing. Well before then, she had to make one of the most difficult decisions of her life.

To risk being hurt by Mike—or to live with the pain of being without him.

"Ms. Torrance?" the older woman asked. "Are you all right?"

Denise forced a smile. "Yes, Velma, I'm fine thanks. You said Mike Ryan called?"

Her secretary smiled knowingly and shook her head. "No, *Patrick* Ryan."

"Oh." The rush of exhilaration slipped away as if it had never been. She should have known better. Mike had made himself perfectly clear on their last night together. He wouldn't be calling her again.

He had thrown the ball into her court.

"What did Patrick want?" she asked, though at the moment, she didn't really care what Mike's twin was up to.

"It was very odd," the older woman said. "He's taking a three-week leave of absence. Asked me to have you inform your father."

"A leave of absence?"

"That's what he said."

After almost a four-week vacation, he needed a leave of absence?

"Did he leave a number?"

"Nope," the secretary shook her head again. "Just said he would keep in touch."

Denise scowled to herself. Maybe Patrick wasn't as different from his brother as she had thought. "Fine, but the next time he calls, get a number."

"Yes, ma'am."

Continuing on down the hall, Denise muttered disgustedly about men in general and Ryan men in particular.

The secretary's phone rang several minutes later. Velma smiled when she recognized the man on the other end.

"Hi, Velma," Mike said. "How is she today?"

"She seems fine. A little pale, maybe. Distracted. But busy."

Pale. Mike frowned thoughtfully and sat back on his couch, putting his feet up on the low coffee table in front of him. He hated not being with Denise. Knowing firsthand how she was feeling. But until he made her see what they had together, the best he could get was daily updates from a secretary with romance in her soul.

It wasn't enough, dammit. He had hoped to hear from Denise before this, but she was just stubborn enough to wait until after the baby was born to come to her senses. Maybe what she needed was one more push in the right direction.

"Velma," he said thoughtfully, "tell me more about this cocktail party you mentioned yesterday."

Chapter 12

"I can't believe Patrick Ryan would be so unprofessional as this," Richard Torrance muttered blackly. "To simply take a leave of absence with no thought as to how it will affect this firm."

Denise sat in the deep leather chair opposite her father's desk. "Obviously something he hadn't counted on came up."

"Something more important than his responsibilities here? To us? To his clients?"

She had been listening to her father rant now for more than ten minutes. Her head hurt. Her stomach was upset. And if she had Patrick Ryan in front of her, she would kick him in the shins. Some friend he was, leaving her to break the news of his absence.

Mike never would have done that.

She blinked, surprised as that thought shot through her mind. It was true. Mike would have called Richard Torrance personally and told him straight out that he needed some personal time. And if her father had dared lecture him on his responsibilities, Mike would have quit on the spot.

He wasn't the kind of man to sit back and let life happen. He rushed out to meet it, refusing to be put off by dangers or fears.

It would have been interesting to see Mike and her father go head-to-head. Odd, but she had the feeling that once over the initial shock, Richard Torrance would probably like Mike. At the very least, he would respect him.

She smiled to herself. One thing she couldn't fault Mike on was his courage. He had even had the nerve and will to admit that he loved her—despite all of the ridiculous arguments she kept throwing at him.

Ridiculous?

She frowned, then slowly nodded to herself.

Yes. Denise sat up straighter in the chair. Absently, she noticed that her father was still talking, complaining about Patrick. But she didn't care. Something was happening here. Something monumental.

Looking past her father, she stared out the tall windows at the ocean beyond. On the horizon, a low bank of thunderheads gathered. A hard, cold wind made the sea choppy, but still there were at least a dozen sailboats sprinkled across the deep blue waves.

Others, unafraid to take a chance.

She swallowed hard. Her heartbeat skittered, then began to beat in a quick double time. In the pit of her stomach, a curl of worry unwound, but she deliberately fought it down.

It was time, she decided suddenly, that she stood up and

took her chances like the rest of the world. Time to stop hiding behind old fears and older wounds.

These last four days without Mike had finally taught her something. Strange that she hadn't even acknowledged it until now. Four days of emptiness were quickly balanced against the time spent with Mike.

The scales were easy to read. Even to a woman who had managed to keep blinders on for most of her life. Another smile crossed her face briefly. It didn't matter what her parents had done with their lives. It only mattered what she had found with Mike. What they could create together.

If she hadn't waited too long.

Denise jumped up from her chair.

"Where are you going?" her father barked.

"I have to leave early today," she said as she walked hurriedly to the door.

"Just wait one minute, young woman. You can't leave yet. We haven't finished—"

"Father," she said as she turned to face him. "I don't have time to explain. I'll tell you all about it another time, all right?"

"Tell me now, blast it."

The tone of voice was the same, sharp commanding tone she had always responded to. Until lately.

"No."

His mouth opened and closed rapidly, but he didn't say a word. Amazing. All she had ever really had to do was to speak up to him. Why had she always been so afraid of doing it? She had wanted him to love her. To care about her.

But how could he have? He didn't even know who she was. She had spent most of her life trying to be whoever Richard

Torrance wanted her to be. Too afraid to be the person she was for fear it wasn't good enough.

Mike had been wrong about one thing. It wasn't about trust. It was about courage. The courage to ask for what you wanted and then to fight to keep it.

She wondered now if things might have been different— if her *life* might have been different—if her mother had demanded Richard Torrance's love and respect.

"Did you love my mother?" she asked abruptly.

"What?" A rush of color filled his cheeks as he fell back into his chair. He stared at his daughter as if he didn't recognize her.

He probably didn't.

"It's an easy question, Father. Did you love mother?"

He looked at her for a long, silent minute. Denise tensed, not sure what she would hear.

"Yes," he said. "I did."

Relief washed through her. "Why didn't you ever spend time with us?"

He scowled and shifted his gaze from hers. Ducking his head, he picked up a sheaf of papers from his desk and busied his hands by straightening the pile.

But she had finally managed to ask the question. Now she had to hear the answer. "Father, why? Was it because of me?"

He dropped the papers and looked directly at her. Obviously horrified, he blurted, "Certainly not. You were a child, Denise. What was between your mother and I had nothing to do with you."

Nothing to do with her? At twenty-nine years old, she had made most of the decisions in her life based on what she had seen growing up.

She came back into the room, placed her palms on the edge

of his desk and leaned towards him. "It had *everything* to do with me. Don't you think I ever wondered why you were never at home? Why Mother was always so unhappy?"

His features twisted into a mask of pain and briefly, Denise regretted even opening the subject. But it was finally time to be honest. Long past time, really.

He flattened his palms on the desktop and stared down at the backs of his hands as if fascinated. After a long, thoughtful moment, he said softly, "Your mother was a...*delicate* woman. She seemed to prefer being off by herself." He shook his head slowly, lost in memories. "Whenever I was at home, she was forever fluttering around the house...unable to sit still a minute. Always nervous. Always tense." He sighed heavily. Regret coloring his voice, he added, "My presence seemed to upset her so that I finally just stayed away more and more."

"She loved you."

His gaze lifted to his daughter's. "She never said so."

A deep well of sadness opened inside her. Too late for them. Her parents had missed so much. Neither of them had been willing to talk to the other. To admit the truth of what they felt and to ask for what they needed.

So instead, they had spent their lives together, yet alone.

Denise pushed up from the desk and smiled at the man she had misunderstood for so long. There was no place here for blame. Not anymore. Besides, there had been enough unhappiness between the Torrances. "I love you, too, Father."

She thought she saw a glimmer of moisture in his eyes, but it was so quickly gone, she could have been mistaken.

"Then you'll tell me why you're leaving work in the middle of the day?" he asked, obviously hoping for a change of subject.

She grinned at him. "Nope."

"Denise…"

"I'll talk to you later, Father," she said and left the office, sailing through the open door. She didn't have a moment to lose. She had already wasted four precious days.

"Where is he?" Denise asked out loud as she drove slowly past Mike's house. Again.

In the three days since finally clearing the air with her father, Denise had tried every way she knew to get in touch with Mike. She hadn't been able to find him.

He was never home when she called. Never returned her messages. She dropped by the motorcycle shop only to be told that she had "just missed Mike." He had to be deliberately avoiding her.

Now, here she was, the night of the firm's cocktail party and instead of being at the hotel welcoming their guests, she was cruising a beach neighborhood looking for Mike Ryan.

Her father was going to be furious.

Sighing, Denise turned her car around and headed for the downtown area. She might as well go and face the music. Once she had her father calmed down, she would leave the party and look for Mike again.

If he thought she was going to give up easily, he was mistaken. It might have taken her forever to make up her mind what it was she wanted…but now that she had, she wasn't about to give it up.

Music rushed out through the double glass doors and onto the circular drive outside the Sea Sprite Hotel. Denise stepped out of her car, took the parking slip from the valet and walked toward the entrance.

Crystal chandeliers hung from the ornate ceiling, spilling hundreds of watts of light on the elegantly dressed men and women attending the party. The hotel lobby, sprinkled with tapestry love seats and overstuffed wing chairs had become a meeting place where local businessmen gathered in tight knots exchanging cards.

Denise smiled, nodded to a few of her clients, and kept walking, heading for the stairs and the ballroom on the second floor. The skirt of her red silk dress swung around her knees as she climbed the marble steps, her mind still on the problem of locating Mike.

Why was he doing this? Had he changed his mind? Was he sorry now that he had ever asked her to marry him in the first place?

No. She wouldn't believe that. He loved her. He loved their baby.

Then why was he making himself invisible?

"Denise," Richard Torrance muttered as he hurried to meet his daughter at the head of the stairs. Taking her arm he led her to the edge of the ballroom where several couples were dancing already. "You're late."

"I know." Denise looked past him at the milling crowd. She usually enjoyed these annual parties. But tonight, her heart just wasn't in it. "I had something I had to do."

He waited a heartbeat for an apology that wasn't coming. Then he shook it off and said, "People have been asking for you. You'd better get in there and start mingling. Be sure to speak with Mrs. Rogers about her accounts, she…"

"I'm not staying, Father," Denise interrupted.

"What do you mean, you're not staying? Of *course* you're

staying." He waved one hand at the revelers. "Even Patrick realized that he had a duty to be here."

"Patrick's here?" she asked, looking from her father into the mass of people just beyond the threshold.

"Didn't I just say so?"

"Where?" Denise asked, craning her neck to see over the heads of the people blocking the entrance to the room. Patrick? Patrick had wanted a leave of absence. He wouldn't have returned simply to attend a cocktail party, no matter how important.

Would he?

"He's in there somewhere." Richard paused and pointed at a small group of men. "There. In the gray suit."

Denise looked at the man's back. Short, black hair. Wide shoulders. Nicely tailored suit. It *could* be Patrick, of course. She couldn't be sure until he turned around.

"No more of this *leaving* nonsense, Denise," her father said hotly. "This is the Torrance party. *You* are a Torrance."

Denise smiled at him. "For now," she said.

"What is *that* supposed to mean?"

She kept her gaze fixed on the tall man in gray. Silently willing him to turn and look at her, she went on talking to her father. "You might as well know everything," she said. "Someone asked me to marry him a week ago."

"What?" Confusion settled on Richard's features. "Who?"

She tore her gaze from the man just inside the ballroom and looked directly at the older man standing beside her. Courage, she thought. Taking a deep, steadying breath, she said, "The father of my child."

Richard Torrance's eyes widened until she thought they

might pop from his head. His brow furrowed and bright splotches of color stained his cheeks.

A couple of weeks ago, she would have been terrified. Now, she only hoped he wouldn't have a heart attack or something.

"You're…you're…"

"Pregnant," she finished for him. "With your first grandchild."

His jaw dropped.

Denise patted her father's arm gently. "It's all right *Grandpa,* you'll get used to it."

"Grandpa?"

"The only problem here is," Denise said and shifted her gaze back to the man in gray. He seemed to have drifted a bit closer, though his back was still turned to her. "I don't know if he still wants me."

"And why wouldn't he?" Richard wanted to know.

She threw him a quick smile. "Because I drive him crazy, he says. I kept insisting that we were all wrong for each other. That he was the wrong man for me."

"Well, is he?" Richard demanded.

"No, Father," she said, her gaze locked on the man in gray. "He's the only *right* man for me."

"Well then, he'll do the right thing by you, too."

"Whether he does or not, you should know that I'm going to raise this baby. All alone, if I have to."

"Don't be foolish, Denise," her father snapped, loudly enough that several heads turned in their direction.

She looked up at her father, but before she could speak, she heard a familiar, deep voice say, "You can't talk to her like that."

Denise and her father turned at the same time to watch Patrick Ryan walk up to them, a furious scowl on his features.

"This is *family* business, Patrick," Richard said. "I'll thank you to keep out of it."

A small crowd formed around them.

Denise noticed them, but didn't care. She only had eyes for one man. Mike Ryan, masquerading as his own twin. She watched his jaw twitch with the effort to keep from shouting at her father.

Her gaze moved over him quickly. He had cut his hair, bought a suit and was pretending to be someone he wasn't all for her sake. Shame rippled through her. Because she had been a coward, the man she loved had given up a part of himself to be what he thought she wanted him to be.

"You didn't have to cut the ponytail," she whispered.

"It doesn't matter," he answered, oblivious to the people around them.

"Everything about you matters," she countered and instinctively walked toward him. Reaching up, she pulled his head down close and kissed him. Hard.

Mike fought down the urge to hold her. To grab her to him and keep her so tightly against him that she would never be able to get away again. It had been hell, avoiding her for the last three days. But he'd had to.

They had had to face each other at this cocktail party. With her in her element. He had thought it would be the one sure way to know if she wanted him. But it had been a stupid idea. Nothing was solved. Yes, she was kissing him in front of everyone. But was it only because tonight, he looked the part of the rising young businessman?

Denise finally pulled back from him and looked up into his eyes. He stared down into those blue depths and felt his soul move into hers.

Smiling, she reached for his tie and quickly undid the careful Windsor knot. Then she unbuttoned his collar button and lifted one hand high enough to ruffle her fingers through his perfect haircut.

"I love you," she whispered, speaking directly to his heart. "The *real* you. Motorcycles, black leather, ponytail and all."

A tentative smile lifted one corner of his mouth. "You don't need suits and ties in your life?"

She shook her head "I never want you to change for me, Mike. All I want is for you to love me."

His chest tightened. Pride and love swelled up inside him as he reached up to yank the hated tie from his neck. Tossing it into the air, he grinned. "No problem, baby," he said, through a suddenly dry throat.

"Denise, are you going to tell me what is going on here?" Richard sounded exasperated, but surprisingly calm, all things considered.

"Dad," she announced loudly, taking one of Mike's hands and setting it at her waist, "I'd like you to meet *Mike* Ryan. He owns Ryan's Custom Cycles and is probably the best bike mechanic in the state." She grinned at her father then. "He's also Patrick's brother and the man I'm going to marry—if he'll still have me."

For an answer, Mike spun her around in his arms. Looking deeply into her eyes, he spoke quietly, not caring who heard. "I didn't want to love you, Denise. But now I don't want to live without you." He smoothed his fingertips down the line of her cheek. "Marry me, baby. Marry me and let me love you forever."

Tears swam in her eyes. He held his breath, waiting. When she nodded, he yanked her into his arms and bent his head to claim a kiss designed to sear her soul.

A woman in their audience sighed plaintively.

At last, Mike lifted his head to smile down at his almost wife.

"Custom Cycles, eh?" Richard said, loudly enough to get his soon-to-be son-in-law's attention. "You could probably use a good accounting firm, my boy."

Mike grinned. At least the man had the sense to surrender when there was nothing left to do. Tucking Denise close to his left side, Mike stretched his right hand out to his future father-in-law. As the other man took it in a firm shake, Mike told him, "Thanks. But I've already got a good accountant."

Silly to have waited so long to get married, Denise told herself as she turned to look up into her groom's eyes. But she'd wanted to clear all of her client's business affairs so that she and Mike could take a real honeymoon. Now she and the gorgeous, ponytailed man in the black tuxedo were just four hours away from their flight to Tahiti.

His gaze moved over her hungrily, lovingly and she felt the shock of amazement right down to her toes. Not only did he enjoy the changes her body was going through, this miraculous man actually seemed to find her swollen belly erotic. At that salacious thought, she tightened her grip on the bouquet she still held in her right hand and stretched out her left to Mike, eager to finish the ceremony and start the marriage.

He inhaled sharply as her fingers touched his. His thumb smoothed across her knuckles as the justice of the peace solemnly intoned the words that would bind Mike Ryan to this woman for the rest of his life.

She looked beautiful. Her off-white dress—she'd insisted on ivory—was cinched beneath her breasts and draped lovingly across the mound of his child. A simple wreath of yellow carnations and white daisies encircled her head, making her look like an ancient goddess of summer.

How in the hell had he *ever* gotten this lucky? he wondered and grinned down into blue eyes that held all the answers to every question he'd ever asked. Behind them, a small group of family and friends held their collective breath expectantly as Mike slid a plain gold band onto Denise's finger.

When the deed was done and all was official, they smiled at each other just before Mike gently placed his right hand on their baby. "I swear I will love you both forever," he whispered.

She covered his hand with hers and rose up on her toes. When his mouth claimed hers, Denise realized that marriage was a *very* sexy thing!

Epilogue

"Take it easy, Mr. Torrance." Tina Dolan looked up at the older man pacing around the dimly lit hospital waiting room. "She's only been in there an hour or so. We could be here all night."

"All night?" Richard paled and slumped down onto one of the hard plastic chairs littering the room. "This waiting business was a lot easier when I was a younger man," he mumbled.

The late night quiet was overwhelming. Besides the Dolans and Richard Torrance, there was only a handful of people sprinkled around the big room.

"Talk to him," Tina told her husband. "Take his mind off of things. This has got to be hardest on him, waiting for word about his only daughter."

Bob Dolan never had to be asked more than once to start talking. Getting up, he walked across the room and took the chair next to the other man. "Y'know," he said, "I've been thinking about setting up some retirement accounts for me and Tina."

Richard glanced at him from the corner of his eye.

"Not gettin' any younger, y'know. Got to get a hedge on those 'golden years'."

"That's a very good idea," Richard said and tossed an anxious glance at the double doors leading to the maternity ward.

"So, what do you think we ought to invest in? Have any good ideas?" Bob prompted the man, hoping to strike a financial nerve. From what Mike said about his father-in-law, the man *loved* to talk business. "I was thinking about maybe sinking some cash into land."

Richard's heavy gray eyebrows lifted slightly. "Property is certainly one way to go about safeguarding your future," he said. "But let me give you a few more tips…."

"C'mon baby," Mike whispered close to her ear. "You're almost there. One more good push and you'll be finished."

She looked at him and nodded. A sickly green cotton gown covered his T-shirt and jeans and he wore a matching cotton cap to cover the ponytail that was now fully grown back. She held his hand tightly and thanked God that he had wanted to be a part of the delivery. She didn't know how she would have gone through all of this without him.

Denise's breath came in short, harsh, rasping breaths. A tearing discomfort settled low in her body and every instinct she possessed told her to push. But she was so tired.

Not only was the baby arriving two weeks early, but the time from the first indication of a labor pain to this overwhelming pressure had taken only three hours. She had always thought a first baby took forever to be born. She had thought she would be prepared.

She wasn't.

"Mike," she gasped in the brief interval between pains, "what if we screw up? What if we're lousy parents?"

He grinned at her. "Are you kidding?" he asked. "We're going to be *great!*"

"All right, Mrs. Ryan," the doctor said. "Get ready to bear down and see your baby."

"It's two weeks early," Denise managed to say as another pain began to build deep within her. "Will it be all right?"

Kathryn Taylor smiled gently. "Two weeks is nothing to worry about."

"Oh, Mike," Denise complained, "your parents will be so disappointed that they weren't here. And your brothers, too."

"Patrick's here," he soothed her. "As for the others, when they do arrive, they'll have the pleasure of meeting the baby without having to wait."

The pain grew and blossomed, opening inside her, making her strain and grit her teeth for battle.

"I see the baby's head, Denise," the doctor crowed. "Almost there."

Denise's breath came in short, hard gasps. Concentrating on her task, she only nodded to the doctor.

"Now," Mike asked as he braced her into an almost sitting position, "aren't you glad we waited to find out the baby's sex?"

Denise didn't answer him. She was far too busy. She felt Mike's strong arms holding her. She heard the doctor's encouraging voice. She felt a last incredible burst of energy rush through her body and when it came, she gathered it to her, gave one last mighty effort and pushed her child into the world.

An indignant scream filled the room and someone laughed.

She looked up into Mike's green eyes and found them teary. "Did you see him?" he whispered. "It's a boy, baby. We have a son."

A son.

She turned her face into his chest and his arms came around her in a gentle, fierce hug. In moments, a nurse was there beside the gurney, holding an incredibly tiny person wrapped up in a pale blue blanket.

"Mr. and Mrs. Ryan," she said and placed the baby carefully into Denise's outstretched arms. "Meet your bouncing baby boy."

Mike leaned down, kissed his son's forehead, then turned to kiss his wife. A wife. A son.

"Have I thanked you lately?" he asked, oblivious to the rest of the people in the room.

"For what?" she said through the tears blurring her vision.

"For loving me."

"You're welcome."

"Hey, Mike!" A deep voice called from the doorway.

They turned to see Patrick's head poke around the edge of the delivery room's double doors.

"Pat!" Mike shouted.

"Get out of here right now," one of the nurses ordered.

Patrick only laughed at her. "So, what is it? Boy? Girl? *Triplets?*"

Denise groaned dramatically.

Mike said proudly, "It's a boy."

The nurse rushed forward flapping a surgical towel at Patrick as if she were a bullfighter in the ring.

Immediately, Patrick pulled his head back. But not

before shouting, "I'll go tell everybody. I'll let *you* call Mom and Dad!"

Turning back to his family, Mike shook his head and said ruefully, "How could we ever screw this up when we have so much help?"

Denise accepted the kiss he gave her, then handed him his son. Mike held the tiny bundle as if his son were made of spun glass. When he looked at her through eyes that were filled with teary pride and happiness, Denise knew that sometimes loving the *wrong* man is the only *right* thing to do.

* * * * *

We hope you enjoyed reading

THE BEST IS YET TO COME

by

New York Times bestselling author

DIANA PALMER

This story was originally from our Silhouette Desire® series

Look for six new passionate romances each and every month from Silhouette Desire®

We hope you enjoyed
our bonus book

MATERNITY BRIDE

by

USA TODAY bestselling author

MAUREEN CHILD

This story was originally from
our Silhouette Desire® series.

*Look for six new passionate romances
each and every month from Silhouette Desire®.*

Choose the romance that suits your reading mood

Passion

Harlequin Presents®
Intense and provocatively passionate love affairs set in glamorous international settings.

Silhouette Desire®
Rich, powerful heroes and scandalous family sagas.

Harlequin® Blaze™
Fun, flirtatious and steamy books that tell it like it is, inside and outside the bedroom.

BESTSELLING AUTHOR COLLECTION

WE HOPE YOU ENJOYED THIS TITLE FROM
THE HARLEQUIN
BESTSELLING AUTHOR COLLECTION.

DISCOVER MORE GREAT ROMANCES FROM HARLEQUIN® AND SILHOUETTE® BOOKS.

Whether you prefer romantic suspense, heartwarming
or passionate novels, each and every month Harlequin® and
Silhouette® have new books for you!

AVAILABLE WHEREVER YOU BUY BOOKS.

*Use the coupon below and save $1.00 on the purchase of
any Harlequin® or Silhouette® series-romance book!*

$1.00 OFF the purchase of any Harlequin® or
Silhouette® series-romance book.

Coupon valid until Aug 31, 2010. Redeemable at participating
retail outlets in the U.S. only. Limit one coupon per customer.

U.S. RETAILERS: Harlequin Enterprises Limited will pay the face value of this coupon plus
8¢ if submitted by customer for this specified product only. Any other use constitutes fraud.
Coupon is nonassignable. Void if taxed, prohibited or restricted by law. Consumer must pay
any government taxes. Void if copied. For reimbursement, submit coupons and proof of sales
directly to: Harlequin Enterprises Limited, P.O. Box 880478, El Paso, TX 88588-0478, U.S.A.
Cash value 1/100 cents. Limit one coupon per purchase. Valid in the U.S. only. ® and ™ are
trademarks owned and used by the trademark owner and/or its licensee.

5 65373 00076 2   (8100)0 11652

FFUSCPNR

BESTSELLING AUTHOR COLLECTION

WE HOPE YOU ENJOYED THIS TITLE FROM
THE HARLEQUIN
BESTSELLING AUTHOR COLLECTION.

DISCOVER MORE GREAT ROMANCES FROM HARLEQUIN® AND SILHOUETTE® BOOKS.

Whether you prefer romantic suspense, heartwarming
or passionate novels, each and every month Harlequin® and
Silhouette® have new books for you!

AVAILABLE WHEREVER YOU BUY BOOKS.

*Use the coupon below and save $1.00 on the purchase of
any Harlequin® or Silhouette® series-romance book!*

Choose the romance that suits your reading mood

Home and Family

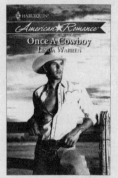

Harlequin® American Romance®
Lively stories about homes,
families and communities like
the ones you know. This is
romance the all-American way!

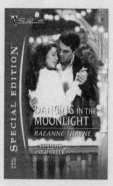

Silhouette® Special Edition
A woman in her world—living
and loving. Celebrating the
magic of creating a family and
developing
romantic
relationships.

Harlequin® Superromance®
Unexpected, exciting and
emotional stories about
homes, families and
communities.

THE HARLEQUIN BESTSELLING AUTHOR COLLECTION

CLASSIC ROMANCES IN COLLECTIBLE VOLUMES
FROM OUR BESTSELLING AUTHORS

Six *New York Times* bestselling authors bring
readers some of their classic romance stories in
the Harlequin Bestselling Author Collection.
Each book also includes a bonus story by
some of our top series authors—
a true treat for romance readers!

Available March 2010

The Best Is Yet to Come by Diana Palmer
Almost Forever by Linda Howard

Available June 2010

Sweet Memories by LaVyrle Spencer
Forever My Love by Heather Graham

Available September 2010

Dream Mender by Sherryl Woods
Part of the Bargain by Linda Lael Miller

Available wherever books are sold.

www.eHarlequin.com

NYTLISTBPA10